ACCIDENTAL MAGIC

MYRTLEWOOD MYSTERIES BOOK 1

Iris Beaglehole

CHAPTER
ONE

Rain bucketed down outside the rusty old car. Rosemary groaned.

"It's just water," Athena said from the passenger seat, picking at her chipped purple nail polish.

Rosemary sighed and looked at her teenage daughter. Athena's red hair hung over her face, the same fiery tone as Rosemary's but straighter and easier to tame.

"Just water...sure," said Rosemary. "Easy for you to say. You're not the one who has to get out of the car." She smoothed down her curly locks in anticipation of the rain that was sure to make them even more wild and frizzy than usual.

"What are you, a cat?" Athena teased with a smile.

"Just because you've always loved the rain, it doesn't mean the rest of us have to."

Athena patted her mother's shoulder. "You used to love it too. Back before..." She didn't finish the sentence and she didn't have to.

There was a moment of silence before Athena added gently, "You do need to go in."

Rosemary felt a chill that had nothing to do with the weather.

1

"Can't you come with me?" she asked.

"You know that wasn't the instruction," Athena said. She put on a posh voice and recited, "Rosemary Thorn, granddaughter of Galderall Thorn, must come alone to meet with the lawyer administering the estate."

"You should go into comedy," Rosemary said, laughing at her daughter. She looked up at the old building with its stone gargoyles. "I don't get it. Why would she do this?"

"She was *your* grandmother," Athena replied. "How should I know? I hardly knew her."

"But there are other family members who should probably be here too, not that Granny had a lot of money to leave behind or anything, but I don't know why she asked for me, in particular."

"Maybe she had something sensitive to tell you…" Athena said.

Rosemary grimaced. "Maybe I'm not ready to find out there's a deep dark family secret."

"Stop being silly, Mum."

"Or is it that I was really adopted and not part of the family at all – you know it's something I used to wonder since I never fit in."

"Mum…"

"You know, even our hair colour is different."

"What about Granny? You said she used to have red hair like us."

"Well, yes. But if it wasn't for that I'd be absolutely sure we weren't related to those other nasty Thorns, and perhaps we aren't. Maybe this is my formal disowning."

"Stop being paranoid."

Rosemary mock-pouted. "How dare you say that to your mother on the day of her formal disowning."

"Mother!"

"Alright, alright." Rosemary opened the door and a gust of wind whipped the rain into her face. "Yuck!" She tried to pull the door closed, but Athena was too fast and gave her an encouraging push, jolting Rosemary out into the weather where she made a dash towards the lawyers' office.

ROSEMARY RAN THROUGH THE RAIN, using her arms to ineffectively shield her head.

Despite the dark moods that had plagued her lately, there was a ray of hope that she had been hiding from Athena. It was just possible that her late grandmother might have bequeathed her something, anything...and even a small sum of money might be enough to give them some respite from the hole they were in.

That ray of hope shrivelled up like a deflated balloon as she saw the huge plumes of smoke pouring out of the building. An alarm rang out, deafeningly loud. Rosemary covered her ears as she watched the people scurrying out of the lawyer's offices, ducking their heads against the rain.

She stood there for a moment, stunned.

"What the..." Athena came to join her.

"Just when you thought things couldn't get worse," Rosemary yelled, through the rain and the screeching alarm and the sirens as the fire brigade arrived.

"Hey – at least you aren't in there, somewhere," Athena said.

"Too true, kid," Rosemary said, wrapping her sopping wet arm around her daughter. "Let's get out of here. It's not like we can do anything to help and the lawyers certainly aren't going to be in any mood to meet with us now."

The drive back to the flat was a quiet one. Athena seemed either dejected or lost in thought and Rosemary was too caught up in her own worries to find out which particular teenage mood her daughter was in.

Athena let out a long sigh as they pulled into the driveway of the dingey flat, which, despite its unpleasantness, they could barely afford. "I don't suppose there was any inheritance waiting for us in that building anyway."

Rosemary let her shoulders slump. "I didn't want to even bring that up as a possibility," she admitted. "I didn't want to–"

"Get my hopes up?"

"Something like that. I mean, I can't have you running wild with fantasies of inheriting a dynasty or anything."

Athena sighed. "I don't need a dynasty, Mum. I don't think you even know what that means. But it would be nice to go back to something like our old life in Stratham."

They went inside and took turns to shower under the pathetic trickle of water from the old broken fixture in the mouldy dilapidated bathroom before getting into dry clothes and watching broadcast TV on the couch, sipping the cups of hot cocoa that was Rosemary's specialty comfort drink.

"You know, you should really sell these," Athena said holding up her drink.

"Wow, things must be bad," Rosemary replied.

"Why do you say that?"

"The situation must be pretty dire if my sixteen-year-old daughter is trying to cheer me up."

"You make me sound like a monster," Athena squinted at her mother and then laughed. "I'm serious though. You make the best hot chocolates, and it wouldn't kill you to dream a little – maybe about creating a chocolate dynasty."

"Now that's a deluded fantasy I can get behind," Rosemary said. "My speciality would be Turkish delight flavoured hot chocolate – you know, the one I make with the rosewater."

"Tastes like soap," Athena complained, wrinkling her nose. "Actually…" Her voice became more serious. "Wasn't there a strange soapy smell in the air, outside that building?"

"Was there?" Rosemary asked. "I can't recall."

"Yes, something a bit like lily of the valley."

"That can't be right," Rosemary said. "I would have noticed that. It would have reminded me of my cousins. You know, the Bracewell-Thorns."

"Yes, I know. You always said they smelled like that flower. How do you think I recognised it? Remember, when I was a child you told me and I insisted you take me to the perfumery to see what it was like – you even got me a little bottle of the scent."

"Nasty stuff."

Athena crossed her arms and pouted. "That's what you said whenever I wore it."

"Well, you reminded me of my nasty cousins. They always smell like that icky poisonous plant."

"That's not a polite thing to say...hey, you don't think there's a chance that they were there today?"

Rosemary thought for a while. "Well, they weren't supposed to be there, unless they had a separate appointment right before ours with Granny's lawyer."

"Do you think that..."

"You're not implying my wealthy cousins could be arsonists?" Rosemary said, raising her eyebrows. "It seems like a stretch, even for them."

But the thought wedged its way into Rosemary's brain and refused to dissipate. Something strange was definitely afoot.

CHAPTER

TWO

Rosemary lay awake that night, in her uncomfortable bed. She let the full force of the disappointment wash over her.

She didn't want Athena to see her cry, but that meant holding back so much. Granny had always been so sweet and kind and patient. Even though Rosemary hadn't visited her in Myrtlewood Village for years — which she regretted dreadfully — she'd always appreciated the endless empathy Granny provided.

Rosemary felt the ache of the fragmentation inside her. She couldn't remember where it started, but she knew it intuitively. There were two disconnected parts of Rosemary Thorn. This, at least, was how she explained to herself the wide berth between her actions and her inner world. Things could make sense inside her mind, but as soon as she tried to enact them or speak them, they'd scramble and warp and scatter into erratic nonsense. It wasn't easy to hold down a solid job or parent a teenager under such conditions. It was hard enough just to look after herself.

It must have been after Dain had left the first time, that Rosemary had stopped visiting Granny as often. It was the shame of it all — not the separation itself, but all the debt that he had dug them into that just kept getting worse.

Rosemary hadn't been able to bear the look in Granny's eyes – was it pity? Rosemary didn't want to take money from an elderly relative, no matter how much Granny had insisted. She couldn't bear the thought of being indebted to anyone, especially not the only living relative she really connected with.

Granny's generosity was the reason that Rosemary felt some hope about the meeting with the lawyer. But all her hope had gone up in smoke along with the lawyer's office.

There's no will now... Rosemary thought. *It probably burned along with everything else. I don't have a hope in Hades of getting out of this debt, and it's not going to disappear all on its own.*

It wasn't a good night of sleep that Rosemary woke from – and it wasn't a gentle waking either.

"What the heck?"

She opened her bleary eyes and tried to shake the feeling of shame and dread from her body. There was a sound. A terrible, horrible sound. It was some kind of yodelling.

It was her phone ringing.

"Athena!" she yelled down the hall. "I told you not to change my bloody ring tone!"

Rosemary grabbed her cell off her bedside table and mashed the icon to end the call, only she missed and hit the little green phone instead.

"Drat!" she yelled and then remembered there was someone on the other end of the phone, listening. *Oh well, too late to turn back now.*

She held the phone up to her ear. "Uhh, yes? I mean...Hello."

Not for the first time, Rosemary wished that she was a morning person, but who on Earth was calling at this hour on a Saturday?

"Miss Thorn."

"Ugh...Speaking."

"Apologies for...disturbing you," the silky and rather old-fashioned male voice on the other end of the line said. Rosemary pictured an elderly man in a velvet smoking jacket. "It seems we missed our appointment yesterday. Unforeseen circumstances."

"We did?" Rosemary said, wondering who this strange caller was.

"Allow me to introduce myself," the caller purred. "I'm Perseus Burk, of Clifford and Burk Associates."

"Clifford and...oh blast, you're from the law firm."

"Indeed."

"I had nothing to do with that fire," Rosemary said, a little too quickly. "I mean, my daughter and I had just arrived and – I mean... umm. I'm glad you're okay. Are you okay? Of course, you are okay enough to call, but I saw those big flames and...and I'm...I'm rambling. Sorry." She ended rather meekly.

"Thank you for your well-wishes. I assure you we are fine. We have rather sophisticated fire-proofing, believe it or not. And I can assure you I'm not calling to in any way accuse you of arson. I'm merely aware that we had an appointment yesterday, which I intend to reschedule at your earliest convenience."

"You're calling me on a Saturday to reschedule an appointment when your whole office just went up in flames?"

"Something like that, yes."

"Why?"

"I'm a lawyer, Miss Thorn. When I make an appointment, I intend to keep it. And as things did not go according to plan yesterday..." he said, with a tone of disapproval.

Rosemary was unsure if he was disapproving of the fire itself or of her missing an appointment in order to avoid being torched alive by an inferno. Judging by his tone, either was possible.

"I decided to call to reassure you that we can meet as soon as you are able," he continued. "I assume you still want to attend this meeting?"

"Oh...oh yes," Rosemary said. "But...uhh, your office is kind of charred right now."

"Indeed it is. Our main offices in Burkenswood will be out of commission for at least a few weeks, however we have a smaller office in Myrtlewood."

"Myrtlewood?" It took Rosemary by surprise to hear the name of her grandmother's village spoken aloud by someone in a fancy accent. It was a small town, a place that hardly anyone knew of. "I guess it makes sense you'd have an office there if Granny was your client, because she was always saying everyone should shop local and support the businesses. She even insisted on buying locally made loo paper made by old Marjie Reeves out of recycled newspaper, even though it was like wiping your arse on sand– oh...I'm doing it again, aren't I?"

"Indeed, you are," Perseus said. "And while I'm sure the rest of that sentence would have been endlessly fascinating, let us return to the matter at hand, shall we?"

"At hand?"

"Yes, our meeting. Your grandmother, Madam Galderall Thorn, insisted that you have a private meeting for the reading of her will, as you may recall."

"Yes," Rosemary said, feeling too embarrassed to say much else lest she begin rambling uncontrollably again.

"And when would you like this meeting to take place?" Perseus Burk prompted.

"Oh, uhh...as soon as possible?" Rosemary suggested, suppressing a tiny squeak of excitement.

"Very well, let me check my diary. How about this afternoon?" Perseus said. "Three o'clock."

"Oh...okay," Rosemary said. "I didn't know lawyers worked on Saturdays."

"I find Saturday much like any other day, Miss Thorn."

"I guess it is," Rosemary said, and then literally held her tongue with her hand to stop it from misbehaving.

"I'll see you at three o'clock this afternoon," He said with a hint of amusement in his voice, as if he could tell exactly what Rosemary was doing to keep herself from blathering on. Rosemary ended the call, the full ramifications of the lawyer's words hitting her as she wandered out of her room.

"Oh, crud!"

"What is it, Mum?"

"I told him we'd be there at three," Rosemary said, still bleary-eyed as she entered the small dishevelled kitchen where Athena was pouring muesli into a chipped bowl.

"Told who?"

"The guy."

"You're not being very specific," Athena said.

"You know – the legal guy."

"Granny's lawyer?"

"That's the one," Rosemary said and sighed, sitting down at the table.

"What's wrong with that?" Athena asked.

"Oh...nothing, just that I told him we'd meet him in Myrtlewood, and I don't think the old car will make it that far without overheating. The last time it happened the mechanic said it would need more serious repairs, only we couldn't afford that, and unless you have a carriage of fine stallions or maybe a pair of racing llamas we can ride..."

"Okay, okay, I get it," Athena said. "So, reschedule."

"But I'm dying to know what's so important that he called me on a Saturday."

"So, we'll take the train," said Athena.

"The train?" Rosemary asked. "Since when do you take trains?"

"You always said you took the train to Myrtleweed when you were a kid."

"It's Myrtlewood."

"Whatever."

"Fine," Rosemary said. "We're taking the train."

"Why do I have to come?"

"Moral support. Plus, it's a really cute town. I know we haven't been there since you were very small, and you probably don't remember but..."

"Yeah, I know. You go on and on about it."

"It's settled then."

"Fine," Athena shrugged. "It was my idea, anyway. Besides, I'm dying to get out of this awful hole."

Just as she spoke those words, a kitchen cabinet door swung loose and fell right off its hinges, clattering loudly to the floor.

"Point taken," said Rosemary.

IT TURNED out there was only one train on Saturday afternoon, so Rosemary convinced Athena that they'd have to stay the night in an affordable inn before catching the Sunday train back. Athena had consented, provided Rosemary could guarantee there would be no bed bugs. They'd had a rather unpleasant and traumatising experience at a boarding house once. Rosemary made bed bug promises that she wasn't entirely sure she could keep, but what choice did she have? She didn't want to leave her teenage daughter all alone in a dodgy neighbourhood, and they hardly had any close friends they could call on at short notice.

They packed their bags and boarded at the Burkenswood train station. Rosemary felt a nostalgic thrill – the excitement of being twelve again and going to visit Granny Thorn in the countryside. Young Rosemary had felt so grown up, leaving her parents behind and travelling on the train all by herself.

Athena was quiet as she took her seat. Rosemary followed her daughter's lead, stowing away the luggage before sitting silently by the window. She savoured the sound of the horn blowing and the rhythmic sound of the train as it began to make its way along the track. There was something so peaceful about a train-ride, a gentle inevitability that the train was going to take her exactly where she needed to go. All she had to do was relax.

Rosemary liked that it was an old-fashioned train – not one of those new fandangled super-fast beasts. This one was more fitting for Myrtlewood.

She listened to the soft whistling of the wind through window and watched the countryside fly past, enjoying the sight of orchards and little villages here and there. As the ride progressed, she even caught glimpses of ocean.

At some point, Rosemary dozed off and dreamed of Granny Thorn serving her tea. She awoke to the scent of lily of the valley, though she couldn't tell if it was from her dream, or whether it was actually in the carriage. She looked across to check if Athena could smell it to find that her teen was fast asleep, slumped over on the padded bench.

The smell had disappeared. Rosemary poked her head into the passageway, just to check. Walking away, quite far down the aisle, was a thin woman with light-coloured hair that looked slightly familiar.

It was possible that Elamina was there on the train, but Rosemary considered it highly unlikely that her snobbish cousin would deign to travel via public transport. She would have brushed it off entirely as just her imagination playing tricks on her, but then she recalled Athena smelling the floral perfume during the fire.

It doesn't mean anything, Rosemary told herself. *Even if Elamina is hanging around, it's probably more to do with the lawyers and the inheritance than it is to do with me.* She hadn't spoken to her cousins in years, and had no desire to after the way they'd always treated her.

The train continued to roll along, and Rosemary enjoyed the view out the window, despite now feeling oddly unsettled. Occasionally, she glanced at her daughter. There was a strong family resemblance between them; the same green eyes and high cheekbones. Athena's features were more delicate and her skin a darker shade from her father's side. Dain never said anything about his heritage other than that he was "Eastern". He'd grown up in foster homes and Rosemary knew not to ask too much. Besides, she reasoned, he probably didn't know much about his birth parents, anyway. Rosemary certainly didn't have that problem. The Thorn family tree was long and lengthy, including a number of quirky characters.

Athena slumbered, blissfully unaware of all their problems. She wore a purple dress that contrasted with her hair along with stockings covered in holes that Rosemary thought were tacky. Of course, Athena thought that Rosemary's trusty jeans and t-shirt combo was drab and unoriginal.

Athena knew they were poor, but she didn't know how far below the black line they were. Rosemary wasn't treading water financially; she was drowning, and the debt just kept mounting up, the interest accruing faster than her measly pay-check from the grocery shop could keep up.

Athena's life was already busy and complicated enough with schoolwork, and dealing with the mean kids, and trying to fit in and find proper friends even when no one seemed to quite understand her.

All that was enough for a teenager to worry about, and so Rosemary was determined to protect her from the truth as much as possible.

The carriage darkened. Rosemary looked back out the window to find they were trundling through a dense forest. She vaguely remembered this part of the journey.

We're getting close to Myrtlewood.

It was a thrilling realisation, a feeling of home-coming that Rosemary hadn't anticipated. There was a hint of something resembling connection, as if the town might hold a balm capable of healing her life. She'd been blocking out her memories of the village and of Granny Thorn in order to protect herself from regret and grief, but she hadn't realised she was also shutting herself off from feelings of joy. Now that she was getting nearer to Myrtlewood, a part of her didn't ever want to leave. It was the very same sensation she'd had as a child every time she had to return from her holidays with the wild and wonderful Granny Thorn, who always had a pantry full of contraband treats that Rosemary's parents would consider sinful and indulgent.

Granny would take young Rosemary to the beach or foraging in the forest or into the Myrtlewood village for dances and fairs. There was always an adventure to be had, and Granny never judged Rosemary for anything she did or for anything she wanted. It was the only time she'd ever felt truly free.

As soon as the forest opened up into bright sunshine and prairie again, the train began to slow.

Athena stirred and stretched, opening her eyes. "Are we there yet?"

"Yes," Rosemary said. "Almost."

"It's...like a fairy tale," Athena said, looking out the window at the row of silver birch trees lining the railway tracks on both sides, tied with ribbons and arrangements of spring flowers in white and pale pink and yellow.

"What is this place?"

"Oh yes. I should have told you. Myrtlewood village is a pretty special place."

"You did tell me that – only about a million times!"

"Well, for the million-and-oneth time, it's special. It's hard to explain exactly how, but this is one of the things they do – they celebrate the seasons. This must be for the early spring festival."

"It still feels like winter to me," Athena said, crossing her arms and shivering.

"Spring often does," Rosemary pointed out.

"So, you're saying they celebrate the spring by cutting down spring blossoms and tying them to other trees?"

"Yes," said Rosemary, matter-of-factly. "They do other things as well."

"Like dancing naked in a circle?"

"Possibly. We'll have to stick around to find out."

"Ugh. No, thank you."

"Look, here's the station," Rosemary said as the train pulled to a stop in front of an old-fashioned brick railway building.

"It is very cute," Athena admitted. "In a kind of old-timey way."

They exited the train and made their way from the station to the town square.

"Where's the lawyers' office?" Athena asked.

"I don't recall, or maybe he didn't say."

"You've got to be joking," said Athena.

"Well, Myrtlewood is a small place. I'm sure we'll find it. Anyway, it's only quarter-past-two. We should have a spot of late lunch and a cup of tea before I go to the meeting."

"Fine," Athena said, in that sullen teenage tone that Rosemary had become accustomed to.

"Look, we can ask this man for directions." A short but somehow lanky chap with close cropped hair approached. He looked to be in his thirties and had an unusual gait, as if he was deliberately trying to keep his back impeccably straight. He wore wire-rimmed spectacles and a chocolate brown cap with a matching brown jumper tied around his neck.

Athena's eyes widened in concern, as if interacting with this slightly odd man might affect her social status for the worst, despite being many miles from school.

"Excuse me," Rosemary said, waving him down as he walked with purpose along the footpath.

"You're excused," the man said.

"Uh, uhm, thanks," Rosemary stuttered. "But can you tell me how to get to...what was it, Thistle and Burk? Borgen and Balks? You know, the lawyers."

"Clifford and Burk?" the man asked in a slightly nasal voice.

"That's it! That's the one."

"Oh," the man said, frowning.

"Don't tell me it's on fire," Rosemary said.

The man looked surprised. "No. Why would it be?"

"Long story," said Athena. "Can you just tell us where it is?"

Rosemary smiled at her daughter, half pleased that she was eager to step in to stop her mother making a fool of herself with terrible rambling, and half embarrassed that this was so often required.

"I could," said the man and kept walking.

Rosemary and Athena followed behind him.

"Why are you following me?" He asked.

"You said you'd tell us where the lawyers' office is," Rosemary reminded him, trying to keep her tone calm and patient, even though she was feeling frustrated and confused.

"I said I *could*," the man corrected. "I didn't say I would."

"Well...will you?" Athena asked, flashing him a smile.

"Oh...fine. If you really must know!" The man blustered. He turned back around and led them back in the direction in which they were originally walking.

He waved his hand, as if flicking water off it, towards a corner of the town square. "Over there!" he yelled. "And that horrible man is probably there, too. Whatever you do, don't trust him. I doubt he's even human."

"Uh, thank you, Mister..." Rosemary said.

"Ferg is the name," the man responded, quickly recovering his composure and reaching out a hand towards Rosemary. She cautiously shook it.

"Thank you, Ferg. I'm Rosemary."

"Rosemary," he said. "Of course you are." And with that, he walked off.

"What an odd man," Rosemary said to Athena.

"You can say that again."

"What an odd–"

"It's an expression, Mum!"

"I know, but I'm still processing, and I thought it might be helpful to say it twice."

Athena sighed. "It's still only two thirty. What are we doing now?"

"Look – over here. It's a teashop," Rosemary said. "I'm sure they'll have something to eat. You can settle in there and read while I go to the meeting, and then we can check in at the inn."

"I hope you at least made reservations for us to stay," Athena said.

Rosemary shot her a look that revealed she hadn't.

"Mum!"

"What? It's out of the way – a small town. I thought they might give us a special deal if we just showed up."

"You're always looking for special deals," Athena protested.

"So, what's this all about, then? The letter said that Granny's will instructed you to meet with me alone."

"Indeed, it did."

"And...?"

"Miss– Rosemary," Perseus said.

She smiled, both at the fact that he was clearly struggling to break out of his usual way of doing things, which amused her, and also because he was trying, which was satisfying.

He cleared his throat. "You may be aware that the circumstances around your grandmother's death were...unusual."

"Unusual how?" Rosemary said, the sinking sensation returning to her along with the roaring in her ears.

"I'm not permitted to discuss any details that may still be under investigation by the authorities," Perseus said.

"But there is an investigation?" Rosemary asked. "Someone hurt Granny."

A sense of panic erupted inside her that she tried to dismiss as illogical. After all, she had already been told this, more or less, just a few minutes ago. Then an even more reasonable voice in her head assured her it was a normal part of grieving to experience these waves, meanwhile, she realised she was speaking all this aloud while crying inside the lawyer's office – the very same lawyer who was looking mortified at her apparent display of insanity and emotion and handing her a box of tissues.

"Thank you," Rosemary said, dabbing her eyes. "It was a risk to have me come here without my chaperone. She usually stops the worst of it."

"Your chaperone?" Perseus asked, looking even more mortified.

"My daughter, Athena. She knows when to shut me up."

"Oh," he said, recovering and letting out a little chuckle, as if finally realising Rosemary was joking.

"But why was it you wanted me to come all the way here today? Is this to do with the 'suspicious circumstances'?"

"My apologies, Rosemary. I should have explained better from the beginning." He pulled out a stack of old papers. "Your grandmother's will states that you, and your daughter, are the sole heirs to her entire estate, which she intends for you to look after with great care and pass on to your descendants."

Rosemary's jaw dropped open.

"Are you quite alright?"

"Excuse me?" Rosemary said. "I didn't quite catch that last part. It sounded like you said Granny left everything to me. But that can't be right. I hadn't even seen her in years!"

"It is, in fact, right," said the lawyer, his tone dry. "It seems the late Madame Thorn had a very old will."

"Oh – well, I guess that makes sense," Rosemary said. "We used to be close. That's the sort of thing other relatives might contest, isn't it? I mean, if there's actually any money involved, which I'm sure there isn't much. Granny's house was quite old and the upkeep must have been far too much for her to manage alone. It might well be in a shambles by now. I'm sure there are hefty land taxes so there's probably more debt than there is value. That's what they always say with pensioners – a penny saved is a penny in the coffin or something. Maybe I just made that up."

Rosemary was aware that she was talking herself down from a ledge of potential disappointment, only she was doing it out-loud and the lawyer seemed perturbed by her continued rambling.

"I'm sorry," she added. "You can blame Marjie – she spiked my drink, though actually this is how I normally behave so it's probably no excuse."

"If you'll allow me to finish," Perseus said. "Her will *was* very old, however she changed it just two months ago..."

"Oh," Rosemary said. "So I don't inherit– "

Perseus cleared his throat again.

"Sorry," Rosemary said. "I'll shut up now."

"That might be wise if you want to hear the rest," he said, curtly. "To continue. The older version of Madame Thorn's will dated back to the year before you were born and prescribed an equal division of all her wealth between her decedents, aside from the manor, which was to go to one particular descendant: the oldest granddaughter."

"But that's me," Rosemary said.

"Yes," Perseus said, patiently. "However, as I said, just two months ago Madame Thorn came to us – her lawyers – and asked for a new will, one that bequeathed her entire fortune to you."

"Fortune?"

"It is a sizeable inheritance, Mi– Rosemary. Some might call it a small fortune or even a medium-sized fortune. It all depends on context. And that is referring to only the cash assets. There are also significant artifacts of value. And the house, too, will be worth a tidy sum. However, as you mentioned, it is old and falling apart, and as you're not local, I assume you probably want to sell it, despite what it says in the will."

Rosemary felt numb.

A fortune! Whether small or medium-sized, a fortune must surely be enough to get her out of debt and more.

"Can I have a look at that?" Rosemary asked, gesturing to the will Perseus Burk was holding. He handed it over, and Rosemary read it several times, not quite believing her eyes. It didn't contain any details about the size of the fortune. However, it did clearly state exactly what the lawyer had just told her.

"Now, it isn't for me to judge," Perseus said. "And please understand that from our legal perspective, Madame Thorn was of sound mind at the time she composed this will. However, just between you and me, the police may find it suspicious."

"Suspicious?"

"Suspicious that she changed her will significantly only weeks before her death – which they also consider *suspicious*."

"Oh, I suppose it is," Rosemary said, folding her arms and frowning.

"If you know of any *reason* that she may have done so, I'd be happy to discuss the legal ramifications with you, free of charge – off the record, of course."

"Reasons?! Are you implying tha–"

"I'm not implying anything," Perseus said silkily, interlacing his fingers and leaning back in his chair. "I'm merely offering you support – just as I intend to offer you support to sell the house."

Rosemary was taken aback. *Sell the house.* Thorn Manor was indeed a rambling old building that needed a lot of work, but Granny was quite specific in her wills – both of them – that the house was to go to Rosemary, the eldest granddaughter, and that she was supposed to take good care of it. And that was exactly what she intended to do – or at least as much care of it as she could afford.

"I don't think that will be necessary," Rosemary said. "I can't very well honour Granny's memory if I'm selling her house the moment I inherit it."

"Take you time; think it over," said Perseus. "In fact – here are the keys."

He handed her a large keyring, full of rusty old keys.

"Why not spend the night there and think about it," he said. "You might find that it's more work than you're willing to take on. And I must inform you that the inheritance is all pending the police investigation. It will be a while before the funds from your grandmother's accounts can be released to you."

"You mean, they have to clear me of any wrongdoing?"

"Something like that. I'm afraid I can't tell you much more. The house isn't officially yours yet, however as you are family of the late owner no one is going to stop you from staying there – though consider yourself warned, it is in quite a state."

Rosemary reached out to take the keys, and her finger brushed against Perseus Burk's hand, which was frightfully cold. She shivered. "Are you alright?" she said.

"Why do you ask?"

"Your hand – it's freezing."

"It's just a condition I have," Perseus said, turning away. "It affects my...blood-pressure. I'm prone to cold extremities."

"If you say so," Rosemary said. "Uhm. Thank you, I guess."

"It has been a pleasure, Miss Thorn," he said, and he didn't even try to correct himself that time.

Rosemary left the lawyers office feeling worse than ever that Granny had died before she'd had gotten the chance to visit her again, but it was wonderful to feel so acknowledged by her grandmother – to be left everything, while the rest of her miserable conniving family got nothing.

Serves them right, after the way they treated me.

She didn't like to dwell on the past. It was too uncomfortable and heart-breaking, and anyway, she had just inherited a medium-sized fortune.

Rosemary was practically jumping for joy as she skipped along the street to meet Athena who was sitting contentedly at the teashop, exactly where Rosemary had left her. Marjie was in full flight, gesturing wildly as she regaled Athena with a story.

"We was just sitting down for tea when young Rosemary came screaming into the living room, waving her hands in the air, certain there was a bear after her...only it was just my Herbert in the shed with his circular saw!"

Athena bent over the table, laughing. Her cheeks were rosy, and Rosemary was happy to see it.

"I see you're having a jolly old time at my expense," she said, coming to join them.

"You look like you've perked right up," Marjie said. "I told you my special tea was just the ticket."

"It was certainly *something*," Rosemary said. "What did you put in it, anyway?"

"Now that's a family secret I'm not willing to share," Marjie said. "But trust me, it'll do you some good."

Rosemary sat back down at the table and examined her watch to find that only half-an-hour had passed, and her cake was still good.

She took another mouthful, letting the delicious tart lemon curd revive her senses while Marjie went off to make her a fresh pot of tea.

"So?" Athena prompted.

"Where do I start?"

"What do we inherit?"

"Umm, everything!" Rosemary said. "And I didn't even realise there was anything much."

"Money?" Athena asked. "Really?! Will it be enough to make us not-poor?"

"It sounds like it might be," Rosemary replied. "Though the lawyer was a bit vague on the details – something about the investigation still pending."

"Yippee!" Athena crowed. "We can go back to Stratham, and I can go back to my old school, and we can live in a nice normal house, and everything will be wonderful! I'll have friends again!"

"Well...here's the thing."

"Oh no – don't use that voice."

"What voice?"

"That how-can-I-let-you-down-easy voice. You always talk like that when you're about to disappoint me."

Rosemary sighed. "Really?"

"Really."

"But I try so hard to protect you from the harsh realities of the world."

"That's exactly your problem, *Mother*. Trying to protect me only disappoints me more. I'm not a baby – just tell me the truth."

"So, the thing is, Granny left us her big old house."

"That's okay," Athena said. "You can sell it."

"You sound exactly like him."

"Like who?"

"That ridiculous man with his silky voice and his nice Italian suits."

"The lawyer? He was good looking, wasn't he?" Athena narrowed her eyes.

"How can you tell?"

"That's the voice you use for good-looking men."

"Oh – shut up! The thing is, it's a special house. It was special to Granny Thorn, and it was special to me as a child."

"But you haven't even visited for years."

"You know I regret that. Don't rub it in."

Tears sprang up involuntarily in Rosemary's eyes, and she did her best to suppress them.

"I'm sorry," Athena said, more gently. "It's just that...you're hardly a handy-woman. How are you going to take care of a big old house that probably needs loads of work?"

"I don't know," Rosemary admitted. "But Granny left it to me in her will with specific instructions to look after it."

Athena crossed her arms. "You're kidding?"

"No. Not kidding."

"You want us to move *here*?"

"Well, I don't know yet. It's all a bit sudden. Let's just go and check out the house. I have the keys from the lawyer. We can even stay there tonight and save money on the inn."

"I thought the inheritance would mean that we don't have to scrimp and save anymore."

"Well, we still will for a while. I don't know when the investigation will be through and anyway, being frugal is a good thing, isn't it?"

Athena rolled her eyes. "Fine. We'll stay in the big old house that belonged to your dead grandma tonight. It better not be haunted."

A strange sensation passed over Rosemary, an almost-yearning feeling as if she hoped Granny was still around, haunting the place. At least that would give her a chance to properly say goodbye.

And with that yearning came a hint of destiny.

FOUR

Thorn Manor was only a short walk from the town centre, but what might have normally taken ten minutes took a lot longer with Rosemary and Athena both lugging their bags. Athena grumbled and complained, but Rosemary was too busy enjoying the sights of the village as it gave way to countryside again. It was lovely to be back, reassuring somehow, as if the world didn't have to be as tough as it had been for the past few years.

"Here it is," Rosemary said, as they drew up to an overgrown driveway.

"Here *what* is? All I can see are trees and vines."

"That's exactly how it should be," Rosemary said. "That's what Granny used to say. Plants want to grow and there's no use in trying to get them to follow human rules."

"She sounds a lot like you," Athena said.

"Thank you."

"It wasn't a compliment."

"I know, but I choose to take it as one."

Rosemary took in the familiar scene, the rambling bushes and wild weeds giving way to the forest that surrounded Thorn Manor. Though she couldn't see the house yet, she could almost sense its presence, and something else, a feeling of being watched. Rosemary shivered and glanced around, though no one else was in sight.

"So, what am I looking at?" Athena asked.

"This is just the entrance to the driveway," Rosemary said.

As they stepped closer, they could make out the shape of the old house, through the trees, on the hill.

"It's like something from a movie, isn't it?" Athena said, and Rosemary thought she detected a faint tone of awe in her daughter's voice.

"It's pretty special," Rosemary said. "Let's go."

As they stepped onto the driveway a flock of tiny gold butterflies took flight and the wind whistled past, ruffling the bushes as if the land itself was breathing a sigh of relief to be inhabited by its rightful guardian again.

The gravel driveway was steep as it wound up the hill into a forested area overlooking the sea. Athena had stopped complaining, giving Rosemary an uncommon sense of peace. She watched a little robin flit from branch to branch on the path ahead of them, welcoming them home.

*Home...*It certainly felt that way. Rosemary hadn't felt at home for so many years, having to move from flat to flat, each seeming more squalid than the last. Her life had felt so caged in, so cramped and desperate. Here, things were so open and calm, wild and wonderfully free.

They neared the house. Rosemary could tell it was much more dilapidated than the last time she'd seen it. The shutters hung at odd angles from their hinges, and vines were taking over the east wing. The lower roof appeared to be caving in, and the tower had seen better days.

"This is definitely the part of the fairy tale where we meet the witch," Athena said.

Just then, a crashing sound startled them.

"Is someone in there?" Athena asked as Rosemary raced towards the house. "Mum! You're supposed to run *away* from the scary noise. Honestly, this is just like a horror film."

"Don't be silly," Rosemary called out, as she reached the building. "It was probably just a cat. But if someone is in there burgling our inheritance, they've got another thing coming."

Rosemary peered in through the front windows at what used to be the parlour. It was bad. The house was practically a ruin. Inside, it looked dingy and dusty.

"It looks as if no one has lived here for years," Athena said, joining her.

"I can't believe I left Granny here to rot."

"Can't we just go back to the village?" Athena asked. "I don't want to go in there. It doesn't look safe. What if the roof caves in, or the floor gives way?"

"Just let me..." Rosemary said, fumbling with the keys, "take a look."

"Fine," said Athena, crossing her arms again. "But I'm waiting out here in case I need to call the emergency services to get you out."

Rosemary found the green key, which she assumed was the right one for the green front door, and tried it. It fitted perfectly, and as the lock turned, a small sparkle appeared.

Rosemary stepped back and squinted at it, not sure whether to believe her eyes.

"Is it electric or something?" she muttered to herself.

"Not bloody likely," Athena said, standing a few metres away at what she must have considered a safe distance from the crumbling old house.

"No," Rosemary said. "Look!"

"I am not coming any closer," Athena insisted.

The sparkle began shimmering out in a radius around the door knob, leaving it a deeper, darker green. It continued out, appearing to clear the dust and years from the wooden door frame leaving it looking fresh and polished.

"I must be hallucinating," Rosemary said.

"Well, at least you're finally admitting it," Athena quipped.

"What on Earth?" The shimmer continued to radiate out until the entire front of the house looked fresh and well-maintained. Rosemary took a step back to see that even the roof pushed itself up and back into rows of orderly tiles. "Are you seeing this?"

"Seeing what?" Athena asked.

"Oh, crud. That special tea must have had some kind of psychedelic component."

"Uh, Mum, are you alright?"

"Of course I'm alright," Rosemary said. "I'm just not used to seeing houses fix themselves."

"What are you talking about?"

"Look?" Rosemary gestured back at the house, only to find that it had returned to its dilapidated state. "Oh...well. Never mind," she muttered, pushing open the door. "I might need a lie down and a cup of non-special tea."

Inside, the house was dark, but not quite as bad as Rosemary had feared. The floor was still solid and so were the walls. There were a few noticeable vines growing inside, but at least it seemed safe to enter. Her vision had mercifully returned to normal. There were no more shimmery sparkles to deceive her. It felt reasonably dry and almost inhabitable, but it still upset Rosemary to think that Granny had lived like this, with the roof caving in and the vines growing indoors.

She stifled a sob and suppressed a well of guilt at not coming to help.

Granny's much-loved ornaments and china were strewn across the filthy floor. Mildew covered the wallpaper, and paintings of landscapes and still-life bouquets hung askew on the walls, where they remained up at all.

As she passed the open door to the room which used to be her grandmother's library, Rosemary had a sense of foreboding, as if something was lurking there in the dark. She stepped quickly past and came to the staircase. It, at least, looked solid. The banister was gleaming under a layer of dust. Rosemary took the steps, two at a time, the way she used to as a child. She reached the top story to find everything largely in-tact and quite a lot tidier than it had been downstairs.

This must have been where Granny was spending all her time, she thought as she walked along the hallway. The realisation gave her a sense of relief. *It's much more inhabitable up here. At least she wasn't living in total squalor.*

Rosemary checked the other rooms, which all looked fine, even her old bedroom from when she was a child with its floral patchwork quilt. The room wasn't dusty, as if Granny had kept it there waiting for her. The thought brought a tear to her eye.

Rosemary didn't want to go into her grandmother's bedroom. She wasn't quite ready to face it yet, but as she returned down the hallway, prepared to update Athena on the state of affairs in the house, Granny's door creaked open, and Rosemary couldn't help but take a peek.

The bed was perfectly made with Granny's lavender quilt. Even the windows were clean, letting bright sunlight shine in. The wood-panelled walls glowed warmly, as if recently oiled.

Rosemary noticed a piece of folded cream paper sitting propped up on the bed, as if waiting for her.

She entered the room, and the door closed softly behind her, giving her an eerie feeling.

"Is that you, Granny?" she whispered. "Are you still here in some form?"

There was no response, but Rosemary comforted herself with the knowledge that if anyone could stick around beyond the grave, it would certainly be Granny Thorn with her sharp wit and strong character.

Rosemary picked up the letter, written in her grandmother's long sloping cursive.

MY DEAREST ROSEMARY,

My time on this earthly plane is almost up. I can feel it drawing nearer, and it is also time that you knew the truth. You know I've never been one to dither about, and so I'll put it bluntly.

You, my dear, are a witch – yes, really, a witch – just like we all are in the family, like it or not.

The reason I couldn't tell you before is due to something that happened many years ago. I had to make a tough call to bind your powers – all the powers in the family, including most of my own magic. It was decades ago, and you won't remember because I had to bind your memory as well. I'm afraid it might have had a detrimental effect on your mind, but let's just say you have plenty of character development yet to do!

I'm so sorry for all this secrecy, and I'm sorry for the distance as well. It was a side-effect of the spell that, as it took hold, you became more and more removed from this place so that it was even hard for you to visit. It was the only way to protect you and young Athena – to keep you away from this place and removed from the source of your powers. I know you felt awful about abandoning me, but you see, dear, it really wasn't your fault.

Now the danger is truly upon us. I've done my best to keep it at bay for this long, and now I know I cannot hold this fortress of energy any more. I only wish I could have told you about it, properly – that I could have taught you – but I was naïve – yes, even old biddies like me can be naïve. I thought I could hold it back for much longer – just to give you a little more time and a shot at normal life.

I'm sorry that I was wrong, and now I can only hope that you are able to free your powers. You will need them if you are to have any chance of fighting the enemy. I cannot say much here, lest someone finds this note before you, however, I will tell you this:

They come by tooth, claw, and fang.

That is all I can say.

I love you infinitely, and I wish you all the blessings I can muster.

Eternally yours,

Granny.

. . .

Rosemary read the note through twice and then sighed, feeling even more guilty than before.

Granny was mad and senile, and I didn't even think to find out...I did nothing to help her.

She took the note back downstairs, through the grimy entrance way and walked out towards where Athena was waiting for her.

"Took you long enough," Athena grumbled, then she stopped when she saw the look on Rosemary's face. "What's wrong?" she asked. "You look like you've seen a ghost."

"It feels a bit like that," Rosemary said. "Look at this."

Athena took the thick cream paper and read it. "So...we're all witches and we're in danger from some kind of beast with claws?" she summarised.

"That's certainly what Granny seemed to think before she carked it. I can't believe I abandoned her here – senile and living in squalor."

"So, it's just as bad inside?" Athena asked.

"Downstairs is pretty dire, but upstairs is actually quite nice."

"Are you still going to be a tight-arse and make us stay here instead of paying for the inn?"

"What, stay here and risk you running off to find refuge at Marjie's cottage without me?" Rosemary said.

"You've got me there. I was just wondering if the old bird had a spare room I could kip in."

Rosemary sighed. "I guess not. I have to admit, it's a lot worse than I thought – well, outside and downstairs is, anyway. Upstairs is almost exactly as I remember it. It doesn't really make sense."

"Are you sure you didn't just hallucinate it being nicer upstairs?" Athena joked. "You and your magic tea!"

"Hey, that wasn't really my choice. Marjie just handed me the tea, and it seemed rude not to drink it. But yes. I'm sure. This time, there was no magical shimmering. It was just normal. Anyway, we can head back to town and stay the night there before leaving on the train in the morning."

Rosemary looked out at the darkening sky. They'd be lucky to make it to town before proper nightfall. Movement caught her eye. She glanced towards the forest to see the glint of eyes staring back at her from the darkness. Her heart raced, but she reassured herself it was probably just some wild animal, a squirrel or ferret perhaps, even a fox. The woods around here were full of such creatures. Nothing to alarm Athena over.

The sound of an engine distracted Rosemary, and she turned to see what looked like an old-fashioned police car rumbling up the driveway. She glanced back, but the creature, whatever it was, was gone.

An officer got out of the car, dressed in a uniform that also looked like it was from another time. He seemed to be in his fifties and slightly rotund, with greying hair that curled around his ears and steel-grey eyes.

"Good day, Ma'am...Miss," he said, nodding to both of them in turn.

"Uh, hi," Rosemary said, confused. "If you're looking for a hen's party you've come to the wrong place."

"Excuse me?" he said. "Hen's party?"

"Well, you're hardly an ordinary copper in that uniform or with that car, so I figured you must be a stri–"

"Mum!"

"What?"

"Just let the man speak before embarrassing us both!"

"Oh, sorry."

"I see, I see," the officer said, with an unduly serious expression. "I'll have you know I am a real copper. We just do things differently in Myrtlewood, see. We're off the beaten track here, and no one ever checks up on us to see if we've got the latest doodaddys, so we do as we see fit."

Rosemary giggled, but the police officer retained a serious face.

"Now look here, I'm Constable Perkins," he said, raising his hand in a small wave. "And you must be Galdie Thorn's relatives – you certainly look like her."

"I'm Rosemary Thorn and this is my daughter, Athena."

"The goddess and the plant," Constable Perkins said.

"Excuse me?"

"Oh, you know – Athena, the goddess, and rosemary is a plant – I have some in my back garden, come to think of it."

"How can we help you, officer?" Athena prompted, clearly used to getting conversations back on track.

"Oh right, well. I'm gonna have to ask you a few questions."

There was a pause while Rosemary and Athena waited for the questions. When none came, Athena prompted again. "Such as?"

"Such as what?"

"What questions do you have for us?"

"Oh...such as, where were you on December the twenty-second?"

"We were in Burkenswood, getting ready for Christmas," Athena replied.

It was true, though the memory saddened Rosemary, as it had been such a pitiful Christmas due to lack of funds.

"And I don't suppose you have an alibi?"

"Each other?" Rosemary suggested.

"How convenient," Constable Perkins said. "Anyone else?"

"Our neighbours, I guess," Athena said.

"And I suppose if I was to check with those neighbours, they would corroborate your story."

"I suppose they would," Rosemary said, though she wasn't sure that old Marcy Podge would remember seeing them, given she was blind drunk at any opportunity, whereas their neighbour on the other side, Mr Finch, was just plain blind.

"Very well, very well," Constable Perkins said, pulling at his suspenders. "When was the last time you saw Galdie Thorn?"

Rosemary's shoulders slumped and Constable Perkins got a gleam in his eye.

"Well, well. Is this the body-language of guilt I see here?"

"It is," Rosemary said. "But not for the conclusion you might be jumping to. It's just that I hadn't seen Granny Thorn in years. Not since Athena was a toddler. I've been such a terrible granddaughter."

"And yet she left this whole place and all her money to you, I hear," Constable Perkins said, suspicious. "Not to that other lot who visit every month."

"What other lot?" Rosemary asked.

"*You* should know. They're *your* relatives."

"I...I don't know," Rosemary admitted. "I don't know why she left it to me, other than, maybe it was something about me being the oldest granddaughter – isn't that what she put in her original will?"

"How do you know that?" Perkins asked. He furrowed his brows, glaring at Rosemary.

"The lawyer told me."

"Did he, now? What else did that Mr Burk tell you?"

"Not much," Rosemary admitted. "I wish I knew more. Really, I do. Was it my cousins who were here visiting Granny so regularly? Elamina and Derse?"

"Could be," Perkins said, leaning back on his heels. "I'm not at liberty to say."

"Either that or he can't remember," Rosemary said quietly, under her breath so that only Athena could hear. Athena nudged her to shut up.

"What was that, Ma'am?"

"Nothing," Rosemary said. "I just...I don't know my cousins very well. That's all."

"Interesting," Perkins said, taking a small notebook out of his pocket and jotting something down. "I'll be back to continue this investigation," he said. "Consider yourself warned. Don't leave town."

"What?" Athena looked aghast.

"But..." Rosemary said. "We just came to visit for a night."

"And you can stay visiting until all this is over," he said, sounding very satisfied with himself.

Rosemary and Athena watched as Constable Perkins walked slowly back to his car, pausing every few steps to look back and shoot them suspicious looks. It was almost comical. They would surely have been trying not to laugh if they hadn't been feeling so stressed.

"What the heck was he on?" Athena said, as the police car rambled back down the driveway. "Stay here – in this cooky little town until he finishes his 'investigation', which sounds more like a wild goose chase than anything. How dare he suspect us when we have nothing to do with it. It's just not fair!"

"Easy on," Rosemary said. "I'm the one who's supposed to ramble like that. You're supposed to have the quick quips, remember."

"But..."

"I know."

"This trip just keeps getting weirder!"

"Yes, it does, but hey – we're set to probably inherit a smallish fortune," Rosemary said. She had downplayed the already-vague sum of money so as not to get Athena's hopes up, and also because she still didn't want to reveal the exact state of the current hole in their accounts.

"If we don't get thrown in jail for murder first. And given his uniform, I bet their local jail still has dungeons and torture implements."

"At least today can't get any worse," Rosemary offered.

As if in response to her statement, the sky above them darkened and thunder rumbled overhead, followed quickly by a deluge of icy-cold rain.

"You shouldn't have said that," Athena said.

"Quick, let's get inside!"

Rosemary grabbed her bag and took her daughter's hand, then ran with her towards the house.

"I'm staying in the entranceway," Athena said, as Rosemary pushed open the door. "I don't want to go in there. It's creepy."

"Oh, it is not," Rosemary said, peering into the dark house. "And besides, the rain is coming in sideways, so you'd better get indoors or you'll catch a cold."

"Fine," Athena said, although she didn't sound fine at all.

The shadowy interior of the house looked to be in better shape than when Rosemary had come inside only a handful of minutes before.

"It's not that bad," Athena admitted. "It looks worse on the outside. It just needs a good dusting in here."

"See, I told you," said Rosemary, though she was concerned that somehow she'd imagined all the additional cobwebs and disarray she'd seen before.

Maybe that special tea is still affecting my senses.

"The lights don't work," Athena said, flicking a switch too many times.

"No. I suspect the power has been cut off. It's been a while since Granny was around to pay the bills."

"So, what do we do?"

"Look." Rosemary pointed to a candlestick on the mantlepiece. "We can do this the old-fashioned way." She found a box of matches and lit the three white tapers, sending candlelight cascading around the room.

"It's actually kind of nice in here, in a creepy-old-house kind of way," Athena said.

"Nice and creepy?"

"Pretty much. So, what do we do now?"

"I'm going to try to make some tea," Rosemary said, walking to the kitchen.

"But the power has been shut off."

Rosemary held up the matches and rattled them.

"Please don't build a bonfire to make tea," Athena said.

"I'm not," Rosemary assured her. "Granny has– I mean *had* an old wood-fired stove as well as a more modern one. I guess it's ours now, along with the rest of this stuff."

"Is any of this valuable?" Athena asked, following Rosemary towards the stove.

"Don't even think about hawking your great grandmother's possessions."

"I was just asking," Athena said defensively. "And surely we don't need all this old stuff."

"The lawyer did mention that there were...uhm...what did he call them? Artefacts? Something like that. Maybe just antiques. He seemed to be interested in them – actually he tried to buy the whole house from me." Rosemary said all this before she could stop herself.

"Perfect! So sell it to him!" Athena said. "We don't need this old junk and you know you bloody well can't take care of an old house like this. You can barely change a lightbulb."

"Granny managed it alright," said Rosemary. "And it was just her here with her old patchwork cat, Molly."

"What happened to the cat?" Athena asked.

"Molly? She probably died years ago," said Rosemary sadly, as the realisation hit her. "She was old even when I was a child."

"Alright, sorry about that," said Athena. "But you have to sell the house. It's our chance to have a normal-ish life, and you're not exactly handy. An old house like that would just crumble around us."

"Athena."

"What? It's true."

"Can we please stop talking about selling my grandmother's house when she's only just willed it to us?"

"But—"

"Please? At least for the night. I'm just...there's only so much I can handle."

"Fine, but we're talking about it tomorrow."

"We can talk about it, sure," Rosemary conceded, and she rummaged around in the cupboards. "Just please understand that the house has a lot of sentimental value for me. It's special."

"I'm going to have to call the psychiatrists and tell them my mother is in love with a house, aren't I? They're going to have to come and drag you out of here before you end up living with a hundred cats and the whole place falling down all around you."

Rosemary shrugged. "You have always wanted a cat."

"That's true," said Athena. "Can I have a cat? Especially if you're going to end up with hundreds. It would be unfair if you get all the cats in your new ramshackle cat lady lifestyle."

"I won't rule it out," Rosemary quipped as she found some kindling and began lighting the old wood stove. "It wouldn't be my worst life choice."

"No – that would be Dad."

"Don't rub it in."

The fire crackled to life and Rosemary stood back to admire her handiwork. "See, your mother is not completely useless."

"I'm actually kind of impressed," Athena admitted. "But just because you can set fire to stuff effectively, that doesn't mean you can look after an old broken-down house like this."

Rosemary sighed. "You're probably right," she said, picking up the old kettle and filling it with water from the tap. "But this place is important to me – it was important to Granny, and I can't just sell it. I already feel guilty enough.

Athena put her arm around her mother. "You really like it here, huh?"

"You really don't, huh?"

"It's creepy, and even if there's money to pay for the restoration, a house like this will require constant upkeep. The money won't last, and it will be about as fruitful as pouring water into a bucket full of holes."

"Since when did you get so wise?" Rosemary asked her daughter.

"Since forever."

"And even if we could afford it, you wouldn't consider moving to Myrtlewood?"

"Mum, we've already moved so many times because of *your* money problems."

The accusation stung, and Rosemary took a step back as if slapped. It was true that Athena wasn't the cause of their financial woes, but it hardly seemed fair to blame her mother when it wasn't her who set off the whole big mess of debt.

Of course, Rosemary had chosen to shack up with Dain in the first place, though it had always felt out of her control. That man had a power over her she couldn't explain, and even after he left her – multiple times – she still inexplicably took him back. It was only with Athena's intervention that she'd finally put a stop to the vicious cycle.

Rosemary didn't like to think of herself as a weak woman who'd throw her life away for a man, and yet in Dain's presence, she melted like goo. It was pitiful. Athena said it was disgusting how she gave away all her power like that, and Rosemary couldn't argue with that. It was one of life's great mysteries that this man could walk all over her and then leave, and she would welcome him back. The bastard.

"You're thinking about him, aren't you?" Athena said. "You're thinking about Dad."

"How did you know?"

"You always have that dazed look on your face when you think of that man...and you're right. Our problems are mostly his fault, as I keep reminding you – but you are the one always letting him get away with it."

Rosemary could feel the sharp edge of the rift in their mother-daughter relationship, the one caused by Dain. As a young child, Athena had idolised her father, but once she hit teenage years, she saw through him.

"You just forget everything bad he does," Athena continued, her hands on her hips. It was something she'd pointed out several times before. "You have this weird memory blind spot when it comes to him. When he does something sneaky or flaky, you'll get mad for a few minutes, sometimes even to the point of plotting revenge, and then it all disappears."

"Surely, I'd remember something like that," said Rosemary. "And besides, if I forget things, it's not my fault. My memory had been addled, remember?"

"It's still your responsibility."

Rosemary let her shoulders slump. "Is it one of the laws of nature that teens must blame their parents for everything?"

"I believe so," Athena said. "Though being a teen doesn't come with a handbook. Sometimes I wish it did. I just want a normal life, you know, like when we lived in Stratham and I actually had friends?"

The kettle whistled, interrupting their slightly stilted conversation. Rosemary made the tea, thankful for finding a carton of long-life milk in the pantry, so that it didn't have to be served black because the tannins gave her a headache.

The rain bucketed down outside and the sky darkened even further as Rosemary and Athena sipped their tea on the window-seats in the alcove near the front door.

"It doesn't look like this is going to let up anytime soon," Rosemary said. "We'd better just kip here. Like I told you, the rooms upstairs are much nicer and cleaner than downstairs."

"Can't we just call a ride-share or something?" Athena asked hopefully.

"You think they have Uber all the way out here?" Rosemary laughed.

"Well, it was worth a shot."

"Come on," said Rosemary. "I'll show you."

She led a hesitant Athena up the staircase.

"You're right. It's not even dusty up here," Athena said. "It looks almost like a normal house."

"Enough with the 'normal' already."

Rosemary wondered, for the millionth time, what was so good about 'normal' anyway. Her parents had desperately wanted a normal life, moving her away from Myrtlewood and away from the eccentric Granny Thorn and devoting themselves to their Christian church. They were humble people who cared more about God than anything else, unlike Granny, who said God better watch out because she had designs on the job. Being such devout Christians made her parents abnormal in Rosemary's eyes. It also meant they tithed all their additional earnings to the church and were never in a position to help their daughter out, not that they would have, anyway. They'd disowned Rosemary in her early twenties, the moment they realised she was having a child out of wedlock, pushing her further into the arms of the man who was to be her ruin. This was the kind of thing Rosemary tried to spare Athena the details on, saying as little as possible about her parents' rejection.

"This is my old room," Rosemary said, showing Athena in. "You can sleep here if you like. It's very cosy. I'll take the guest room."

"Why don't you sleep here since it's your room, and I'll take the guest room?"

"Okay. Sure," Rosemary said putting on a cheerful voice, though it meant taking the single bed instead of the double. "If that's what you want."

She showed Athena next door to the room Granny kept made up for guests. She had often enjoyed the company of unusual guests in Rosemary's youth. Sometimes they wore cloaks and capes, other times, top hats or old-fashioned embroidered dresses. When Rosemary had asked her grandmother about the strange clothes her friends wore, Granny had just mumbled something vague about "medieval fairs and other such things."

The guest room was done up in matching forget-me-not blue. It was perfectly clean and tidy like the other rooms upstairs.

"It's nice," Athena said. "You're really going to take the single bed and let me stay in here?"

"Sure, why not?" said Rosemary.

"Or there's that other room – I guess that was hers."

"Granny's room. Yes. No. I'm not going to stay in there."

"Too soon?"

"It feels like it will always be too soon," Rosemary said.

Athena patted her gently on the shoulder.

"Are you hungry?" Rosemary asked.

"Starved."

"I saw some tins of beans downstairs, and I bet there's other stuff we can have for supper."

"At this point, I'd eat anything."

Supper was indeed cans of beans on toast, a favourite food of Athena's, growing up. Rosemary had very frugally brought half a loaf of bread from home to save it going stale and to provide at least one meal on their trip. She toasted two slices each, using the toasting fork over the fire while the can of beans simmered in a pot on the stove.

"This is good," Athena said, as they ate their make-shift meal at the kitchen table after Rosemary had cleared it of a thick layer of dust. "Do you think it tastes better because we had to toil over it?"

"Toil?" Rosemary laughed. "What kind of fairy tale are you living in? I did all the cooking, you just stood there telling me that it wasn't going to work."

"I'll have you know that took a great deal of concentration," Athena quipped.

"Alright then, you poor toiling teen – time for bed."

They made their way upstairs, feeling exhausted, and said good-night on the landing.

Rosemary slipped into her childhood bed and fell quickly asleep.

CHAPTER
FIVE

A loud bang startled Rosemary awake, followed by a shriek from the next room.

Athena!

Rosemary's mind raced with awful possibilities of dangerous intruders and natural disasters. She leapt out of bed and flung open the door to find her daughter standing there in the dull moonlight, pale and trembling.

"What? What is it?"

"Didn't you hear that noise?" Athena asked.

"Of course I heard it. Why else would I be standing here?"

A loud crash sounded from downstairs.

"Oh...crud," Rosemary said. "We really are being burgled, aren't we?"

"Shh!"

"Oh sorry," Rosemary said in a whisper. "You're right. We don't want them to know we're here."

"Obviously!" Athena hissed. "Where's your phone? Call the police."

"It's downstairs, I think," Rosemary said. She didn't mention that it was probably out of battery as she'd forgotten to charge it because that was exactly the kind of irresponsible thing Athena always grilled her about.

"Crud," Athena whispered. "So is mine."

"Is this a bad time to wish you were always glued to your phone like normal teenagers?" Rosemary muttered. "I'm sure they don't leave their phones in downstairs."

"Shush, Mum," Athena hissed. "What's the point in me being glued to my phone when I have no friends?"

There was another crash, and another, interrupting their pointless and frustrating conversation.

"Do you think we should try to sneak up on them?" Rosemary asked, quietly. "You know – startle them with the element of surprise. Hit them with a bat?"

"Do you *have* a bat?" Athena asked.

"No, but I do have..." Rosemary looked around before picking up a heavy-looking lamp from the sideboard. "This."

"Great, we'll startle them with a lamp."

"Have you got a better idea?"

Athena shrugged. "Wait 'til they go away?"

"That's great, but what if they don't?" said Rosemary, trying hard not to show how terrified she felt and failing miserably. She'd never seen Athena so scared, her teeth chattering and eyes wide.

"Listen," Rosemary whispered.

"To what?"

"Exactly. There's silence now. Maybe they've gone away – or maybe it was just an animal or something, a broken shutter blowing in the wind."

Athena looked doubtful, but it was true. The rain had stopped outside, and the house was completely silent. "Uhm...Mum."

"What?"

"If it was just a shutter in the wind, then how do you explain that sound?"

"What sound?"

"It's like...music of some sort."

Rosemary strained her ears to listen, and sure enough, there was a sound a bit like chimes.

"This is way too creepy," Athena said, reaching for Rosemary's arm as if she were still a small child needing to hang onto her mother.

"It's probably wind chimes or something."

"I didn't hear any wind chimes earlier, did you?"

Rosemary shook her head. "Look, let's just check it out, okay?"

"Okay, but you're going first and take that stupid lamp with you."

They crept down the staircase, treading softly to try to avoid any creaking steps. It was so dark, looking down into the ground floor of the house, that Rosemary almost turned back, but Athena urged her on.

"It might be dangerous," Rosemary hissed. "There could be a serial killer with an axe down there just waiting for us."

"Don't you think a serial killer would have just wandered on up here and chopped us into tiny little pieces by now?" Athena whispered back. "Let's just go and figure out what's causing that sound. I have to know now. There's no way I'm going to sleep without finding out."

"Fine," Rosemary said. "But I notice you're not curious enough to go first."

"You're my mother. It's literally your job to protect me."

Rosemary took a deep breath and breathed out slowly, just like the online anxiety videos told her to do, though those had not specifically envisioned a situation where one was holding an old lamp in preparation for confrontation with the musically inclined axe-wielding serial killer that her imagination was busy fabricating.

The house remained silent, apart from the chiming sound that continued to ring out, softly, as if beckoning them closer.

Rosemary and Athena followed the sound down the staircase and along the passageway to a closed door.

"Not in here," Rosemary said and shuddered.

"Why not? What's in there?"

"I just got a feeling, earlier – like there's something big and powerful there."

"Was that when you were trippin' on magic tea?" Athena jibed.

"Probably," Rosemary said. "But that doesn't mean I was wrong."

"What is that room, anyway?"

"Granny's library. She never let me go in there when I was a kid."

"Look. It's probably just an old music box or something," Athena said, pushing open the door.

The room was just as dark except for a rectangular shape in the centre that looked to be glowing. Light shone out from it revealing an intricate pattern, which looked lacy, illuminating the glossy surface of Granny's big wooded desk.

"It *is* a box...of some sort," Athena said, taking a step forward. Rosemary reached out and tried to hold her back.

"It might be dangerous."

"It's a freaking box, Mum."

"Maybe it's an explosive or something."

"Mum!"

"What?"

"Stop being ridiculous – it's just an old music box. It probably got disturbed during the storm or something."

"You know that doesn't make sense, right?" Rosemary said.

"Well, what do you think it is?" Athena asked.

The box continued to chime, and after a moment, Athena pushed her mother forward.

"Hey! Watch it."

"Go on," Athena said.

"What do you want me to do?"

"Open it, of course. Let's see what's making the sound."

"Fine then," Rosemary said, noticing that her own voice sounded as petulant and teenage as Athena's was when she was in a sulk.

She took a step forward and reached out towards the box. As her fingers brushed against it, the lid flew open, blasting the whole room in blinding white light.

"What the...?" Athena said.

Rosemary ducked, pulling Athena down beside her, terrified that this was some kind of explosion after all, but as the light faded to a golden glow, she saw the sparkling that she'd assumed she had hallucinated earlier.

It was moving faster this time, radiating out, clearing the dust from the big desk and then moving further into the room.

"Do you see that?" Rosemary asked, rubbing her eyes.

"Of course I see it!" said Athena, no longer bothering to keep her voice down.

"Get back," Rosemary said. "It might be some kind of bacteria."

"Bacteria?" Athena said, doubtfully. "Really?! You think this is dust-eating bacteria?"

"Well, what do you think it is?"

"Some kind of hallucination we're both having. Did you slip me some of that special tea?"

"No. Of course not."

"Well, if this 'bacteria' eats dirt and grime, we'd better both get out of the way. We're not exactly sparkling clean," Athena said.

They both stepped back as the shimmering golden light put the room to rights – not just dusting, but also plumping the cushion on the chair and straightening the books that clung to the shelves encasing the room.

"This is really weird," Athena said as they promptly exited the room, walking backwards. "I can't stop watching; it's too cool – like Mary Poppins or something. I should have had some of that tea *earlier*."

"I told you I didn't dose you," Rosemary said.

"Well, someone did. This can't possibly be real."

"Even if we are both hallucinating, how likely is it that we're seeing the exact same thing?"

"I don't know," Athena said. "I'm hardly an expert on psychedelics."

Just then, the shimmering glow reached the boundaries of the library. It slowed and then burst out – illuminating the house around them, cleaning, clearing, tidying and fixing everything in sight.

"This is impossible!" Athena said as they ran outside to get away from the flying household objects – including a broom, a chair, several books, and the cups and plates they had carelessly left by the window seats. "What kind of house tidies itself?"

"The perfect house?" Rosemary suggested.

They stood outside and watched as the exterior of the house received a rapid makeover, turning from weather-worn and crumbling into what appeared to be gleaming paint and freshly scrubbed stonework. The lower roof pushed itself up, and every tile slipped satisfyingly into place, and the tower re-built itself.

"Super weird," Athena said.

"Yep," Rosemary agreed. "It's just like before – and that only lasted for about thirty seconds. Let's see how long this lasts."

"You mean this hallucination?"

"Or whatever it is."

"What else could it possibly be?"

"Who knows, kiddo," Rosemary said, draping her arm around Athena's shoulders. She couldn't help but recall her grandmother's note from earlier – *you're a witch. We all are in the family.* The words echoed in her mind as the house continued to bloom like a rose, restoring itself back into a pristine state, the shutters pulling them-selves up by the hinges, and the ivy creeping back to a slightly less chaotic level.

"No freaking way," Athena said. "This is some potent drug we're on, huh?"

"I don't think it's a drug, love," Rosemary said. "But I also can't quite believe it's real. Do you think we could be dreaming?" She pinched herself but found she didn't wake up.

"Must be," Athena said. "Ouch."

"You pinched yourself too, huh?"

"Theoretically, it's possible to pinch yourself in a dream and feel pain, right? It would just be dreamed pain," Athena said, as the house finally stopped righting itself and stood, calm and still and grand before them set against the blooming light of the early dawn.

"I guess," Rosemary said.

"You must be in *my* dream," Athena said.

"No, you're definitely in mine," Rosemary argued.

"That's just what dream-Mum would say."

"Very well, oh wise and powerful master of this dream, do you think it's safe to go back inside the house? I think it's starting to rain again, and my feet are cold and squidgy."

Indeed, a light pattering of rain had begun to fall all around them.

"I guess," Athena said. "Or maybe it's super dangerous and the danger will wake us up."

They trod back into the house. Every surface was spotless and gleaming in the low light. Their eyes were wide as they made their way upstairs. Rosemary insisted on them wiping their muddy feet with towels from the linen closet, despite Athena's insistence that it wasn't going to matter when they woke up, anyway.

"Can you sleep in the same room as me?" Athena asked. "This has all been way too freaky, and I don't want to be alone in case something even freakier happens."

"Freakier than a house fixing and tidying itself?" Rosemary asked.

"...maybe?" Athena said.

"Sure. We can both fit in the big spare bed, but you have to promise not to kick me."

"I make no such promises," Athena said.

They got into bed and immediately felt drowsy.

"It's strange," Athena said with a yawn. "I don't think I've ever gone to bed before in order to wake myself up."

And with that, they both fell fast asleep.

"THE BIRDS ARE TOO LOUD," Rosemary moaned into her pillow. "And the light is too...light."

"What time is it?" Athena asked, sitting up in bed.

"I don't know. My phone is downstairs, remember."

"Well, according to the clock that's still ticking on the chest of drawers over there, it's nine o'clock."

"It's a Sunday," Rosemary grumbled. "They should start the day later."

"That's not how it works, Mum," Athena said, getting out of bed. "Hey, I had the weirdest dream last night."

"You mean – that there were loud noises and then music and a bright exploding light box, and then the house fixed and cleaned itself?" Rosemary asked.

"You dreamed it, too?!"

"Uhm, Athena," Rosemary muttered, still half asleep and dazed.

"What?"

"If that wasn't a dream, then why do you think we're sleeping in the same room?"

"No...way!" Athena shouted. "It's not possible."

She jumped out of bed and ran out of the room. Rosemary heard her footsteps down the stairs, but despite her daughter's excitement, she still wished the daylight would just go away and let her sleep for an extra hour. The thumping of footsteps sounded again, and Athena burst into the room.

"No way! No way!" she said, jumping up and down.

"Hey, settle down," Rosemary said. "I'm trying to sleep here."

"Mum. Get up, now!"

"But..."

"Now!"

Athena grabbed her mother's arm and started pulling.

"Hey! Leave me alone."

"Mum!"

"Fine," Rosemary said, and pushed herself out of bed.

As she made her way down the staircase, it slowly dawned on her that Athena was right to be excited. The house, including the ground floor, really was clean and as lovely as Rosemary remembered it being on her earlier visits when Granny was still alive.

The wallpaper was spotless and fresh-looking. The paintings all hung exactly as they should, and even the vases, crystals, and crockery on display on the hall cabinet up ahead looked to be in order, as if Granny had just dusted that very morning. Rosemary bit back the hope that Granny's death had all been a terrible misunderstanding and that she'd emerge at any moment to tell them to take their grubby shoes off and put the kettle on immediately. Grief had a funny way of defying all logic, and though Rosemary knew in her mind that her grandmother was gone, her heart had other ideas.

"How do you explain this, then?" Athena asked. She was standing at the top of the staircase with her arms crossed, looking at her mother as if Rosemary was a naughty child and Athena was the parent who'd just caught her with her hand in the biscuit tin.

"How do *I* explain it?" Rosemary said. "How do *you* explain it?"

"Either we are still hallucinating now, or we were when we first arrived," Athena suggested weakly.

"Or the house magically restored itself after I touched that...thing."

They both turned in the direction of Granny's library. On closer inspection, the box still sat on the desk, innocently. It had somehow closed itself and looked like an ordinary carved wooden item.

They both took a step closer and then looked at each other cautiously.

Just then, a rumble sounded outside. They turned back to the front of the house. Through the now-clean window, they could see a pale pink car making its way up the driveway towards the Thorn Manor.

"Not another visitor," Rosemary said.

"At least it's not that cop again," said Athena. "He was hard work."

Rosemary sighed. "You'd think being out in the middle of nowhere in a dead-lady's house would be enough reason for people not to visit."

"Come on, Mum. Let's just go and find out what they want."

"But it's raining again."

Rosemary and Athena watched from the window as the car door opened and a navy blue sensible-heeled shoe popped out below it, followed by another. Then an umbrella appeared, and the door closed, revealing a rather short, dark-haired woman with a perfectly straight fringe. She wore a navy-blue pencil skirt and a pale pink cardigan, which matched both her car and her handbag.

"It's like something out of a cartoon," Rosemary said, as the woman paused and eyed the house before resuming her approach.

"Shush, Mum. Just because it's not your style, it doesn't mean you have to judge."

"Well, then why are you always judging my sense of dress?"

"Because you have none."

"Ouch."

"What?" Athena asked. "It's true. Look at what you're wearing."

Rosemary looked down at her worn blue jeans and dark red long-sleeve t-shirt. It was a perfectly normal outfit, but Athena often judged such an ensemble as drab.

"So rude!" Rosemary said, poking Athena in the shoulder. "How did I raise you to be so insolent? Anyway, what's wrong with jeans and a red t-shirt?"

"It's not even a style. You just throw on whatever clothes you find first. Take a good long look at yourself," Athena joked.

There were three sharp knocks at the door, and Rosemary went to answer it.

"Hello?" she said.

"Why, good morning, Madam," the woman said in a high, slightly raspy voice. "Allow me to introduce myself. My name is Despina Crepe, and I'm from the local estate agency in town."

"I didn't know Myrtlewood had an estate agency," Rosemary said. "Next thing you'll tell me, they have their own zoo and prison, too. Everything you need – right here— ow!"

Athena had jabbed her in the ribs. Rosemary scowled.

"Are you quite alright there?" Despina asked.

"I'm fine, thanks," Rosemary said. She wasn't exactly fine. In fact, Rosemary had a mild phobia of estate agents, brought on through some bad experiences when she was younger, and the particular anxiety she got around them sometimes made her break out in hives. This had led her to believe she was allergic. At that very moment, she noticed a slight itch near her wrists, cementing her urge to cut the interaction as short as possible.

"Very well," said Despina. "May I come in?"

"Uh...well, actually, we were kind of in the middle of something, so if you don't mind," Rosemary tried to shut the door, but it bounced back. Despina had already wedged her shoe inside.

"Well, I shan't be a minute," Despina said. "And your name is?"

"Rosemary Thorn, and I really must be going," Rosemary said, trying to will the itch away.

"Rosemary – of course! Now, I heard you inherited Galdie's old place. I must say, I came to have a look the other day, and I'm sure it was in much worse repair. You must have worked your magic on it," she winked.

What does this woman know? Rosemary wondered. *And why does she give me the creeps – as well as hives?!*

Despina smiled a sickly sweet smile. "Well, I can't imagine city people like you two would want to live in an old place like this. I won't keep you any longer, but know that I'm here anytime you want to talk about selling. Here's my card."

She held out a pale pink business card. As she did, Rosemary noticed a flash of something silver. It was a brooch in Despina's lapel, bearing a circular coat of arms with a crow, snake, and wolf, as well as a symbol that looked like some kind of Celtic knot. It was unusual enough for Rosemary to do a double-take despite her itching desire to get the woman out of her vicinity.

"That's an interesting brooch," she said.

"Oh, this old thing?" Despina said sweetly, clutching it. "Just a family heirloom. You get a lot of that kind of thing around here. This whole village is just full of old stuff. I bet there's plenty of junk you want to get rid of in that big old house." Her eyes gleamed as she tried to look past them into the house.

"Not really, no," Rosemary said.

"Mum!" Athena nudged her mother.

"Got to go now," Rosemary said.

Despina removed her foot from the doorframe and Rosemary quickly closed it before the estate agent decided to try anything else.

"What?" Rosemary asked as Athena glared at her.

"That could have been your chance."

"My chance to what?"

"To make some cash, so we can get out of here and go back to a normal life."

"Oh," Rosemary's shoulders slumped. "You're still fixated on that idea, huh?"

"Of course. Why wouldn't I be?"

"I just thought that after last night..."

"You mean the hallucinations?"

"Or magic?"

"Are you serious?" Athena asked. "You're supposed to be the adult here."

"I was just thinking that...wait a minute."

"What?"

"We haven't eaten."

"So?"

"So – remember how our brains stop working properly when the blood sugar runs low?"

"Speak for yourself," Athena said. "My brain is perfectly fine. Yours is just as odd as it always is."

"No. I'm getting the woozy feeling."

"Okay. Let's have some food, and then you can call that woman and tell her you're interested in selling."

The problem was, Rosemary wasn't interested in selling at all. In fact, calling the estate agent was pretty close to being the last thing she wanted to do, but her blood-sugar was too low for her to properly articulate any of that.

In the sparkling clean kitchen, they found not just the old wood burner stove but a new-looking oven, and to their astonishment it turned on – as did the eclectic kettle.

"I thought the power was off," Athena said.

"It was!" Rosemary insisted. "Maybe it was a power cut because of the storm? I'm sure most of this stuff wasn't here last night."

"It was quite dark," Athena said, but her tone was uncertain.

Rosemary laughed.

"What?" Athena asked.

"Don't you think it's funny that we're freaking out over a kettle after what we saw last night?"

"I don't think any of this is funny."

"Oh, love, you're always so serious when you need to eat. Let's see..."

Rosemary opened up the previously bare pantry, looking for the rest of the bread she'd stored there the night before, only to find it now contained an assortment of canned food. She checked the refrigerator and found various edible items in there too. Upon examination, nothing was past its expiry date.

She decided to keep all this from Athena, at least until after they'd eaten. She cooked up some bacon and eggs and served them on toast with cups of tea. Athena was so hungry she didn't even think to ask about the ingredients until after she'd wolfed down her breakfast at the polished wooden kitchen table.

"Where did all that come from, then?"

"It was in the kitchen – though, I don't remember seeing it..."

"Must have just been another thing we missed last night." Athena said, settling on the most plausible explanation. "Alright, so now that you've gotten us both fed, it's time to call that Despina woman."

"No."

"Why not?"

"You know I'm allergic to estate agents," said Rosemary.

"Oh, come off it. You are not!"

"They give me a rash."

"That's preposterous and you know it."

"So, I'm preposterous, then."

"Mum!"

"That's not the only reason," Rosemary admitted. "I don't want to sell the house. In fact, I love this place."

"More than you love me?"

"Athena!"

"What?"

"Don't be ridiculous."

"Don't you want me to be happy, Mother?"

"Of course I do, and I'm not going to make you move here, but I'm not going to sell it either. It's all I have left of Granny." Tears welled up in Rosemary's eyes, and her voice took on a high note as she braced herself so as not to completely break down.

Athena sighed and put her arm around her mum.

"Hey, I get it. It's okay," Athena said. "You don't *have* to sell the house."

"Thanks for your permission," Rosemary said, wiping her eyes.

"Well, I didn't want you to have a full melt-down."

"I'm serious, though. Thank you."

"For what?"

"For understanding that this is important to me."

"What are daughters for?"

"Clearly they are for making their mothers another cup of tea."

"Oh, fine," Athena said, taking their cups and plates to the kitchen.

Rosemary smiled to herself and got up from the table. She shook out her arms and legs and then wandered around the ground floor, looking at Granny's things while Athena put the kettle on.

At the wall facing the bottom of the staircase, Rosemary came eye-to-eye with the familiar portrait of a slightly younger Galderall Thorn than she'd ever met. It was deftly painted in oils in that classic romantic style, though it also held something so lifelike about the visage. Out of the corner of her eye, Rosemary could have sworn she saw her grandmother wink at her.

"Weird."

"What?" Athena said, coming to join Rosemary bearing a laden tea tray.

"The painting. It's just so lifelike."

"I'm not sure how your eyes work, but this image does not represent what I see of life," Athena said. "It's too misty and swirly."

"She must have been, what? Forty-something when this was painted? That's only a little bit older than me."

"So, this is the famous Granny Thorn, is it?" Athena said. "She looks...different to how I imagined."

"You met her, you know."

"Oh sure, when I was what? Two?"

"Probably."

"Two-year-olds aren't known for their attention to detail, Mother."

"I wish you had got to spend more time with her," Rosemary said. "She was...she was amazing."

Rosemary thought the painting in front of her might have just smiled slightly, but decided that they'd had enough excitement for one day already and did not try to bring up the possibility with Athena. Instead, she followed her daughter back towards the kitchen and then sat with her on the window seats, drinking tea.

"So, what now?" Athena asked. "Can we pack up and go back?"

"I guess we have to. You have school tomorrow."

"Oh, don't remind me. School is awful at the moment."

"That bad, huh?" Rosemary asked.

Athena didn't usually tell Rosemary much about her school life these days. She was at the age where she preferred to withhold a lot of information about her life from her mother.

"It's not just the teachers or the classes," Athena said. "I mean, they're alright. It's more..."

"The social stuff?" Rosemary suggested.

"Yeah, it sucks being an outcast."

"Tell me about it, kid."

"Wait a minute," Athena said. "Didn't that police guy say we had to stay here until he'd finished his investigation?"

Rosemary scratched her head, trying to remember a detail as far back as yesterday. "I think he did. But surely, he can't stop you from going to school – I mean, what power does he have to get us to stay in the village? The country, sure, the region, maybe, but the village?"

"It does seem strange," Athena admitted. "But everything about this place is."

"So, what do we do?" Rosemary asked.

"Uhm, you're the adult, remember?"

"Oh yeah...crud. I don't know."

"We can go and check in with him, see if he actually meant it," Athena suggested. "Maybe ask to speak to his supervisor. That guy must surely be a rogue cop."

"So sensible," Rosemary said.

"Why am I trying to get myself *into* going back to school, when by all rights, I should be trying to find a way out of it?" Athena asked.

"I thought you hated this freaky place and wanted to get as far away as possible."

"That might be true," Athena said. "But then you brought up school, and that's a whole different kind of freaky that I'd rather avoid."

"Tough luck, kid," Rosemary said. "Let's get dressed and pack up and we can figure out how to continue your gainful education."

"You know, when you put it like that, staying in Myrtlewood isn't such a bad idea."

"I know you are only saying that because you hate Burkenswood," Rosemary said. "So, don't get my hopes up that you would move here when you really want to be in Stratham."

"Things were just better in Stratham," Athena said.

"You always say that, but you forget that it wasn't all roses there either. Your friends kept falling out with each other, and it upset you a lot."

"At least I had some friends."

"You'll make more. I promise."

"What if I just stayed here and hid away from the world?"

"Not going to happen. If we do decide to move here, you'll have school here to look forward to. Let's go back into town and see if we can shed some light on what we're actually allowed to do while 'under investigation.' If we don't get back to Burkenswood soon, I'm going to lose my job!"

"Maybe you won't need to work behind a counter after you inherit that small fortune."

"Gosh, I hope that's the case. If I never have to deal with another coupon again, it'll be too soon."

They put on their coats and shoes and locked up the house, then made their way into town, enjoying the views of the countryside. The weather had fined up and the birds all seemed to be out, singing to one another as if gossiping about the rainstorm the night before.

"Can we go back to get more cake?" Athena asked wistfully.

"After that woman spiked my tea? I don't think that's wise," said Rosemary, but as they entered the village, Marjie popped her head out of her shop door and greeted them warmly.

"Come in for some lunch," she said.

"Uh, no," Rosemary replied. "We really have to be going. We have some errands to run."

"Nonsense," Marjie said. "You have plenty of time to run errands once you've been fed and watered."

"The thing is..." Rosemary said, struggling to find the words to raise her grievance, especially since Marjie was so warm and kind. "Yesterday you slipped something into my drink."

"Oh that," Marjie said, with a dismissive wave. "Just a special blend of lemon balm and cardamom. It wasn't alcoholic, if that's what you were thinking."

"I did think that, originally," Rosemary said. "Really, it was just ordinary herbs and spices?"

"And a little charm of my own," Marjie said. "It should have given you a nice bright warm feeling, that's all."

Rosemary looked at Athena, who shrugged.

"Any chance it could have caused me to...err...see things?"

"See things, dear?"

"Yes – you know...like hallucinations? I mean...Athena and I both saw some strange things last night."

"Certainly not," Marjie said, ushering them into the tea shop and setting them up at the table. "That's not something I would do, and anyway, it was just you I gave the charm to, not your girl."

Rosemary and Athena looked at each other, perplexed as Marjie brought them both menus.

"What kind of strange things did you see, dear?" Marjie asked.

"Oh, it's hard to explain." Rosemary said, perusing the menu and settling on the mushroom pie. Athena ordered the bangers and mash, and Marjie went off to the kitchen to tell her husband, Herb, to get cooking. She was back a moment later with a tray of tea, which she assured them was perfectly normal this time.

"It was the house, wasn't it?" Marjie said knowingly.

"Excuse me?" Rosemary asked.

"The house – Thorn Manor – it was playing tricks on you, wasn't it?"

"Playing tricks, how?" Rosemary asked.

Athena looked alarmed at the possibility of a sentient house. It wasn't something Rosemary would have considered possible either, though the experiences of the previous night had set a whole new bar for what "possible" meant.

"Is it...alive?" Rosemary asked, and Athena kicked her gently under the table.

"Not in the way you or I are," Marjie said. "But it has a certain presence...a power, a will of its own, one might say. What exactly happened, dear?"

Rosemary wasn't sure whether she ought to reveal the details of the very strange occurrences to anyone else yet, not even a close friend of her grandmother's like Marjie. The last thing she needed was rumours flying around that she was bonkers when she was apparently involved in a murder investigation.

It did strike her, though, that Marjie might hold the key to interpreting Granny's note, which was seeming more and more reasonable as her world became less and less so.

Is "witch" a code for something else, or is it really what Granny was talking about?

Rosemary wanted to ask, but held back, unsure. She resolved to make a note of all her questions and then bring them up at a later date, preferably when Athena wasn't there to kick her.

CHAPTER
SIX

R osemary and Athena stopped talking as they enjoyed the delicious food that Herb had brought out with a curt nod.

"He's a man of few words," Marjie explained. "You'll get used to him." Then she spun around on her heels and squealed. "Oh, it's just so good to have you home!"

After that, Rosemary had to forgive Marjie completely for the magic tea incident. It was impossible to hold a grudge against someone so genuine and warm and welcoming, and yes, Myrtlewood did feel a lot like a home, at least to Rosemary.

They finished up their meals and made their way over to the police station, which Marjie had told them was across the town square. The building looked just as old-fashioned as Constable Perkins' uniform.

As they crossed the square, two rows of young children wearing pastels were walking in a circle, holding wicker baskets. Rosemary also noticed a tall, thin woman in a bright red cape, who wore her black hair pulled back in a tight bun.

"Such a strange place," Athena said as they pushed open the doors to the police station. The foyer was empty, and the whole building was still and silent.

Rosemary walked up to the front desk and rang the silver domed bell that sat in its centre. She jumped back at the sudden movement as a dark shape emerged from behind the other side of the counter.

"What the...!" Rosemary and Athena both shrieked.

"Hello there. How can I be of service?" Constable Perkins said, straightening his cap.

"You!" Rosemary said.

"Oh, it's you," said Constable Perkins.

"What were you doing under there?" Athena asked.

"I'll be the one asking the questions, young lady," Constable Perkins replied, taking his small notebook out of his breast pocket and clicking his pen.

"But we were the ones who came to see you," Athena argued.

"Oh, right," he said. "So, what can I do for you?"

"Okay, so here's the thing," Rosemary said. "Yesterday you came to the house and told us not to leave town until you're finished with the investigation, but we live in Burkenswood. Athena needs to get back to school and I need to go to work."

"That may be the case, Ma'am, but we can't have you running off while the investigation is ongoing. How am I to know if you might just skip the country or not?"

"Really?" Rosemary said.

"Really. You must stay in Myrtlewood until you've been cleared of any wrongdoing."

"But that doesn't make sense for us – I have to work for a living, and if I don't turn up, I don't get paid," Rosemary said, feeling desperate. She didn't know when the inheritance money would come through, or how much of it there actually was.

"That's not my problem," said Constable Perkins. "I'm just here to be a professional and...professionally do my job of upholding the law...professionally."

"I'll be speaking to my lawyer about this. I don't even think it's legal to hold people in a particular town."

"Be my guest, Miss Thorn," said Constable Perkins. "But I think you'll find we do things differently in Myrtlewood, regardless of what any fancy-schmancy lawyers say."

Rosemary looked at him, aghast that a uniformed police officer would use a term like fancy-schmancy.

"I want to speak to your superior," Rosemary said.

"I think you'll find that no one is superior to me," Constable Perkins said, flicking his moustache.

"I mean, your manager."

"I manage myself just fine, thank you," he replied.

"Are you saying there isn't a police chief or anyone above you I can ask?"

"Oh, there was, but he retired and moved to Bath."

Rosemary and Athena left the police station feeling bewildered.

"On the bright side, I don't have to go to school," Athena said. "But then again, I'm trapped in this insane little town in the middle of nowhere that's a kind of parody of itself, where things behave in ways that defy the laws of science."

"So, you're finally coming around to the fact that the house did, indeed, fix itself?" Rosemary asked.

"I don't know what to believe anymore."

Rosemary wrapped her arm around Athena. "The problem is, we have no idea how long this investigation is going to take. If it's going to be months, then you will need to enroll at the local school so you don't get too far behind before exams."

"Oh, no. Please don't say that!" Athena said. "I've changed schools too many times already, and I bet the school here is hopeless."

"Come on then, let's go to the lawyer's office and see if they can give us better advice on what our rights are."

"But it's Sunday," said Athena.

"Well, he was the one who insisted I come here on Saturday, so maybe the office is open on Sunday as well."

They walked down the road towards the Myrtlewood branch of Clifford and Burk, which was indeed open. A pale, thin woman who looked far too young to have silvery hair sat behind the reception desk with a frown on her face. She seemed to be solving complex mathematical equations on the notepad in front of her.

"Hi," Rosemary said.

"How can I help you?" the woman asked, though she looked disgruntled about being interrupted from her equations.

"I'm wondering if Perseus—I mean, Mr Burk, is available."

"Do you have an appointment?"

"No."

The woman frowned again and rifled through an old-fashioned leather-bound appointment book. "He's not due in the office today," she said. "He's in Burkenswood and is...err...golfing this afternoon."

"Of course he is," Rosemary said, before she could stop herself.

"Pardon me?"

"I just mean, isn't that the stereotypical thing that lawyers are supposed to do on Sundays? Come to think of it, why are you even open?"

The woman's frown deepened, and she muttered, "We're always open. That's part of the problem with this place."

"Okay, very well. We'll just be going."

"Message?" the receptionist asked.

"What?"

"What message shall I leave for Perseus?"

"Oh...uh," she looked at Athena, who nodded encouragingly. "You can just tell him that Rosemary Thorn wanted to ask him about some things."

"Very well," the woman said and went back to her equations without writing the message down.

CHAPTER
SEVEN

A thena followed her mother out of the lawyer's office. The sky above was overcast, and the air was slightly muggy, giving her the sense that the clouds were cloaking the land in a snuggly blanket. It was the kind of observation she seldom shared with her mother, partly because she didn't want Rosemary to get carried away with even more unusual thoughts, but mostly because she wanted to maintain the air of seriousness about her that commanded respect.

Rosemary was the silly one. Athena was the logical one.

This was part of the game Athena played in her head that allowed her to feel slightly more in control of a life that was often uncontrollable. Athena knew it was only partly her mother's fault. Rosemary, at least, tried. Her father, on the other hand, was a total loose cannon, and Athena had vowed to stay away from him and anyone like him.

This went some way to explaining why she'd never had much of an interest in boys. But as they'd left the lawyer's office and headed towards the town square, Athena couldn't help but notice him. His dark hair flopped across his face as he sat under a stark leafless tree, reading a rather large hardback book.

There was something insatiably romantic about the image of him sitting there. He was so lost in his book that Athena felt he might never notice her, and the thought caused a slight jolt of pain through her chest that she wasn't expecting.

As if in response to her emotion, he looked up, his pale blue-grey eyes meeting hers.

It was definitely a moment of...*something*.

Athena had no words for what to call it, but the boy was looking at her as if seeing her...all of her. She almost felt he could reach right through her mind, into her memories, seeing everything laid bare...*but of course, that's impossible,* she told herself.

She realised she was staring and blushed. Then she quickly wrenched her eyes away from him and hurried to catch up with Rosemary.

Something in her mind whispered: *I see you...*

As Athena walked away, she glanced back in the direction of the boy, only to find he had disappeared.

CHAPTER
EIGHT

Athena trailed behind as Rosemary made her way across to the town square so preoccupied with worries that she walked right into someone.

"Sorry," Rosemary said, taking a step back.

"Sorry for what?" the man asked. Rosemary recognised him as Ferg, the odd chap who had given them directions the day before. Only, he was wearing a blue cap with a matching blue sweater draped over his shoulders, rather than yesterday's brown ensemble.

"Sorry for bumping into you, I guess," Rosemary said.

"We meet again, Rose Thorn."

"Rosemary," she corrected.

"If you insist," he said. "Next time you should look where you're going, you know." He said the comment not as an admonishment but offhandedly, as if it were an idle fact.

"I intend to," Rosemary assured him

"Very well. While you're here, you Thorn women can assist me with something."

"Uh...we can?" Rosemary asked, looking at her daughter, who had been oddly quiet since their visit to the police station. Athena merely shrugged.

"Yes. With the festival preparations for Imbolc," Ferg said in his somewhat wooden tone.

"Imbolc?"

"Yes. Imbolc is the festival of first light. It marks the ending of winter, the first signs of spring. That's why we have the flowers. We must honour the goddess, Brigid."

"You say first signs of spring," said Athena, "But it looks like the season's already in full flight with all these blossoms and daffodils everywhere."

"When we honour the gods and goddesses, they show us favour in turn," Ferg said.

Rosemary and Athena gave each other a puzzled look, as if trying to work out if Ferg was serious or speaking in metaphor.

"What is it exactly that you want us to do?" Rosemary asked.

Ferg raised his arm, revealing he'd been holding on to dozens of pastel-coloured ribbons. "Tie these to the trees around the town circle."

"You mean the town square."

"No, the circle – the circle of trees and the big round lawn within the square."

Rosemary looked across the square to see that a large circle of trees was dotted around inside it.

"Oh...well." She looked at Athena.

"We'd love to help," Athena said.

Rosemary stared at her, shocked. That was not the reaction she was expecting from her teen.

"Great!" Ferg said. "Here you go." He handed them the ribbons he was holding, plus another bag of them. "Just tie them in bows. It shouldn't take very long."

"All of them?" Rosemary asked. Eyeing the bag full of ribbons. "There must be at least a hundred in there."

"Yes, all of them. You can tie them with your hands or with your magic if you're in a hurry, but I don't want to see a rushed job."

"My magic?"

"That's what I said."

"Ohh...kay."

Ferg gave her a strange look. "The whole town knows, you know."

It was a slightly creepy thing to say, and Rosemary had the urge to get as far away from this strange man as possible, but he seemed to mean whatever it was in quite a matter-of-fact way.

"I don't know what you're talking about," Rosemary said. Only perhaps, she did. It was all starting to fall into place in her mind: the letter from Granny insisting the family were all witches but saying that she'd had to bind their power years ago, the house fixing itself, the box on Granny's desk that lit up like fireworks. *Could it all really be magic?*

Ferg nodded slightly, as if he'd understood Rosemary's thought-process. She gave him a funny look, hoping that he wasn't actually a mind-reader or she'd have to remember to keep as far away from him as possible.

"So, what is this Imbolc festival like?" Athena asked, changing the conversation as she took some of the ribbons from Rosemary. "Will the whole town be there?"

"Of course," Ferg said. "But as for the details, you'll have to wait and see. We have to have some surprises."

"As long as there are no human sacrifices or naked dancing," Athena said, and this time, it was Rosemary who gently kicked *her*.

"That would be hugely inappropriate," said Ferg. "It's hardly the season for them. Too cold. And anyway, that's not the modern way of doing things," he shook his head sadly, as if lamenting the loss of tradition. "If we burn anything in rituals these days, it's just herbs and the occasional wooden figure that goes on the autumn bonfires for Samhain."

"Err...very good then," Athena said, though she looked as if she wasn't so keen on helping anymore.

"Just start in the east and move around the circle sunwise," Ferg said, not seeming to notice that he'd said anything strange or off-putting.

He walked away, leaving them standing there with the ribbons.

"How did we get landed with this?" Athena asked. "This place is even weirder than I thought."

"You were the one who enthusiastically volunteered to help."

"Yes, but that was before I heard Ferg's nostalgia for the good-old-days of human sacrifice."

"That *was* decidedly uncomfortable," Rosemary agreed. "Let's get started, though. Otherwise, he'll come back to find us, and we'll have to talk to him again."

They got to work, tying ribbons on trees. It was more enjoyable than Rosemary had expected. In fact, in performing the simple act, she felt she might also be tying parts of herself back together, even if it was rather clumsily and haphazardly. It wasn't a permanent fix, more like an old muscle being stretched for the first time in ages. It had been a while since she had done something quiet and relatively solitary. She and Athena divided the ribbons and took different trees, then moved between them, trying the silky strips of satin into pastel bows. Just as she was tying a lemon-yellow ribbon to a silver birch tree, her phone rang.

Rosemary was astonished at the sound. She was absolutely sure her phone battery would be well flat by then, having only charged it for a few minutes that morning.

"Hello?" she answered, her tone cautious.

"Mis– Rosemary," a familiar voice said.

"Mister Burk?" Rosemary asked.

"Please, call me Perseus. If you want me to refer to you on a first-name basis, then it's only fitting."

"Alright then, Perseus. How can I help you?"

"I was actually wondering how I could help you," he said. "You called into my office, remember."

"Oh yes," Rosemary recalled. She'd somehow forgotten, even though it must have only been fifteen or so minutes before. "I figured you were busy with your golf and wouldn't call me back on a Sunday. What is it with lawyers and golf, anyway? Is it some kind of status thing or is it possible you actually enjoy it? It seems a bit dull – no offence. Are all lawyers born liking golf or is it a learned thing?" She wondered out loud, then clamped her hand over her mouth to stop herself from rambling any further.

"I beg your pardon, Rosemary. I called to see how I could help, not to be casually insulted."

She could hear the smile in his voice, and it made her laugh.

"I'm sorry, Perseus," she said. "Next time I'll be sure to insult you more formally."

"I appreciate it," he said. "Now. What it is you need?"

"They won't let us leave town," Rosemary said, recalling what pre-empted the visit to the lawyers.

"Who won't?"

"The police...Constable Perkins said we couldn't leave Myrtlewood until we were cleared from the investigation. The thing is, we have lives in Burkenswood. Athena has school. I have what passes for work, though it pays terribly. I still need that terrible pay to, you know, pay the rent and not be homeless."

"Rosemary, you just inherited a rather large home and a medium-sized fortune."

"Kind of," she said. "Like you said, it isn't coming through yet, and we don't have any money until...well, who knows when. You don't seem to know. Anyway, it's disruptive for Athena to miss school, and she doesn't want to live here."

"She doesn't?"

"No, not really. She doesn't much like Burkenswood either, but she likes Stratham more and wants to move back there if possible."

"And what do you want?"

"It hardly matters what I want at the moment, does it? We have no choice, apparently. We can't leave here and...well...can we leave? Is this even legal?"

"I'll look into it for you," Perseus Burk said. "Though I'm afraid that while this investigation continues, you are likely best placed to stay in town and help...err...resolve the issues."

"What on earth do you mean by that?"

"Things appear to be quite complicated, and you may have vital information that will find the person – or people – who harmed your grandmother," he said, and then hesitated. "Not only that, but I've just received word of another unexpected development."

"What kind of development?" Rosemary said through rising dread.

"Your cousin Elamina has issued a legal challenge on the will of Galderall Thorn."

"You're joking!" Rosemary said. "What would Elamina want with an old house? It's certainly not cash. She's loaded."

"She has not stated a particular objective, just that she believes the new will made by Madame Thorn is compromised, somehow."

Rosemary's mind was racing...*compromised? Is she implying that I tried to twist Granny's arm into giving me her entire fortune?*

The thought of the implied accusation made Rosemary furious. "Well, she can go suck on a toadstool," she said. "I didn't even speak to Granny in all that time, let alone try to manipulate her. Elamina was the one who was visiting her regularly according to that cop. Maybe it was just her personality that turned Granny off."

"That could well be the case," Perseus Burk said. "Though it does create certain...complications for you."

"How do you mean?"

"Well, given the suspicious nature of Madame Thorn's death..."

"Oh no – no, that's just great! Maybe that's what all this is about. Elamina is trying to frame me!"

"I suggest refraining from jumping to conclusions," Burk said. Rosemary had tried but could not really think of him by his first name. He was far too formal. "I do not seek to alarm you," he continued. "Just to make you aware of the risks. The police, after all, will be looking for a motive. A legal challenge to the will such as this will rouse their suspicions."

"So, tell me then, who would stand to gain if I was thrown in jail for murder? Who would inherit then?"

"I expect the will and estate would have to be re-litigated before a judge," he said. "Depending on how good your cousin's lawyer is, as the second-oldest granddaughter, Elamina might well stand to inherit the property. Or it could be sold and the money would likely be divided up equally among eligible family members."

"So, there's Elamina's motive!" Rosemary crowed. "That's what I'll tell that ridiculous constable."

"I understand you're upset, Rosemary," Burk said.

"Upset? No. I'm livid. Can you even imagine being thrown into this situation?"

"As a matter of fact, I can," Burk said calmly. "I was in a similar situation some years ago with my own family, and based on that experience, I advise you not to throw stones. Avoid making any strong accusations until you have concrete evidence, and if you want to raise your concerns with the authorities, do it subtly."

"You've got to be kidding," Rosemary said. "There's nothing subtle about being framed for murdering the only family member – aside from my daughter – that I actually love!"

"Rosemary. The police like to think they are clever. They like to be the ones to work things out. That is the only reason I'm advising you of this as your legal counsel. It's practical advice. If you subtly lead the authorities to work it out 'on their own', they are much more likely to see things your way than if you accost them with furious and spurious accusations."

Rosemary sighed. "I suppose you're right."

"Very well. Is there anything else I can help you with?"

"No," she said, then added a slightly sullen "Thank you."

"I'm happy to help, as I said. Anytime you need legal advice, please do call me. Golfing advice, however, is not included."

Rosemary laughed and hung up the phone.

"What was all that?" Athena asked from behind her.

Rosemary turned to find her daughter smirking.

"All what?" she asked. "I was simply seeking legal advice."

"You were flirting!"

"Oh, nonsense. You know I don't know how to flirt!"

"Well...you *were* doing it badly."

"Athena, this is hardly the time to be accusing me of more things. We are in the middle of a murder investigation."

"Oh, that old chestnut."

"Yes. That old rotten, slippery, slimy chestnut that keeps getting worse."

"What *are* you talking about, Mother?"

"Elamina is contesting Granny's will, which makes it look like we are guilty of something."

"Great...but by 'we', you mean 'you', right? I didn't murder anyone."

"Thanks for the support, kid," Rosemary hissed. "But I'd like to remind you that neither did I! And furthermore – keep your voice down when you say suspicious things like that. You never know when that oddball policeman is going to pop up with his notepad and use our silly jokes against us."

"Sorry," Athena said, raising her palms in surrender.

They both looked around, but Constable Perkins was blessedly nowhere in sight.

"So, I take it we can't just leave town?" Athena asked.

"Apparently 'it is in our best interests' to stay," Rosemary said. "Whatever that means."

"I expect it means exactly what it sounds like."

Rosemary shrugged.

"So, what do we do then?" Athena asked. "We can't just stay here in limbo and do nothing."

"That's it!" Rosemary said, excitedly.

"What?"

"We are going to solve this damned investigation ourselves!"

"Mum, you can't 'solve' an investigation. You *carry out* investigations, you maybe *conduct* them. You solve problems."

"You know what I mean. We will figure it all out."

"You're sure about that?" Athena asked sceptically.

"Yes," said Rosemary, feeling more and more determined. "We just need to gather all the evidence together and figure out the patterns and the motives and stuff. Surely, it can't be that hard."

"Uh, Mum, you've been watching too many murder mysteries on the telly. In real life, this stuff is really hard. That's why people train to do it – professionally!"

"Are you saying you don't think we could make a better go of it than old Perkins over there?" Rosemary said, gesturing towards the police station.

"You might have a point," Athena said. "So, what do we do?"

"We talk to people, ask questions, not like an interrogation, but just as if we are friendly people."

"I'm not friendly, and I'm not a good actor," Athena said.

"Oh, yes, you are – on both counts – when you want to be. We'll get information together and when we work it out, we'll drop subtle hints to Constable Perkins just like Perseus suggested."

"Perseus?" Athena said, raising her eyebrows. "You're on a first-name-basis with the lawyer?"

"Long story," Rosemary said. "Though I still want to just call him Burk. He's kind of stuffy. And stop giving me that look. It's not going to happen."

"So, what exactly did *Perseus* say? Why are we dropping subtle hints instead of being more to-the-point?"

"Because cops have big egos," Rosemary improvised. "And they want to figure everything out themselves. If you tell them something directly, they will assume you're wrong because they think they're smarter than you. So, you have to kind of approach things sideways and lead them without their knowledge, so that they think they are the clever ones working everything out."

"That's an overly complicated way of putting it," said Athena. "But I think *Perseus* might just be onto something."

CHAPTER
NINE

They finished up tying the ribbons and made a quick stop at the grocery store as Athena had convinced Rosemary that they were sorely in need of snacks.

"We've got food back at the house," said Rosemary. "It would be better if we didn't waste money."

"Ninety nine pence on Jaffa Cakes is hardly going to break the bank," said Athena. She was selecting a second packet, much to Rosemary's disapproval, when a voice startled them.

"Rosey?"

She turned to look straight into the blue-green eyes she remembered from long ago.

"Liam?"

"Of course," he said, brushing his light sandy hair out of his eyes. Rosemary recalled that he always did seem to have a problem with getting haircuts on time, but the look also suited him. Liam had been a gangly youth, but he'd bulked up to the point where he was almost embarrassingly attractive in a slightly rough way, as if he belonged in a Men's magazine photo shoot about living in a log cabin. Rosemary took in the stubble frosting his chin and the definition of his muscles evidenced even through his shirt.

She was awash in old memories – that first mid-winter carnival in Myrtlewood, where she and Liam had snuck away from the crowd to kiss, sweetly and innocently, under the mistletoe when they were only fourteen. The summer they had spent together, after getting to know each other through a year's worth of letters. It had been bliss – walking down by the river, holding hands in jubilant teenage infatuation. The autumn where Rosemary had realised it was never going to work – her heart ached from the long-distance and their letters had become few and far between. Furthermore, another young man had caught her eye. She'd called Liam to tell him it was over, hearing his voice shatter into tears on the other end of the phone.

The other young man had turned out to be very, very bad for her, and it always made her wonder what would have happened if she'd stuck with sweet and earthy Liam.

"You're still in Myrtlewood," Rosemary said, blushing slightly.

"Of course, as far as I'm concerned, it's the best place I could possibly live, and you?"

"Oh..." Rosemary said. "Well..."

"We're here for the moment," Athena added, trying to help her mother find the right words without launching into the whole murder investigation thing.

"You must be...?" he said, looking at Athena.

"This is my daughter, Athena."

"Oh gosh," Liam said. "I heard you had a daughter, Rosey, but I didn't realise time had..."

"It does pass quickly, doesn't it? Especially when you're not a parent."

"Mum!"

"Anyway, as Athena said, we're here for the moment."

"Of course," said Liam. "Your grandmother. I was so sorry to hear about that."

He looked down at the floor, as if unable to proceed.

"Yes," Rosemary said, trying to hold back from launching into the entire story, then she realised that, as a local, Liam might have helpful information. "Actually, I'd like to know what you've heard about the situation. We've had a few...mixed messages."

"From Madame Thorn?"

"No. How would Granny be sending us messages?" Rosemary said and then recalled the box and the note and the strangely smiling painting. "Never mind. I was thinking more about what people are saying 'round town. Who do they think might have had a role in her... well, you know."

"I'm not one for gossip, but this is a small town and people do talk," Liam said. "All I know is she was found up at the house. I heard there were animal footprints of a few different kinds – could have been birds and dogs."

"Oh," Rosemary said, feeling herself growing pale. "I wasn't expecting that."

"Sorry, Rosey," Liam said. "I didn't mean to..."

"No, it's fine," she said, though she didn't feel particularly fine. "Anyway, we best be getting on."

"Look – here's my card," Liam said, handing her a small yellow square of card with 'Haversham Books' on the front.

"Your...card?"

"Yes – I run the bookshop just across the way. Pop in anytime you want to chat or...you know, call me if you need anything."

"Thanks, Liam."

Rosemary watched as he walked away, then turned back to Athena.

"What was all that?" Athena asked.

"What?"

"All that gushing, *Rosey*! All the doe eyes!"

"Don't be silly. He was a childhood crush. That's all."

"Are you going to *call* him?"

"Not like that, Athena. You know I don't date. Anyway, he's probably married or otherwise occupied."

"You always make excuses like that."

"Athena!"

"What?"

"Can we please just stick to the matters at hand? Such as, oh, I don't know – solving a murder so we don't get blamed for it?"

"Oh fine, spoilsport," Athena said, plucking two bags of crisps from the shelf to add to the basket. "Let's get back to the house, then. We can't keep talking about murder all around town, or we'll look even more suspicious."

They left the grocery shop and made their way back to Thorn Manor.

The house still looked grand and well-maintained. Rosemary was grateful that it had not regressed back to a run-down shambles, though how the house had seemingly fixed itself in the first place remained a mystery.

"I suppose we have to let my boss and your school know that we won't be in tomorrow," Rosemary said.

"I guess," Athena replied. "It still seems so weird. I don't particularly want to go to school, but it feels like we're trapped here, and I don't like it."

"I know, love," Rosemary said. "It's an unusual situation, but I believe we are up to the task. Let's solve this mystery and get our freedom back."

"How do you suggest we start?"

"A cup of tea?" Rosemary suggested. "Yes, that's always the best way to start: a cup of tea and we can chat about the things we've learned so far."

They went inside and Rosemary put the kettle on and readied the teapot. When the tea was brewed, they sat in the window seats and thought through some possible suspects.

"Who would stand to gain from the situation?" Athena asked. "Apart from us, I mean."

"Well, there's obviously Elamina," Rosemary said. "She's certainly up to something – who does she think she is, contesting the will? I bet it's all her fault. Her and her brother Derse and their hoity-toity parents, aunt Cecilia and uncle Cyril. The constable said that some family had been visiting Granny regularly. I bet it was her, trying to wear Granny down."

"I thought you said she didn't need money. That side of the family is loaded."

"Maybe they made some bad investments, got into money troubles, or maybe there's something else they want. They were always so competitive. I bet they just can't bear to lose anything. Including the old family manor."

"We'll put them down as *potential* suspects, okay?" Athena said, writing in her notebook. "But don't get too obsessed with thinking it's them. That's how they always miss the real killer on telly. You know, it's a red-herring or something. Puts you off the scent."

Rosemary shrugged. "Fine, who else is there?"

"What about the people who want the house? There was that really odd estate woman."

"Ugh, don't remind me," Rosemary shuddered. "I feel the tingle of an itch on my hands just at her mention."

"Don't be such a hypochondriac," Athena said. "There is no way you can actually be allergic to estate agents."

"You don't believe your own mother!"

"Would you, if grandma said something like that?"

"Oh, probably not," Rosemary conceded. "Okay write her down. Look—" She picked up the pink card off the coffee table. "Here she is: Despina Crepe."

"Of course, it could be her or someone else who she's an agent for," Athena suggested.

"Oooh...like a double agent," Rosemary said.

"No, Mum. A single agent. That is literally her job."

"I guess you're right. Maybe we can ask her more questions to see what we can ascertain about the prospective buyers she has in mind, pretend we might be interested in selling so that she gives us more information."

"Good idea," Athena said. "And we can find out more about your cousins too. We could even ask them questions directly."

"Oh, yes. That's going to go well," said Rosemary. "Hey Elamina, how are you? It's been so long. Did you change your hair? It looks nice. Oh, and by the way, did you happen to kill Granny?"

"No, Mother. Not like that. Just a normal conversation where we can figure out if they are tense or nervous about anything."

"We don't have normal conversations," Rosemary said. "A normal conversation in our family is us talking about each other separately, in our separate homes. I'm sure they are having their normal conversation about how hopeless I am right now."

Athena sighed.

"Okay, okay," Rosemary conceded. "It's a possibility."

"Who else is there?" Athena asked. "Has anyone else shown an interest in the house?"

"Well, Marjie's interested in everything," Rosemary said.

"Come on, Mum. She can't possibly be a killer."

"It's always who they least suspect," said Rosemary.

"That's on television, not in reality," said Athena. "Although she did dose you with that 'charm' or whatever it was. What if she dosed Granny too?"

"Why? Why would her best friend do that?"

"You're right. That's too creepy," said Athena. "Besides, Marjie is not the murdering type."

"How would you know that?"

"I'm a good judge of character, remember...unlike some people I know. Anyway, who else was interested in the house?"

"There was Burk," said Rosemary.

"You mean your lawyer friend, *Perseus?* He wants the house, too, does he? *Interesting.*" Athena said it in *that voice* and Rosemary gave her an evil glare.

"When we first met, he was very keen on me selling it, that's all. It seemed strange since I hadn't even come out here to see it at that point."

"I'll write him down, but now you can't date him."

"Since when do I date anyone?" Rosemary asked. "And why not?"

"It would be a conflict of interest," Athena insisted. "Oh, actually... you should date him!"

"So consistent."

"No, seriously. That would give you a reason to get to know him and ask questions."

"Like, please pass the salt, and by the way, have you committed any casual murders lately?"

"In a non-suspicious way," Athena said. "You know, ask about how long he's been around here and why he's interested in the house."

"It certainly is an interesting house," Rosemary said, looking around at all the gleaming wood. "Yesterday, I have to admit, I was terrified of it, but now it just feels so..."

"Cosy?" Athena suggested, looking around the room at all the doilies and ornaments.

"Yes, and welcoming. As if it's here to look after us."

"Well, I hope that's the case, since there's a murderer on the loose. What other suspects do we have?" Athena asked.

"I can't think of any just yet, but maybe after we chat with other people around town, we can add more. Hey! Why don't we find a big piece of paper so we can write down all the names and all the connections, like one of those police whiteboards on telly."

Rosemary got up and looked around for something to use. Of course, Granny's library was the obvious place to look for paper, but she'd been avoiding that room since the light-box-house-fixing incident.

She peeked around the door, but the scene seemed quite ordinary. Even the box sitting on the desk appeared to be innocent and wooden. She pushed the door open wider, cautiously stepping into the room and giving the box a wide girth as she walked past.

The library was well-stocked with stationery. It didn't take Rosemary long to find a large piece of paper on one of the shelves behind the desk. She turned back, intending to take it straight out to Athena, but the box caught her eye again. Rosemary was curious to know what was inside and what could have happened the night before to spark such a reaction.

How dangerous could it possibly be? Her curiosity got the better of her. She set the paper down on the desk and reached for the box. As she touched it, the sound of a chime rang out.

Rosemary stared at the box. She could detect a slight glow inside that hadn't been there a moment earlier.

Part of her wanted to run away as quickly as possible, but the other part wondered if this was some kind of message from Granny.

She thought back to the note telling her about the family's supposed magic powers, and the painting that seemed to smile at her, and the light from the box that somehow repaired and cleaned the old house.

If this really is magic and it somehow cleans a house, how could that possibly be a bad thing?

She thought about calling out to Athena, but then again, she didn't want to scare her.

"Granny?" she whispered. "Is that you?"

The interior of the box seemed to glow brighter.

"Granny?"

Rosemary reached back out towards the box. As her hand touched it, the glow started to spread from the tips of her fingers and up her arm.

She wanted to pull back in surprise, but the light was warm and pleasant and soothing, reminding Rosemary of the way Granny would sing her to sleep as a young child. Instead of pulling away, Rosemary leaned in further. The light flooded through her entire body. This time, there was something else in the box. Her index finger brushed against its cool, hard surface.

Rosemary grasped the object, lifting it up away from the bright light to see she was holding a quartz crystal.

It glowed brightly in her hand, and the room around her faded to black.

She was standing in a void.

"Athena?" she called out. Her voice echoed into the empty space around her. Rosemary's heart raced. *What just happened? Where am I?*

She walked tentatively into the dark. The crystal glowed like a lantern in her hand, radiating light that fell into the darkness without illuminating anything around her.

It all just seemed like nothing, a vast black emptiness. The ground beneath, at least, was solid but just as pitch black as everything else.

"Hello?" she called out, and then fear caught her heart. If anything dangerous was out there, she was alerting it to her presence. As if the light was not enough.

She cupped the crystal in her palms, trying to mute its glow. It stubbornly continued to shine from between her clenched fingers.

Another source of light flickered close by. There was a flurry of movement, and Rosemary froze, but so too did whatever she was looking at. As her eyes adjusted to the new light source, she realised that it was some sort of mirror – a reflection of her. It breathed when she did and turned its head in time with her, but this woman was wild and confident, clad in intricate dusky lace with beautiful tattoos of botanical plants up her arms.

Rosemary stared at the woman in the mirror, who was both her and not her. The woman stared back, so strong and confident. Rosemary felt a deep tug, as if the woman she was staring at was the long-lost part of her she'd been searching for, imprisoned in the glass, or perhaps a future self, waiting to unfurl like a wild blossom. Another light flickered up ahead, and the reflection dispersed like smoke. Rosemary stepped towards the brighter light. It seemed welcoming and safe, drawing her in.

Up ahead, another woman stood on a platform of stone, stooped and slender, wearing light grey robes. She had long white hair, half-plaited and trailing down her back. She held a large bowl made of stone. Her smile was genuine, warm, and somehow familiar.

"Who are you?" Rosemary asked. "Do I know you?"

"Of course, dear," the woman said. "You are of my line and like-

90

ness. My blood flows through you, as it has through generations before you."

"You're...my ancestor?"

"I am your elder," the woman said, nodding. "And it's time for you to reconnect with your life blood."

"What do you mean?" Rosemary asked.

"Here," the woman said. "Drink of this to regain your link with the family line."

The woman took a silver goblet and scooped it into the stone bowl she was holding. Shimmery liquid, like mercury, dripped from the sides and Rosemary wondered if this was a trick, an enemy, trying to poison her...but the woman's smile was so kind and, really, what choice did Rosemary have? She had no idea where she was or how to get back.

Rosemary reached out for the goblet, taking it into both palms. She eyed the liquid, which seemed to move as if it had a life of its own. She lifted it to her lips and took a great gulp then closed her eyes to savour the complex flavour.

It tasted like rust and honey, and cool summer nights, and fresh cut grass and elderberry wine. It tasted like Granny's mince pies and Sunday morning lie-ins, and late nights at the beach, and lolling out on a blanket underneath the stars in the throes of youthful infatuation. It tasted like secrets and velvet, and coming out of the cold rain to drink hot toddies. It was bitter and tart and sweet and a little bit salty. It was delicious and also slightly painful to drink, and yet Rosemary wanted more.

Rosemary opened her eyes to find the woman had vanished. She was in the dark again. She called out, but nothing responded. She felt a distinct discomfort...a creeping fear, and then—

"Mum!"

Athena was shaking her awake, and Rosemary opened her eyes to the blinding daylight of the library.

"I wasn't ready," Rosemary said.

"What?" Athena asked. "You fell asleep."

"No. I was...I was somewhere else, and I drank a potion and then it was dark and uncomfortable but...I get the feeling something else was supposed to happen."

"What are you talking about?"

"Oh, never mind," Rosemary said, picking herself up off the floor. "I'll explain later."

"Did you at least find the paper?"

"Oh...oh yes, paper," Rosemary said, reaching out towards the desk. Just as she did so, the paper twitched and then flew straight into her hand.

"Did you just see that?" Rosemary asked. She turned to see Athena's jaw dropping. "That was weird. Let's get out of here."

"No," Athena said. "Try it again."

"Why?" Rosemary asked. "It was weird enough the first time."

"Just try it," Athena said. "I want to see if you can actually move paper with your mind or if it was just the wind of something."

"Right. It's blowing a gale in here," Rosemary said into the perfectly still room.

"Or static electricity. I don't know. Just try it."

Rosemary held out her hand towards the stack of paper on the bottom shelf, willing it to come to her. Everything remained still and ordinary.

"What did you say last time?" Athena asked.

"Uhm, paper?"

Still, nothing moved from the shelf.

"Try it again, but more commanding," Athena said.

"Paper!" Rosemary cried. The stack of paper remained perfectly still, and Rosemary, despite her initial hesitation, was oddly disappointed. "Maybe it only works sometimes," she said.

"What works sometimes?" Athena asked.

"My magic," said Rosemary. "The elder restored it. At least I think that's what happened. She gave me some kind of silver potion to drink from a goblet which tasted like...well, like everything good with just a tinge of sadness."

"Did you hit your head, or something?"

"No, I'm serious," Rosemary said. "You saw it with your own eyes. That paper moved. It came to me."

"I saw something, but I'm not convinced it's magic."

"And the house!" said Rosemary. "You saw the house fix itself."

Athena shook her head, as if trying to shake off cobwebs. "Come on," she said. "I think we need another cup of tea."

"Seriously," Rosemary said, following her daughter out to the kitchen. She reached into her pocket and pulled out the note from Granny. "Remember this?"

"You thought she was mad and senile, remember?"

"Sure, I did, at first...but with everything that's happened."

"You really think it's magic?" Athena asked. "That you're magical?"

"Our family is. That's what Granny said in this letter, only somehow, we lost it. There was some grave danger and Granny bound the family's powers. That's why we never knew, and that's also why I stopped spending so much time in Myrtlewood. Granny says here that it was all part of the spell."

"Convenient that she basically excuses you for neglecting her," Athena said.

"Ouch. That's harsh."

"Well, you were going on about how guilty you felt, and then all of a sudden, you have a reason for your actions."

"I'm not trying to use it as an excuse," Rosemary said.

Athena had filled the electric kettle with water by this point. She tried to put it on, but the switch didn't light up. "It's not working. Maybe it's another power-cut. Drat. We'll have to use the wood-burner again." She started filling the old-fashioned kettle instead.

"Or we could use the gas stove," Rosemary suggested, gesturing to the gleaming stainless-steel oven with gas hobs on top. "We'll just need to use matches to light it. It will be a lot quicker than lighting the wood-burner."

"Then why didn't we do that when we first arrived?"

"I don't think the gas stove was here," Rosemary said.

"Oh, nonsense. Here." Athena passed the filled stove-top kettle to Rosemary.

"You really don't believe me, do you?" Rosemary said, still holding the kettle. "I mean...I can understand why. It's not easy to believe this stuff...but when you've seen it with your own eyes."

"It's ridiculous, Mum,"

"I know it's ridiculous!" Rosemary said. She could feel a slight tingling in her fingers, which were unusually warm, but she ignored it in favour of continuing the impassioned conversation. "Don't you think I realise that? I'm a grown woman. Why would I make this stuff up?"

"I never said you made it up," Athena said, using her calming voice. "I just think you're getting carried away."

"Carried away?!"

The kettle started to whistle in her hands around the same time that Rosemary realised it was unbearably hot.

"Ouch," she dropped it down on the unlit stove. "What...?!"

Steam billowed out of the kettle, which continued to whistle and then died down, as if the stove had been turned off beneath it.

"No way!" Athena cried. "No freaking way. Did you just boil the kettle with your *hands*?"

"I...I think so," Rosemary said.

"Is the water safe to drink?" Athena asked.

"I don't see why not," said Rosemary.

"You might have magicked it to be all weird."

Athena picked up the kettle and poured a little of the hot water into the sink, just to check it, but it was quite ordinary looking. She made the tea and carried the tea tray over to the window seats, while Rosemary wrung her hands and paced around, muttering undiscernibly to herself.

"The tea tastes fine," Athena said. "I hope it doesn't make us hallucinate again."

"I think we've established that it wasn't a hallucination," Rosemary said.

"Do you think you can do it again? Boil the water, I mean."

"Oh, I don't know," Rosemary replied. "I couldn't make the paper move when I tried to do it deliberately. Maybe this is the kind of magic that only words by accident."

"That's a *kind*?" Athena asked. "Oh, hello, Rosemary, what type of magic do you practice? Just the accidental kind."

"Oh, stop it," Rosemary said. "You know about as much as I do."

"Give me that letter then," Athena said.

Rosemary begrudgingly handed it over, though she was at least satisfied that Athena finally seemed to believe her.

"It says it's family magic," Athena said. "So where are *my* powers?"

"I don't know," Rosemary said. "It's all to do with that box in the library, I think, but the elder also said that magic would be restored to the family line. Maybe you have the magic, too, and you just haven't accidentally used it yet."

"We could ask Marjie about all this," Athena suggested. "She seems to know about charms and the like."

"We could, but we haven't completely ruled her out as a suspect yet," Rosemary reminded her. "I really hope she isn't the one who hurt Granny, because that would be awful. Her own best friend."

"It won't be her," Athena said.

"How do you know?"

"I told you, I have an instinct for these things."

"You mean you've watched too many crime dramas?"

"No. In a crime drama she would be a likely suspect, but in real life she can't be."

"And why is that, madame investigator?" Rosemary asked.

"She's too...good," Athena said. "You can just tell with her. She's good and kind and warm through and through. There's no way she's the one who killed your grandmother."

"Well, I'm not quite so hasty," Rosemary said, retrieving the large piece of paper. "Let's get started on this. We have to be methodical. Who were the people in Granny Thorn's life that might have hurt her? Who had it in for her? Who had something to gain from her passing?

There's that estate lady. Despina. Who else?" She began scrawling on the paper.

"What about that lawyer man you like so much?" Athena said, teasing.

"Perseus Burk. Yes, I suppose we can't rule him out. He did seem strangely eager to help with all this, and he was keen on me selling the house. Okay. That's two. Then, of course, there are our dear relatives, the Bracewell-Thorns. I'll write down Elamina and Derse for now, though their parents are just as bad, but more distant. I have a feeling that if it was them, they'd all be in on it together. Oh...and that constable. He was a weird one. I wonder if he has something to hide.?"

"Surely, there are a bunch more people that we just haven't heard of yet," Athena said.

"You're right. We need to start asking questions, and what better excuse than to go into to town for dinner and strike up innocent conversations to find out more details."

"You've got to be kidding me," Athena said. "*You* having an *innocent* conversation? You're bound to put your foot in it. Besides, you keep saying how broke we are, but you keep suggesting we go out for food."

"I'm too tired to cook," said Rosemary. "A pub meal is hardly going to make much of a difference to our financial situation." Not compared to the masses of debt, anyway. "But you're right. I *am* bound to say something stupid. I'll try to be careful."

"Oh, fine," Athena said. "Let's go. I'm starved."

CHAPTER
TEN

Athena and Rosemary put on their coats against the chilly wind and made their way towards the Myrtlewood village.

It was late afternoon, fading into early evening, and the sky was just beginning to darken. Athena delighted in seeing a snowy owl, who watched them from a hollow in a nearby tree. They paused to admire it.

"Maybe it's not so bad here," Athena said.

"Oh, okay, so you don't take my word for it, but trust in this owl."

"Of course, owls are innately trustworthy," Athena said, but just as the words escaped her mouth, they heard a loud scratching sound from the stand of trees nearby, followed by an unearthly squawking.

"Let's get out of here!" Athena whispered, and Rosemary agreed. They hurried on, and both breathed a sigh of relief when they reached the village. Marjie's tea shop was closed, as were most of the other shops, giving the whole place an eerie dusky feeling, but the lights were on, and jolly sounds were booming from the building called the 'Witches Wort', the only pub in town. They made their way, gratefully, into the warmth.

All the other patrons turned their heads to watch as they entered.

There was a hush and all Rosemary could hear was the sea shanty playing quietly over the speakers.

The woman behind the bar smiled at them. "Welcome," she said. "And who do we have here?"

The woman was not much older than Rosemary, with a round face and long strawberry blond hair, which she wore in a plait.

Rosemary wasn't used to such a personal greeting from someone she didn't know, but she decided to go along with it. After all, this was a small town.

"Uhm, I'm Rosemary," she said. "And this is my daughter Athena."

"Why, I never...Rosemary Thorn!" the bartender said. "You don't remember me?"

"Uh, no," Rosemary admitted.

"I'm Sherry Hume. I used to help your grandmother out around the house when I was a kid. I'd give you piggy-backs around the garden."

Rosemary smiled, a flicker of memory helping her to nod in agreement, though it was so vague she never would have recognised this woman without prompting.

"Sit down, sit down! I'll bring you two some menus."

Rosemary and Athena took their seats in an empty booth.

"Well, that's gone and put a dampener on our investigations, hasn't it?" Athena said.

"What do you mean?"

"The whole town knows who we are now, and who we're related to. They're hardly going to spill the beans and tell us they killed granny."

"Well, the murderer isn't," Rosemary whispered, trying to encourage Athena to keep her voice down. "But they probably weren't going to waltz up and tell perfect strangers about their terrible crime, either. The thing is, there are probably tons of people here who know a thing or two and would want to tell us because they want the crime to be solved – for Granny's sake."

"I didn't think of it like that," Athena admitted.

Sherry brought them the menus as promised, along with two small brown pottery mugs that were steaming and smelled delicious – sweet and spicy.

"What's this?" Rosemary asked. "We didn't order drinks."

"On the house," Sherry said. "This is some of our famous mulled mead!"

Rosemary looked at Athena whose eyes were wide as she stared at the unusual beverage.

"—and don't worry," Sherry continued. "It's not too alcoholic, more like a ginger beer, I promise."

"Uh. Okay," Rosemary said. "It's not spiked with...anything else, is it?"

Sherry cackled. "Oh, you've been spending too much time with Marjie, haven't you?"

"Some," Rosemary admitted.

"Look, I'll level with you," Sherry said. "Our mulled mead is made with an old and very secret recipe, and it does involve a little bit of magic – nothing serious. It's just something to give you a bit of a pick-me-up and protect you from the cold, that's all."

"Magic," Rosemary said. "Of course."

Sherry smiled again and left them to consider the menus.

Rosemary took a sip of the mulled mead. It really was delicious and warming. Athena did the same and smiled. She looked in Sherry's direction at the bar.

"So, it really is just something they talk about casually here," Rosemary said, looking around the pub. "Magic – as if it was needlework or tennis or Szechuan pepper."

"So it seems," said Athena. "Unless it's a metaphor."

"You're too sensible for your own good," said Rosemary.

"These prices are good," Athena said, ignoring her mother and scouring the menu.

"It's just as well," Rosemary replied. "We are short on cash for the foreseeable future. Payday isn't until Thursday, and it won't be much if I can't get back to do more shifts. We won't be able to afford meals out like this – or anything else – if we're not lucky."

"All the more reason to figure out what happened to Granny Thorn," Athena said. "If we can solve that mystery, then maybe we can get our freedom back and—"

"'scuse me," an old woman said, stumbling into the booth. She had wild hair and an eye patch. "Allow me to introduce myself. My name is Agatha Twigg and I couldn't help overhearing what you young ladies were saying about old Galdie."

"Oh, yes?" Rosemary said, blanching. She didn't realise they'd been talking loud enough for anyone else to hear. "You knew my grandmother, then?"

"'course I did," Agatha said, shaking her head sadly. "And what a shame it was to lose her in her prime like that."

"In her prime? She was in her eighties,"

"Exactly," said the old woman. "I bet she had a good few decades left. She was a strong 'un."

Athena raised her eyebrows at Rosemary in a way that suggested they'd be better off not believing anything the old woman said, but Rosemary was less incredulous. After all...magic was probably real. Who knew how long a magically enhanced life-span might be? And Granny Thorn had always been fit as a fiddle.

"Do you know anything about what happened to her?" Rosemary asked. "We want to know, you see. As family, it's so hard to think of her passing without even knowing what happened."

"It wasn't me, if you're asking," Agatha said. "I mean, Galdie had her enemies, but I wasn't one of them. I'd know better than to cross someone so powerful."

"Enemies?" Athena asked, seemingly forgetting her own distrust for a moment. "Who were her enemies, then?"

"Well, she didn't like all that many people, see. She never got along with the police force around here, or the postman, for that matter. She loathed courier companies. She didn't like that bloke at the bookshop – kept muttering about how he didn't know real magical books from the fake ones. She was definitely offside with the Bloodstone Society..."

"The what?"

100

"Oh, you know. No one is supposed to know they exist, but naturally, everyone does. They're just one of those secret societies. Think they're better than anyone else. Old Galdie hated them with a passion. Told them to stay away from her house."

"It seems like lots of people were after her house," Rosemary said. "I mean, I've already had a few people trying to buy it, and it's not even mine."

She'd meant to say "yet," but something told her to hold her tongue. After all, she didn't know if she could really trust this unusual stranger.

"O'course, lots of people want that house. Legend says that's where the power is hidden."

"What power?" Athena asked.

"The old Thorn magic. Y'see, you'd both be too young to remember it, but once that power was so obvious. You could feel it miles away. Then, probably only a few decades ago, it vanished from the radar. The house was still there, and Galdie was still there, but though she still seemed to have a bit of power for odds and ends, there wasn't the great loads of it there was before. The Thorns were one of the old magical families, see, and the power just grew and grew over generations. Now, don't get me wrong, Myrtlewood is a special place, and just about everyone here has a trace of some kind of power or other, but it's nothing compared to that old magic...nothing," she muttered.

"Are you ready to order?" Sherry said, and Rosemary realised she must have been standing within earshot for some time. "Sorry if Agatha is bothering you. She's a great story-teller, this one."

"Yes, I'm starved." Athena said. "I'll have the fish 'n chips, please."

"Great, and for you, Rosemary?"

"I'll have the same, thanks."

"Anything else?"

"No thank you," Rosemary and Athena choroused at the same time.

"That young lass is too big for her britches," Agatha grumbled. "Thinks she owns the place. Well...she does. But that's only because old Merle died and left it to her. No one knows why he didn't leave it to his own kids. It was right suspicious if you ask me, but try telling that to the local law enforcement. What a joke."

Agatha Twigg took a big swig of her pint and then toddled away, muttering to herself.

"Well, I supposed we should take all that with a grain of salt," Rosemary said.

"Or a bucket load," said Athena. "Perhaps a whole salt-lake full of saline."

"I'm pretty sure half of what she said made absolute sense," Rosemary said. "I'm just not sure exactly which half."

"Oh, don't mind old Aggie," Sherry said. She was back again holding two plates full of delicious looking golden deep-fried food.

"That was quick!" Rosemary and Athena both exclaimed as both plates were placed down on the table in front of them.

"Well, I have my ways," Sherry said, tapping her nose. "She, on the other hand." She gestured back to where Agatha was now standing, near the bar, accosting a young couple who sat there. "Well, she's a troublemaker. Pay no mind to anything she tells you."

"She talked about Granny Thorn," Athena said. "You wouldn't happen to know anything, would you? About what happened to her?"

"I've heard some whispers that her own magic might have back-fired," Sherry said. "Other people in here say that wasn't it, but I can't bear to think that someone would hurt that lovely old woman intentionally."

"Agatha said she had enemies," Athena added, clearly fishing for more information.

"Oh, don't we all?" Sherry said. "No one can please everyone, and Agatha least of all. She and Galdie never saw eye to eye."

Rosemary cleared her throat. "Agatha said she wasn't counted among Granny's many enemies."

"Of course she'd say that," said Sherry. "No one wants to be seen as the enemy of the dead, especially not when that death was suspicious."

"So, you do think it was suspicious?" Rosemary asked. "Not just her own...accidental doing?"

She couldn't quite bring herself to say "magic", despite the way everyone else around Myrtlewood seemed to talk about it, as if it was as plain as daylight.

"It's not up to me now, is it?" Sherry said. "I'm no expert, but one thing is for sure. It was magic that killed your Gran."

"How can you tell?" Athena asked.

Rosemary wasn't sure if she was bluffing or starting to get her head around the magic thing.

"I went up there the next day," Sherry said. "I was supposed to drop off some pickles for Galdie. When I arrived, the police was blocking the entrance. I didn't see nothing, but I could feel it in the air. That was definitely some strong magic. So, either Galdie was messing with something more powerful than she should have reckoned with, or someone was using some strong forces against her. Anyway, enough of me. I'll let you eat."

As Sherry walked away, Rosemary and Athena gave each other a significant look.

"It couldn't possibly be us," Rosemary said.

"Uh, Mum, we knew that already, remember?"

"*We* knew it already, but the authorities? All we have to do is convince that constable that we don't know the first thing about magic, and that therefore it couldn't have been us who hurt Granny."

"Sure, but how are we going to explain that to the coppers? Hey, so we didn't even believe in magic until five minutes ago, therefore we couldn't possibly have killed an old lady with it."

"That's exactly what I want to say," Rosemary said. "But in different words."

"You're really going to go to the police and talk about magic?" Athena asked. "They'll lock you up for being mad."

"Not just any police," said Rosemary. "The Myrtlewood authorities. You know they're already at least half-mad, so my insanity shouldn't bother them too much."

Athena shrugged. "You have a point. Shall we eat now?"

They tucked in to their meal to find it as crispy and satisfying as it looked, and still piping hot despite all their distracting conversation.

"We'd better be getting back," Rosemary said, after they'd finished up their dinners. "It's still slightly light outside, but it will be completely dark soon, and I'm not sure there are street lights."

"Couldn't we stay just a little bit longer?" Athena asked. "Surely, there must be some kind of taxi service here."

"What's got into you?" Rosemary asked her. She followed her daughter's gaze across the room to where a pale, dark-haired boy sat. He looked only slightly older than Athena, and he was definitely looking back at her.

"Oh…I see," said Rosemary, smiling. "Your sudden affection for the Myrtlewood pub has nothing to do with the fine dining experience, or even the warm small-town atmosphere, and almost certainly something to do with a certain—"

"Shut it, Mum!" Athena said in an urgent whisper. "It's none of your business who I fancy."

"I knew it! You fancy him!"

"Keep it down, will you? I want to leave here with some shreds of dignity intact."

"Oh, fine," Rosemary said, folding her arms in a sulk. "But we really do have to be getting out of here soon, and I'm pretty sure there are no taxis in Myrtlewood."

"Did someone say taxi?" Ferg appeared at the side of the table.

"Uh…" said Rosemary, taken aback.

"Yes!" said Athena. "We'd like to catch a taxi a bit later, but we don't know if there are any in Myrtlewood."

"I happen to run the only preeminent taxi service in town," Ferg said.

"Is it preeminent if it's the only one?" Rosemary muttered.

Athena kicked her, and not as gently as usual.

"Ouch."

"So, you can take us home then, in about half an hour?" Athena asked.

"I can, indeed. I basically spend my evenings here waiting to see if anyone needs a lift home. Can't condone drunk driving, after all," said Ferg.

"Uh, how much will it cost?" Rosemary asked. "It's only a five or ten-minute walk to Thorn Manor, so it will hardly take a minute to drive."

"The first trip is free," Ferg assured them. "After that it's 20p per minute."

"That's very reasonable," Rosemary said.

"Thank you," said Ferg. "People don't often call me that." He saluted like a sailor. "I'll be back in twenty minutes."

"That was quite strange," Rosemary said. "Are you sure you want to ride in a car with that man?"

"Oh, he's harmless," Athena said. "I'm a good judge of character, remember, unlike *some* people." She gave Rosemary a significant look.

"Hey, how long are you going to blame me for your father?"

"I don't know. How about forever? I have to live with his genes, after all."

"Huh, fair enough," Rosemary said. "But you turned out alright." She reached out to pat Athena's shoulder but was quickly brushed away as Athena gave her a significant look and then turned her attention back towards The Boy.

Rosemary sighed and got up from the table. She figured she might as well pay the bill before Athena decided she wanted dessert and cost them extra money they didn't have. She took a final swig of the mulled mead, emptying the cup and enjoying the spicy warming sensation, then she mumbled something to Athena about getting ready to leave soon, but was deliberately ignored.

As Rosemary approached the empty bar, Sherry re-emerged from the back room.

"Just settling up," said Rosemary.

"Oh no," Sherry insisted. "This was your first meal here for a donkey's age. You can't expect me to charge you for that."

"Can't I?" Rosemary asked, perplexed.

"Certainly not. We have our customs in Myrtlewood, and the first meal is always free for people who move here."

"But..." Rosemary said. "We may not be moving here. We're just here because of Granny..."

"Oh, nonsense," said Sherry, matter-of-factly. "You belong here. It's obvious. And your daughter will see that soon enough. See, she's already getting friendly with the locals."

Rosemary looked back and was slightly alarmed to see the boy from across the room had approached Athena and was standing by their booth, chatting to her. He wasn't smiling though, as Rosemary thought he ought to be. Instead, he had a sullen, brooding look. *Teenagers!*

"You know what?" Rosemary said, turning her attention back to Sherry. "I really hope you're right. I do love it here. It's so different from the rest of the world – or at least the other places I've lived. Myrtlewood is special. It's like a cosy blanket and a hot cup of tea on a cold rainy night."

"That it is," Sherry said.

Rosemary glanced back across the bar to see Athena was still chatting away to the glum young man. She would have given her pinkie toe to know what they were talking about, but she knew better than to try to eavesdrop. Athena would have none of that. She tried not to stare, but something else caught her eye. In the corner booth sat an ominous, hooded figure. Whoever it was had the hood of their cloak – yes, cloak – pulled forward so far that it obscured their face.

She turned back to Sherry to ask after the strange character only to find her busy pulling a pint for another patron.

"You look like you've seen a ghost," Sherry said, bustling back moments later.

"Oh, it's just..."

Rosemary turned to gesture towards the corner booth only to find it empty. The hooded figure had disappeared. "Oh, you get a few strange characters in here, don't you?" she asked Sherry.

"We're all strange characters here, love," Sherry said warmly.

"Touché," Rosemary replied. "It's just—"

"Look, Rosemary, I've been meaning to tell you something since you first walked in," Sherry said. "Only, it's probably not going to make a lot of sense."

"What is it?" Rosemary asked. "I mean, I'm used to not making any sense, if it's any consolation. I don't know if that increases or decreases my chances of misunderstanding whatever it is you're going to tell me."

"So, the thing is, old Galdie knew something. Something she shouldn't have known at the time. In fact, most people still don't know it. I only know because she confided it in me one day when I was delivering some dinner to her. She liked to order the mutton stew, and I never minded running it up to her. One day, about a month or more ago, I go to deliver the stew, see, and she's in a right state. She wasn't too clear about what it was, but she'd been down at the council buildings to pay her rates earlier that day and walked in on...Oh, I don't know what it is, but it was something to do with the town mayor. I'm dead certain he was up to no good."

"No good as in embezzlement, or an affair or..." Rosemary still couldn't bring herself to suggest magic, even though it seemed more and more likely over the past twenty-four hours.

"I don't know the details. That's why it doesn't make any sense, really. I just thought you should know, in case it helps. It sounds like you've been poking around, trying to figure out who had it in for her."

Rosemary blanched again. *So much for our secret investigation...*

"So, you think she witnessed something bad at the council office, and the mayor then went to great lengths to shut her up?"

"You didn't hear me say anything of the sort, mind," said Sherry. "I won't go on record with anything like that, in case it comes back to bite me in the bum."

"I see," said Rosemary.

"The thing is, it might not have even been intentional. The mayor, Mr June, is just not very good at spells. He's all pomp and ceremony, sure, and no one else wants the job of listening to the complaints of every Tom, Dick and Harry, so he's had no competition. He just keeps getting re-elected, but if he did go up there, trying to erase your Granny's memory, it might have backfired on him."

"Interesting theory," Rosemary said. "And yes, we are trying to figure out what happened to Granny Thorn. It's awful not knowing."

It was also awful being a potential suspect, too, but Rosemary didn't exactly want to broadcast that to the entire pub.

"I suppose we'd better get going," Rosemary said. "Apparently, Ferg is our taxi driver for the evening. Is he trustworthy?"

"Who? Fergus?" Sherry said. "Oh, aye, he's a good lad. A bit odd, but who am I to judge?"

"I'll take your word for it," Rosemary said.

"Very well, but where's your young girl?" Sherry asked.

Rosemary looked back towards their table to see it empty. Athena was nowhere in sight.

CHAPTER
ELEVEN

Athena sighed as her mother prattled on about her largely unwarranted suspicions. She took another bite of her fish 'n chips. It was good food – magical or not. The whole magic thing was starting to sink in, though Athena's logical mind wanted to dismiss it completely.

Things had been getting weirder and weirder inside her head, and she didn't want to tell Rosemary about it. The pub was fairly crowded, and that only made things worse.

There were strange sounds, as if her mind was a radio station being tuned in and out – and being around people made it worse.

It would have been easier if the sounds were comprehensible, but they were mostly gibberish, half-formed sentences and single words out of context. She sometimes felt as if she was hearing bits and pieces of people's thoughts, but nothing clear enough to be interesting, just incoherent noise. Athena worried she might be losing her marbles.

It had all started when she'd seen that boy.

I see you...

That was the first time she'd heard a voice in her head and been sure that it wasn't her internal monologue. But he'd disappeared oh so quickly, and Athena was left with only questions and incomprehensible sounds.

She'd begun to wonder if the boy had ever existed at all, or had he merely been her mind playing tricks on her? *Have I become so lonely that I'm making up imaginary friends?* She wondered and then stifled a laugh. *Even my hallucinations don't want to talk to me.*

Rosemary gave her a strange look, but Athena simply looked back blankly, and they continued to eat in silence.

There you are...

The voice said again. Athena froze. She looked across the table at her mother, who seemed focussed on her chips and clearly hadn't noticed anything unusual. Athena made the most of the small moment of privacy where Rosemary was so engrossed in fried food that she didn't notice her daughter scanning the bar, looking for someone in particular.

*He has to be real...*she thought to herself. *And if he is, Mum will see him, too.*

There he was. Sitting at the edge of a booth across the room was the boy from earlier. Athena recognised his dark hair. He turned towards her, flashing those grey-blue eyes in her direction.

*It's you...*Athena thought.

Yes, it is, came a surprising reply in her head.

Athena shook herself, relieved that Rosemary was still preoccupied with scoffing dinner. Only a moment had passed, but it felt like an age.

She turned back to the boy.

You can hear me? Athena asked.

The boy nodded from across the room.

Athena blushed, wondering how she could possibly drown out her thoughts so as to retain some privacy around someone who was clearly a mind-reader and...*a mind speaker? Is that even a thing?*

She refocused her attention on finishing her dinner. All the while, her heart was racing, as was her mind.

Am I totally nuts? Is it possible that I just had a telepathic conversation with a stranger? I need to stop thinking...He can probably hear all of this!

She took a gulp of the beverage Sherry had brought them and felt it soothing her.

Don't worry, the boy's voice said in her mind. *I can't see everything in your head. I can just hear the thoughts you broadcast clearly. Think of it like a conversation.*

Oh...okay... Athena thought back.

I can help you learn to master it, if you like, the boy offered.

Just then, Rosemary said, "We'd better be getting back. It's still slightly light outside, but it will be completely dark soon, and I'm not sure there are street lights."

No... Athena thought. *I was just starting to figure out the mystery.*

She wasn't ready to tell her mother about what had been going on in her head. Firstly, because she wanted to maintain as much privacy as possible, and secondly, because she didn't want to worry Rosemary – not after everything else that had happened recently. There was already far too much to worry about!

"Couldn't we stay just a little bit longer?" Athena asked. "Surely, there must be some kind of taxi service here."

"What's got into you?" Rosemary asked.

Athena couldn't help it. Her eyes darted in the direction of the boy.

Rosemary followed her gaze across the room to where he sat.

"Oh...I see," said Rosemary, smiling. "Your sudden affection for the Myrtlewood pub has nothing to do with the fine dining experience, or even the warm small-town atmosphere, and almost certainly something to do with a certain..."

"Shush!"

Athena tried to stop herself from blushing. She was relieved that, at least, her mother could see the boy. He wasn't a figment of her imagination, after all. However, she did not appreciate Rosemary's tone.

Athena already had too much on her mind and being heckled for fancying a boy wasn't helping. It wasn't even that Athena fancied him. She didn't know anything about him at all except for his unusual ability, but she wasn't about to tell her mother any of that.

Nevertheless, she needed to resolve the mystery and was relieved when that unusual man, Ferg, offered to taxi them home. It was even better moments later, when Rosemary went over to the bar to pay and became distracted by a conversation with Sherry. Athena finally had time alone to think, or at least that was what she thought.

Finally, alone, his voice said in her head.

Yes, what of it?

Good. Can I come over and talk to you?

I guess so, Athena replied, though she felt a nervous jolt at the proposition. Her nervousness only worsened as she watched him get up and walk towards her. Though she was sitting down, she could tell he was around a foot taller than her, and his hair hung over his eyes in a cool way. She gulped, not knowing what to say.

"What's your name?" he asked.

"Athena," she replied, looking down at the wood grain on the table to stop herself from staring into those stormy eyes.

"Athena, goddess of wisdom," he said.

"Something like that," Athena replied. "What about you? What's your name?"

"Finnigan," he said.

There was a moment of silence, in which a thousand deafening thoughts rushed through Athena's mind, creating a roaring effect.

"So..." she said, finally. "Why did you come over here if..."

"If I can already talk to you in here?" he said, pointing to his temple. "I wanted to meet you properly." He twirled his hand in an elaborate gesture and bowed.

Athena laughed, surprised.

"I can't see you smile inside your head," he said.

Athena gulped. *Is he...flirting with me?*

"So, what is this, anyway?" she asked. "Telepathy?"

"Shh," Finnigan said, raising his finger to his lips. "You really don't know anything about it?" he asked.

Athena shook her head, unsure what was okay to say aloud.

"Come with me," said Finnigan.

"Where?"

"Just out of here."

"But..." Athena said.

"We won't be a minute."

Athena hesitated. She knew next to nothing about this boy, and yet she absolutely needed to figure out what was going on inside her head, and he seemed to have the answers. She glanced up to the bar to see her mother still focussed on talking to Sherry.

"Okay," she said, though she wasn't sure if Finnigan could hear her since he'd already walked away. She got up quickly, and followed him.

CHAPTER
TWELVE

"Athena? Athena!"

Rosemary called out across the bar. Many heads turned her way, but none bore the face she wanted to see. Her heart raced.

How long does it take to abduct a teenager? She wondered. *Probably not very long, especially if the teen has gone willingly! How could Athena do this? She is supposed to be the sensible one – at least in her mind she is. She's always telling me off for being careless and brash. Now look at her, disappearing in the night off to goddess-knows-where!*

Rosemary strode furiously around the pub, checking in all the corners and booths, but Athena was nowhere to be found. She looked outside the front door, but there was no one in sight. The empty street chilled her blood.

At least I hope she went willingly, Rosemary thought, her anger quickly transmuting into terror. *What if someone – The Boy – threatened her? What if he had a weapon, or used some kind of bewitching charm!*

Her fury was now firmly aimed at The Boy, and she intended to make him regret he ever looked at her daughter. She turned back to the pub, hoping that Athena would blossom out of the woodwork or emerge from the bathroom and tell her to stop being so silly, but the stalls were empty. She strode back out into the main room again and checked the table to see if her daughter had left a note. Nothing.

"Athena!" Rosemary called out again. She turned back towards the door, only to walk straight into something solid. It was a large, tall man, with a scarred face and greying scraggly hair. He gently gripped Rosemary by both arms and said in a quiet voice, "Calm down, lass. She's just out here."

"Oh, thank goodness!"

Rosemary gratefully followed the man towards a side door.

"Here," he gestured through the window.

Athena was sitting on the stoop next to The Boy, his hand lay on the stone beside them and her hand rested on top.

She's holding hands WITH A BOY!

Rosemary took a deep breath and reminded herself that this was quite ordinary teenage behaviour. So normal, in fact, that she should have been more surprised that Athena hadn't taken much of an interest in boys previously – as far as she'd told her mother, anyway. But this was a boy she'd just met!

"Thank you," she said to the older man, not taking her eyes of her daughter this time.

"A pleasure to do a good deed," he said. "The name's Covvey."

"Covvey," Rosemary muttered. The name sounded familiar, but Rosemary couldn't think why.

"You ever need anything, I'm happy to help." Covvey said. "Galdie did me many a favour, and I owe her more than my life."

"Thank you," Rosemary said, risking a glance at his wrinkled and scarred face before turning back towards her daughter again.

"I'm Rosemary."

"I know you are," Covvey said.

Rosemary turned back towards him, wondering if she'd known him years ago, but all she could see was his back as he limped back towards the bar.

Rosemary took a deep breath and pushed open the door.

"Excuse me, young lady. Exactly what do you think you're doing?"

Athena jolted away from The Boy. "Such a cliché, Mum! Give me some privacy."

"I'll give you privacy when you show me enough respect to let me know where you're going before I tear the whole pub apart looking for you in a right panic!"

"Woah, take a deep breath!" said Athena, embarrassment blooming on her cheeks in a bright blush.

"I already did."

"Ready for your transportation?" a reedy voice said from behind Rosemary's left shoulder.

"See? Time to go!" Rosemary said, reaching for Athena's arm. "No time for privacy – or anything else." She glared at The Boy, who gave her a disinterested stare in return.

Teenagers!

Athena brushed off her mother's hand but got up just the same.

"Fine, I'll go, but let me at least say goodbye to Finnigan."

"Finnigan," Rosemary repeated, under her breath, trying to remember the name so she knew who to track down if Athena made any other unexpected disappearances. "Fine. Say goodbye. You have two minutes, and I'll wait right inside, by the door."

"Mum!"

"Don't push it."

"Ugh!" Athena huffed, crossing her arms.

Rosemary stepped back inside the blessedly warm pub to find Ferg standing there, holding her jacket for her.

"Oh...uh, thank you," she said.

"You left it at your table, Ma'am."

"I didn't realise this taxi came with the full valet service."

"Pardon?"

"You know, valet – like in fancy hotels where they drive your car for you."

"I think you'll find I do not know about the val-aye," Ferg said. "And no one drives my car but me. Sorry to disappoint."

116

"Uh, never mind," Rosemary said. "I'm not disappointed, don't worry."

Athena reemerged from the side door, glaring daggers at Rosemary, and followed her glumly out front to where a bright orange VW bug was waiting. Ferg opened the door.

"Just like a valet," Athena joked, clearly recovering from her bad mood.

"No, you may not drive my automobile, young madam," Ferg said.

Athena shot a confused glance at her mother.

"Don't ask," Rosemary replied. She was still feeling quite scratchy and mad at Athena, though she couldn't entirely explain why.

"What's got your goat?" Athena asked her.

"You gave me a right scare back there. I'm starting to wonder whether it was a good idea trying to get us to move to Myrtlewood in the first place."

"You are the one who loves it here," Athena said.

"You're right. This place seems like a dream come true, but it could so easily turn into a nightmare. Maybe I've been too hasty in wanting to move."

"Oh, don't start this now," Athena said. "I was just starting to like the place, and also..." She gestured to Ferg, who had a serious expression, as if he was concentrating hard on the road. "Keep your voice down," Athena whispered.

"So now you like it here?" Rosemary said, not caring if Ferg heard her. "And what am I supposed to do if you go off the rails?"

"Don't be silly, Mum. You're totally overreacting. We went outside to look at the stars for five minutes! Finnigan was showing me the constellations."

"Well, that's just lovely. Stargazing while I was running around frantically through the pub, calling your name. Feeling like an awful mother, scared you'd been abducted for Pete's sake."

"It's not my fault you overreacted," Athena said.

"Overreacted? Really? And what if you had been abducted, in a strange town in the middle of nowhere?"

"But I hadn't been."

Rosemary sighed. "You've never done anything so careless before, and yet, within a day or two of being here you're throwing caution to the wind and stepping outside with a boy you don't even know without telling me!"

"Oh, come on," Athena said. "I didn't want to have to go up to you and explain...Can't you give me a bit of privacy?"

"I hate to break it to you, love, but in a small town like this, there's no privacy."

"She's right, you know," Ferg said from the front seat.

Athena looked at Rosemary, mortified.

"See, I told you."

"Do you want some advice?" Ferg asked.

"No!" Rosemary and Athena said at once.

"Suit yourselves," said Ferg, as he turned the car down the driveway to Thorn Manor.

"That took longer than I was expecting," Rosemary said, trying to keep a neutral tone as it wasn't really Ferg she was annoyed with.

"I took the scenic route, since you're new in town."

"At night?"

"It *is* night," said Ferg.

"Oh...well, thank you," Rosemary said, as they pulled up at the house.

Something looked different. Rosemary could tell, even from the car. Thorn Manor seemed more imposing than usual – ominous and dark, against the blue-black sky.

"I do hope you'll be in attendance at the spring festival next Saturn day," said Ferg.

"Saturday?" Athena suggested.

"I prefer not to use the shorthand for the day of Saturn. I revere the gods."

"Oh, okay, fair enough," said Athena, shrugging.

"Here's my card, in case you require any more transportation." Ferg held out the card for Rosemary to take. She slipped it into her pocket and thanked him. Then both she and Athena got out into the chilly night air and made their way towards the house.

"Is it just me, or does the house look different?" Athena asked.

"It's not just you," Rosemary said. "And don't think you're off the hook for what happened earlier."

"Oh, come on, Mum!" Athena said, shivering in the cold. "What is up with you? It's really not such a big deal. I shouldn't have slipped out without telling you, and I'm sorry for that. But *you* should have trusted that I can look after myself for five minutes. I didn't go far. I was being responsible."

"Oh sure," said Rosemary. "You were fine – you were being responsible – but what about him? What about The Boy?!"

"Finnigan was fine, too."

"I don't know anything about him, and neither did you. He could have been a total creep."

"I'm a good judge of character," Athena muttered under her breath. "And as much as I should have told you where I was going, you shouldn't have freaked out like that. It's daft."

Rosemary huffed, too ruffled for a response as she fumbled with her cold fingers on the house keys. The front door swung open to reveal...nothing.

A swirling black void was the only thing visible inside the house. The darkness had engulfed everything. At its edges, silvery waves shimmered as they circled in a chaotic vortex. It seemed to pulse with its own kind of life force, which gave Rosemary an ominous feeling. She definitely did not want to mess with it.

"What the...?"

Rosemary pulled the door closed immediately.

"What just happened?" Athena asked as they both took several steps back from the house for good measure.

"You really expect me to know?" Rosemary asked, her voice acerbic.

"Well, no, I guess I can't expect you to know, or to be reasonable. I can't expect much from you at all."

"Oh, Athena."

"Stop being so mad at me," Athena grumbled.

Rosemary folded her arms against the freezing night air and gave Athena a stern look, certain her daughter was hiding something from her.

"Oh, I give up," Athena said, throwing her arms in the air. "Don't you think we have bigger problems right now, like the fact that our newly-inherited house is a gaping void of doom?"

They stood in silence for a moment, their breath fogging up in front of them, looking up at the house which seemed to loom above them.

"You might have a point," Rosemary admitted. "It might well have been a normal teenage thing, and I might well have issues, which are being triggered."

"I'm glad that's settled then," Athena said, crossing her arms. "Now, back to the other pressing matter at hand. What do we do about the house?"

Rosemary took a few deep breaths to calm herself, and thought about their situation. "We could call someone to help us," she suggested.

"That Ferg man? He gave you his card."

"I'd rather not," said Rosemary. "And why is it that every second person in this town has a business card? What are we in a corporate 80s movie or something?"

"I hope not," Athena said. "My hair is far too flat."

"Well, mine is all frizz today, so I'll fit right in."

"If not Ferg, then who?" Athena asked. "We don't have anyone's number here."

"Haven't you ever heard of a telephone directory service?"

"Actually, no. What's that?" said Athena.

Rosemary was taken aback. "It's like a phone book, but you look it up online or you call a person and they just put you through."

"Really? That sounds like a massive violation of privacy."

"Well, I think it only works on landlines," Rosemary said.

"People still have landlines?" Athena asked. "You're lucky I know

120

what *they* are. We haven't had one since we lived in that big old shared house in St Austell, and that was *years* ago."

"Well, these outdated technologies turn out to be quite helpful at times like these," said Rosemary. "Oh drat!"

"What is it?"

"No reception."

Athena checked her phone too. "Me neither."

"Great," Rosemary said. "So, we're stuck out here, in the middle of nowhere, cold and exhausted...and the house is a swirling doom vortex, and it's too dark to walk anywhere else."

"That about sums it up," Athena said. "Strange, I'm sure I had reception earlier."

"You think *that's* strange?" Rosemary laughed. "Wait 'till I show you to the kitchen."

"Do you want to try again?" Athena asked.

"The door, you mean?"

"Sure, why not. What do we have to lose?"

"I'd say the stakes are quite high, really," Rosemary said, finding this all suddenly absurdly amusing. "We could lose our entire selves into a great spiralling abyss."

"True," Athena admitted. "How about you try the door, and we'll hold onto the veranda posts just in case the house tries to suck us inside. They look reasonably solid."

"Do you really think that's such a good idea?" Rosemary asked.

"Mum, it's freezing out here, and if we don't get out of the cold soon, we might just die of hypothermia."

"I suppose you're right. Okay. Here goes."

Rosemary approached the door, cautiously, and took hold of the veranda railing with one hand while she fitted her key into the lock with the other. "Ready?" she called to Athena, who was standing a much more comfortable distance back.

"As I'll ever be," Athena replied.

"Right. Hold on tight!"

The two Thorns braced themselves against the unknown potential powers of the house's new vortex. For a split second, Rosemary was awash with fears of giant beastly creatures escaping the void to eat them, but she pushed through her terror and turned the key. The door swung open, with an innocent creak to reveal a perfectly ordinary entrance way.

Rosemary sighed with relief.

"Now that's the kind of anti-climax I can get behind," Athena said, stepping closer.

"Wait," Rosemary said. "What if it's just an illusion?"

"You think it's more likely to be an illusion now that we're seeing the normal house that we've been in before than the glimpse of absurd mayhem we saw, briefly?"

"Probably not *more* likely," Rosemary admitted. "But I'm not sure I trust it."

"Fair enough," Athena said. "Let's just go in, slowly and carefully for now, and we'll dash back out if another vortex appears, alright?"

"Alright."

They stepped tentatively into the house, grateful to find the floor was solid beneath them. It was also blessedly warm and toasty – much warmer than it probably should have been, but Rosemary wasn't about to begrudge it that oddness when they needed to warm up. She found the light switch and flicked it to reveal that everything seemed to be as it was when they'd left earlier.

"Tea?" she asked, walking to the kitchen to put the kettle on.

"Yes please," Athena said. "I need to warm my insides. It's freezing out there. I'm glad the house is warm. Is there central heating or something? I'd have figured a place as old as this might just rely on fire places."

"Given the experience we just had, I really hope it's just central heating. I've had enough of all this magic stuff to last a lifetime. I'm seriously hoping to get back to normal life as soon as possible."

"I'm just starting to enjoy it," Athena said.

"Really?"

"Yes. I mean, it's not every day you discover your mother has magic powers. Hey...you don't think that..."

"What?" Rosemary asked.

"Maybe it was you who made it weird in here."

"I certainly did not."

"But you were all flustered, Mum."

"Flustered? You should have seen me back at the pub. If I could create a void of doom in here, then why didn't I turn the entire establishment into magical chaos?"

"Good point," Athena said. "Maybe your magic is connected to the house."

"How so?"

"Well, it only seemed to work – accidentally – when we were here earlier. Nothing odd happened when we were in town. Maybe it's kind of – *bound* – here."

"It's a good theory, though I can't be made responsible for whatever that thing was. I mean, firstly, we don't know I definitely caused it – there could have been any other number of factors – and secondly, even on the off chance that I did, I had no idea!"

"I'm not blaming you, Mum," Athena said. "But please try to keep a calm temper, just in case."

"Alright. Fair enough," Rosemary said, yawning as the full exhaustion from the day caught up with her. "But don't go off gallivanting with surly young men without my knowledge or permission."

"I wasn't gallivanting. The real question is, why is it so triggering for you?"

"Oh fine," said Rosemary. "It's just that you reminded me of your father."

"Harsh."

"No..." said Rosemary. "It was something he was known for doing. He could walk into a bar and have women pawing at him in five minutes flat."

"You're joking!" said Athena.

"I wish I was. It was like...like he had some kind of power over them. And maybe he really did, now that we know magic is real."

"That's ridiculous."

"That may be so, but it's also the truth. You blame me for going back to him, over and over...or rather, for taking him in every time he turned back up in our lives, but the thing is, I never felt I had much power over the situation. Dain just had this charm that dissolved all my defences."

"That's gross, Mum."

Rosemary sighed. "Not like that."

"I'm not Dad," Athena said firmly. "I'm not like Dad at all."

"In many ways, that's true," said Rosemary. "But you have to admit, tonight was...well it was unusual. You were gazing over at that boy you'd never seen before in your life."

"That's not true. I saw him earlier."

"What? When?"

"When we were leaving the lawyers' office. I saw him sitting under a tree, with a book, and he looked so...well, anyway. I saw him. He saw me." Athena shrugged.

"There was a moment?" Rosemary suggested.

"Yuck. Please don't say sappy things like that. But yeah, I guess. Then I saw him in the pub, and it seemed like...oh, I don't know. It was a nice co-incidence, I suppose."

"So, you looked at each other," said Rosemary. "That part is normal, but what happened next is just a little bit strange. He came over to your table, and then you went *stargazing*!"

"It was totally normal, Mum," Athena said, though Rosemary noticed her voice was rather defensive. "He came over and introduced himself and said he didn't recognise me, was I from out of town?"

"Shy and brooding teenagers just do that, do they?"

"Sometimes."

"Just don't do it again, please?"

"Fine."

They drank their cups of tea in silence, overcome by tiredness, which was compounded by the lack of sleep from the night before.

Rosemary yawned. "Bed time."

"What's that?" Athena asked, sounding scared.

"What?"

"Out there. I'm sure I just saw eyes watching us from the woods."

"It's probably just a fox or a rabbit or something," said Rosemary, looking out into the darkness. "I saw something like that before when we first arrived."

"And you didn't tell me?"

"The woods are wild around here," Rosemary said. "There will be loads of creatures out there. But don't worry."

"Sure, Mum. Way to make me not worry."

"They're harmless," Rosemary insisted as she got up from the couch and made her way cautiously upstairs, but everything on the upper level seemed to be in order, too.

"Do you want me to kip in your room again?" Rosemary asked.

"No, I'm safer alone," Athena said. "Given how out-of-control your newfound magic powers are."

"Fair enough."

"It's not really fair though, is it?" Athena said, crossing her arms.

"What are you referring to?"

"You get to have powers, and I don't."

"You can have mine," Rosemary said. "I don't want them."

"Are you serious?" Athena asked. "You really don't want to be magic?"

"It's more trouble than it's worth, trust me."

"That's even more unfair. You don't even want your powers, and I want them, but what do I get?"

"Oh, just go to bed, will you?" Rosemary said, smiling warmly at her child. "Let's hope this all makes more sense in the morning."

"I appreciate your wild optimism," said Athena. "And I am sorry about before. I promise to let you know where I am next time we're in a strange small town and I meet a boy."

"I appreciate that," Rosemary replied, lifting her arms for a hug. "I'm sorry for going off at you – and you are really not much at all like your father."

"Thanks, Mum," Athena said, returning the hug.

They parted ways. Rosemary went back to her childhood bedroom and remembered to plug in her phone, which had miraculously regained its reception.

"Figures," she muttered to herself, as she got changed and climbed into bed. "It's never there when you need it."

She closed her eyes and drifted off to sleep, praying to any magical deity who might be listening for things to settle down and become safe.

CHAPTER
THIRTEEN

A howl tore through the night air, waking Rosemary just in time to be jolted by a loud crash.

"Oh, no...not again!"

She jumped out of bed, pushed back the curtains, and peered out into the night.

"Something's attacking the house!" Athena cried, rushing into Rosemary's room.

"Shhh. I'm trying to see what it is."

"Isn't it downstairs again?" Athena asked. "Like last night."

"Could be. I heard something out here. Look!"

A bright orange flame burned in the darkness, quickly building in size as it moved closer.

"It's heading for the house!" Athena shrieked. "Duck!"

They both ducked as another crash sounded. The house trembled and Rosemary peeked up to check the damage, expecting to see flames.

All was dark and still again outside.

"Weird," she said. "It's like nothing happened."

"You spoke too soon," Athena said. "Look, there's another one."

Another bright fiery ball had appeared and was heading directly towards them. They watched this time, bracing themselves for impact, but too curious to duck down completely. Just as the great ball of fire reached the perimeter of the front lawn it seemed to flatten, as if it had collided with something invisible in the air.

"Holy cow!" Athena exclaimed. "It's a forcefield!"

"No way!" said Rosemary. "Did I do that?"

She looked at her hands as if examining them for magic powers.

"Not bloody likely," Athena said. "Remember we're in a house that can fix itself. Well, chances are it can also protect itself from stupid thugs."

"Thugs?" Rosemary asked. "Is that what you think is going on?"

"How else did the fireballs appear, Mum?"

"I don't know. I'm unfamiliar with fireball lore and etiquette." She squinted down into the forest where the fire had originated from. "I think I can see something moving around down there."

"Look. There they are!" Athena pointed to the far side of the lawn.

Rosemary could see what looked like people, clad in black, moving like shadows in the night. "They've gotten through the forcefield!" she cried.

"Maybe it only deflects magical attacks, not just people wandering in," Athena suggested.

"How did you get to be such an expert?"

"It's just a bit of calm rationality, but I don't expect *you* to understand that," Athena said.

A rattling sound came from below, followed by the tinkle of breaking glass.

"Oh, drat. This hardly seems like the time to be calm," said Rosemary, keeping her voice low so as not to attract the attention of the intruders.

"Someone is definitely breaking into the house this time!" Athena said in an urgent whisper. "Do you think it's the same people who made that racket last night?"

"Sounds plausible," said Rosemary. "I wonder if all that scared them off, or if the house has more defences than just a forcefield."

"Should we leave them to it?" Athena asked. "I don't much feel like confronting burglars, if that's what they are – especially ones with big fireballs at their disposal.

"Not a chance," said Rosemary, adrenaline pumping through her body along with righteous rage, making her feel at least fifty percent braver than usual. "Offence is the best defence, remember, and I'm not going to take the chance that they might come up here. Where's my trusty lamp?"

She found said trusty lamp on the dresser and began inching her way downstairs. "Stay back," Rosemary said. "I'm only doing this to keep you safe."

"I don't know if you're brave or just foolish," Athena muttered, following at a safe distance.

Rosemary made it to the foot of the stairwell to find absolute silence. It was too quiet, in fact. She took a tentative step out, towards the west side of the house, where she suspected the breaking glass had been.

"Ahh!"

Rosemary ducked as a winged creature flew at her, clawing at her face and arms. She lifted the lamp up and tried to fend it off.

"What are you doing?" Athena whispered from the stairwell.

"Ahh – this beast! It's attacking me," she shrieked.

"It's just a crow, Mum," Athena said, trying to suppress a giggle.

"It's evil!" Rosemary cried, trying to whack the crow with her lamp. It managed to find purchase, and at the same time, golden sparks flew out of her fingertips, paralysing the bird mid-flight. It fell to the ground, dazed, and Rosemary breathed a sigh of relief. She raised her hands up to her face to feel only minor scratches left by the bird.

"What a show," a man's voice said. Rosemary turned to find a dark silhouette standing in the doorway to the kitchen. She couldn't see his face in the shadows, though something about his voice was familiar. She could tell he was leaning casually against the doorframe – far too relaxed for what this situation warranted in her view.

"Excuse me?" Rosemary said. "What are you doing in my house? Get out!"

"This isn't your house yet," the man said. "And I suspect, with those killer instincts it never will be. You'd be better off hopping on the next train out of town – if you want to live, that is."

"How sweet of you to have my best interests at heart," Rosemary sneered. "Now get out or you'll meet the same fate as that crow. You saw what I did to it."

The man laughed. "You have no mastery over your magic. You hardly have any access to it at all. Your powers are more of a danger to you than they are to anyone else. I, on the other hand..."

"Oh, no..." Rosemary said, as the man held his palms about a foot apart and began chanting. Fire flared in the centre, and she was NOT prepared to deal with fireballs in the house.

The flames flickered and then puttered out.

"What?" the man asked, clearly gobsmacked.

Rosemary smiled.

"It seems you've underestimated the Thorn family magic, after all," she said, patting the wall near her in appreciation for the house.

"No matter," the man said. "I have other advantages."

He lunged towards her, all muscle and strength, which clearly meant he had the upper-hand over Rosemary's fairly un-muscly frame, but she centred herself just like her self-defence teacher had told her, planting her feet. She lifted her lamp high in the air and sent it crashing down onto the intruder's head.

The lamp cracked into pieces, and Rosemary's powers crackled through it, glinting in the dark. She smiled, triumphantly, hoping that would be enough to stun the man, but though it seemed to addle him somewhat, it only enraged him more. He lashed out, kicking Rosemary to the floor. She instinctively rolled away and then crouched down, ensuring her balance was stable. When the man turned back and lunged at her again, she was able to grab hold of his arm, swinging him around and sending him crashing into a side-table.

Gran's knickknacks scattered across the floor, and Rosemary hoped there wasn't anything too special on display that had been permanently damaged. She was surprised at her own strength, and fighting instinct for that matter. She didn't know if it was the adrenaline pumping through her veins or the magic somehow giving her the advantage over her clearly more muscular opponent.

The man righted himself and growled. Fangs popped out at the corners of his mouth.

"No sodding way," Rosemary said. "You've got to be kidding me. This is not some paranormal teen drama. How can it possibly be real?"

"You'll find real-life in Myrtlewood is far more dangerous than you expected."

"I'm starting to get that impression," she replied as the man...*or vampire?* Lunged towards her again.

This time, she simply ducked and stepped to the side, allowing him to crash directly into a wall, splintering the timber panelling.

That's it...I'm definitely being helped by magic in this fight.

Rosemary decided to embrace her newfound power. The man pulled himself up to attack again and was met by several kicks to the legs and chest, followed by a sharp punch in the face.

"Ouch!" he cried, hopping back.

"Bet you didn't expect that now, did ya?" Rosemary said, hopping up and down and pumping her fists in the air like a boxer.

She jumped forward, sending another swift kick towards the area Granny would have referred to as his nether-regions. The intruder doubled up in pain, and Rosemary shot a satisfied glance up towards the stairwell where Athena was cowering on the landing.

Big Mistake.

She turned back to the vampire and saw a predatory gleam in his eyes as he caught sight of the teenage girl.

"Oh. No. You. Don't!"

Rosemary grabbed at him, intending to haul him in another direction, but it was too late. He had escaped her grasp and bounded towards the stairwell.

Wood. Granny's voice rang out in Rosemary's mind.

Of course, she realised. *Wood kills vampires.*

Rosemary snapped out her hand and grabbed the closest piece of wood: a splinter of panelling that happened to be just the right size to wrap her fist around. *Thank you, house.*

She jumped higher than she thought possible and lunged towards the man as he clambered up the stairs, mounting his back like a bull-fighter. She raised the wooden makeshift stake up high and stabbed it down, driving it into the man's back.

He let out a groan of pain and turned his head toward her, terror in his eyes. Up close, in the low light of the stairwell, Rosemary could see a clear resemblance in his face to Perseus Burk, just before the intruder burst into a cloud of dust, sending her thudding down onto the steps.

"So...vampire?" Athena asked, coughing.

"I guess so," Rosemary replied, feeling slightly mortified.

"That was awesome!" Athena said. "You're a freaking superhero."

"Oh, nonsense," said Rosemary. "And keep your voice down. We don't know if it was just one intruder – and his crow – or whether there are more fights to be had. I sincerely hope there aren't."

"But Mum," Athena said, more quietly this time. "You're the chosen one."

"Cut that out."

"Seriously, Mum, even the scratches on your face have healed up. You do have superpowers."

Rosemary reached up to trace her fingers across her cheek where the scratches had been, only to find smooth skin. "What the..."

Athena giggled softly. "In every generation, a slayer is born." Then she held her ribs, doubling over on the stairs, trying to muffle her own hysterical laughter.

"Will you stop with the Buffy references?" Rosemary hissed. "This is a serious situation. We're sitting in a dark house with no idea if any other intruders are about to attack or what kind of...special abilities... they might have."

As if in answer to her words, all the lights in the house suddenly flickered on.

Rosemary and Athena looked at each other in surprise.

"The house?" Athena asked.

Rosemary shrugged.

They waited in silence for a few moments, but there were no unusual sounds, so they got up and began to investigate.

As Rosemary stepped away from the downstairs landing, she tripped over something.

"Oh, blast," she said, regaining her balance. Then she realised what it was. "Blast. Blast. Blast!"

"What is it?" Athena asked.

"It's...a body?" Rosemary said.

Indeed, a man's form lay on the floor, clad entirely in black.

"I thought he turned to dust," Athena said. "Did he actually just teleport or something?"

"Just teleport?" Rosemary said. "As if it's the more ordinary of the two options?"

"Oh, you know what I mean."

"It's a different man," Rosemary said, examining his face, which did not at all look like Burk. This man had dark cropped hair with smaller eyes and thick dark eyebrows with a scar on his cheek. She pressed her fingers to his neck. "And he's not dead, either, which I guess is a good thing?"

"How do you figure that?" Athena asked.

"Well, we are in the midst of a murder investigation." Rosemary reminded her. "I suspect the less murder we *actually* commit, the better."

"Fair call," Athena said. "Hey! He's surrounded by feathers. You don't suppose this is the crow?"

"Is that another Hollywood reference?" Rosemary asked.

"Well, sort of," Athena said. "I mean, if vampires are real, then maybe shapeshifters are too. I think this guy might have been the crow that attacked you before."

"It seems a bit far-fetched," Rosemary said dismissively. "Anyway, wouldn't he be naked if he was a crow a minute ago?"

"Mum, surely if magic can transform him into a crow, it could make him clothed too, and all of this is far-fetched. Get with it!"

"Oh, fine," Rosemary said as she began to wander around the house, checking rooms. "I'll consider it a possibility. At least it doesn't look like there are any other intruders to worry about. Maybe if there were more, they've already run away when they saw how strong I am."

Athena laughed. "That part is the most far-fetched of the lot."

"Hey! I took self-defence classes," Rosemary said. "My instructor said I showed great promise."

"Was that before or after you broke his nose with your handbag?"

"That was a prime example of self-defence!" Rosemary insisted.

"Well, it might have been if you weren't supposed to be in hand-to-hand combat with someone entirely different."

"Oh, shush. Don't remind me. Anyway, let's go and have some tea."

"And just leave old crowy here?" Athena asked.

"He's out cold. We'll figure out what to do with him. I'm in strong need of a cup of tea to help my brain work," said Rosemary.

"Let's at least tie him up first," Athena said. "Before we wander off, leaving ourselves open to another attack."

"Good point," said Rosemary. "I was going to think of that."

"Sure, you were," Athena said. She'd already rummaged in a drawer and found some thick twine. "This will do for now."

"I suppose we should call the police."

"Actually, we should have done that about an hour ago when we first saw the fireballs," Athena pointed out.

"You're probably right. For some reason, Constable Perkins didn't cross my mind when faced with imminent danger."

"Fair enough," said Athena, following her mother to the kitchen to make tea.

Rosemary put the kettle on and then sat down at the kitchen table and rested her face in her hands, pressing gently against her closed eyes in the vain hope that she might wake up from this very strange dream.

"It's all a bit much, isn't it?" Athena said gently.

Rosemary nodded.

"I'm sure things will settle down soon, Mum. I mean, surely those attackers were the ones who killed Granny Thorn. It's too much of a co-incidence otherwise. Call Constable Perkins and tell him what happened."

"Do you think he'll even believe us?" Rosemary asked.

"He'll have to, once he sees the damage, plus there's old crowy over there."

"Alright," Rosemary said. "I'll call him. But I still don't like our chances staying here. What if there are more of them, whoever *they* are? What if they come back to finish the job? What if they hurt you?"

"I'll be fine, Mum."

"It's too dangerous," Rosemary said. "We have to get out of here."

"Typical."

"What?"

"When I hate the place, you want to stay, but as soon as I start liking it, you want to get out of here as fast as you possibly can."

"For good reason," Rosemary grumbled. The kettle whistled, and she got up to make tea. While it brewed, she looked up the number of the local police station and gave them a call. Even though it was just before dawn, Constable Perkins answered, sounding as if he'd just woken up. Rosemary wondered if the police station phoneline re-directed straight to his bedroom! She gave him the short version of what happened. He told her wearily and warily that he would be right over after he saw to some urgent business, which she assumed was his morning routine.

Rosemary poured the tea into cups at the table, but was too restless to sit still. She got up and paced around, sipping her tea and darting anxiously from thought to thought, then decided to assess the damage by the stairs.

"Oh...drat!"

There was an ominous space on the floor, surrounded by several black feathers and twine, where the intruder should have been lying.

"What is it?" Athena called out as she approached Rosemary.

"He's gone."

"No!" Athena shrieked. "But we didn't hear a thing!"

Rosemary felt her spine prick in cold fear at the possibility that the man was still in the house – in humanoid form or any other. She looked around, but there was no sign of him. She checked through most of the house, but could not shake the eerie feeling. Even when she was satisfied he had gone, there was the possibility that he might return at any moment, and this time they might not be so lucky.

"This is all too much," she said. "Athena, pack your bags!"

"What? Where are we going?"

"Away from the vampires and were-crows, for Goddess' sake! This is no place for a young woman to live!"

"But I like it here!"

"Athena!"

"Come on, Mum. That was way more exciting than Burkenswood has ever been, and you were awesome. You totally kicked arse."

Rosemary couldn't help but glow at the rare praise.

"I did, didn't I?"

Athena nodded. "Very impressive."

"Still, as your mother it is my prerogative to keep you out of danger. We have to get as far away from this place as possible."

"And what do you suggest we do at four thirty in the morning?" Athena asked. "I'm not lugging my bag all that way again. It nearly put my back out last time."

"Fine," Rosemary said. "I suggest we get dressed and pack. Then, to save your delicate back, we call Ferg to take us to the train station. We'll catch the next thing that will get us out of here – train, bus, broom – I don't care what it is."

"What about Constable Perkins?"

"We'll tell him what happened and then explain that we have to get out of town as soon as possible for our own safety, unless he's prepared to hire armoured guards for the house 24/7, which I can guar- antee is out of budget for a small town like this. We are leaving whether he likes it or not, and I don't care if I have to go to court to overrule him."

"But..."

"No. This is non-negotiable. We both could have died just minutes ago."

"Oh, you're no fun."

"That's just tough, isn't it? We're going."

Rosemary cajoled Athena into following her upstairs. They packed their bags in silence.

"You're going to regret this, you know." Athena grumbled as she hoisted her bag back downstairs.

"Oh, yeah?" said Rosemary. "I'm going to regret protecting my daughter's life by getting her away from danger, am I? And why is that?"

"Because this town is special – like you kept saying. I actually think it's the only place you've ever fit in...that you've ever felt at home."

"You're just saying that because you want to see the dashing and broody Finnigan again," Rosemary teased, though a part of her knew that Athena was right. Myrtlewood had always felt like home, so much so that Rosemary had yearned for it sometimes when she was away, never quite understanding why it was she couldn't stay in the quaint, quirky village for long.

I suppose I have Granny's spell to thank for that, she thought to herself as she lugged her own bag, following Athena. *And now that the spell is broken, I still can't stay here. Typical.*

It had been a common pattern in Rosemary's life that the things she wanted moved out of her grasp just as she thought she could reach them.

She sighed and looked out the window at the lightening sky. *Surely, it's late enough to call Ferg now. If it goes straight to voicemail, he could come as soon as he gets the message, and the sooner we get out of Myrtlewood, the better.*

Ferg picked up on the second ring. "Ferg's Useful Services, how can

I help?" said the unusual voice that had already become rather familiar.

"Good morning, Ferg."

"Is it?"

"Well, perhaps not. Anyway, it's Rosemary Thorn here. Athena and I need to get to the train station and could use your taxi services."

"Right away, Ma'am," Ferg said and hung up the phone before Rosemary could try to exchange anymore unsuccessful pleasantries with him.

"He's coming now," she said to Athena. "Let's wait on the porch."

"Please reconsider," Athena begged.

"Not a chance. We are not staying here a moment longer – and we are not coming back until we know for sure that it's safe."

She approached the front door and tried to unlatch it while still carrying her bag, but was unsuccessful.

"Oh, bother," she put her bag down and tried again, but the latch didn't move. "What is wrong with this door!?"

"Is it stuck?" Athena asked.

"It's more than stuck. It's not doing anything at all! I bet those intruders did something to it. They wanted to trap us in here so they could come back and finish the job."

"Or maybe it's the house."

"Of course it's the house, Athena. The door is part of the house."

"No – I mean, maybe the house is trying to stop us from leaving. It wants us to stay."

"That's even worse!" said Rosemary. "We will not be trapped here because of a stubborn sentient building! If the house is really acting in our best interests, it would let us make choices for ourselves. I can't believe I just said that. See what this place is turning me into? I'm over it. I'm over all of it. I want to get as far away from Myrtlewood as possible."

She looked frantically at Athena.

"I'm sorry to hear that, dear," Granny Thorn's voice said, coming from the direction of the door.

Rosemary snapped her head back in shock to see her grandmother's likeness imprinted on the gleaming mahogany surface in front of her.

"Granny?"

"Oh, of course it is. Who else would it be?"

"Are you...a ghost?"

"I don't seem to have a corporeal form, so yes, I suppose so."

"Uhhh..." Rosemary shot Athena an even more frantic look. "Are you seeing this, too?"

Athena smiled nervously and nodded.

"It's good to see you," Rosemary said. "Even if you are...disembodied. I've missed you."

"I've missed you too, love, but there isn't much time. I'm using up a lot of my energy just to speak to you now, and I need you to understand that you must stay in Myrtlewood."

"Oh," Rosemary deflated. "Not you too! Can't you see it's dangerous?"

"I'm afraid I do see that...a little too clearly, actually."

"Oh...sorry, of course you do," said Rosemary.

"So, then why do you want us to stay?"

"It is with great regret that I had to lead you into this danger," Granny Thorn said. "However, it was only in order to protect you and many others from an even greater risk."

"Well, that's just spiffing then," Rosemary said, sarcastically. "Isn't there anyone else who can deal with this while we nip out of town?"

"No, Rosemary. You are the only ones who can wield the Thorn magic. I do not trust your cousins and neither should you. There is no escaping what has been set in motion. If you were to leave town now, the danger would follow you. However, you wouldn't be as well-protected as you are here, in my house."

"Drat," Rosemary said.

"Stay in Myrtlewood, Rosemary," said Granny's ghost. "It is your rightful home, and I'm sorry that I created such distance, that I kept you away for so long. It was out of fear for your safety and Athena's, but now that you are both powerful women, you are ready."

"I'm not ready," Rosemary insisted. "And Athena is absolutely not ready. She's only sixteen."

"A powerful age."

"Too powerful, if you ask me," Rosemary grumbled.

"Let me look at you, dear," Granny said, beckoning Athena closer.

The girl stepped tentatively forward.

"Oh, yes. You are indeed powerful."

"I don't think so, Granny Thorn...I mean, Mum is the one with the superpowers."

"You don't know it yet, but it's right beneath the surface, and not just from our side of the family, either," Granny said, winking. "You're a special one."

"Granny," Rosemary said. "As much as I love and respect you, I really can't subject Athena to this. It's not right. You should have seen the men who invaded this place – your home – last night. They had fireballs and fangs and...uhm, birds."

"Our enemies are trying to drive you out. Don't you see?" Granny replied. "They think you're weak. They're trying to scare you off."

"But why? Why would they go to so much trouble? I don't understand," said Rosemary.

"Don't tell anyone else you saw me. I can't have every Tom, Dick and Harry calling me up to ask for help with magical odds and ends."

Granny's image in the door was fading fast. "No! Don't go!" Rosemary cried. "We need you!"

"I'm sorry, dear. My energy is running out. Much love and blessings to you!"

With that, she vanished into the polished mahogany.

"Drat!" Rosemary said. "Drat, drat, drat! We didn't ask her who her killer was!"

"Mum!" Athena said. "That should have been so obvious! Not to mention, it would have saved us a whole lot of trouble. What were you thinking?"

"I didn't hear you ask her, either," Rosemary said, glumly.

"You're supposed to be the adult here."

"Well, according to Granny, we are both strong women, and you're special. What on earth was she talking about, saying it wasn't all from our side of the family? I mean, your father is...he's *special* in his own way, but it isn't generally a *good* way."

"I have no idea," Athena said. "I like to think I didn't inherit any traits from him at all."

"He's not magic, though, is he?" Rosemary asked. "I mean, he's got enough charm to woo all the ladies, but he's never had sparks fly out of his hands or fought a vampire and won, as far as I know."

"It's not a competition, Mum," Athena said. "Anyway, how do you know we can trust her?"

"Granny? Of course, we can trust her. She's the most trustworthy person I know."

"Except for the fact that she hid the family magic from us and cast a spell to drive us away from this place?"

"Well, she had good reason to do that," said Rosemary, but a bitterness lingered on her tongue as she realised Athena had a point. Granny was at least partially responsible for all this, and she hadn't bothered to let them know anything while she was alive. Rosemary felt an uneasy crumbling of one of the few things in her life she'd felt was certain – her relationship with her beloved grandmother. All the while, Athena nattered on, oblivious to her mother's inner turmoil.

"Even if that's the case and Granny Thorn did have good reasons, how do we know that...that apparition on the door...was really her?"

"It was definitely her," Rosemary muttered. "There's no one quite like Granny Thorn, and it's not something you could fake."

"Not even with magic?"

"I don't think so," Rosemary said, though she wasn't entirely sure, herself. "We have to get her to come back!"

"What?" Athena asked.

"Yes – that's it," said Rosemary. "We can get her to come back and ask her who killed her straightaway and then we can think of a test that only she would know to make sure it's her and not some kind of trick."

"How do you suppose we do that?"

"Granny!" Rosemary said to the door. "Granny! If you can hear me...uhm...knock three times?"

Just then, there was a knock at the door.

Rosemary looked triumphantly at Athena.

"Uh, Mum," Athena said, glancing around through the side windows.

"What? It worked!"

"No, it didn't," Athena assured her, in a furious whisper. "Not unless you were really trying to summon Constable Perkins!"

"What!?"

Rosemary glanced through the window to see that the strange police officer was indeed standing on the doorstep.

"Oh bollocks!" Rosemary cursed under her breath. "What's he doing here?"

"You called him, remember?" Athena whispered.

"That seems like years go."

Constable Perkins knocked again.

"More like an hour. What do we do?" Athena said, keeping her voice low.

"I suppose we have to let him in," Rosemary said. "I mean...we can show him the mess that the intruders made and everything...That's why I called him, after all."

"Of course, you have to let him in!" Athena said. "What else would you do?"

"Pretend we've already gone?" Rosemary suggested.

"Oh yeah, and when he comes in to investigate, what then?"

"I didn't think of that."

"Just let him in," Athena said. "And try not to say anything too ridiculous, or we'll end up in even more trouble."

"What about the door?" Rosemary said. "It wasn't working before."

"Just try it."

"Fine," Rosemary said, turning the handle and latch to find they clicked open effortlessly.

"Took you long enough," Constable Perkins grumbled. "Now what's all this about?"

"It's..." Rosemary began and then lost her train of thought.

"There were intruders, Sir," Athena chimed in, perhaps sensing the immediate danger of her mother spouting off more incriminating nonsense.

Constable Perkins shifted his disapproving gaze on Rosemary into a more mollified glare at her daughter. Evidently, he liked being called "sir."

"Go on," he said.

"We were sleeping in the bedrooms upstairs, and we heard noises," Athena said, attempting to walk him through the chain of events.

"Loud crashing, howling noises!" Rosemary added enthusiastically.

Athena nudged her subtly with her foot.

"They woke us up, Sir. We went to the window to have a look, and we saw some people out there, all wearing black."

"More than one?" Constable Perkins asked.

"At least two," Athena said.

"But it was dark. How can you be so sure?" he asked.

"We know there were at least two because they came inside the house, and we saw them," Athena said. "Mum fought them off. It was actually quite impressive."

Rosemary gave a satisfied smile until she remembered the fate of the vampire she dusted. She wished that Athena hadn't mentioned how many there were, just in case. Still, the story was vague enough that there was a chance that particular dusting wouldn't be traced back to her.

"Where did all this happen?" Constable Perkins asked.

"Over there, by the landing," Athena said gesturing down the hall-way, towards the staircase. "I'll show you."

"Wait a minute!" Constable Perkins said in such an abrasive and accusatory tone that Rosemary wondered if he'd somehow already figured out the vampire homicide.

"What's with the bags?" Constable Perkins asked, pointing to the bags that still lay on the floor nearby. "You weren't thinking of skipping town, were you? After I specifically told you not to?"

"We certainly weren't going to stay in a house plagued by intruders," Rosemary snapped. "We were going to stay...oh I don't know, somewhere else in town, maybe? I suppose we could ask Marjie. Anyway, we're not the ones you should be suspicious of. I'm pretty sure whoever broke in last night were the exact same culprits that killed Granny, or were strongly connected to them."

"Hang on, hang on. I'm the one who does the accusing around here," Constable Perkins said. "What if you made all this up, so you'd have an excuse to leave the country and never return?"

"Constable Perkins," Rosemary said in her mum voice. "As much as you might inexplicably despise me, please believe me when I say I have no intention of becoming an international fugitive."

Athena gave Rosemary an alarmed look that told her to shut up now.

"You Thorn women are so cantankerous, the lot of ya," the police officer grumbled. "Now show me the damage, then."

"Damage?" Rosemary asked.

"From the fighting you supposedly did in the middle of the night."

"Uh, of course. Right this way," Rosemary said, leading him towards the stairways. "Oh, blast!"

"What is it, Mum?" Athena asked, following behind the constable.

"This was a right mess before!" Rosemary exclaimed. "Honestly! I never thought it would be such trouble to have a self-fixing house."

The whole area below the stairs looked perfect and polished without even a crow's feather to mess up the floor.

"What are you on about?" Constable Perkins asked.

"It's..." Rosemary tried to find a good excuse but quickly gave up. "Oh, sod it. It's just – this house kind of fixes and tidies itself. I know that sounds mad—"

"No," Constable Perkins said. "Not mad, just magic. And I do believe this is the most honest you've been with me since we first met."

"You...do?" Rosemary asked.

"I can always tell when people are hiding things from me, and you have secrecy written all over you," he grumbled. "That's another problem with you Thorn women, you always seem to hide the truth. Even if you think it's in other people's best interests. It's not."

"So, you believe me?" Rosemary asked.

"About the house fixing and cleaning itself, sure. That sounds plausible."

"*That* sounds plausible?"

"It would be just like old Galdie not to want to do her own house-work and maintenance," he said. "Though it's a mystery to me how she keeps her spells going after she's already gone to the other side."

"Good," Rosemary said. "So that clears things up, then."

"It most certainly does not," he replied. "You're still hiding things from me. I can't believe what you say about the intruders because there's too much secrecy getting in the way. The one thing I do believe is the house is self-fixing, but everything else is just a story as far as I'm concerned."

"But it's true...and...and..." Rosemary was grasping at straws, trying to remember the other thing she had been meaning to tell the police officer. "We can't possibly have killed Granny!" she said triumphantly.

"Oh yeah, and how's that then?" Constable Perkins asked, suspiciously.

"Well...well...someone told us her death was definitely caused by magic. Powerful magic. You see, so it couldn't be us. We didn't know about any of this stuff before we arrived back in Myrtlewood."

"Any of what stuff?"

"Magic," Athena said, trying to help fill in the blanks in Rosemary's haphazard explanation. "We didn't live here before, you see, Sir. We lived in ordinary towns where people don't believe in spells and charms or anything like that, so it wasn't until we came to Myrtlewood and stayed here, in this house, that things started happening that we couldn't possibly explain except through magic. Everyone talks about it around here as if it's the most normal thing in the world – like sunshine or electricity."

"I never did trust electricity," Constable Perkins grumbled.

"Uh...anyway," Rosemary said. "Athena and I are telling the truth now. You must be able to tell with your...ability. We honestly didn't know about magic before we came here on Saturday."

"Fair enough, fair enough," Constable Perkins said, tugging at his suspenders as he shifted from side to side. "I've seen enough, here."

"You have?" Rosemary said, hopefully. "Does that mean we're cleared?"

"Certainly not," he said. "I'm yet to carry out the full investigation. Just because you tell the truth about a few specific things, it doesn't mean much on the whole. You're still hiding some things." He looked at them suspiciously. "I need to get the full picture, you see."

"Oh...okay," Rosemary said, following the police officer out of the house to find Ferg standing on the veranda, this time wearing a yellow cap and sweater.

"Hello there," he said. "Taxi to the train station, ready and waiting."

"To the train station, eh?" Constable Perkins said, his voice dripping with suspicion. "I thought you said you were going to stay with old Marjie."

Rosemary sighed. She was backed into a corner, and she knew there was nothing for it but the truth. "Actually, to be perfectly honest, I was in a right tizz this morning, and I wanted to get as far away from Myrtlewood as possible."

"Oh, you did, did you?"

"I was going to tell you," she said. "I mean – otherwise why would I have called you?"

Rosemary's voice sounded a tad more doubtful than she intended it to.

Constable Perkins raised an eyebrow. "Why indeed?"

"It was just...terrifying. I was scared for my life, but most of all, I was trying to protect Athena. One of the attackers...he lunged at her."

"Oh, yes," Constable Perkins said, scratching his chin as if he'd just remembered a small detail he'd forgotten to ask about. "These attackers, what did they look like?"

Rosemary's gut seemed to form into a stone at the question. "Uh...well, like Athena said, they were wearing black...and it was dark, so I didn't see much. They were men, though...erm...with short hair."

"You seem nervous," the police officer said.

"I was terrified," said Rosemary, wondering whether it was considered a heinous crime to dust a vampire or more of a community service. She wasn't about to take the chance of finding out for herself. "And I still am. What if they come back? I mean...it seems likely, especially if they're the ones who killed Granny. Maybe they're after us or looking to steal something she hid in the house...I really don't know."

"You know more than you're letting on, that's for sure," Constable Perkins said. He nodded at Rosemary and Athena. "Make sure you *do* stay in town."

He tipped his hat at Ferg, who saluted in response and said "Good day, Sir."

As Constable Perkins's car puttered away down the driveway, Ferg looked from Rosemary to Athena. "I take it we are not going to the train station now?" he said.

Rosemary had the sensation of the entire world spinning around her. The last few hours had been such a rollercoaster of terror and anger at the intruders, of stubbornly wanting to escape Myrtlewood, of seeing her Granny again. Even if it was in two-dimensional ghost form, which gave her a pang of loss and happiness and confusion all at the same time. Granny had told her to stay, and that was more powerful than anything the constable might have said.

"I guess we're staying," said Rosemary, looking at her daughter, who shrugged but looked rather pleased all the same.

"Very well," said Ferg, walking backwards towards his orange car.

"Actually, I could do with some breakfast," Rosemary said. "How about you, Athena?"

"Yes! I'm starved," Athena said.

"Ferg, instead of the station," said Rosemary. "How about you take us down to Marjie's, so we don't have to walk? It has already been a full morning, and I don't know if we have the energy to get there ourselves."

"Very well," Ferg replied. He walked over to his car and opened the back door for them.

"Yellow is a good colour on you, by the way," Rosemary commented as she followed Athena into the car.

Ferg shrugged. "It's Monday."

Rosemary waited for him to explain the relevance of Monday to his choice of clothing, but Ferg got into the car without elaborating.

"Is Monday something to do with yellow?" Rosemary prodded, trying to make small talk despite her creeping sense of exhaustion.

"Of course," Ferg said. "Monday is the bright day where the week starts. I wear a different colour every day. Saturn Day is brown, Sunday is blue, Moon Day is yellow, Tuesday is orange, Wednesday is purple, Thursday is green, Friday is red."

Rosemary and Athena looked at each other in astonishment.

"Great," Rosemary said. "So, I can tell which day of the week it is based on what colour you're wearing."

"If it suits you," Ferg said.

"It's like a rainbow," said Athena

"No."

"But—" Athena started, but Ferg interrupted.

"No, it's deliberately not in that order – and it includes brown. Rainbows don't have brown," Ferg insisted.

"Okay then," said Athena.

"I'm an individual."

"That, you are," said Rosemary with a slightly amused grin. She was no longer amused. However, an hour later when she checked her phone to find a message from her boss, telling her she had been fired for not turning up for her early shift that morning.

Rosemary pressed her palms to her face. She didn't want to tell Athena, not just yet. It was mostly her fault. She'd meant to call and tell him they were staying away for longer, but either she'd put it off or forgotten, probably both. Of course, it was possible that she would have been fired for missing the shift either way, even with good reason, but now it was too late. Fate had made up its mind for her.

FOURTEEN

They pulled up outside the tea shop just as Marjie was putting out the "open" sign.

"Hi Marjie, ready for your first customers?" Rosemary asked, as she and Athena got out of the car.

"Absolutely!" Marjie said. "Get yourselves inside and out of the cold, and I'll bring you both some tea. It looks like you need my special blend today."

Rosemary shrugged. "Actually, you might be right. It has been one shocker of a morning."

"Say no more, say no more," Marjie said, ushering them inside.

As Marjie bustled about in the kitchen, making tea, Athena nudged Rosemary's arm.

"What?" Rosemary asked.

"Do you think we should tell her?" Athena asked, keeping her voice quiet so that Marjie wouldn't hear.

"Tell her what?"

"Everything," Athena said.

"Why on earth would we do that?" Rosemary asked.

"We need an ally," Athena explained. "We need someone we can trust who lives here, someone who understands this place inside-out who can help us to get our head around all this."

"What if we can't trust her?" Rosemary asked.

"Oh, come on, Mum. Does it look like Marjie was outside our house sporting a black ninja outfit last night? What do *you* think?"

"No, that's not what I was implying," Rosemary said. "It's just... what if her loyalties don't lie with Granny? What if she's some kind of mastermind...behind the whole thing?"

"Does that seem like a criminal mastermind to you?" Athena said, gesturing in the direction of the kitchen where Marjie was busy donning a floral apron.

"No, but..."

"I think at this point, the benefits of having an ally outweigh the risks of Marjie being a dark wizard," Athena said.

"Oh, fine. We'll tell Marjie."

"Tell me what, dear?" Marjie said, as she approached with a tea tray laden not only with tea but with toast and soft-boiled eggs in little floral egg cups.

"You brought us breakfast!" Athena said, with much more enthusiasm than Rosemary was used to from her teen.

"Of course I did," Marjie said. "The two of you need fattening up. Now, what was it you wanted to tell me? I'm all ears."

Rosemary took a sip of Marjie's special blend and instantly felt warmed and reassured. She began the long story about the house: the noises and the magic box and the self-fixing and the attacks and the intruders, omitting only the part about the vampire staking, which she wasn't sure was a safe topic to broach at that point.

Marjie smiled and nodded and ummed and arred, her expression growing gradually more concerned as they explained about the attacks to the house. She looked quite impressed with that last detail.

"You really fought him off, did ya?" Marjie asked, with more than a hint of pride in her voice.

"So, it seems. I guess it was something to do with the magic. I still don't understand it very well," Rosemary said.

"Oh, magic isn't for understanding up here." She tapped her head. "All that logic will do you no good. You have to understand it here." She held her palm to her heart. "That's where magic really lives."

"I see," Rosemary said, though she wasn't quite sure she got it.

"I'm surprised you don't want to skip right out of town after all that, though," said Marjie.

"I did want to, actually," Rosemary admitted. She wasn't sure if she should tell Marjie about Granny appearing and decided to err on the side of caution. "Constable Perkins has forbidden us from leaving town."

"I'm glad you haven't left us," said Marjie. "You'll be a lot safer here. But rest assured, I'll be giving that Constable Perkins a piece of my mind for troubling you."

"Who's troubling whom, now?" a rich booming voice sounded from the door.

"Now, now, Mr June. You're early this morning!" Marjie exclaimed.

Rosemary turned to look at the customer who had just entered. He wore a black embroidered jacket with a royal-purple collar, and though he might have been about her age, he carried a black stylised walking stick with a silver top. His hair was slicked back. The look was so old-fashioned that Rosemary assumed he was actually older, or that he was going for a particular goth look. She couldn't tell which.

Marjie left to fuss over Mr June instead, bringing him his usual English breakfast tea and a slice of carrot cake.

"The doctor says I have to eat my vegetables," he boomed, taking a large bite of the cake.

Rosemary and Athena gave each other a questioning look.

"Perfect, as always, Marjoram," Mr June said, smacking his chops. "And who are your lovely lady guests? I don't recognise them. You'd think, as mayor, that I'd have a good handle on all the goings-on in town, but it's quite frankly not the case."

Mayor...alarm bells rang in Rosemary's mind. She couldn't quite remember what it was she'd heard about the mayor of Myrtlewood, or who had told her. She racked her brains, wanting to ask Athena if she recalled anything, but not wanting to appear suspicious by whispering. Athena did not look suspicious, just perturbed by the unusual character.

"Why, this is Rosemary Thorn and her daughter Athena, of course! Can't you see the family resemblance?"

For the first time, Rosemary wished that Marjie wasn't quite so friendly, especially after everything they'd just told her about the past few days. She wished she'd had a mind to let Marjie know the entire conversation was in the strictest confidence, and now it would be hard to say anything. She tried to shoot Marjie a warning look.

"Of course! The Thorny descendants," Mr June said. "See what I did there."

"Yes, uh, very clever," Rosemary said.

Athena rolled her eyes, and Rosemary was grateful that the mayor didn't notice. It was her turn to kick her daughter softly under the table, an action that earned her an angry glare.

"Here to check out the old house, I imagine," Mr June continued. "I expect you'll want to put it up on the market as soon as possible. An old manor like that is a lot of work to maintain."

"Actually," Rosemary said. "We have decided to stay in Myrtlewood."

Athena looked at Rosemary, startled by the certainty in her mother's voice.

"Oh, ugh," Mr June spluttered, choking on his tea.

Rosemary wasn't actually quite as sure as she had tried to sound. She was really just trying to gauge the mayor's reaction to see how likely he was to be their prime suspect, but it was starting to seem likely they'd stay in Myrtlewood. After all, she'd just lost her job and there wasn't much to go back for, plus she trusted Granny's instincts.

"Really?" he asked. "Because I know a few people who'd be willing buyers – people who love old heritage houses like that."

"Really. We're staying." Rosemary said.

Mr June looked perturbed for a moment, and then he clapped his hands together enthusiastically. "Two new members of Myrtlewood! Two new constituents! Welcome!"

He strode over to their table and shook hands with both of them.

"Thank you, Mr June," said Rosemary.

"Oh please, call me Don," the mayor said.

"Don June?" Rosemary asked, trying to suppress a giggle.

"That's my name. What of it?" he asked.

"Nothing," said Rosemary. "It's just...an unusual name, is all."

"I pride myself on being extraordinary," he said, tugging at his purple collar.

"I can see you're successful at it," Rosemary said, trying to sound complimentary rather than mocking. After all, he could well be a murderer whose bad side she didn't want to get on, and even if he wasn't, it would pay to have an official on their side if things got worse with Constable Perkins.

"Now, if you'll excuse me," Mr June said. "I'll be over there, reading my paper. It's the best way to start the day – a cup of tea and the morning paper, don't you agree?"

Rosemary and Athena both nodded enthusiastically, hoping he'd clear off and leave them in peace. They ate the rest of their breakfast in silence, while more customers arrived and the noise around them built up.

After a while, the mayor folded up his newspaper with a flourish and announced to Marjie that "duty calls" before striding out of the tea shop.

Rosemary turned to Athena. "What do you think?" she asked. "Suspect?" She gestured to the table where Mr June had been sitting moments before.

"I don't know," Athena said. "Why do you say that?"

"Someone told me something dodgy about him, only I can't, for the life of me, remember what it was. Do you know?"

"Mum, your memory is shocking, but honestly, how would I know?"

"Well, chances are you were there with me when they said it."

154

"Not ringing any bells. What was it?"

"I told you, I can't remember. If I could recall who said it, I could go back and ask them. Hang on, that's it!"

"What's it?"

"It was right before you went missing. That bar woman told me something, and it must have been so interesting I took my eyes off you for a minute too long – big mistake."

"Hey! I thought we were over all that."

"We're over some of it," Rosemary corrected. "I'm still processing. Anyway, what was her name?"

"Sherry," Athena said. "And I only remember that because I thought it was funny that she worked in a bar with a name like that. That's this place all over though, isn't it? I can't believe you are now so sure we're moving here. This morning you couldn't get away fast enough."

"Well...I'm not a hundred percent sure, but Granny told us to stay, so we're here for now. I was just trying to test him."

"Test who?"

"The mayor, of course. I wanted to see the look on his face. If he was trying to scare us off, then he wouldn't be happy about us sticking around, now, would he?"

"He seemed pretty happy about it to me," Athena said.

"Actually, at first, he looked shocked and choked on his tea, remember? Only after he recovered from that did he come over and roll out the welcome wagon."

"So, what did your test tell you?"

"I'm not sure yet."

Rosemary took another sip of tea and watched as a smile spread across Athena's face.

"We're really staying, then?!"

"So, it seems."

"Don't you have a job to get back to?"

"Uh, about that..."

"What?"

"Apparently I don't have a job. Not anymore."

"What? Oh no...you didn't!" Athena said. "You forgot to call Mr Lindon, didn't you?"

Rosemary sighed. "Don't give me a hard time, okay. It's been a rough few days and...I'm sure he was likely to fire me even if I did call up and tell him I couldn't make it in for days – or weeks – without a good non-incriminating explanation or an idea of when we'd be able to leave. And, well, *you* wanted to stay here, anyway. You should be pleased."

"I am pleased," Athena said. "But it's the principle of the matter."

"And that principle is?"

"You're always wrong," Athena teased.

"Harsh!" said Rosemary, giving her a playful push.

"But true," Athena insisted. "What are we going to do about money now that you're gainfully unemployed?"

"We'll figure it out," Rosemary said. "We always do."

CHAPTER
FIFTEEN

They thanked Marjie for breakfast and Rosemary tried to pay, to no avail.

"Your Granny wouldn't approve of me charging you," Marjie insisted. "You Thorns are like family to us, Reeves. There will be no charging going on what-so-ever."

Rosemary felt terribly guilty, though her dwindling bank account would have expressed gratitude if it could.

"Well, at least let me return the favour and treat you sometime," said Rosemary.

"Oh, if you must," Marjie said.

"Thanks again, Marjie. You're brilliant." Rosemary said, giving the older woman a peck on the cheek.

"Oh, it's nothing really," Marjie insisted.

"Come over for dinner, sometime," Rosemary said as she turned to go, then remembered the other thing she needed to tell Marjie. She turned back. "Uh, and please don't tell anyone what's been happening to us up at the Manor. It's strictly confidential, all right? It's not that we have anything to hide. We just don't want the attackers to find out through the grapevine that they've ruffled us."

157

"O'course not," Marjie said. "Mum's the word."

Rosemary and Athena left the shop, slightly reassured by Marjie's promise of a secret kept, though they really knew so little about her it was hard to tell how loose her tongue was.

"She could be the town gossip, you know," Rosemary pointed out on their walk back to the manor.

"Your Granny trusted her. That should be good enough," Athena reminded her mother. "Besides, what were you thinking, inviting her over for dinner like that? What if we're attacked again?"

"Actually, that's a brilliant idea!"

"What!? Being attacked is not something you aspire to." Athena scolded.

"Not being attacked, per se, but dinner."

"Dinner is always a good idea," Athena agreed. "What's your point?"

Rosemary lowered her voice and looked around as they neared the edge of the village. "We'll have a dinner party and invite all the suspects and watch them to see what they do and who is acting suspicious."

"So, you want to get all the potential murderers in the same room as us, and feed them?" Athena asked.

"Yes."

"Ridiculous! What if they slip you poison or attack you?"

"I'm hoping the house will help us a little," Rosemary said, sheepishly.

"A great lot of good it did Granny Thorn," Athena muttered.

"We can invite that police officer, too," Rosemary said. "And everyone who is being friendly to us, so that there are more pairs of eyes watching for anything untoward."

"You really want to do this?" Athena asked.

"Yes. Just think about it. It will be our hello-to-Myrtlewood party. We can invite all the suspicious people like the mayor and that lawyer, Burk..."

"I thought you liked him," Athena said with just a hint of teasing in her voice.

"I thought he was okay," Rosemary admitted, looking around the picturesque countryside as they walked, to make sure no one was listening to what she said next. "But did I tell you how much that vampire guy I dusted looked like him?"

"No, you did not," Athena said. "Do you mean to inform me that you managed to dust a lawyer?"

"No, love. It wasn't him, but there was a definitive resemblance."

"Well, that's incredibly suspicious."

"Yes, and I bet he knows more than he's letting on."

"So, you really think this dinner is a good idea?" Athena asked.

"Of course it is. We'll hold it in the formal dining room."

They had reached the long rambling driveway to Thorn manor, and Rosemary once again had a creeping feeling of being watched.

"What will we serve them? Jaffa cakes and crisps?" Athena asked, clearly not noticing Rosemary's discomfort, which was probably for the best. She didn't want to worry her daughter.

"No. I'll cook."

"Really, Mum? It's been ages since you've cooked properly. You know I miss your cooking...well, especially the desserts."

"You never much liked my fancy dinners when you were younger, you fuss-pot. I got out of the habit of making proper meals when all you wanted was baked beans on toast."

"It's normal for little kids to be fussy. I'm not so bad now. I even eat a variety of vegetables," said Athena as they reached Thorn Manor.

"Sure," Rosemary said. "A somewhat limited variety..."

"Anyway, how are you supposed to cook a fancy meal and host the party at the same time? That's more than one person can do – let alone spotting nefarious villains."

"It will be fine, Athena. I'll just make most of the food ahead of time."

Athena sighed and followed Rosemary into the house, and they went directly to the kitchen to put the kettle on, as usual.

"We better at least get that big piece of paper and make sure we've got all the suspects. I guess it needs updating now." She retrieved the list and set it down on the kitchen table while Rosemary made tea.

"So, we need to add Mr Don June the mayor, and...who else? Burk is already on here because he asked about you selling the house. Why does everyone seem to want you to sell it?"

Rosemary shrugged. "It's a pretty special house."

"Yes, but do they all know about how it fixes and cleans itself, or was that one of Granny Thorn's many secrets?" Athena asked.

Rosemary shrugged.

"And why does it do that?" Athena continued. "Where is the magic coming from? Maybe if we understand that, we'll know why everyone's so interested in buying the house."

"Your guess is as good as mine," said Rosemary. "In Granny's letter it seemed like she thought it was to do with the family magic, remember? She bound the family magic years ago because people were after it, and those people eventually came after her."

"Are you sure they're people?"

"Hey, vampires are people too," Rosemary said. "Even if they're not humans."

"You're the expert...Buffy."

"Oh, shut it!"

"Hey. Do you think you've released the magic, like Granny Thorn's letter told you to do? I mean, there was that thing with the box and then you said you went to another world and met an addler."

"An elder!"

"Whatever. Did that release the family magic, or just part of it? You've definitely got some magic, at least when you're in the house."

"I see what you're getting at," Rosemary said. "The power must still be bound up in here, and people who are after that power want to buy the house so they can get at it."

"*Finally*, Mum," Athena said, bemused. "You know you're not the sharpest tool in the shed."

"Did you just call me a tool?" Rosemary said. "How rude."

"Ha, ha. Very funny," said Athena.

"Seriously, though. We need to figure out how this magic works. We need to know more than our enemies."

"Up until a couple of days ago, our only enemy was Dad," said Athena.

"He's not an enemy, just a...problem."

"A big problem, Mum. And if he ever tries to come back, I'm casting a spell on you to stop you falling for his codswallop again."

"That sounds like a wise course of action," Rosemary admitted. "Though I seem to be the only one with magic at this point."

"Don't rub it in," Athena said. "It's *so* not fair that you get super strength to fight off vampires with sparks flying out of your hands and the power to move things and boil a kettle—"

Just then, the kettle whistled.

"It wasn't me that time," Rosemary said, going to make tea.

"Still not fair," said Athena.

"None of that was my choice," Rosemary said, carrying the freshly made pot of tea to the table to sit next to her daughter. She glanced at their makeshift investigation map. "Is there anyone else we're missing?"

"I don't know, you were the one catching up on all the pub gossip. What else did Sherry say?"

"If only I could remember," Rosemary said. "Everything she said was overshadowed by your sudden disappearance."

"Stop bringing that up, already."

"I will not," Rosemary said. "As your parent, I have rights...and that includes the right to hassle you about your behaviour."

"I suppose it's only fair, seeing as I hassle you about yours."

"It should be a right that only *I* have," Rosemary grumbled.

They sipped their tea and then spent the next few hours going over the details of what they knew.

"There was some kind of group someone told me about that Granny didn't like," Rosemary recalled. "The Blueblood Clan? The Bluetooth Group? Something like that."

"They sound like a tech firm," Athena scoffed.

"Yes, I'm sure a tech firm is trying to embezzle our magic for their own nefarious digital purposes."

"Stop saying nefarious all the time," Athena complained. "It's a stupid word."

"But it seems so *fitting*," Rosemary protested.

She poured their tea, and then the two of them sat in silence for a while, sipping and pondering.

"We have to go back to the pub, don't we?" Athena said.

"I suppose so, but only if you don't run off without telling me where you're going."

"I won't!" Athena insisted.

"Promise."

"I promise not to run off without telling you, not even if I'm only five metres away."

"Very good. Thank you," said Rosemary, patting her daughter on the arm.

Athena grimaced and pulled away.

Teenagers! Rosemary thought. *Grossed out at any show of affection... unless it happens to come from a mysterious boy!*

"Let's hope Sherry is working again tonight," Rosemary said. "We could even bring this piece of paper to write down what she says."

"What an idea, Mum. Bring a huge piece of paper so that everyone can see that we're conducting our own investigation and probably get in the way. You know this town is full of weirdos and busybodies just waiting to give us their opinion on everything and lead us off-track, accidentally or on purpose."

"You just reminded me of something," Rosemary said. "Remember that woman? The strange old bat who came over to our table last night? What was it she said?"

"Granny Thorn had enemies, some other nonsense."

"It could have been useful nonsense," Rosemary lamented. "I just wish I could remember it!"

"Your memory is like a sieve at the best of times," Athena said.

"Don't worry about it. That woman was clearly batty. Didn't Sherry say as much?"

"Sure, but how do you know we can trust Sherry?" Rosemary asked.

"This isn't Cluedo, Mum. Be reasonable."

"I am being reasonable. It really could be anyone – even Marjie – and now we've gone and told her almost everything."

"Well, whoever is responsible would already know half of what we told her, since they were the ones who planned the attack," Athena said. "Come on. Get your coat."

"Where are we going?" Rosemary asked.

"To the pub, for lunch," Athena replied.

"Good call," Rosemary said. "We can ask Sherry whatever it was she said last night."

"Plus, I'm starved," Athena added.

"Already? We only just had breakfast."

Athena shrugged. "Blame it on a growth-spurt, if you must."

Rosemary took a snap of the large piece of paper with her phone just in case they wanted to refer to it inconspicuously at the pub. They put on their walking shoes and headed out the door and back into town.

It was lunch time when they reached the pub, and it was bustling with customers, but to their disappointment, Sherry wasn't behind the bar. A man was there, instead, standing with his back to them, polishing the glasses. Rosemary noticed his muscular frame and his casual sandy hair before he turned towards them, flashing familiar blue-green eyes her way.

"Liam?" she said. "You...work here?"

Liam looked startled. He put down the glass he was holding and straightened his apron a little. "Rosey. Hi. Uh...not usually. I just help Sherry out sometimes on the days that the bookshop is closed."

"Where is she?" Athena prompted.

"Oh, yes," Rosemary said. "Where is Sherry today? We were hoping to have a wee chat with her."

"She's come down with something," Liam said. "Excuse me."

He turned to a customer at the bar and began pouring pints.

"I wonder if she's okay," Athena said.

"It's probably just a cold," Rosemary replied. "I'm sure she's fine."

"Knowing this town, it's some kind of magical malady," Athena said. "Or worse – what if the people who came after us have gone after her too?"

"Don't be so paranoid," said Rosemary.

"Paranoid about what?" Liam asked.

Rosemary turned back to find him leaning on the bar, smiling. "Sorry – didn't mean to eaves-drop," Liam said. "It's a bad habit, I know. I'll just go over there and sort the cutlery."

"Hang on a minute," said Rosemary. "Don't go just yet. While you have a minute, is Sherry alright? What's she come down with?"

"I tried to find that out myself," Liam said, blushing slightly. "But she fobbed me off, didn't she? Typical Sherry. She told me she'd be right as rain in no time."

Rosemary felt somewhat reassured by that explanation. At least Sherry was well enough to talk and be stroppy. Even Athena looked somewhat satisfied.

"So, what brings you two to this fine establishment?" Liam asked. "Lunch?"

"Oh, yes," Rosemary said. "Yes, please."

"Take a seat." Liam handed them a couple of menus. "I'll be over in just a jiffy."

"Shall we go back to where we sat last time, or are there too many bad memories for you?" Athena asked Rosemary.

"We'd better take the same seat," Rosemary replied. "Seeing as it's the only booth that's empty, and I'll just have to push through the bad memories and make good ones – you know – get back on the bicycle."

"Gross, Mum!"

"It's not gross. I do not think you know what that phrase means."

"It sounds sordid."

"Well, it's not, it just means, you know...when you fall off, you should get back on, so that you keep riding and don't develop a phobia. At least I think that's what it means."

"Still sounds gross," Athena said, noticeably scanning the bar before sitting down.

"I give up," Rosemary said. "What do you want to eat?"

They both scanned the menu, Rosemary occasionally glancing at her daughter to see if she was looking out for anything else the pub had to offer, namely The Boy, though he was nowhere in sight.

"Maybe the pie," Athena said. "It's steak and mushroom today."

A man's voice interrupted them. "The steak and mushroom pie is excellent."

Rosemary looked up to see Burk standing next to their table.

"Oh...hello," she said, cautiously.

"I'm glad you decided to stick around town," Burk said. He glanced at Athena.

"Uh, Athena, this is the lawyer I told you about, Perseus Burk," said Rosemary. "This is my daughter, Athena."

"It's a pleasure to meet you," he said, holding out his hand to Athena, who reluctantly shook it, a puzzled expression on her face.

"I take it you've had quite an eventful time," Burk said.

"How do you figure that?" Rosemary asked, suspicious. She wasn't about to let a handsome lawyer throw her off track.

"Constable Perkins informed me. As your lawyer, I have a duty to know what's going on."

"But you're not..." Rosemary said. "I mean. It's very generous for you to offer to help, but you're not officially my lawyer. You were Granny's lawyer, but I never signed anything to say you were mine."

Burk looked taken aback. "I thought you were taking up the offer of my legal assistance," he said. "You called me, after all."

Yes...but that was before your evil twin attacked me! Rosemary thought, though she managed to hold herself back from saying it.

"I did," Rosemary said, coolly. "And thank you for your offer, but I feel uncomfortable about you talking to the police behind my back."

Athena shot her mother a look of warning that said: *keep your mouth shut. Don't start rambling. This is serious.*

"It wasn't...it wasn't like that," Burk said, noticeably ruffled for the first time since Rosemary met him, which admittedly hadn't been that long. "The constable actually came to me this morning, concerned for your welfare. I told him I would check in to see if you were okay. I was about to give you a call after lunch, but then I saw you were already here."

"How thoughtful of you," Rosemary said, smiling politely, but not warmly. "What exactly did Constable Perkins tell you?"

"He said that there had been a disturbance at the house – that you'd told him you were attacked by intruders. I'm suspecting they had something to do with your grandmother's passing."

"We suspect so, too," Athena said. "But how do we know we can trust you?"

Rosemary kicked Athena under the table.

"I suppose you don't know that," Burk said.

"Perhaps you could refrain from speaking to the authorities about us for the time being?" Athena suggested.

"But...I'm sorry...Rosemary...?" Burk stuttered.

"Is this man bothering you?" Liam asked, approaching the table.

Rosemary watched as a look of challenge passed between the two men.

"We were just chatting," Burk said.

Liam looked from Rosemary to Athena.

"It's fine, Liam," Rosemary said. "Perseus was just leaving."

Perseus Burk gave her a slightly pleading look and then raised his palms in surrender and walked away.

"That man is a right prick," Liam said. "He struts around here as if he owns the place.... Just because he's some fancy-pants lawyer...Sorry he was bothering you."

"It's fine, really," Rosemary said. "Can we order some lunch?"

"Of course," Liam said, seemingly remembering why he was standing there. "What will you have?"

"Steak and mushroom pie?" Rosemary asked Athena.

Athena shook her head. "Actually, I think I'll just have the pumpkin soup, thanks."

"Well, I'll have the pie," said Rosemary. "And a ginger ale."

"Make that two ginger ales," Athena said.

"Perfect," said Liam. "It won't be long. The cook here is magic."

Rosemary smiled, assuming Liam meant that literally.

"I think I'm starting to get used to Myrtlewood, with all this para-normal-normalness," she said to Athena.

"It's a wonder, with how open they are about it, that you didn't pick up on it earlier," Athena said. "You spent summers here as a kid; did it all just sail over your head?"

"I presume it was part of Granny's spell that I didn't remember," Rosemary said, frowning. "Maybe she's responsible for my sieve-like memory. Hey!" her expression brightened. "Maybe when we've unbound the magic, it will fix my memory."

"It's magic, not miracles," Athena said sceptically. She glanced around the pub again.

"He's not here, you know," Rosemary said.

"Who?" Athena asked, feigning innocence.

"Your Finnigan chap."

"I wasn't looking for him," Athena insisted. "I'm just...you know... looking for suspicious behaviour."

"Sure, sure," Rosemary said. "Speaking of suspicious behaviour. What do you think all that was about before, with Burk and Liam?"

"So he's Burk now?" Athena asked. "Moment's ago, he was Perseus. 'Oh Perseus, do you think I should order the steak and mushroom pie?'" said Athena, batting her eyelids and putting on a cartoony accent.

"Oh, shut it," said Rosemary. "I did not say – or sound – anything like that. From the tense interaction before, I was sure that both men knew something. I bet one, or both is involved with the plot to steal our magic."

"Seriously, Mum?"

"What?"

"Are you that blind?"

"What are you talking about?" Rosemary asked.

"They're both keen on you, and they're getting all weird and blokey and territorial over it."

"Don't be silly," Rosemary said. "Burk is just Granny's lawyer, and Liam...well he's an old adolescent flame, sure, but I'd be surprised if he's not seeing Sherry. Did you see the protective way he responded before when we asked about her?"

"Still..."

"No." Rosemary said. "Neither of them are my type, and besides, I don't date, remember."

"Do you even have a type – except for drop-kick?"

"Athena, it's rude to talk about your father that way."

"Rude, but true."

"Come on. Dain's not that bad. He just has issues – lots of them."

"Dad's not the only one with issues," said Athena, giving her mother a meaningful look.

"Here you go," said Liam, appearing back at the table with a laden tray and placing their meals and drinks in front of them.

"That was quick," Rosemary said. "No wonder you have this whole place under control with just you behind the bar."

Liam beamed. "Sherry has this whole place under control, even when she's bedridden," he said with a look of pride in his eyes.

Rosemary shot Athena an I-told-you-so glance.

"About Sherry," Athena said. "We'd love to see her when she's well. Could you pass on the message?"

"Of course," Liam replied. "I'm sure she'd love to pop 'round to the old house. She's always adored that place."

Rosemary's expression changed to one of suspicion, but Athena subtly shook her head.

"Thanks, Liam," Rosemary said. "Tell her to give us a call and pop around when she's well, or we'll catch up with her here."

"No worries," Liam said and made his way back to the bar.

Rosemary and Athena had just started tucking into their meals when another interruption arrived.

"Rosemary Thorn!"

Rosemary looked up at the sound of the woman's voice to find her heart sinking, and her hands starting to itch.

"Oh, hi...Despina?"

"That's the one!" the estate agent said. She was entirely clad in cornflower blue this time, with a matching bow on her head. "And this is my...niece, Geneviève."

A young girl stepped forward who couldn't have been more than about twelve, though she was wearing much more mature clothing than her aunt – a mauve suit, more appropriate for a professional office than a country pub, and certainly not commonly worn by tweens. Her curly chestnut-coloured hair was pulled back into a tight bun, and Rosemary empathised. It was so hard to tame curly hair. She herself had entirely given up and let her hair do its own wild thing, but when she was younger, she'd slaved for hours to try to control her locks, to no avail.

"Hi Geneviève," Rosemary said with a smile.

Athena frowned from across the table.

"We were just popping in for lunch," Despina said.

"Yes. Can we join you?" Geneviève asked.

"Oh...uhm," she glanced at Athena, who stared bloody murder back. "Well..."

"Oh, come now, Gen. I'm sure Athena and Rosemary are enjoying quality time. They wouldn't want to be interrupted by people they hardly know."

Geneviève looked downcast, pulling at Rosemary's heartstrings.

"Maybe not today," Rosemary said. "But we are planning a dinner for later this week, a sort of welcome-to-the-town kind of thing. We'd love for you to join us."

Rosemary felt a sharp kick to her shins. She grimaced to stifle a yell and then managed to turn her expression into a smile.

Geneviève's face lit up. "Really?"

"Yes, *really*," Rosemary said, giving Athena a meaningful look.

"How wonderful," said Despina. "We look forward to further details. Enjoy your lunch." She gave a little wave and then ushered the young girl away.

"What was *that*?" Athena said. "You looked like you were about to adopt that brat!"

"Oh, don't be jealous," Rosemary said, dismissively.

"I am not!"

"You always hated it when I held other babies when you were little. I don't see how this is any different."

"You were just instantly all gooey over little miss twelve-going-on-thirty-two. It was weird and inappropriate. I can't believe you invited them to our party!"

"She's charming," Rosemary said. "I wish I could say the same for her aunt." She shuddered and scratched at her hands. "And besides, Despina is on our invite list already, remember. She's a suspect, as someone who's expressed an interest in us selling the house."

"That's because she's a freaking estate agent!" Athena hissed. "It is *literally* her job to sell houses. She's almost the least-suspicious person we've encountered, apart from Marjie."

"So why are you getting so riled up, then?" Rosemary asked. "If she's not guilty, she'll just be another guest. It's going to be my problem, really. I don't know how I'm going to tolerate a whole evening with itchy hands. The rash might even spread to my—"

"I do not want to hear about your imaginary rashes, or where they might spread," Athena snapped. "Nor do I want to spend an evening with that child, who clearly thinks she's an adult. How tiresome!"

"Oh, you've always hated younger kids," Rosemary said.

"And you've always loved them."

"It's probably because you're an only child, you know."

"And thank goodness for that," said Athena. "Imagine if I got a younger sibling who dressed like Margaret Thatcher."

"Thatcher always wore blue, you know."

"Not the point, Mum."

"So, what if I liked the kid? She's a much snappier dresser than her aunt."

"And that's what's important to you, is it?" Athena teased. "If only I knew...I could have been gaining parental approval points just from power-dressing."

"Since when have you ever cared about *my* approval?" Rosemary asked. "You know, I love you very much, but you were practically born with a judgemental glare."

"Harsh, Mum."

"It's not a bad quality to have," Rosemary assured her. "You're naturally shrewd, and it has only increased with your teenage brain-changes. It probably kept you out of danger fairly well, aside from the other night."

"You mean, last night? In which I was perfectly safe? And five meters away?"

"Without telling your mother, yes," said Rosemary. "Anyway. Your judgement can be an asset. Like you say, you are a pretty good judge of character. You just have to learn to keep it in check."

"If I'm such a good judge of character, then why don't you trust my judgement on little miss-high-flyer?" Athena asked.

"Because you're being petty," Rosemary said. "And it shows."

Athena sighed and focussed on quietly slurping her soup.

Rosemary properly dug into the steak and mushroom pie up until that point she had only picked at the chips and salad, which were rather nice, but the pie itself was exceptional. Burk had been right about that, at least.

CHAPTER
SIXTEEN

While Rosemary ate, savouring every mouthful of the delicious meat pie, she gazed over to the far corner of the bar. She wasn't paying attention at first, but by-and-by, she noticed a couple of people had walked out through the shadowed door with its red-velvet curtains, into darkness. Though they had not returned, however, different people had walked in.

It was perplexing, as it wasn't marked with an exit sign like the other doors. It also had a whiff of secrecy about it. She wondered if it was a secret gambling room, or perhaps something more magical. She thought about asking Liam, but he was nowhere in sight.

Rosemary was startled when Despina and Geneviève both walked out that way, clearly not staying for lunch, after all. For a moment she worried about the young girl being taken through a door like that into some dark, sinister location, perhaps frequented by multiple estate agents. Rosemary shuddered.

"What?" Athena asked her.

"What do you think that is?" she asked Athena, pointing to the unusual door.

"Erm...a doorway?"

"Don't you think there's something...shady about it?"

"Not really, Mum," Athena said, clearly not in the mood to chat.

Rosemary decided to investigate. She took her last mouthful of pie and excused herself. She went to the loos first, hoping not to look too suspicious, then she skirted the room so that she ended up near the mysterious door.

There was a slight cavern to one side of it, like a badly lit cloak room. She stepped into the shadows and listened.

Nothing.

Rosemary tentatively pushed open the door, only to find her wrist seized as, from out of nowhere, she was shoved firmly but politely back into the far corner of the shadowy alcove.

"What the...!" Rosemary said, blinking in the darkness in an attempt to see the gentle assailant who was still gripping her arm, holding her up against the wall.

"Do *not* open that door," a familiar silky voice said. "Whatever you do."

"Mr Burk?"

"Perseus," he corrected.

"What do you mean by this?" Rosemary asked.

"I can't explain," Burk said, stepping back. "Just trust me, please."

Again, there was a vulnerability in his voice that bordered on pleading, but that Rosemary instinctively responded to, intuiting that he was trying to protect her.

"I don't understand," she said. "I just saw Despina and her little niece go through there."

"They have their reasons," Burk assured her.

"And I'm not allowed to know them?" Rosemary asked, feeling stroppy. She pushed herself away from Burk, though a part of her had enjoyed the intimacy of having someone so close. As she did, she noticed how cold his hand was on her wrist. *Poor circulation...*that's what he'd said back at his office, but now Rosemary wasn't so sure.

"Something strange is going on here, isn't it?" she said.

Burk laughed. "In Myrtlewood? Of course."

"But everyone is so open about magic here. Why won't you tell me what's going on behind the door?"

"I have my reasons," Burk said. "And they are chiefly concerned with your safety." He bowed his head slightly.

"Fine," Rosemary said. "But I do intend to find out, one way or another."

She stepped back towards the light, but Burk's hand shot out, lightning quick, and barred her way.

"Wait, Rosemary."

"Call me Ms Thorn," Rosemary said, feeling it was only appropriate to rescind the invitation to use her first name given the distance she intended on putting between herself and Mr Burk.

"Ms Thorn..." Burk said.

Rosemary had to brace herself against the discomfort of the polite title. It was almost as unpleasant as being in the presence of estate agents.

"What?" Rosemary said, and there was a harshness to her tone that even she didn't expect.

"Is there a reason for your being so distant, all of a sudden?"

"There might be," Rosemary said. "But I don't have to explain myself to you."

"That's fine," Burk said. "I do have one other question, though. And then I promise I'll stop bothering you."

"What is it?" Rosemary asked.

"Constable Perkins told me about the attack, but he couldn't describe the intruders to me."

Rosemary's gut tightened, recalling the face of the vampire just as he burst into dust, the face uncomfortably similar to the one directly in front of her.

"It's confidential to the investigation," Rosemary said.

Burk visibly deflated. His expression was so sad that Rosemary was caught off guard, and her wayward tongue got away from her. "One of them had dark hair and a goatee, I think. Oh, and a scar on his cheek.

The other one..." she paused, managing to restrain herself. "Uh...I didn't see the other one."

"Verikus," Burk said, under his breath.

"Excuse me?"

"Verikus Wyrt," he explained. "He's been a right pain in my neck ever since he learned to walk and talk. I don't suppose my wayward brother was with him?"

Rosemary felt as if her insides had frozen solid.

His brother! I killed Perseus Burk's brother!

She managed to utter a strained, "I told you, I didn't see."

"That would be just like them," Burk said. "If you ever have the misfortune of meeting my brother, run the other way. He's rotten to the core."

And he's a vampire... Rosemary thought before remembering the swiftness of Perseus Burk's movements and the chill of his skin.

Does vampirism run in families?...I have so much to learn.

"My brother makes his money as a hired goon," Burk admitted, bowing his head further, as if in shame. "He'll do anything for a chunk of cash or gold...or even stolen goods. He once took a job against me – *his own brother* – in exchange for a box of smokes and bag of jewellery, probably nicked from some wealthy old woman."

"I'm...sorry," Rosemary said. After an awkward pause, she added. "I have to get back to my daughter."

"Of course," Burk said, dropping his hand.

Rosemary stepped past him and back into the light and bustle of the pub.

"If you ever need anything, the offer still stands," she heard Burk say as she walked away.

"There you are!" Athena practically shouted as Rosemary returned to their table. "You've been gone for ages! I was about ready to send out a search party!"

"Oh, really?"

"No – but if I had disappeared for that long, you'd have had the army out looking for me."

"That's because you're a teenager and I'm your mother."

"It sometimes feels like the other way around," Athena said, crossing her arms. "Where were you, anyway?"

"I'll tell you later," Rosemary said, looking around the pub, which had emptied out, somewhat.

"What? Why? What happened?" Athena looked worried.

"Nothing much," Rosemary said, keeping her voice low. "I just discovered something that I don't want to share in a place where it might be overheard."

"Okay – let's go."

Rosemary took some cash out of her wallet and left it on the table.

"Don't we pay at the bar?" Athena asked, looking around for Liam, who was nowhere in sight.

"Sure," said Rosemary. "I just don't want to get into another argument about why we should or shouldn't pay for meals."

"Despite the fact that you soon won't be able to afford to go out for them? You lost your job, remember?" Athena said.

"Yes, despite that. I still have some shreds of pride left, and I'll just have to find a new job more locally. Until then, we can go back to your favourite childhood meal of beans on toast."

"Great," said Athena, "just when I was starting to like vegetables. I suppose I'll have to regress again."

"That reminds me," Rosemary said. "We need to enroll you in the local school! I can't believe I hadn't thought of that."

"I had," Athena admitted. "I was actually thinking about it a lot, hoping you'd never remember that I'm still school-aged."

Rosemary sighed. "How could I forget something so obvious? I mean, not your age, clearly, but school?"

"Give yourself a break, Mum. It's Monday. It has only been one school day, and you just decided this morning that we're staying here for the time being. Let's take a few days to figure things out."

"I see what you're trying to do there," Rosemary said, putting on her coat as they made their way through the pub and out the front door. "And it's not going to work. I'll call up the local school as soon as we get home. And don't be hoping I won't remember!"

Athena laughed. "Oh well, it was worth a try. The school here is probably bonkers, but it can't be any worse than the one in Burkenswood. Have you forgot we have a flat back there, filled with all our measly possessions?"

"No, I have not forgotten," said Rosemary as they walked back to Thorn Manor. "I've been thinking about that a lot since Constable Perkins insisted we stay in town. I just haven't figured out what to do about it. I mean, our stuff is bound to fit in the car – we don't own very much, and I'm not keeping that terrible excuse for a bed!"

"So, we get rid of the crappy furniture or just leave it in the flat for the next unfortunate tenants?" Athena suggested.

"Unfortunate to inherit the furniture, or the flat?"

"Both," said Athena. "You have to admit, Thorn Manor is a huge leap above anywhere else we've lived."

"That's true," Rosemary said. "And we haven't even explored the house. We've only been in the central part. There are two whole other wings – plus the tower."

"I bags the tower!" said Athena.

"For what?"

"It's going to be my bedroom."

"It'll be freezing in winter," Rosemary said. "With windows all around. Plus, it's tiny. You'd barely get a bed in there."

"I don't care. It's mine," Athena said. "I am determined to have every moody teenager's dream bedroom."

Rosemary sighed. "Impractical and romantic."

"Exactly!" said Athena. "But not in a gross touchy-feely way. Romantic in a classic gothic historical sense."

"If you insist," said Rosemary. "How about, as soon as we get back, I'll ring up about the school and then we can explore Thorn Manor and see what else it's hiding? Granny only used the central part of the house. I do remember wandering around the other wings as a child, but as you know, I don't remember all that much. I'm pretty sure there's an old-fashioned glass conservatory out the back too."

"Cool!" Athena exclaimed. "It's just like something out of an old novel."

"Since when do you read the classics?" Rosemary asked.

"Since now, I guess," Athena said. "I have to get into the spirit of my new home, after all."

Rosemary laughed. "You're full of surprises, you are."

"Wait a minute, you're just trying to distract me, aren't you?" Athena said in an accusatory tone.

"What are you talking about?"

"You're trying to distract me from your mysterious disappearance earlier with talk of the tower and conservatory."

"No," said Rosemary. "I was intending to tell you about that. I...I just haven't figured out the right words."

"Were you accosted in the loos by an assassin woman with a weapon for a handbag?"

"Well...not exactly."

"Then what?" Athena demanded.

"I found out who our attackers were," Rosemary said, keeping her voice quiet in case there were eavesdroppers hidden behind the trees nearby, or perhaps eavesdroppers that *were* in fact trees, given that in a place like this anything could be possible.

"What!?" Athena exclaimed. "How? Who are they?"

"I ran into Burk again."

"Oh, really?" Athena said, raising her eyebrows. "I thought we were staying away from him."

"It wasn't intentional," Rosemary argued. "Anyway, it turns out the crow man is someone called Vikivis or Ver...Verikus? Yes, I think that's it Verikus Wyrt."

"Interesting name. And what about Burk's vampy doppelganger?" Athena asked.

"Well, it turns out they're related. The vamp I dusted was Burk's hooligan brother."

"No way!" Athena cried.

"Shh, keep your voice down."

"Does that make him a vampire, too?"

"I'm pretty sure it doesn't work like that...but...maybe? There are a few weird things about Burk – he's super-fast and his hands are so cold!"

"Super-fast at what, exactly?" Athena asked.

"Nothing like that!" said Rosemary.

"Well, if he is a vamp, then how was he out during the day?"

Rosemary sighed. "It's possible that Buffy lied to us."

"Blasphemy!" said Athena. "Anyway, she was right about the bursting into dust thing."

"That's true – but just because we now believe in paranormal beings and other such things, it doesn't mean they follow the exact same rules as on TV and movies – I mean – even they don't follow the same rules as each other, and I'm willing to bet that vampires do not sparkle!"

"So, do we or do we not think your good friend Burk is a vampire?" Athena asked.

"I don't know! He might not be one, but there is definitely something unusual about him – something supernatural."

"I guess it does kind of kill off your budding romance."

"There *is* no romance, I assure you," said Rosemary, thinking back to the brief brush of intimacy in the dark earlier. It wasn't exactly her idea of romance, though there was a closeness about it she hadn't experienced in a long time...that she was definitely *not* going to inform Athena about. "But yes – 'I murdered your brother' would kind of put a dampener on things."

"You didn't *tell* him?!" Athena cried.

"Of course not. I don't want to incur family vengeance or wind up in prison, if that's even a possible consequence of murdering someone who's technically already dead."

By this time, they had reached the house and Rosemary had definitely *not* forgotten about calling the local school to ask about enrollments. Or rather, she had forgotten several times and then quickly remembered again.

As soon as they got through the door and taken their shoes and coats off, she made the call.

"Well, that's strangely convenient," Rosemary said, hanging up the phone a moment later.

"What is?"

"I called up the local school only to listen to a message informing me that the rest of the week is a holiday due to the Imbolc Festival." She shrugged. "I suppose you can start after that."

"Is that even legal?" Athena asked. "I mean, I'm not complaining, but don't they have to have the same holidays as everywhere else?"

"I suppose, if it's a special character school..." Rosemary said. "Oh, I don't know. Things are different in Myrtlewood. Just take their local police department as an example of that. Besides, I bet you're secretly delighted about going to school here, hoping to see Finnigan again."

"No," Athena said, crossing her arms.

"No?"

"He said he didn't go to school around here."

"I suppose he busses to some fancy private school," Rosemary said. "He seems like the type."

"Now who's judgemental?"

"What? He does! Anyway, I'm relieved about that."

"Why? Because you want me to stay away from him and that will be hard if we're at the same school?"

"Because if he's in boarding school, he'll be locked up safely, far away from you – at least on weeknights, and that alleviates approximately 40% of my worries."

"What are the other 60%?"

"Weekends and holidays."

Athena sighed. "Fine, you've made your paranoia abundantly clear. Can we at least explore the house now?"

"Of course we can," said Rosemary. "It'll do us some good to take our minds off the investigation into Granny's death."

"Thanks. Now that you've put it that way, I'm going to have a lot of trouble taking my mind off it."

But despite Athena's protestations, it didn't take long before she was sufficiently distracted. The magic of the house that kept it clean and well-maintained seemed to weaken the further they moved away from the central rooms. The east wing was covered in a thick layer of dust, which made them both sneeze. And try as they might, they could not find the entrance to the tower. Rosemary couldn't ever remember going up there as a child, and even though it looked like it might stem from the east of the manor, it remained a mystery.

Feeling grimy, with snivelling sinuses, they gave up on the exploration but vowed to return in the near future, armed with cleaning implements – if only they would find the laundry room. They had planned to explore the west wing next. However, assuming it was in a similar state, they searched for the laundry instead.

They found it, just by walking out of the kitchen's back door. It was an old room, but sported new laundry appliances and quite a few different mops and buckets and brooms.

"No witchy brooms, though," Athena said.

"I'm sure *that's* a myth," said Rosemary. "I am not co-ordinated enough to ride one of those things and fly around in the air, even if I do happen to be a witch."

"I'm glad we found this place, though," said Athena. "I'm onto my last pair of clean underwear, and all my clothes need a wash. We were only supposed to stay for a night, remember?"

"Yes," said Rosemary. "And it's only been *two* nights. Can you believe that? It feels a lot longer."

"We are definitely going to need to go back and get the rest of our clothes soon," Athena said. "It's not like we can afford whole new wardrobes."

"Hey – look!" Rosemary said, picking up a set of keys off a hook by the laundry room's back door.

"We already have keys to the house."

"Yes, but these are car keys...I wonder if..."

She pushed open the back door to reveal a poorly lit garage.

"You didn't tell me Granny had a car," Athena said, squinting into the low light. "It looks like there's something vaguely car-shaped in there."

"No...well, she used to, quite a nice old classic Rolls Royce. But I figured she must have sold it. She was far too old to be driving."

Athena switched on the light to reveal a vehicle covered in a large grey sheet. They both stepped forward and pulled the sheet off to reveal a perfectly waxed burgundy and gold Rolls Royce.

"It looks good," Rosemary said.

"Good? It looks bloody brilliant! Is it...is it ours?"

"I guess so, once the will has gone through properly."

"Does it go?"

Rosemary took the keys and opened the car door with them, then she tried the ignition. The engine purred to life. "Sounds like it!"

"Great, so we can drive this back to Burkenswood to pick up our things," Athena said.

"Not now!"

"Okay, first thing tomorrow morning," Athena insisted.

Rosemary sighed. "I guess you're right. We do need to clean up our old life eventually, but for now, try to relax. How about I put the washing on and you can go upstairs for a nice hot bath."

"That sounds like the best idea you've had all day," Athena said.

CHAPTER

SEVENTEEN

Rosemary perched on the window seat, sipping a cup of tea. She looked out at the wild tangle of garden that lay just beyond the front lawn, wondering how hard the upkeep was going to be on the grounds of Thorn Manor.

In that moment, she was convinced that the magic of Myrtlewood wasn't just the stuff of fantasy. It was also something simple she felt deep in her bones, as if being here had begun to knit the disconnected parts of her back together like a quilt, or perhaps like a vine, wildly entangling the order with the chaos, creating something that made its own kind of beautiful sense in her inner world, something that might help her become a coherent person, or at least someone who wasn't objectively a failure in the eyes of the world.

She could hear the subtle hum of the washing machine, and, occasionally, the sound of Athena singing to herself in the bath upstairs. When she stopped worrying about how she was going to mow the lawns, it was all rather relaxing. That was until a car pulled up the driveway – a newer Rolls Royce in gleaming dark charcoal that could only mean one thing.

Rosemary sculled her hot tea and tried to tame the static from her hair. She wanted to present the impression of being on top of things.

The knock came, half a minute later, and Rosemary was already at the door, ready to slam it at any moment.

The overpoweringly soapy scent of lily of the valley wafted into the house, making Rosemary cough. A petite woman with ice-blond hair and an ice-cold gaze stood behind the door, along with a taller man, his dark hair gelled back and a permanent sneer on his face.

"Elamina, Derse..." Rosemary said. "What a surprise."

She couldn't quite manage "nice" before surprise, but lying was never really Rosemary's forte, anyway.

"Rosemary," Elamina said. "It has been too long, cousin."

"Really?" Rosemary asked. "I would have thought ever seeing each other again wouldn't have been too long – for either side. You never gave the impression that you ever wanted to spend any time with me, in particular."

"Still," Elamina said, peering around, behind Rosemary, into the house. "Family is family. Aren't you going to invite us in?" she put on the biggest fake-smile Rosemary had ever seen – which was startling and a little frightening. Rosemary couldn't recall seeing her cousin ever smiling before, outside of a malicious gleam in her eyes when something went her way.

"I don't believe I am," Rosemary said. She wasn't about to let her cousins walk all over her like they had in the past. "I was in the middle of something, so this is not the best time."

Derse coughed and cleared his throat. Rosemary looked towards him, but he didn't say anything.

"But surely, this is a family house," Elamina said. "We belong here as much as you do."

"I don't think so," Rosemary said. "According to both of Granny's wills, the house belongs to me, and in the more recent one so does everything else."

Elamina wrinkled her perfectly smooth and pale face into a

grimace. "I think you'll find we are contesting the will," she said. "Our lawyers advise that our side of the family should get more."

Rosemary laughed. Her grown cousin was about to have a tantrum on her front doorstep, and given the way Elamina had always treated Rosemary, it was a satisfying sight.

"Well, Granny's lawyers don't seem to think so. She was sound of mind when she made both wills, and you get nothing," Rosemary said.

"Rubbish," Elamina replied. "We deserve half the house – at least! Probably more. After all, I was the one who organised the funeral that you didn't bother to attend."

Rosemary winced. She hadn't attended precisely because Elamina had organised an elaborate function near her swanky mansion, not something that Granny would have wanted at all.

"And I visited Granny regularly in her last few months." Elamina pouted and batted her eyelashes. "Where were you?"

"Trying to survive and feed my daughter. Thanks for asking," said Rosemary. She had a right mind to slam the door in their faces and leave it at that, but she couldn't help herself. "Granny knew me, and she knew you. She knew you were just greasing up to her to try to get the house. Lord knows why you need it when you're already filthy rich."

"Oh, poor, sweet Rosemary," Elamina said. "You think this is about money. How crude. If you only knew..."

"I do happen to know about the magic," Rosemary said, testing her cousin.

Elamina's eyes widened.

"How...how do you know?" she stuttered. "Did you find something?"

"More than you can imagine," said Rosemary.

"But the family magic is still bound, otherwise we would..."

"You'd what? Sprout wings and fly around?"

"You think this is all some big joke, don't you?" Elamina said. "I'll tell you this. When Daddy first married Mummy, he knew she was from an old magical family, and it showed! She could do all sorts of things – we all could! But when we were just kids, it all stopped. You must remember that? It was like the well ran dry, and so did my parents' marriage."

"I thought they were still together."

"They are, on paper," Elamina said. "But Daddy is obsessed. He was always hounding Granny to find out what happened to the magic – of course we still have some – from his side of the family, but the Thorn magic virtually disappeared. Only Granny seemed to possess any at all, and even that...well, she was a shadow of her former self."

"Something did happen," Rosemary admitted. "I don't know what it was and I don't know any of the details, so don't ask. Granny was trying to protect herself – and us. That's all I can say."

"From whom?" Derse asked, continuing with his perpetual sneer.

"I had actually wondered if it was from you," said Rosemary. "I'm still not convinced otherwise."

"You think *we* had something to do with Granny's death?!" Elamina cried. "Oh, you must be joking! I know we've never gotten along, Rosemary, but *this*?"

"You have a motive," Rosemary pointed out. "Your side of the family wanted the magic."

"And you didn't?"

"We didn't even know about it. It's hard to explain, but it's all part of what Granny had to do to protect the family magic. She bound it and altered my memory and did something that kept me away from this place. I didn't know about any of this until we came back to Myrtlewood."

"Did she tell you all that?" Elamina asked.

"She wrote me a letter, if you must know." Rosemary wasn't about to tell her cousin about the ghostly apparition as well.

"Can I see it?"

"No, it's private."

"So, I'm just supposed to take your word for it?"

"I'm not going to tell you what you're supposed to do," Rosemary said. "I'm not the hoity-toity one in the family. Go and tell yourself what to do...and do it elsewhere!"

"Rosemary, please?"

"Oh, very well. You can come back on Friday night, if you must."

"Friday night?"

"We're having a dinner party, here, and I thought you might like to come, you know...to meet some of Granny's friends?"

It sounded like a weak excuse, but the cousins were on the big piece of paper, and Rosemary's hairbrained dinner-party was only going to work if all the key suspects were there. If the killer was not among them it, it would just be a party of oddballs – entertaining, but useless for their cause.

"You're inviting us to dinner?" Elamina said the words as though they left a foul taste in her mouth, and Derse's sneer deepened.

"That's what I said." Rosemary held her ground, waiting in silence until they caved in.

"Oh, very well," Elamina said. "What's the dress code?"

"I don't know, Elamina," said Rosemary. "How about 'dress as your true self?'"

"What's that supposed to mean?"

"Think about it," Rosemary said. "You'll figure it out." Though, by the time the words had escaped her lips she had already become confused about what she'd meant.

"Fine. We'll see you Friday. What time?" said Elamina.

"Seven p.m.," Rosemary replied.

"Seven it is." Elamina lifted her palm and gave a little wave. She turned and sauntered down the front steps, through the car door that was being held open by the chauffer, and into the back-seat. She didn't look back at Rosemary as the car backed to turn around and drove away.

CHAPTER
EIGHTEEN

The rest of Monday evening flew past, blissfully uneventful.

Rosemary prepared the customary Thorn delicacy of beans on toast, and while they ate, she filled Athena in on the visit from her unpleasant relatives, with much ensuing laughter.

"You should have called out to me," Athena said. "I would've loved to see that."

"Well, you'll have your chance to get reacquainted with the Bracewell-Thorns," said Rosemary. "I've invited them to our dinner party."

"Really?"

"Yes – they're on our big piece of paper."

"And they accepted?"

"They did indeed."

"I would have thought snobs like them wouldn't stoop to dine with us," said Athena.

"Under normal circumstances, I think you're right – but they want the magic, so they'll be here."

Rosemary and Athena went to bed early and slept peacefully that night, with no loud disruptions for a change. They got up early the next morning in preparation for the trip back to Burkenswood to retrieve the rest of their belongings – aside from the terrible furniture.

"Shall we go?" Rosemary asked first thing in the morning.

"What about breakfast?"

"I thought we could stop in at Marjie's on the way. We should tell her what we're up to – so someone knows to come looking for us if we don't return."

Athena shuddered.

"I meant that as a joke," Rosemary said.

"That may be so, but it's too close for comfort. Anyway, aren't we going to get in trouble with that coppa for leaving town?"

"We'll be back before he even realises we've gone," Rosemary said.

The engine of Granny's old, but well-maintained Rolls Royce purred to life, and they cruised into Myrtlewood village, to Marjie's tea shop.

They were the first customers to arrive again.

"Making a habit of this!" Marjie said, kissing them both on the cheek. "You'll be my best customers!"

"Only if you let us pay," Rosemary said.

"Oh, nonsense," said Marjie. "Your presence is payment enough. Now what'll you have?"

"Anything, really," Rosemary said. "Just whatever is convenient for you. We want to be quick. We're driving back to Burkenswood to pick up the rest of our things from the flat – since we're going to be staying in Myrtlewood for a good while."

"Very good, very good," Marjie said. She brought them a big pot of Earl Grey tea and disappeared into the kitchen again.

"So, we'll go straight to the flat and clear out everything we want and then I'll call the landlord to say I won't be renewing the lease," said Rosemary.

Athena nodded. "And we'll be back before nightfall, won't we?"

"I should think so. Why is that?"

"I don't like the idea of travelling at night," said Athena. "Given the danger we're in."

"Fair enough, though logically, we'll be at more risk at the house. That's where all the attacks have been so far."

"Yes, but it's also where my mother has superpowers to protect me with," Athena said.

"Inconsistent powers that I can't seem to control," Rosemary reminded her. "I'm just a normal person most of the time, remember."

"Normal is a stretch. Anyway, what's your plan when we get back to Myrtlewood? It's now Tuesday, and you told the Bracewell-Thorns our dinner is going to be on Friday...so we have a couple more days to prepare for all these people – some of whom you actively dislike – to descend on the house. How is that going to work again?"

Rosemary sighed. "Well, first I have to invite them all."

Athena sighed. "Yes, that is something you should have already done by now. It's only a few days away. And what if our true villain doesn't come?"

"They will," said Rosemary. "They won't be able to resist a peek inside the house and a chance to steal the magic."

"Very well," said Athena. "Exactly what do you think this dinner party is going to achieve – how are you going to spot the murderer?"

"I haven't figured that part out, exactly," said Rosemary. "I just thought it would be a good idea to get everyone in one place and watch for clues."

"That is a very vague plan," Athena said. "I've got no idea what could go wrong because there are just so many possibilities. Inviting all the suspects to the very same house that the villain has been trying to break into...?"

"Exactly!" said Rosemary. "Someone is bound to sneak off, looking for the source of our power."

"Which is...? The box?" Athena asked.

"Perhaps," said Rosemary. "It certainly seems to be a big connection point for everything that's happened so far...maybe we should have brought it with us to keep it safe."

"Really, Mum? You think it would be any better protected with us in the car than in a big magical house? That's absurd. Plus – Granny's ghost is there to haunt anyone who comes in."

"I hope you're right," Rosemary said.

"Anyway, back to your dinner party," said Athena. "So, it's some kind of test? Oh – I have an idea – we hide the real box and have something similar on display, which we say is an important family heirloom that Granny left us, only we don't know why."

"Actually, that's brilliant. Good work, kiddo!"

"Don't call me that!"

Just then, Marjie returned, bearing a tray laden with eggs, sausages and fried tomatoes.

"Oh Marjie – this is...a lot of food," Rosemary said. "Thank you. It looks delicious."

"I have to feed you up for your big journey," said Marjie. "Also, I couldn't help overhearing..."

Rosemary and Athena gave each other a worried look.

"Now, don't fret. You can trust me," Marjie said. "I want to get to the bottom of Galdie's death almost as much as you do. She was very dear to my heart, you know. Anyway, I think it's wonderful you're trying to solve the mystery. I'm only nosing in to make a little suggestion."

"What's that, then?" Athena asked.

"Well...I like the idea of the dinner party, but don't you think a little spell might be in order, you know, to help determine which attendee is the killer?"

"Go on," said Rosemary. "What kind of spell?"

"Perhaps something to reveal the truth?" Marjie said. "I'll look into it for you, though bear in mind that they might have armed themselves against magic and my spell might not work."

"Thank you, Marjie. That would be brilliant," Rosemary said.

Marjie's face lit up and then she bustled off, humming to herself, while Rosemary and Athena dug into the hearty breakfast spread.

The tea shop was buzzing with customers by the time they finished eating, and Rosemary didn't get a chance to properly say goodbye to

Marjie, but she did slip some money under her tea cup to cover the meal, knowing full well that Marjie wouldn't dream of charging her.

"Stop doing that, Mum," Athena said. "People will think we're Americans."

"Oh, don't be silly," Rosemary said. "How else are we supposed to pay our way around here?"

"I thought we were broke."

"Well, I am rather short on cash, but I have a bit of wiggle room left on my credit card, which will at least get us enough petrol to make it to Burkenswood and back with aplenty for food along the way. When I get back, I seriously need to get a job as quickly as possible, even if that means competing with Ferg in the local taxi industry."

"If you do that, you'd better offer the luxury service. I don't think we can get by on 20p per minute."

"Deal," said Rosemary, putting her coat back on. "Let's go."

They climbed into Granny's car and made their way smoothly out of the town square and towards the main road, heading out of town.

"This car drives like a dream," Rosemary said. "Not that I'm a car person, but it's so nice. I'd love to keep it, if we can afford it."

"I do feel a bit like a member of the royal family, riding in this thing," Athena admitted. "Surely we can afford it once the inheritance comes through."

"I guess that depends on how successful Elamina's challenge is," said Rosemary. "And on whether I'm cleared in the investigation. Otherwise, the Crown might seize everything."

"How awful would that be?" said Athena. "Just when we're so close to a life of luxury – you'd be thrown in jail and I'd be sent to juvenile detention or something."

Rosemary shuddered. "Don't talk about it. We aren't guilty and we're going to do everything in our power to prove it. Wait – what's that?" Something was blocking the road up ahead. As they drew closer, Rosemary realised what it was. "Oh, crud!"

Constable Perkins's car was parked across half the road, and he was checking every car as it drove by.

"Just my luck!" said Rosemary. "The one time we're actually leaving town, he happens to be conducting a road block."

"Is it just luck, though?" Athena asked. "Or something more sinister?"

They grew quiet as they pulled up to where the officer was standing, hands on hips, glaring at them. Rosemary reluctantly wound the window down.

"And just where do you think you two are going when I've expressly forbidden you from leaving town?"

"Uh, good morning, officer. We were just popping back to Burkenswood since we need to pick up our possessions if we're going to be staying in Myrtlewood for a while."

"Oh…you are, are you?" Constable Perkins said. "Not on my watch!"

"But we need our clothes!" Athena cried. "I can't wear the same two outfits every day forever!"

"That is not my problem, missy," he replied sternly, then turned to Rosemary. "And you, Ms Thorn, should know better. How am I supposed to know you're not secretly skipping the country?"

"Because I promise I'm not, and because you have some magical truth-seeking power?" Rosemary suggested.

"Not good enough," the police officer said.

Rosemary sighed. "What are we supposed to do, then, sir? We have our whole lives, as they were, back at the flat in Burkenswood."

"Surely, someone who isn't one of you could fetch you any items you deem necessary," Constable Perkins suggested. "I have a right mind to arrest you just for attempting to breach my orders."

"No. Please don't," said Rosemary. "We'll turn right around and go back to Thorn Manor – and if there's anything else we're not sure about we'll check with you first. I promise. Actually, to make it up to you, why don't you come to our dinner party on Friday night?"

Athena glared at Rosemary from the passenger seat.

"It wouldn't do for me to muddy an investigation like that, Ms Thorn."

"Well…you'd actually be doing me a huge favour. You see…we've planned a little gathering – not much, just a kind of housewarming – but now Athena is worried that whomever is responsible for the attacks might be one of our new Myrtlewood friends. So…having you there – as a strong and competent police officer would really set her at ease."

Rosemary wasn't looking, but she could feel Athena's glare intensify.

"You're really that worried about your safety?" Constable Perkins asked.

"Of course we are!" said Rosemary. "After the other night – the attack on the house. We both could have died, just like Granny."

"Let me think about your kind and generous offer to invite me to a party to be your personal bodyguard…" Constable Perkins said.

"It's not like that," Rosemary insisted as the officer waved a few other cars past that had backed up behind them. "I just wondered if it would be in your best interests, too. I mean, if the killer is there, you might be able to catch them red-handed, stealing whatever it was they wanted to take from Granny."

"How do you know they don't already have it?" the officer asked.

"Why would they keep coming back, if that was the case?"

"Fair point," he said. "Alright. I'll think about it. But I suspect I'll either come as a civilian, wearing my mufti clothes, or I'll wear my uniform and patrol around outside waiting for any funny business – and that's only if other duties don't call me away."

"Thank you, officer," Rosemary said. "That sounds marvellous."

"And no more funny business from you two!"

"Absolutely not." Rosemary started the engine and began to turn the car around to head back to Thorn Manor.

"What was all that about?" Athena asked. "I am *not* the one terrified for my life – that would be you. Don't you remember he has the power to tell truth from lies?"

"It just kind of slipped out," Rosemary said. "But I don't think any of it was a complete lie – you should be fearing for your life after all."

"Why not just tell him the truth about the dinner – that we are deliberately inviting suspects?"

"Because he'll think we're being vigilantes and he'll put a stop to it," Rosemary said. "Remember, everything has to be *his* idea."

"And you wanted him there, why?"

"Well, I'm not a hundred percent sure that he's not the one who hurt Granny for one – I mean, that would be awfully convenient, wouldn't it? He could pin it on us. He has the power."

"What would his motive be, though?" Athena asked.

"Power? The same as everyone else?"

"I don't get that impression from him, though," Athena said. "I mean...he's a terrible communicator, and a grumpy old git – but he's not sinister or evil or anything."

"I'm glad you don't think so," Rosemary said. "But we are not basing the entirety of our investigation on your gut instincts."

Athena sighed. "Back to another important matter," she said. "How on earth are we going to get all our things collected from Burkenswood? It's not like we had any friends to speak of back there who could just run them a couple of hours down the road for us. We've moved around far too much to have any real friends."

Rosemary thought about that for a while. It was true – they didn't have any close friends in Burkenswood who'd likely be up for that kind of favour.

"The people in Myrtlewood are so nice they might well do it," Athena continued. "Though we've only really just met them, despite some family connections."

"Hmm," Rosemary said. "You're right. I bet Marjie or Liam would do it for us, if they could, or Sherry, when she's better, but it seems rude to ask when we hardly know them. Besides, any of them could be the killer."

"I thought we'd agreed that Marjie is definitely not the killer," Athena said defensively.

"Well, how else did Constable Perkins know to set up a road block right when we were leaving town?" Rosemary asked. "Marjie was the only one we told."

"That's true," said Athena. "But it could have just been a massive coincidence – or maybe he used magic...or someone else is watching our every move. All of those things seem far more likely."

"Even still," Rosemary said. "I'll be keeping an eye on her on Friday. She's the only one who knows about the test – so we'll have to create a slightly different test, just for her."

"Fine, but none of that helps us get our clothes and stuff, Mum."

"There's always Dain."

"Oh...no. No, no, no! We are not calling Dad. No way!"

"He's actually quite good in a pinch," Rosemary reasoned. "The amount of times I've had to call him to jump-start my car..."

"And then he sticks around for a week and eats all our food, and your money mysteriously goes missing..."

"Still, what choice do we have?"

"Mum!"

"What?"

"We cannot bring him back into our lives, just when things are starting to improve!" Athena said.

"Do you really call being attacked by demons an improvement?"

"No – not that part."

"Or being accused of murder?"

"Oh, don't be a drama queen," Athena said. "You have not been formally accused of anything."

"Still..."

"No, Mum. I was referring to the smallish fortune and the big fancy house we are in the process of inheriting. That is something we want to keep dad about a million miles away from. It's just as well we've moved addresses already, so he doesn't know where we are."

"Well..."

"Mum! No, you didn't."

"I might have sent him a little text message."

"I can't believe you!" Athena cried, burying her face in her hands.

"He's your father. He deserves to know where you are. I'm pretty sure it's illegal for us to move house without telling him."

"So, now you're all concerned with the letter of the law?"

"As of recently, yes," Rosemary said. "If I'd thought about it properly, I wouldn't have even tried to leave town today. It only makes us look more suspicious."

They pulled up into the garage of Thorn Manor. Athena got out of the car and slammed the door in a huff.

"Tea?" Rosemary asked.

"No," Athena said, stomping into the house.

"Oh, don't be like that, sweetheart. I know he's got issues, but he's still your father."

"That's not my fault," Athena shot back.

"Still, he may be our only legitimate option right now. I might just give him a quick text and see is he's free. Don't worry, I promise I won't tell him about the inheritance – in fact, I won't even tell him about Granny passing, so he doesn't get any ideas. I'll just say we're going to need some things. I can even see if he'll sell that old bomb of a vehicle for us."

"Real smart move, Mum."

"It won't be worth much," Rosemary said. "In fact, he can keep the money in exchange for bringing us all our things."

"Fine," Athena said. "Suit yourself, but you're lucky we don't have anything else worth selling or he'd pawn it all before you could blink."

"Athena..."

"No! I've had enough of you," she said, and stormed upstairs, slamming the bedroom door behind her.

Rosemary sighed. Of course, Athena had a point. She was rational to a fault, and her father was the total opposite. It was actually baffling to Rosemary how she managed to raise such a reasonable and astute daughter, given both her parents' obvious shortcomings in those particular areas. It wasn't that Rosemary was bafflingly irrational. It was more that rationality held little interest for her mind, which preferred to dart from one thing to the next, finding strange connections.

Having Athena around was balancing for her, grounding.

Dain, on the other hand, lived on a different planet entirely most of the time – figuratively, of course. But, as Rosemary had argued, he was good in a pinch, and he had gotten her out of many spots of bother over the years – though not quite as many as he'd gotten her into.

It was true that when he showed up, Rosemary had little in the way of defence against his charm, and he'd inevitably found his way back into her bed and into her heart, only to hurt her again, but not this time. Rosemary was determined – even if she had to look up a magic spell to protect herself from womanisers.

Spells...that's it!

She sent a quick text message to Dain asking for the favour and then decided that magic spells were exactly what she needed to learn about – to arm herself against the charms of her ex or any number of other predators.

She made herself tea and took it with her into the library.

The box was still sitting on the desk, innocuously, despite all the power it seemed to possess.

Rosemary chose to ignore it, seeing as she didn't know what other surprises it might contain. She thoroughly immersed herself in scanning the bookshelves. Befitting her character, Granny Thorn had been quite the collector of interesting reference material. Among the hundreds of titles here were several large volumes of *Material Medica* – detailing the botany and uses of healing herbs, and multiple encyclopaedias and histories of magic, which could definitely come in handy.

Rosemary practically kicked herself for not exploring the library earlier. It seemed obvious that the information they needed would be contained somewhere in these volumes. She got quite cross with herself, in fact, until she remembered it was only Tuesday in the longest week she'd ever experienced. She was only a couple of days into even believing in magic, let alone researching it.

Perhaps there's something about this house...or this town that makes time slow, Rosemary wondered, as she traced her fingers along the spines.

Her nail caught against something not-quite-book-like. On closer inspection, it was a rough piece of paper. Rosemary pulled at the large volume on mythical creatures behind. The paper slipped out and fell to the floor. It appeared to be an invitation of some kind.

You are cordially invited to the symposium of the Bloodstone Society, it read, followed by an address in Burkenswood with a time and date proposed for the sixth of June, though no year.

*The Bloodstone Society...*Rosemary thought. That's what Sherry was talking about the other night. And here they were, inviting Granny to some kind of fancy event.

It must be fancy, Rosemary reasoned. *There's even a wax seal on the back.*

The seal had mostly crumbled off, but the corner of it looked slightly like a shield. It reminded Rosemary of something, though she couldn't place exactly what it was.

"Peculiar and more peculiar," Rosemary muttered to herself, wondering if it was Alice or the caterpillar who had said something like that in the original story.

She carefully took the invitation and placed it next to the stack of useful-looking books she was collecting.

Madame Tuison's Collection of Spells and Incantations certainly looked promising, as did *A Magical History of Myrtlewood* by A. C. Twigg. *Twigg...*that sounded familiar, too.

She also stacked up several books on protective charms and a few volumes of *The Basics of Witchcraft*, seeing as she really was starting from ground zero, here.

It was a pity that Athena was in such a foul mood, Rosemary reflected; going through all these books was exactly the kind of thing the young Thorn would have loved.

Rosemary chose some volumes especially for Athena to look at when she was in a better mood. Perhaps she could even find a spell to repel a deadbeat ex.

Though the books were fascinating, Rosemary couldn't help but glance back at the little wooden box on the desk every few minutes.

It almost seemed to call to her, not in a creepy way, but in a familiar manner that had a hint of destiny about it.

"Oh, alright," she said, to the box. "I'll bite – but no funny business. Nothing dangerous or deadly, only things that will help us solve the mystery and get our lives in order, *please?*"

She left the piles of books on the floor and approached the desk.

The box seemed to be glowing slightly, and Rosemary had second thoughts about touching it, especially with Athena upstairs and blissfully ignorant of her mother's antics. She thought about turning away, taking the books, and shutting the door, ignoring the stupid box, but her curiosity got the best of her.

Rosemary reached out for the small wooden chest and braced herself as her fingers brushed against its surface.

Nothing happened.

She was still standing in the library, holding the box, and then the world around her seemed to fall away in pieces like those of a broken mirror, cascading into darkness and emptiness. The box in her hand glowed brightly in the dark. She glanced down to see it had transformed into the crystal she had seen before.

"Hello?" she said, into the darkness. There was no reply.

Rosemary cleared her throat. "Uhm...elder woman?"

Still nothing but stillness and darkness. Then she heard something...a subtle thud in the distance, echoing like a heartbeat.

There was nowhere else to go and nothing else to see, so Rosemary stepped forward, towards the sound that continued, intermittently, to thud gently.

She could see a soft glow in the distance, which, as she approached, became clearer. The first thing she could make out was a rock face, and she wondered whether she had reached the same place as last time, even though the elder was nowhere to be seen.

As she stepped closer, she recognised creeping green vines, which clung to the rock. And the further she walked, the thicker they grew until they were all around her – a forest of vines.

The thud became louder and louder, leading Rosemary on until she saw a bright white light shining through the dense green foliage.

Rosemary had thought the vines were friendly, or at the very least that they were harmless. But, by and by, she realised that they were holding tight to the bright light, that looked more and more like a larger version of the crystal she held in her hands, suffocating it, choking it. The thrumming sound was the light crystal fighting back or crying out for help.

She reached up, hoping to free it. A voice sounded behind Rosemary, startling her. "No, stop. Don't touch them."

Rosemary turned to see the same woman as before – the elder. Rosemary hesitated, looking at the vines. They seemed malicious now, as if they were watching her, waiting.

"You must release the binding," the woman said. "Before it's too late."

Rosemary glanced back at the vines...

The vines are the binding, she realised. *Not an evil force, on their own, but something created to protect, which has now become too restrictive and is starting to strangle the very thing it's supposed to keep safe...*

"But how?" Rosemary asked. "How can I release it if I can't touch the vines?"

"You must look within," the elder said infuriatingly.

"What is that supposed to mean!?" Rosemary asked. "I want a simple answer about what to do – none of this cryptic and vague rubbish! Look within? A fat lot of good that's going to do me!"

The elder blurred in front of Rosemary's eyes, along with the vines and the light and blackness around them. Everything faded to grey, and Rosemary woke to the sound of Athena telling her off again.

"What the!? Mum! What in blazers do you think you're doing getting yourself knocked unconscious again! You scared me half to death!"

"Oh...sorry," Rosemary said, opening her eyes to see she was back in the library. She felt a heavy sense of dread and a desperate yearning to see Granny again, to talk to her and ask her to explain herself.

"It looks like a tornado came through here," Athena said. "What happened?"

"Well, I was looking through the books to see if there was anything useful – you know – like a spell to protect me from your dad's charms or a recipe for some anti-vampire repellent or something, and then I decided to try the box again."

"You're saying you threw the books all around the room?!"

"No," Rosemary said, coming to her senses to see that the books had, indeed, scattered. "I put them in piles. They must have been knocked over when I passed out."

"Honestly!" Athena said. "You just don't think things through."

"I think we've covered that already," Rosemary said. "Plenty of times, in fact. Now help me take these books to the dining room table. There are some great ones in here – maybe there's even something that can help us contact Granny and talk to her again."

CHAPTER
NINETEEN

"Here's another option, look," Rosemary said. "But it requires a Ouija board. Do you think we could make one?"

"You really won't give up on this contacting the dead thing, will you?" Athena asked. "I told you it was a bad idea."

They sat around the dining room table, which was piled high with books, sipping tea and leafing through the large number of volumes that might have useful information contained within.

"Oh, come on," Rosemary said. "I really have to figure out what's going on with the Thorn magic binding and how to break it. You should have seen what it was like in there."

"Mum, you weren't *in* anything. You were passed out on the floor hallucinating about that elder again."

"I think we're well beyond hallucinations at this point, Athena."

"That might be so, but we can't tell if what you saw was a fair and accurate representation of the truth."

"Don't use legal jargon on me. You know it upsets my allergies," Rosemary said, taking a big sip of tea to calm her nerves.

"No, Mum, your imaginary allergy is to estate agents, remember?"

"Legal jargon is just as bad. Oh, bother. I'm going to have to invite

203

that lawyer over on Friday, too, aren't I?"

"Your special friend, Mr Burk...or should I say, *Perseus?*" Athena teased, picking up another book from the piles in front of them on the table and scanning the table of contents.

"Don't start that again."

"Look," said Athena. "All I'm saying is that we don't know if what you saw is real. It might be a trick...or you might not fully understand it."

"Exactly!" Rosemary said. "And that's why I need to talk to Granny again. She's the only one I can really trust to explain all this."

Rosemary still had absolute faith in Granny Thorn, despite everything. Even though Rosemary now had more questions than ever, she needed to believe that her grandmother had a good reason for her secrecy. If only they could talk to her again to figure it all out.

"Mum," said Athena. "I've seen way too many horror films to ever attempt a séance."

"But we aren't trying to raise the dead or contact anyone creepy," Rosemary insisted. "This is Granny we're talking about."

"At least six of these books warn us to never attempt contacting the dead unless we know exactly what we're doing, and most of the rituals I've found require it to be the festival of Samhain...which I think is in the autumn. Almost the opposite time of year!"

"Still, we know Granny, and we know she's around here somewhere. She seems to be the most likely candidate for us to contact, and I'm not bloody waiting until autumn. That crystal wrapped in vines was pulsing in an unnerving way. It looked like that whole thing was going to blow!"

"You mean explode?"

"Explode or implode...I don't know. It just felt to me like time was running out, and the elder implied as much."

"Oh fine," Athena said. "We'll try your Ouija board idea – but just this once, and..." She hesitated.

"And what?"

"You have to make this protection charm first, to ward off Dad."

"Fine!" said Rosemary, grasping the book that Athena shoved her way. "Altazar's Compendium of Enchantments?"

"You just need a little black square of cloth and salt and..." said Athena, pointing to the ingredients list. "Rosemary...well, that's convenient."

"Convenient that it's my name?"

"No, that's just a coincidence. Rosemary is apparently known for its protective properties. It's convenient because I spotted a big bush of it right by the front door."

"Since when are you the expert in herbology?"

"It's herbalism, Mum, and I'm not an expert. It used to grow at my old school along with lavender. The bees love it."

"Well in that case..." Rosemary said, letting her words train off into thin air.

"Hmm. It says you need some black onyx for this one. Where can we find that?"

"Maybe in one of these cupboards," Rosemary said, putting the book down and opening up some of the cupboards in the various sideboards on which gran kept her paperweights and doilies and other odds and ends. The first two cupboards only contained various old china dinner sets, but the third one Rosemary tried had a whole lot of interesting things. Her eyes fell on a large, smooth wooden board. "Hey look!" she said.

"Did you find onyx?"

"No, but I did find a state-of-the-art Ouija board," Rosemary said, pulling it out of the cupboard and waving it around.

"Be careful with that thing," Athena said, ducking out of the way as it swung towards her.

"Can we use it?!" Rosemary asked, excitedly. "Can we? Can we?"

"Sure, after you've made the charm."

"Oh, fine." She crossed her arms and pouted a little for good measure.

Athena began rummaging through some drawers nearby. "This one's full of crystals!" she said. "Look!"

Rosemary did look to see an entire drawer of sparkly stones. "Very pretty," she said. "You know. I really don't remember any of this from when I was a kid. I wonder if I played with those. I bet I would have loved them."

"I think Granny Thorn kept them as important magical items," said Athena. "Not children's playthings."

"Granny wasn't like that," Rosemary said. "She let me play with anything – and she never treated me like a silly child – everything was for learning about and exploring the world."

"It's a bloody shame she addled your memory then, isn't it?" Athena said. "You might have been a brilliant scientist or inventor or something."

"I've never thought of that," Rosemary said. "Gosh...I hope not."

"Why not?"

"Well, for one, it would mean Granny took away a great opportunity for me to do something important with my life, and secondly, because working in a lab all day sounds dead boring!"

"You're a walking contradiction, you know that?" Athena said. "Look, that black one at the back is probably onyx."

Rosemary picked it up. The small black opaque stone was shiny but unremarkable in her hand, like a polished pebble. "It looks like the picture in the Gem Index. Is this all we need, then?"

"No, let me see. Oh, you also need black pepper – though there's plenty of that in the kitchen."

"Salt and pepper and rosemary. Sounds like we're roasting lamb," Rosemary said. "Ooh, actually, that's a great idea for Friday's dinner. Especially if rosemary does have protective properties."

"I'm not sure it works like that," Athena said.

"I'm sure I can find a way to spell the food to our advantage," said Rosemary. "Anyway, a roast lamb is an easy meal to chuck in the oven and then ignore for a couple of hours while I do other things."

"Suit yourself," Athena said. "But you know I don't eat baby animals."

"Roast mutton it is then!" said Rosemary. "Even better, I'll roast it on a lower temperature for longer so that it's nice and tender. That will buy us plenty of time to get everything sorted for dinner."

They found a piece of black fabric and some black twine in amongst Granny's sewing things which were stored off to the side of the parlour, and then Athena ducked out of the front door to cut a few twigs of rosemary from the bush.

"That's everything!" Rosemary said. She gathered all the ingredients together on the kitchen bench and said the protection chant over and over again as she combined the salt, black pepper, and rosemary leaves inside the black cloth with the onyx.

Earth and air, fire and water, may I be protected from Dain.

She tied the bundle together and waved it over a lit candle, three times, while picturing Dain and what she often thought of as his stupid, handsome face. Then she sprinkled salt water over herself and the bundle, and flicked some at Athena, while picturing calm, tranquillity, and peace, which, in her mind, looked like a windswept beach.

"Hey!" Athena said.

"Quiet – I'm being tranquil here. I want to hear only the sea."

Athena sighed. "Are you quite finished?"

"I think so," Rosemary said. "Now I just have to wear it around my neck for days on end. Lucky black goes with everything."

"That's the spirit," Athena said. "I hope it works."

"Ooh, can we do mine now?" Rosemary asked. "I'm dying to speak to Granny."

"After dinner?" Athena suggested. "I'm starved, and I assume it's not the best idea to contact the dead on an empty stomach."

"Oh, very well then," said Rosemary. "But after that there's no more stalling."

She whipped up a quick dinner of tinned tomato soup and toast, marvelling at how the half-loaf of bread they'd brought with them and the other modest supplies in the kitchen seemed to be lasting so well.

This is the kind of magic I can get behind, Rosemary thought, smiling at the house and patting the kitchen bench in appreciation.

They ate their soup in silence.

Rosemary assumed Athena was thinking about Finnigan, while Athena assumed Rosemary was thinking about contacting Granny, meanwhile they were both actually thinking about each other, and about a potential impending visit from Dain, with their possessions, if he actually came through this time.

After dinner, they cleared the kitchen table and laid out the Ouija board.

"Alright," said Athena. "What do we do now?"

"How should I know?" Rosemary asked.

"You're the one who was reading about all the séances, remember."

"Oh, yes. That's right. So, I think we light a candle, with a clear intention in our minds and then hold hands, thinking of the person we want to contact."

Rosemary retrieved a candlestick and lit it, focusing on getting a clearer understanding of the binding and how to free their powers.

Then she stood back and reached for Athena's hands as they stood over the board.

"Are we supposed to close our eyes?" Athena asked.

"Of course not," said Rosemary. "How on earth would we see the letters Granny spells out if we have our eyes shut?"

"I just meant at first, to focus,"

"Will you two stop bickering for just one moment and give an old woman some peace?"

Rosemary and Athena both glanced down at the Ouija board to see Granny's face materialising there.

"Oh, gosh!" said Rosemary.

"This is way more effective than in the movies," Athena admitted.

"You know you can just summon me by calling my name loud enough?" Granny Thorn said. "You don't need to resort to all this codswallop."

"Hey. It's your board," Rosemary pointed out. "And no, I did not know that. It would have been a really useful thing to tell me last time you appeared to us, just like you could have told us who your killer is."

"Oh – I'd love to!" Granny said.

"Great," said Athena. "Who did it?"

"I'd love to," Granny said, frowning. "But I'm afraid they bound me from doing any such thing – those gormless gits!"

"I see," Rosemary said, her mood sinking in disappointment. "And I suppose ghost testimonies don't count anyway, even in Myrtlewood."

"I'm afraid not. I'm sorry I can't be of more help to you."

"But there's more than one of them – the attackers," Athena said. "You used plurals."

"A smart lass you are, dear," said Granny.

"Thank you," said Athena. "Granny Thorn, is there anything else you can tell us about them?"

"I'm afraid not, love, but I did leave you clues, and I can tell you a smidgeon about *that*."

"Please do," said Rosemary, perking up. "And then also, if you can, tell us about the binding and how to break it."

"The clues are: Blue. Lace. Dance."

"That's it?" Rosemary asked. "Those are the clues?"

"Well, not exactly. They're the clues to help you find the actual clues that I've hidden."

"What is this tosh!?" Rosemary said. "Can't you just tell us?"

"No, dear, I cannot. Mind your tongue."

"Why not?" Athena asked in a much calmer voice.

"The reason is perfectly obvious," Granny said. "I told you, they bound me from revealing who they are. Also, they might well be listening. I've done everything in my power to protect you, including hiding the information that others might use against you."

"You really think they're listening to a conversation in our kitchen?" Rosemary asked.

"It's possible to listen in when people are communicating between realms," said Granny Thorn. "Think of it like radio-waves."

"Well, that's just perfect," said Rosemary, scowling in frustration. "I suppose you can't tell us how to break the binding, either."

"Actually...no. But find the clues and you will figure it all out rather quickly."

"Well, you're a great help," Rosemary muttered, a caustic edge to her voice.

"I'm sorry, Rosemary dear. You did always have a short temper, and patience is not your forte, but please try to push through the frustration. You're going to need to do that in order to break the binding."

"Next, you're going to tell me I have to look within, like that elder," Rosemary scoffed.

"Oh, you absolutely do," said Granny. "But clearly you're not quite ready for that."

"What's that supposed to mean?!"

"Shush, Mum," Athena scolded. "We only have Granny here for a short time – remember – it uses up lots of her energy. Stop getting so cross and be practical."

"Fine, I'll hold my tongue," Rosemary said.

Granny stuck her own tongue out at that.

"Behave yourself, Granny Thorn!" said Athena. "We can't have Mum getting wound up again."

Rosemary glared at both of them.

"Okay," Athena continued. "Granny, you can't tell us how to break the binding, but can you at least explain more about how the whole thing happened – and how you came to bind our powers in the first place?"

"My dears – they've been after us for years. I only wish I saw this coming before it was too late. The binding is very old magic, and I daresay you'll find bits and pieces about it in the books in my library, but casting it is a very different process from breaking it, so don't worry too much about what I did. The main thing you both must focus on is yourselves. Think not too much on the past. Dwell not too much on the future. The answer is in the present. That is very important."

"In the present, I'm talking to a dead woman whom I'm very cross at," Rosemary said.

"Shh," said Athena.

"And with that, my energy is ebbing," said Granny. "I must bid you farewell. Remember that I love you very much, my sweet girls."

Granny faded back into the Ouija board. Rosemary sighed and dropped Athena's hands. "Well, a fat lot of good that did us."

"I think it might have actually been quite useful information," Athena said. "We just have to work it out."

"Always more cryptic messages and riddles!"

"Hey, you were the one who insisted we try to contact her," said Athena.

"That was before I knew she was going to be so infuriating."

"Oh, Mum, really? She tried to be helpful – which was more than you did, throwing a wobbly like that! It was unbelievable!"

"I was just brassed off that she couldn't be straight with us," Rosemary said.

"Through no fault of her own!"

"Oh, fine, take her side."

"We are all on the same side here," Athena said. "And when you're ready to behave like a grown-up, you can come and join us."

"I'm going to bed," Rosemary announced.

"Aren't you going to help me look for the clues? Something blue... lace...dance. It's a bit like a wedding, isn't it?"

"It's silly is what it is," Rosemary said. "I don't want to play games."

"Says the woman with the Ouija board!"

"Bed!" Rosemary said, storming upstairs. "Goodnight," she called down from her childhood bedroom before throwing herself on the single bed. It was silly, she knew that. She was behaving like a child, but surely all adults did that sometimes. Rosemary oscillated between rage that Granny had stolen a piece of her mind from her and sadness that she had been magically excluded. All of this burned above a deep-seated guilt. She hadn't been there for Granny, spell or not. Was that why Granny hadn't let her in on the secret? Everything had happened so fast that she'd barely had a chance to process any of it, and the impending danger only made it that much worse. *We will get out of this mess*, she vowed. *I'm going to kick the arse of whoever threatened my family, and then I'm going to live a life I'm actually in control of.*

CHAPTER
TWENTY

Rosemary lay in bed the next morning, feeling slightly better. She had processed a lot of the anger from the previous night, but still felt a keen sting of betrayal regarding Granny and being deceived for all those years by the person she most trusted.

Is this what looking within is like? Rosemary wondered, swallowing the bitter truth. *I don't much like it.*

She had no idea what the somewhat vague message meant, or how far she'd have to look before things finally made sense and she figured out how to break the binding.

Rosemary flinched at the sound of a knock.

"Yes?" she asked.

Athena pushed open the door, fully dressed and energetic-looking. "Come on sleepy head. Are you ready to help me look for clues yet?"

"Oh, alright."

"Good, because I've already made breakfast and tea."

"Really?" Rosemary asked, pushing herself out of bed and following Athena downstairs. "What did you make? It smells good."

"Just bacon and eggs."

"I can't believe that bacon's still good," Rosemary muttered. "Did you check it?"

"Oh Mum – when are you going to get used to having a magical refrigerator? Of course, I checked it. The food here seems to replenish itself somehow. We might be broke, but we're not going to starve."

"That's great," Rosemary said. "For as long as it lasts, anyway."

"You're such a cynical old lady."

"Well, either we release the binding and who knows what happens to the magic then, or we don't figure out how to and the whole thing implodes...or explodes. I'm not sure which is worse."

"Depends on where you're standing, perhaps," Athena said, serving her mother a plate of fried eggs and bacon on toast.

"Thank you," Rosemary said. "This was very thoughtful."

Athena shrugged. "I was hungry," she said. "And besides, I figured we needed a good meal after yesterday, when we didn't have a proper lunch and just had soup for dinner – and both got so cross at each other."

"You're very wise," Rosemary said.

"Remember that next time we argue," said Athena.

"So, what's your grand plan for today?" Rosemary asked. "Since you're already up and dressed and organised so early in the morning."

"It's nine o'clock, Mum," Athena said. "And my plan for the day is to find those clues that Granny hinted at. Yes, I do expect you to help me."

"Oh, very well," said Rosemary, finishing off her breakfast. "Where do you suggest we start?"

"Granny's bedroom, I think," Athena replied.

"Do we have to? It's all so intimate, going into someone's personal space like that."

"Personal space is something different, Mum, and it would serve you well to get a better grasp of it!"

"You know what I mean," said Rosemary.

"Yes, and yes, we do have to," Athena replied. "It makes sense that Granny would keep something important within reach."

"Or that she'd hide it far away, in the conservatory or something, so that people wouldn't guess."

"People like you would guess that," Athena pointed out. "You just did."

"Okay, fine. We start upstairs, but then I'm checking the conservatory."

"Blue. Lace. Dance," Athena repeated the clues Granny had given them. "Something blue, or lacy, or both – or something that dances?"

"Mmm, hmm," said Rosemary, getting up from the table and following Athena upstairs. "Could be anything, really."

"I'm hoping it will be obvious once we find it," Athena said. "Do you think it's one thing with three clues or three things that make up one clue?"

"How should I know?" Rosemary asked. "Nobody tells me anything useful."

"Oh, stop sulking, Mum," Athena said. "Granny Thorn had her reasons." She turned the handle and opened the door to Granny's bedroom.

Rosemary was taken aback by the nostalgia of it. Everything about this room reminded her of Granny, and it stabbed at her heart, painfully.

Why wasn't I trusted? Why couldn't she have let me in on her big secret instead of robbing me of my memories and keeping everything from me? Even Elamina knew about our family's magic...

Rosemary had always thought she was Granny's favourite, which made it hurt even more that she'd been kept in the dark. Her memories were so personal – her whole sense of self hinged on what she could remember of life, and a part of that had been stolen, which also meant the other parts made less sense. It was no wonder she had felt so fragmented. *It's like my whole childhood was a lie...and my adulthood too.*

She didn't share her lamenting thoughts with Athena to avoid being told off again.

"Look, here's the wardrobe," Athena said, pulling it open and examining the contents. "Lots of black dresses. Did she have lots of funerals to attend?"

"Granny just liked wearing black," Rosemary said, swallowing some of her own bitterness in order to focus on the matters at hand. "She said it goes with everything, so why wear anything else?"

"You do realise that second part defeats the purpose of the first part," Athena pointed out.

"I suppose you're right," said Rosemary. "Granny also said she liked black because it didn't stain easily."

"Very pragmatic. Look there are a bunch of other bright colours in here too: red dresses, green dresses, even purple. Lots of solid colour. I gather she wasn't a fan of prints or pastels."

"She certainly wasn't," Rosemary smirked. "Granny said pastels were what happened when colours gave up the will to live."

"I can't argue with that," said Athena. "She and Marjie must have made a funny pair – Granny in black and Marjie in pastel florals."

"They always said they were like chalk and cheese," Rosemary said.

"There's some black lace in here, but only one solid blue dress."

"Why are you fixated on the wardrobe?" Rosemary asked. "Those clues were so vague they could mean anything."

"Sure, but I figured it might have been a blue lacy dress – you know – the kind she might go out dancing in?"

"Granny did like to go to the local cèilidh dances," Rosemary recalled. "She said they were a whole pile of fun and good energy."

"There you go," said Athena. "But there's no blue lace in here. Hmm. Maybe we're on the wrong track entirely."

They scanned the rest of the room, but there weren't many blue objects, or much lace either, though Athena did discover a rather extensive shoe collection.

"Doilies are lacy," Rosemary said. "You know – like the ones down-stairs...and there are blue paperweights around there, too."

"Worth a try," said Athena. They retreated back down to the ground floor and looked at the items sitting on top of the cabinets.

"This one has a little blue," said Rosemary, holding up a blown glass paperweight. "And it was sitting on top of a doily."

"But what about the dancing?" Athena asked.

Rosemary shrugged. "We could check inside the cabinet?"

They sorted through the contents of the cupboard directly below the blueish paperweight, but all they found was a collection of silly hats.

"Granny Thorn might have worn them out dancing?" Athena suggested.

"Only if it was a fancy dress ball," said Rosemary. "It seems like a weak connection...but even if this was what Granny was alluding to – how are we supposed to find the hidden clue from a bunch of old junk?"

They sorted through the hats for possible leads, and then checked the doilies and the paperweight again, but nothing stood out as obvious.

Rosemary sighed and got up, brushing some dust from her jeans. "I'm going to check out the conservatory," she said.

"What's your obsession with that?" Athena asked.

Rosemary shrugged. "It's where I'd hide things. The conservatory was always such a lovely, lush place when I was growing up. I loved it in there."

"Fine," Athena said, following behind her mother as they left the house, through a side door and made their way around the outside.

"It looks a bit rough," Athena said, looking up at the old octagonal glass conservatory adjacent to the west wing of Thorn Manor. It did appear to be covered in a heavy layer of mildew and moss.

"Clearly the magic that maintains the house doesn't stretch all the way out here," Rosemary said.

"I know, it's just...would Granny Thorn really come all the way out here to hide something? She was old and frail."

"Granny was always active," Rosemary said. "If she was still making it up the stairs to use her bedroom, right to the point of leaving me a note there before she died, I'm sure she could have put on her Wellington boots and clomped out here easily enough.

"Wait, that's right...the note," said Athena.

"What about it?"

"Do you think it might contain any clues or useful information that might help us decipher this puzzle?"

"I don't know," said Rosemary. "I'll have a look at it when we get back inside."

She pushed open the door to the conservatory and winced at the sound of many insects scuttling away to hide.

"Not much in there," said Athena. "Unless you count rather a lot of moss, and what's that fuzzy plant?"

"Asparagus fern, I think," said Rosemary.

"It's...kind of lacy...Oh...that's right!"

"What?"

"Isn't there a plant that grows wild called something-lace?" Athena asked.

"Queen Anne's lace?" Rosemary suggested.

"Yes, that one. Do you think...?"

"Too vague," said Rosemary. "It grows all along the roadsides around here."

"Maybe that's part of the clue," Athena suggested. "Like we're supposed to follow the road with that plant growing along it to find something blue and then do some kind of ritual dance?"

"Are you serious?" Rosemary asked. "Granny was odd, but she wasn't completely potty! Anyway, you'd have to follow every single road, just about."

"Hey – I'm just trying to come up with ideas," Athena said defensively. "Your only idea was to look in here – where there's nothing but old pots and ferns. Nothing blue. No lace. No dancing."

Rosemary looked under a few pots, but as the centipedes and spider scurried away, she thought better of it and retreated back outside.

"It used to be beautiful in there," Rosemary said, sadly. "It was glorious, with all kinds of tropical plants. Granny even grew bananas!"

Athena gave her mother a sympathetic look and patted her arm. "Maybe we can restore it to its former glory," she suggested. "Once the inheritance comes through."

Rosemary smiled at her daughter. "I'd like that," she said as they made their way back to the house. There was so much potential in their lives now. If only they could get through the pressing danger.

CHAPTER
TWENTY-ONE

They searched the house from top to toe, trying to make connections with the prompts Granny had given them.

"It's all so exhausting," Rosemary said as they sat down to a light lunch of kippers on toast.

"Really?" Athena asked. "We've only been looking at old stuff."

"Maybe for you," Rosemary said, "but everything I come across seems to jog my memory, and bring back old feelings – both good and difficult. It all makes me miss Granny, and then I keep remembering that I'm still cross at her."

"That does sound like a rollercoaster," Athena said.

"I'm emotionally exhausted. I might need an afternoon kip."

"Go on, then," Athena said. "I'll keep looking down here, and you go upstairs to have a rest – you poor old thing."

"I'm only as old as I feel," said Rosemary. "Which is about a million years old right now!"

She gave Athena a quick hug and made her way upstairs. Afternoon sunlight was pouring in through her childhood bedroom, warming the air up to just the right temperature. Rosemary got into bed, wondering if she would ever move into Granny's larger room. It seemed wrong to do that, and eerie. Granny's room was Granny's room. Besides, her ghost might want to hang out in there when she built up a bit more strength.

Rosemary yawned, closed her eyes, and drifted off to sleep. She dreamed of the vines – thick vines – choking the light, choking the life right out of her. Rosemary tried to scream and cough at the same time, waking herself up.

She lay in bed, her heart racing, reminding herself that she was fine. Everything was okay.

As her heart-rate slowed, she looked around the room, at the things she had collected as a child, her colourful silk scarves; the shells she had picked up on the beach as a child, sitting in a bowl on the windowsill; the pictures of fairies she'd pinned to the wall.

Her eyes fell on an object on the dresser. It was a music box that Granny had given her as a present, much to eight-year-old Rosemary's delight.

It was a long time since she'd looked inside, but she recalled the box contained a tiny ballerina that danced on a mirror as if by magic – though actually by magnets. She remembered keeping special stones and nick-nacks in there, things she had hoped would one day be valuable, but in all probability were not.

The memory struck a chord.

Dance...

Rosemary got up and opened the box, disappointed to find it empty except for the ballerina. She picked it up and placed it on the mirror in the centre of the box, and then she gasped.

"Athena!" she called out.

Athena came running.

"What is it? Are we being attacked again?"

"No," said Rosemary. "Look at what I found."

"It's...a toy jewellery box?"

"Look closer."

"What am I looking for?"

Rosemary pointed to the lace skirt, worn by the tiny ballerina, then to the blue velvet lining of the box. "This must be it!"

Athena looked sceptical. "Was that Granny Thorn's or yours?"

"It was mine. Granny gave it to me," Rosemary said. "Remember what she said – the answer is in the *present*!"

"But it's empty," Athena pointed out.

"It's really cool. Watch this," said Rosemary, twisting the latch to wind it up. The box immediately began to chime out a song, and Rosemary set it down on the dresser. They watched as the little ballerina started to dance, propelled by her own magnetic stand and the inner workings of the box.

"Granny used to always sing this to me," Rosemary said.

COME AWAY MY LITTLE CHILD,
> *through the forests of the wild.*
> *Feel the pulling deep within,*
> *Trees will dance and trees will sing,*
> *until they die and fall*
> *elemental magic calls,*
> *until we let the light shine though, rise up and seize it all.*

"YOU KNOW that's not how the original poem goes," Athena said as Rosemary stopped singing.

"What poem?"

"You know? The Yates poem. It's really famous – about faeries and stuff."

Athena had a strange, unreadable expression on her face.

"It's funny. I can't remember that either. It might be part of Granny's spell."

"Or your memory could be bad in a perfectly ordinary way," Athena said.

"You're suggesting Granny made this version up?" Rosemary asked. "I wonder why?"

"Maybe she was teaching you how to break the binding this whole time!"

"You mean – that song is the key – like a magic chant?"

"Could be – either that or its instructions."

"What kind of instructions?"

"Like - go into the forest and find an old fallen tree and, I don't know, meditate?"

"Meditate?! What are you, a yoga guru?"

"Yes, meditate," said Athena. "Remember – the elder said to look within, and I'm pretty sure that song says the same thing."

"Oh, bother!"

Despite her resistance, Rosemary felt somewhat buoyed by their discovery.

"You're in a much better mood," Athena commented as they sipped their afternoon cups of tea.

"It's just nice to know that Granny has been teaching me this stuff...all along...leaving me clues for how to break the binding. I wasn't just an afterthought."

"She really went to great lengths to keep all this stuff hidden, didn't she?" Athena said. "Which isn't exactly reassuring. It means that whoever was after her was very bad news."

"It was all so long ago," Rosemary said. "Does that mean we can cross off a whole bunch of suspects who would have been too young a few decades ago?"

"No," said Athena. "They might still be involved. Those guys who attacked us looked relatively young."

"Blast, you're right," Rosemary said. "And here I was, trying to find a way to avoid inviting a bunch of people to dinner."

"You still haven't invited everyone?!" Athena cried. "You'd better get a move on. Friday is only two days away."

"Oh fine," Rosemary said. "I'll do it after I've finished my tea."

And so she did. Rosemary spent a good chunk of the rest of the afternoon sending out messages and making phone calls to the remaining people on their list.

"I hope it's not too short notice," Rosemary said, finally putting her feet up after sending the last message.

"Like you said before," said Athena. "The real culprit is sure to come if they are keen on another look inside the house and a chance to steal the family magic."

"Speaking of that...we need a decoy box."

"Way ahead of you," said Athena. She wandered over to the cabinet and retrieved a small wooden carved box of a similar size to the one in the library.

"Brilliant! When did you find that?"

"While you were off having your nanna nap earlier."

"It's perfect," said Rosemary, examining the empty box.

"Maybe we can sprinkle some gold powder over it to make it look more magical," Athena suggested.

"Oh, yeah?" said Rosemary. "And where are we going to find that? You know all about my aversion to glitter."

"Don't remind me about my school production disaster," Athena said. "But I know where Granny kept a whole lot of strange, coloured powders."

"What? Why would she do that?"

"I suspect they're a magical ingredient," said Athena. "I think I saw something about using powders as a base for charms."

She wandered over to the dining room where piles of books were still stacked up and returned with Altazar's Compendium of Enchantments.

"Your favourite book," Rosemary muttered.

"Look – it says here that powders are an effective vehicle for spells, especially those directed at other people. Hmm...that gives me an idea..."

Athena scanned the following three pages of the book. "This might work."

"What?" Rosemary asked.

"It's a green powder...a spell that reveals malicious intent...only you have to blow it directly into people's faces."

"Sounds delightful," Rosemary remarked.

"It could be a useful tool to have on Friday," Athena insisted. "Especially if your rather vague plan turns out fruitless."

"It does sound like something that might come in handy," Rosemary said. "Though we are not going to make many friends if that's our way of welcoming them!"

"No," Athena admitted, reading on. "It's best left as a backup plan, especially considering its potential side effects are eye burns and vomiting."

"Definitely not my first choice," Rosemary agreed.

The sky outside had darkened by this time, and Rosemary began thinking about what to eat for dinner. She went to the fridge, only to find it stocked with a leg of mutton and half a dozen other new ingredients, which she was certain hadn't been there before.

"Hey Athena!" she called out, waving the large cut of meat around.

"What on earth?"

"I love having a magical refrigerator!" Rosemary crowed.

"How...?"

"Remembered how I mentioned making roast mutton yesterday?"

"No way!" Athena said, bounding over to the kitchen. "Ooh, and look! Cornish Pasties! I was craving them this morning."

"Splendid. This brings the term 'smart-appliance' to a whole new level! Cornish pasties for dinner?" Rosemary said.

"Not sure they're a traditional dinner food," Athena said. "But who cares!"

Rosemary turned the oven on to heat up the pasties and then looked in the pantry for something appropriate to serve on the side. She was interrupted by a knock at the door.

Startled, Rosemary looked at Athena, whose eyes were wide.

"What do you think that could be?" Rosemary asked.

"Nothing good, that's for sure," Athena replied.

"Do you think they'll go away if we don't answer?"

"Actually, I think they'll probably break in..."

"Oh, fine," Rosemary said. "I guess I should go and check to see who it is, at least."

"Wait," said Athena, grabbing Rosemary by the Arm. "What if it's Dad?"

"Why would he be here?"

"You asked him to bring all our stuff, remember?"

"Oh, yeah...That's right. Well, if it's Dain, then we should definitely answer the door and help him to bring things in."

"I don't want you going near that man," Athena insisted.

"Even after the protection charm?"

"We don't know if it works," said Athena.

"So, what do you propose?" Rosemary asked.

"I'll answer the door and tell him you're occupied."

"He's not going to buy that."

"You're sick with terrible di—"

"Enough!" Rosemary said. "I'm not letting you answer the door in case it's someone dangerous."

Athena crossed her arms and pouted as Rosemary pushed past on her way towards the front door. She checked the side windows, just to make sure it wasn't anyone too dodgy looking.

"Well, that's strange," said Rosemary.

"Who is it?"

"It's just...a pile of boxes." She opened the door and looked around. "Yep, all I can see is boxes, which I really hope are our things."

She lifted the lid on one of them to find a pile of her old shoes. "Yep – it's our stuff...but where is Dain?"

"Is he over there in the car, maybe?" Athena asked.

Rosemary squinted into the darkness to see the vague outline of their old rust-bucket. "Dain?" she called out.

There was no answer, and so Rosemary approached the car, looking around warily, in case of attack.

The doors and car boot were open, and the key was sitting in the ignition, but there was no sign of Rosemary's deadbeat ex.

"Dad?" Athena called out, into the night, but only an owl answered back. "That's just creepy," she said.

Rosemary locked up the car, and the two Thorns picked up the boxes and brought them into the foyer of the house, quickly closing and locking the front door behind them.

"Dad must have been here...surely," Athena said.

"But where did he go?" Rosemary asked. "Did someone attack him? Kidnap him?"

"Seems unlikely that they'd do it silently without disturbing us," said Athena. "Maybe your charm actually worked."

"What? You mean it teleported him somewhere else like in the space films?"

"Or...like it made him run away – very quickly?" Athena suggested, with more than a hint of doubt in her voice.

"Oh, well..." said Rosemary. "I guess, that's for the best, as long as he's okay."

"I do not care if he's okay. He can rot."

"Athena!"

"Look – you're cross at Granny when she was actually pretty decent for the most part, albeit secretive and odd."

"That's different—"

"And you don't even talk to your parents."

"Because they only ever want to chat about saving my immortal soul and sending you off to bible camp!"

"So?! Imagine what it's like to have Dain for a father. I'd take bible camp and a secure, loving home any day over Dad nicking off with your wallet again."

Rosemary sighed. "Okay. Point taken."

"Great. So, you're not going to try to pretend he should be in my life anymore?"

"I guess I'll have to leave all that up to you," Rosemary replied. "You're the expert on your life, after all."

"And it's time you started treating me like I am!" said Athena.

CHAPTER
TWENTY-TWO

Both to Rosemary's satisfaction and dismay, every single person she had invited on Friday had RSVP'd as attending. It was good to know that all the likely suspects would make it, as she'd woken in the middle of Wednesday night worrying that the real perpetrator might decline, and instead, use the distraction of the dinner to attack them.

On Thursday morning, Rosemary sat at the kitchen table, making lists of all the things she needed, while Athena painted her nails a deep aubergine purple.

"Do you think the fridge is reliable as a source of ingredients?" Rosemary asked. "And how fast does it even work?"

"How should I know?" Athena asked. "Why don't you test it? Fridge! I want Hobnobs! – Now go check."

"Okay," Rosemary got up and opened the fridge to find that the mutton roast was still there, however Hobnobs had not appeared. She looked at Athena and shook her head.

"Drat," Athena said. "Maybe it only does non-branded foodstuffs."

"You mean, like real food?" Rosemary asked.

"What even is *real*, anymore?"

"I wish I knew the answer to that," said Rosemary. "I might need to go into town and do a quick shop, just in case the magic falls through. Do you want to come?"

"Don't even think of leaving me alone in this house," Athena replied. "Plus, I can't trust you to remember to buy me Hobnobs."

They got ready. Even though the weather was fine for walking, they made their way into town in Granny's car, since they needed to carry all the shopping back somehow.

Myrtlewood village was bustling with people and cars. Rosemary managed to find a park near Burk's office, but deliberately avoided glancing at the old stone building as they made their way through the town square towards the local grocery shop.

"Oh, hello there?" Ferg's distinctive voice rang out from behind a tree.

"Hello...tree-Ferg," Rosemary said.

"I'm just regular Ferg," he said, stepping out from the tree holding old wilted blossoms. He reached down to the large box at his feet and drew out some fresh flowers.

"What are you doing there?" Athena asked.

"I'm replacing the old drooping blossoms in the displays with fresh ones," Ferg explained.

"Why do you start decorating so early if you just have to replace them?" Rosemary asked.

"It's just the nature of this season. It's tempestuous like that," said Ferg. He shook his head sagely. "But you have to do what you can to please the Gods. We must feast for Brigid. Demeter must return to put the world to rights!"

"You really believe in the gods, across multiple pantheons, huh?" Rosemary asked.

Ferg lowered his voice. "Shh. Of course I do! And if you aren't careful, they'll show you exactly how real they are. Now get out of here before they hear your lack of faith and send a lightning bolt this way."

"You're serious," said Athena, shaking her head in disbelief.

"Or seriously superstitious," Rosemary muttered under her breath, only to receive a sharp kick from her daughter.

"So," Ferg said. "I hear you're planning a bit of a get-together tomorrow night."

"Oh…" said Rosemary.

"Did we invite him?" Athena whispered.

"Was I supposed to? I can't remember," Rosemary hissed. "Did we suspect him?"

"I think we suspected just about everyone," Athena whispered back.

"Maybe we'll just invite the whole town and see what happens."

Athena gave her a tense look.

Rosemary turned back to Ferg to see he was clearly awaiting his invitation awkwardly.

"Won't you join us?" Rosemary asked.

"Excellent," said Ferg, skipping up and down on the spot like a fawn. "I'd be delighted to accept."

Rosemary and Athena walked away, slightly disconcerted.

"It'll all end in a flaming pile of eye burns and vomiting and we'll be banished from Myrtlewood forever," Rosemary grumbled.

"That's way more likely than it should be," Athena said.

"We haven't mixed up that powder charm yet," said Rosemary.

"Actually, I did it this morning while you were having a lie in."

"Athena!"

"What? It's a backup plan."

"A terrible one."

"It could come in handy," Athena insisted.

"What *would* come in handy is some kind of defensive spell, like a charm to banish your enemies," said Rosemary.

"I cooked up a couple of those too…" said Athena. "Though I don't know if any of them will work."

"That's excellent. Well done, you," Rosemary said.

Their grocery shopping took longer than expected, as every second person seemed to want to introduce themselves and chat and mention they'd heard about the dinner party on Friday night and then pause awkwardly, waiting to be invited, but Rosemary was onto them and waited out the silence before saying a cheerful. "Got to dash! Nice to meet you," and continuing on her way.

Athena did manage to con her mother into buying a packet of crisps as they made their way around the aisle of the small and independent grocery shop, which was surprisingly well-stocked for a small town.

By the time they made it back to the car, they were both starving.

"Quick stop at Marjie's?" Rosemary suggested. "I'm sure it's dangerous for me to drive with low blood sugar."

"Agreed," Athena said. "I'm sure it's dangerous being in your presence with low blood sugar."

"Dangerous for you, or me?"

"Both," said Athena.

Marjie's tea shop was bustling, and they were lucky to find a table, but as soon as they sat down, Marjie was on her way over with two large roast beef sandwiches and a pot of tea.

"Is this for us?" Rosemary asked.

"Of course it is," Marjie said. "I saw you coming from across the square and thought I knew just what you needed."

"It actually is exactly what I feel like," Athena said. "How did you guess?"

"I have a knack fer these things," said Marjie proudly.

Marjie left them to attend to other customers, and Athena gave Rosemary a pleading look. "See, she can't possibly be one of the suspects. She's way too nice. We have to take her off our list."

"Niceness does not preclude murder," Rosemary said. "Besides, it's not doing her any harm. She doesn't even know about it."

"But what if she finds out?" Athena asked. "It'll break her poor old heart. And I'd feel rotten for going along with all this – accepting her hospitality."

"It's impossible not to," said Rosemary, holding up a wad of cash she found stashed under the teapot. "I tried to pay her the other day, but she's given our money back – with interest!"

"She *can't* be the culprit," Athena insisted. "She's had plenty of opportunities to poison us, plus she could have come to the house any time, and we'd have let her right in, but she hasn't even tried."

They started eating, enjoying the soft fresh bread and tender beef, the tang of pickles and crisp salad.

"How's the lunch?" Marjie said, having clearly just returned from serving other customers.

"Great, thanks!" said Athena, taking another big bite of her sandwich.

"Listen," said Margie, lowering her voice. "I've been meaning to pop in and see you. I have a wee charm prepared that you can use when people arrive tomorrow. It should track their movements through the house, so you'll be able to see anything out of the ordinary. I can bring by the components and show you how it works later on."

"Thank you," Rosemary said. "That sounds perfect."

Marjie beamed at them and then left them to it.

"See..." Athena said.

"She just invited herself around to the house," Rosemary pointed out.

"And you said that was perfect."

"Well, what was I supposed to say? Stay away, foul demon?"

"You obviously don't want her to think we were suspicious of her, because you care about her feelings."

They finished up their meals and drove somewhat solemnly back to Thorn Manor.

Rosemary began the preparation for the following day's dinner party almost immediately, leaving Athena to pour over the books still cluttering the dining table. It was rather peaceful, chopping onions in Granny's lovely wooden-panelled kitchen. It had been a long time since Rosemary properly cooked a meal. She used to love it, but life and stress and being strapped for cash had gotten in the way.

As she began to sauté the diced onions with spices she was

reminded of the year and a half of cheffing school she'd gotten through before her pregnancy with Athena and tight finances had forced her to drop out. She'd wanted to specialise in pastry cheffing and become a chocolatier, for surely there had been nothing better in the world to young Rosemary than good chocolate.

Chocolate... Even her very favourite thing had lost its appeal over the years of struggle for survival. Rosemary hardly ever indulged in it these days, though in her occasional daydreams, she was stirring up her own truffle blends and inventing interesting flavour combinations like passionfruit and coriander, or quince and sage, or blackberries and thyme.

Why does life have to always get in the way of dreams? she lamented.

A knock at the door disturbed Rosemary's truffly dreams.

"Marjie!" Athena called out from the next room.

"Let her in," Rosemary called back.

"Of *course*, Mum!"

A moment later, Marjie bustled into the kitchen with a tray of unusual objects, followed by Athena.

"Hello dear," Marjie said, kissing Rosemary on the cheek. "Now, I won't keep you long. I see that you're busy there." She nodded to the pan of onions that Rosemary had been occasionally stirring as they caramelised.

"No worries," said Rosemary. "I can just turn this down."

She adjusted the heat to very, very low and stepped away from the stove as Marjie placed her tray down on the kitchen table.

"Now," Marjie said, picking up two clear crystals. "You place these two on either side of the front door...like so." She took them over to the door and put them down near the bottom of the doorframe on both sides.

"This one hangs above the door." She held out a little pink bouquet, disguising a bundle in its midst. "I've tried to camouflage it in the flowers to make it less obvious." She passed the bouquet to Athena.

"Clever," said Athena.

Rosemary merely nodded.

"I'll let you hang that up, dear," said Marjie. "I wouldn't want to put my back out, trying."

"Sure thing," Athena said and skipped off to hang the bundle.

Marjie returned her attention to her tray. "And this—" She produced another bundle, which was black this time. "This goes in your pocket when you're welcoming them in. Be sure to shake hands or make some kind of skin contact with every single one of them."

"Very well," said Rosemary. "What's the rest of it for?"

"Oh, the other bundles are to be placed in the key corners of the rooms where the guests are likely to be. I'll let you do that part, too. After the working, we'll be able to see trails for every one of them and where they've been."

"Thank you for going to all this trouble," Rosemary said.

"Oh, it's nothing, dear," said Marjie. "My only concern right now is keeping you both safe."

Rosemary felt a stab of guilt. She badly hoped this wasn't all an act on Marjie's part but even if it wasn't, it felt wrong to suspect her.

"I'm back!" said Athena, bounding back into the room. Rosemary marvelled at her ability to behave like a sullen teenager one minute and like an excited eight-year-old the next. "Hey, Marjie, won't you stay for a cup of tea?" Athena asked.

"Oh, I wouldn't want to trouble you," Marjie said.

"It's no trouble," said Athena, putting on the kettle. "Take a seat."

Rosemary gave Athena a puzzled look. It wasn't that she minded Marjie staying for tea. Indeed, she was slightly embarrassed that she didn't think to offer herself. It was more that Athena was acting out of character. She was clearly up to something.

"While the kettle boils," Athena said. "I just want to try something…"

"Athena," Rosemary said with a hint of warning in her voice. She reached out for her daughter's arm, but Athena shook her off.

Rosemary noticed an instant later that Athena had something hidden in her closed fist.

"Marjie, will you close your eyes for just a moment?" Athena said, walking over to the kitchen table.

"Oh course, dear."

"Athena!" Rosemary whispered urgently, but it was too late.

Athena raised her palm to reveal a sparkling green powder and blew it gently towards Marjie. The powder moved, slower than seemed physically possible, creating a small dust cloud around Marjie, who sneezed. The green turned to orange, and then the powder vanished. She opened her eyes in surprise. The colour was quickly fading back to normal.

"Athena!" Rosemary said sternly.

"What was that?" Marjie asked, surprised.

"Just something I was practicing," Athena said with feigned innocence.

"Trying to prove a point, more like," said Rosemary.

"And it worked! I was right!" Athena crowed.

"Just as well we didn't see any of those side effects!" Rosemary hissed.

"That's why I told her to close her eyes," Athena insisted. "The side effects are more likely if it gets into people's eyes or mouth."

"Oh, come now, you two," Marjie said. "I think I've worked out what that just was."

Rosemary and Athena looked at each other, hoping Marjie was assuming something else.

"Did you really suspect me?" the older woman asked sadly.

There was a moment of tension in which Rosemary felt a great rush of guilt.

"I didn't," Athena insisted. "Which is why I had to show Mum that you're innocent." She scampered back to the kitchen towards the tea things.

Another moment passed where Rosemary thought of a hundred ways to apologise to her grandmother's closest friend for suspecting her of her murder, and all of them fell flat in her mind.

"Well, I suppose you can't be too careful these days," Marjie said cheerfully, sipping the tea that Athena had just brought her.

"You're not cross?" Rosemary asked.

"I don't see why I should be," said Marjie. "I think it's grand that you clever girls are doing such a good job of looking out for yourselves – I can't fault you for that! I care very much about the both of you."

Rosemary smiled. "I *am* sorry," she said.

"No need to apologise, dear. You're doing a great job – and I'm glad I passed your test! Now I'll leave you to your preparation, but do give us a bell if I can help with anything else."

CHAPTER
TWENTY-THREE

Rosemary slept fitfully that night.

She dreamed of walking in the forest surrounding the house, searching...searching for the source of their power.

I've got to release the binding...

The music from the ballerina box started to play, and Rosemary began dancing – dancing...she couldn't stop, even though the dancing was making her younger and younger until she was just a small child screaming out.

Noooo!

Rosemary awoke to twisted, sweaty sheets.

"Mum? Are you alright?" Athena was there, in the doorway.

"Just a bad dream, love," Rosemary said.

"It's the magic, isn't it?" said Athena. "It's getting to you."

"Some kind of tension does seem to be building," Rosemary admitted.

"The whole house feels like it's humming slightly," said Athena.

"It does, doesn't it? But don't worry. We're going to work this out."

The day was taken up by preparations for dinner. Rosemary stuffed the mutton leg – which was thankfully still in the fridge – with garlic and rosemary sprigs, and smothered it in olive oil and sea salt. Then she set to work on an enormous pot of her ratatouille soup, a favourite recipe that she hadn't bothered to prepare in years. Later, when the mutton was roasting slowly in the oven, she peeled potatoes to be served with it, and then prepared several large chocolate treacle tarts, enough for all the guests. Finally, she got to work on the salad course of delicately sliced pears with toasted walnuts, rocket, basil, and parmesan with a mustard and lemon juice dressing designed to protect the pears from oxidising. She kept the rocket and basil aside to add right before serving, lest they wilt.

"This is all very swish," Athena said, coming into the kitchen to see dozens of matching plates and bowls stacked up, ready for the servings of food. Rosemary was toasting the walnuts in one of Granny's many large cast-iron pans.

"You're going to help dish this out, aren't you?" Rosemary said. "I'll have to keep an eye on the guests the whole time."

"Marjie and I have got you covered," said Athena.

"When did that happen?"

"When I walked her out to her car. She insisted on coming back here early to help out with dinner, and I accepted of course – now that we know she's definitely not a baddie."

"But she's already helped us enough," Rosemary said. "I'm going to forever be in debt of gratitude to that woman...and thank you," she said, hugging Athena. "That has actually given me a lot more peace of mind. I'm not sure how else I would juggle all this."

"What are daughters for?" said Athena, hugging her mother back.

"Winding me up and driving me batty?" Rosemary suggested.

"I think you do that well enough on your own."

Marjie did indeed arrive about an hour early, and headed straight to the kitchen to help Athena plate up the salad while Rosemary did a last-minute sweep around the house to check that everything was in order.

She couldn't very well move the box from the desk in the library to hide it, since touching it sent her somewhere else. Instead, she found the key for the library door and locked it, along with several other doors on the ground floor – just so it wasn't suspicious as the only locked door.

Athena had carefully placed the decoy box on the mantlepiece in the parlour. It stood there, gracefully dusted with a little gold power for magical effect and surrounded by sparkling crystals from Granny's drawer.

Satisfied that everything was as orderly as it could be, Rosemary headed upstairs to change into something less covered in food. She didn't have many nice dresses, being someone who preferred to live in jeans, but she had a simple black dress that looked okay if she paired it with a nice necklace and earrings. She chose the amethyst necklace that Granny had given her for her sixteenth birthday and a set of purple dangly earrings to match the colour, and even slipped on some simple black ballet flats instead of her usual boots, sneakers, or bare feet.

By the time Rosemary made it back downstairs, the salad course was resting on the kitchen table and the soup was being ladled into bowls, ready to be kept warm in the oven after she removed the lamb roast.

"Everything's in order!" Rosemary announced, sounding somewhat surprised.

"And don't you look lovely!" Marjie cooed.

"You clean up alright," Athena commented.

Rosemary shrugged. "That's high praise coming from a teenager."

"Stop stereotyping me," Athena said.

Just then, the doorbell rang.

"Now, have you got all the parts of my enchantment sorted?" Marjie asked.

"Yes," said Rosemary, picking up the key bundle from the kitchen sideboard and tucking it into the pocket of her dress. "The number one lesson here is to always buy dresses with pockets," she said sagely.

"Very good."

"Oh...music!" Rosemary cried. "I forgot."

"I've got that sorted," Athena said, bringing up the music app on her phone. "This is hooked up to the surround sound."

Rosemary smiled and then frowned. "What kind of music do you have lined up, exactly?" she asked. "And since when does Granny have surround sound? She doesn't even have a telly."

"Of course she does, silly," Marjie said. "It's behind the big tapestry in the parlour."

"And I made a playlist for exactly this occasion," said Athena, pressing play. Mediterranean acoustic music flooded through the house and Rosemary smiled.

"Now go get that door before everyone gives up on us!" Athena said.

To Rosemary's displeasure, the first guests to arrive were her not-so-dear cousins. Elamina looked resplendent, if icy, in a glittering midnight-toned gown, and Derse was in a three-piece suit.

Rosemary made a great effort not to breathe in Elamina's signature overly sweet floral perfume. She tried to smile, but it turned out to be more of a grimace. "Welcome," she said as she awkwardly reached out to shake her cousin's hands. It wasn't something that she'd normally do, but it was required for Marjie's enchantment to work and Rosemary figured they needed all the magical help they could get.

"Are we quite on time?" Elamina asked, looking at Rosemary's hand as if it was a days-old dead thing, but begrudgingly taking it and giving it a pathetic little shake.

"You are actually a little early," Rosemary said as she grimaced again, this time from the painful force of Derse's handshake. "Uh, haven't you ever heard of being fashionably late?"

Elamina gave a funny little laugh and muttered "fashionably" a few times, as if she was struggling to reconcile the concept with Rosemary's presence.

"Erm, come in, I guess," Rosemary said, taking their coats and leading them through into the parlour where Athena was now waiting as planned to offer them drinks and keep an eye on the general goings on.

"This is your...offspring?" Elamina asked, giving Athena a faint but vaguely genuine smile as she eyed her curiously.

"Yes, I suppose you haven't really met her properly," Rosemary said. "This is my daughter Athena."

"Charmed," Elamina said, holding out her dainty gloved hand for Athena to shake, a gesture that both Rosemary and her daughter found puzzling. Derse merely nodded at the girl and accepted her offer of sherry. Elamina opted for straight whiskey.

The next to arrive was Constable Perkins, dressed in a bright blue blazer and a red bowtie.

"You made it!" Rosemary exclaimed, shaking his hand enthusiastically as she tried to suppress a giggle at his unusual outfit. "Right this way."

She led Constable Perkins into the parlour, enjoying the sight of her cousin's mortified faces as they surveyed their fellow guest. She deliberately introduced him with his police title to ensure they were on their best behaviour, hopefully for the entire evening.

"The cousins, eh?" the police officer in not-so-plain clothes said. "I've been meaning to have a chat with you both concerning your grandmother. Perhaps we can schedule an appointment now."

Elamina glared at Rosemary, who smiled with satisfaction, which was short-lived as another knock sounded at the door. She raced off to let in Liam who arrived with a well-recovered Sherry.

"Sorry, I didn't call or drop by," Sherry said, handing Rosemary a bottle of red wine. "I had so much to catch up on after a few days in bed!"

"No worries," said Rosemary, vigorously shaking their hands.

"So formal," Liam said as he shook back.

"Just being polite," said Rosemary, leading them over to Athena in the Parlour.

Perseus Burk arrived a few short minutes later in a silk shirt and black jacket, no tie. He held a bunch of white roses and another bottle of red wine, which he handed to Rosemary, who quickly put the bouquet down on the sideboard before Athena could see and make fun of her.

"Thank you," Rosemary said, not wanting to make eye-contact for very long with the handsome, yet very suspicious man – if he indeed was a man and not some other kind of creature entirely. She reached for his cold hand, which gave hers a little squeeze. Rosemary pulled back from the intimacy and waved Burk inside. Don June, the mayor, in his usual black and purple outfit was hot on his heels, arriving before Rosemary even had a chance to close the door.

"Thank you for coming at such short notice," she said.

"Nonsense! I'm always keen to socialise with the constituents – do keep me in mind for all future events," said Mr June. "It's just a shame that my husband couldn't make it tonight. He's out of town on business."

"Your husband?" Rosemary muttered absentmindedly.

"Yes, Zade. You'd love him."

"Maybe next time we'll get to meet him," said Rosemary, smiling.

No sooner had Rosemary shaken hands with the mayor and ushered him to the parlour when the door knocker sounded again.

This time, Despina and Genevieve stood on the doorstep, both frowning slightly, flanked by Ferg, who was grinning ear-to-ear.

"Beautiful night for a party!" Ferg said. "I was just pointing out to these two what an odd pair they make; the big one dresses young and the little one dresses old!"

Rosemary smiled apologetically at Despina, who was wearing pastel pink, and Geneviève, who was dressed entirely in black, wearing a long cocktail dress and coat, her chestnut hair falling in carefully tamed ringlets.

Rosemary managed to shake all of their hands and usher them into the parlour.

"Right, that's it then," she said to Athena, who had almost finished handing out drinks.

"Well..." Athena said.

The house seemed to hum at a stronger frequency than before.

Athena's eyes went wide. "Did you just feel that?"

Rosemary nodded and glanced around, but none of the guests seemed to notice the building intensity. They were all engaged in polite, impolite, or odd conversation. "What do you think it could be?" she asked in a whisper. "Is the house reacting to Granny's attacker being here?"

"Well, in that case, why did it start humming earlier before any guests arrived?" Athena asked. "And why did it build up now, after everyone is already inside, rather than when someone in particular entered?"

"You have a point," Rosemary said. "Maybe it's just reacting to having so many people – magical people – inside."

"Or maybe it's to do with the binding," Athena suggested quietly. "You said the energy was building up, and it was going to explode."

"Or implode," Rosemary reminded her.

"I don't much like the sound of either, especially when we're all inside."

"We can't very well conduct a dinner party out in the cold," Rosemary said.

"You could call it off," Athena pointed out.

"And waste all the effort we've put in just because the house is humming? I don't think so."

Rosemary turned back to the group and cleared her throat. Heads turned towards her, but then the door knocker sounded again, and she had to excuse herself once more.

Who on earth could that be?

Covvey Dunne and Agatha Twigg from the pub stood in the door-way, dressed in what Rosemary assumed were their fancy going-out clothes. Agatha wore a green sequined dress and Covvey had on a smoking jacket over a t-shirt and jeans.

"Erm, hello?" said Rosemary. She certainly did not remember inviting them.

"We're here for the party," Agatha said, bustling past.

"Oh..." Rosemary said. It was too late. They were both inside, and she hadn't managed to shake their hands. She thought about trying to turf them out, but then wondered if they'd come because they were involved with the sinister plot to steal the family magic. Of course, under normal circumstances, that would be more than enough to send people packing, but Rosemary felt some urgency in getting to the bottom of the mystery, since her freedom was at stake. She was not going to be jailed, especially for a crime she'd never ever want to commit. She shook hands with them, hoping that the charm worked once people were already inside, and led them to the parlour where they proceeded to glare at many of the other guests.

Rosemary rushed back to the kitchen.

"Any chance of adding a couple of extra plates?" she asked Marjie who was setting the mutton to rest.

"You can't count?" Marjie asked, smiling cheekily.

"More like gate-crashes," Rosemary said.

"Who are they?" asked Marjie.

"That Covvey man and Agatha Twigg."

"Typical trouble makers," Marjie said. "I love them both, but they can't manage to mind their own business. Always sticking their heads in where they're not welcome."

Rosemary shrugged. "Is there enough food to go around?"

"I think you're forgetting I have a certain knack for this thing," said Margie. She twiddled her fingers and two more bowls filled with soup and salad appeared.

"You just made that?"

"I replicated them – making them from scratch would be too hard, but a little replication is easy as pie. Now, get out there and attend to your guests. Poor Athena is in there all alone with that lot!"

Rosemary gave Marjie a quick hug. "Thanks so much for all your help."

"It's nothing, dear. Now go!"

Upon returning to the parlour, Rosemary picked up a glass and teaspoon and tinkled them together in the universal sign for making a speech.

"Thank you all for coming," she said. "In a moment, we'll go through to the dining room for dinner, but I just wanted to say a few words first."

She had practiced the carefully designed speech, but was sure it would come out garbled. The important thing was creating the right level of intrigue about The Box.

"Granny Thorn was very dear to me," Rosemary said. "And though I miss her very much, it's an honour to be here, in her house, surrounded by many of her friends and loved ones."

Rosemary noticed that Elamina and Derse were glaring at her, but she pushed on. "When we first came to Myrtlewood, it was just for a meeting. We only packed for one day – that was almost a week ago, though it feels much longer and not entirely in a bad way," she smiled warmly. There was a small murmur of laughter from the group.

"But Myrtlewood has won our hearts over in this short time, and we are delighted to stay here as caretakers of Granny's house and all her unusual things."

Another little murmur of laughter, though none of it from the cousins, who looked even angrier than before.

"For example, the refrigerator seems to fill itself, quite as it pleases, and we've hardly had to do a lick of housework. Trust Granny to find a way out of dusting!" Slightly louder laughter rang around the room. "Or this box," Rosemary said, gesturing towards the mantlepiece. "Granny told us it was extremely important, yet she didn't even say why, so we just keep it here on the mantlepiece, hoping it does whatever it needs to do."

There were many curious looks towards the decoy box sitting innocently between the crystals.

"Anyway, I'm sure you're all starved," Rosemary said. "So, without any further delay, come through and eat!"

She opened the side door to the parlour, which led directly into the dining room. The big wooden table had been beautifully laid out with dark blue cloth napkins, polished silver cutlery, and Granny Thorn's special crystal glasses.

Everyone took their seats as Rosemary and Athena poured wine they'd found in Granny's cellar for those who wanted it, and offered grape juice as a non-alcoholic option.

When Rosemary got to Geneviève, she didn't bother offering her wine, but went straight to the grape juice. The girl scowled at her. Rosemary gave her a cheeky grin. "Maybe in a few years, I'll be offering you wine," she whispered.

"If you survive that long," Genevieve said through gritted teeth.

Rosemary looked at the girl, who flashed her a charming smile and giggled, and Rosemary giggled back, slightly baffled by the joke.

As she continued round the table, there was another knock at the door.

"Oh no!" Rosemary said under her breath to Athena. "What now?"

"It's probably just Finnigan," Athena said. "Don't worry. I'll get it."

"I forgot about him!" Rosemary said.

"I wish you forgot about him earlier and stopped giving me a hard time," Athena hissed and bolted towards the door. Rosemary stuck her head out of the parlour to check if the new arrival was indeed Finnigan. The broody teen stood in the doorway, eyes locked on Athena.

Satisfied that it wasn't any other uninvited guests, Rosemary ducked back to the kitchen to tell Marjie it was time to serve the salad.

"Way ahead of you," Marjie said, holding a big tray of salad bowls.

Rosemary picked up a second tray of salads and headed back to the dining room, passing the teenagers, who seemed to be hovering by the door.

"I have to leave," Finnigan said.

"But you only just got here."

"Sorry." He turned to Rosemary, looking awfully pale. "Thank you for your hospitality, uhm, be careful."

"I'll...see him out," Athena said.

Rosemary shook her head in astonishment. "Teenagers are so peculiar," she muttered to herself, but as she wandered back towards the dinner party, she felt a creeping suspicion about The Boy.

CHAPTER
TWENTY-FOUR

Athena was relieved to escape the noise and bustle of the dinner party, even if it was only for a few minutes. Despite the comparative peace outside, she walked Finnigan out with a jumble of questions circulating in her mind.

"What was all that about?" she asked when the front door was closed.

"Shh," Finnigan whispered. *Not here. Some of them have powerful hearing.* He said in her mind.

He took Athena's hand and led her around the side of the house. She felt even more perplexed and slightly concerned.

"This should be far enough away," Finnigan said, still keeping his voice low. They had passed the conservatory and were almost at the back of the house, near the forest.

"What is going on?" Athena asked. "And why do we have to keep our voices down, can't we speak telepathically?"

"It doesn't come easily to you yet," said Finnigan. "There's too much of a risk of getting things mixed up, and I want to make sure that doesn't happen."

"Things are about as clear as mud," Athena said. "Why couldn't you stay for dinner? What's wrong?"

"There are enemies in your midst," Finnigan said.

"How can you tell?" Athena asked suspiciously. "Actually, there are supposed to be enemies at the dinner party. That's all part of the plan."

"You plan to dine with evil-doers?"

"Why do you speak in such an old-fashioned way?" Athena asked.

Finnigan shrugged. "Athena, they are our mortal enemy."

"I still don't understand what you're talking about," said Athena. "Can't you tell me? Who are the enemies? We've just invited all the suspects who might have killed Granny Thorn, but we don't know which one it is."

"They are not one," said Finnigan cryptically. "They are many."

"Why are you speaking in riddles? It's almost like you're not even able to tell me the truth." This thought upset Athena so much that tears pricked the corners of her eyes. After all, this was a life and death situation – not a time for playing games.

"The truth is bound," Finnigan said, just as a gust of wind blew his hair away from his grey-blue eyes. He turned as if responding to a sound that Athena could not hear and stared off into the forest as a thick mist started to descend over the trees.

"Come with me," he insisted. "I can keep you safe from them."

"No," Athena said. "I can't. My mother would kill me, and anyway, I hardly know you."

There was a moment of silence, and then Finnigan spoke. "I must go now. I wish I could protect you. Please be safe. Do whatever you can to get them out of your house. You're much more powerful than you realise."

"Finnigan..." Athena reached out for him as he walked backwards into the forest.

"Goodbye Athena. Take care."

"Wait!" Athena said, but it was too late.

Finnigan had slipped away into the mist. She watched as it curled around him, and for a moment, Athena could have sworn his features flickered into something more ancient and beautiful and slightly frightening.

As he disappeared, his voice echoed inside her mind.

You are one of us. Stay away from the enemy. They will only do you harm.

CHAPTER
TWENTY-FIVE

Rosemary walked into the dining room to start distributing the salads with Marjie right behind her.

"Psst! Rosemary!" Marjie hissed from the side of the room, where she'd put her tray down on a cabinet.

"What?"

"Come with me for a minute."

Rosemary followed Marjie just outside the door and out of earshot of the guests.

"I can't believe you're trying to feed vampires human food!" Marjie said, quietly but urgently.

"What?" Rosemary said. "I realise my cousins are very pale, but I don't think they're vampires."

"Oh, not them!" Said Marjie. "But several of the others!"

"Who?!" Rosemary asked.

"It's not polite for me to say," said Marjie. "They get rather cross if you start telling people about their...condition. Vampires are very private."

Rosemary frowned. "Honestly, Marjie – how was I supposed to know?! It's not like I'm asking about their sexuality or anything," she said. "I simply want to know which of my guests want to drink my blood." Rosemary gulped, trying to ward off her own rising panic. There was too much new information to process, and she felt flustered. Athena was nowhere in sight, and the guests were no doubt getting hungry.

"Leave it to me," Marjie said. "I'll just enchant a few of these bowls so that they're vampire-friendly and everyone will be none the wiser."

"What happens if they just eat regular food?" Rosemary asked.

"You don't want to know," said Marjie. "It gets very messy. You just go and check on the chocolate tarts, and I'll sort this out."

Rosemary headed off to the kitchen, feeling flustered. The chocolate tarts were cooked, so she removed them from the oven to set and then headed back to the dining room, where the salads were all laid out. All of them looked completely normal, and Rosemary eyed the guests warily, wondering which of them were vampires.

Athena was still mysteriously missing, but reappeared moments later, blushing slightly. Rosemary was too relieved at her return to be cross about her temporary vanishing act. It had probably only been a few minutes, but still she wasn't too happy about the short time she'd spent not knowing where her daughter was.

Get used to it, Granny's voice said in the back of Rosemary's mind.

What? Granny? Is that actually you?

'Course it is, Granny replied. *Now eat something before you get low blood sugar and completely lose it.*

Rosemary scoffed down her salad, wondering how much Granny knew, or how much she could reveal about the present situation.

Which ones are vampires? Rosemary asked in her mind.

It's rude to say, Granny replied. *But you can probably work it out easily enough.*

I cannot tell. They all look perfectly normal to me. Rosemary surveyed her oddball guests. *Well, not normal, but not evil.*

Don't stereotype vampires like that, said Granny. *That's also rude. They're no more evil than human beings...well, most of them.*

Granny's assertion was slightly reassuring to Rosemary, who had felt rather prickly about having vampires at her dinner table. She surveyed the guests to see if she could tell which ones weren't breathing.

They certainly were an odd bunch. Constable Perkins was getting slightly sloshed, looking even more clown-like and attracting disturbed glances from Elamina and Derse, who had only just recovered from their shock when Marjie – who they must have assumed was a servant – sat down on the other side of them to eat. Burk appeared to be wrapped up in a conversation with Liam and Sherry.

Rosemary thought about it for a while. She hadn't seen Sherry during the day, only at night at the pub. Did that mean...? The only other two guests she'd never seen during the day were the gate-crashers, Covvey and Agatha, who both seemed harmless, if a bit rough around the edges.

Rosemary wondered if that meant that they were the vampires here. *Is it common for vampires to invite themselves to dinner? Don't they need to be invited in?*

She would have appreciated a reply to these questions, but Granny seemed to have vacated the space she'd been occupying in Rosemary's mind.

Of course, there was still Burk with his cold hands and his supernatural speed, though Rosemary had seen him in his offices during the daytime and in the pub at lunch. She really knew so little about vampires outside of fiction and wished she could ask Marjie or Granny more questions.

As Athena and Marjie served the soup course, the whole house seemed to tremble, making some of the glassware tinkle subtly. The guests looked at each other and then at Rosemary, who merely shrugged, though a concerned glance passed between her and Athena.

What's going on with the house?!

Rosemary watched the guests carefully for anything suspicious. Just as they were finishing up the soup, Burk excused himself and got up from the table, saying he needed a pit-stop.

Rosemary had been waiting for just such an occurrence.

Aha! she thought. *He's trying to steal the decoy box!* She got up from the table a moment later, saying she was going to check on the main course, leaving Athena to keep watch over the other guests. Instead, she made her way directly to the parlour, only to find it empty. The box was still exactly where it ought to have been, undisturbed.

Panic shot through Rosemary. She felt an urgent need to check the library, but as she headed in that direction, she noticed a tall, dark figure standing by the stairwell. She froze, her mind darting back to the crow man, but as her eyes adjusted to the lack of light, she realised it was Burk standing there.

"Uh, hello?" Rosemary said. "The loo is the other direction."

Burk turned towards her, a pained expression on his face. "He was here, wasn't he? This was where it happened?"

Rosemary gaped as an entirely different kind of panic floored her. *He knows!*

"I don't know what you're talking about," Rosemary said, trying to play dumb.

"My brother..." Burk said. "He's been missing for days, which wouldn't normally be too unusual. But I was wondering after the attack on your house..."

"Perseus..." Rosemary tried to think of a million reasons why she couldn't possibly have killed his brother, but none came.

"I can sense his essence," he said. "It was here that he...that he died. The dusting, it leaves a residue, you know."

Rosemary coughed. "Oh...gross..."

"Tell me the truth," Burk said, his voice steady and even, but chafing around the edges. "It was you who did it. You killed him, didn't you?"

There was nothing for it. "Yes," Rosemary said. "He attacked us. He went after Athena..."

Burk's eyes were dark as onyx and Rosemary wished she could take back her confession for fear of retribution. What was she thinking, incurring the wrath of the Burk family so openly and readily? They'd surely come after her and make the rest of her life a living nightmare, for as long as it lasted, anyway.

But Burk just grimaced, tears gleaming in corners of eyes. "I suppose he had that coming," he said.

"You—you're not mad at me?" Rosemary stuttered.

"He would have killed you," said Burk. "You know what we are, don't you?"

"I knew what he was, but..."

"You must have known. You fed me blood-enchanted food."

"That was Marjie," Rosemary insisted. "She told me there were vampires here, but that it would be rude to tell me who they were."

Burk gave a dry chuckle. "People in this town are so polite. But you must have suspected me."

"I didn't think it was genetic," Rosemary said.

"It's not," said Burk. "It's a long story as to how we both got turned."

"I have all night, I guess," said Rosemary, only to be interrupted by a loud scream from the direction of the parlour, followed by another great tremble from the house. "On second thought, maybe we can save the story for another time!"

Rosemary ran back to the dining room to see the guests disbursing out into the hallway. Her eyes widened as she looked through the open door at the carnage as she was buffeted back by strong winds.

Terrifying darkness quaked from the centre of the room in the form of a vortex. This one was even more intense than the one that had appeared at the front door days earlier, and it seemed to have opened up in the centre of the table. An ominous, low vibration underscored the swirling black darkness inside. Gales of wind blew in both directions at once, sweeping out of the room, around the sides of the chasm, and pulling in through the centre. Rosemary braced herself against the strong currents of air, checking for everyone's safety but mostly looking for her daughter.

"Athena!"

Several of the dinner guests clung to the side of the room. Elamina and Derse gripped tensely onto the windowsill, and Constable Perkins was wrapped around the cabinet on the other side of the room, groaning softly.

"Athena!" Rosemary called.

Suddenly, her daughter was at her side.

"The house can't hold all these people!" Athena called out. "I knew this was going to happen!"

"It's the family magic," said Marjie, from behind them. "You've done something to start the unbinding process, but it's only partially complete. It needs to be released fully or..." Marjie's words trailed off.

Rosemary didn't want to know what came after the "or". She could guess well enough that more chaos and danger would ensue.

"You can do it, Rosemary," Marjie said. "You're the one with the power here."

"Yes, Mum, you can. This is our magic – and you're the one Granny Thorn chose to inherit it after all."

"But I don't know what to do!" Rosemary shrieked, beside herself with panic. Suddenly the burden on her shoulders was overwhelming, and she felt shattered, as if the disconnected parts of herself would never reunify into a cohesive whole. Anxiety was a vise in her chest, tightening her breathing.

"Just calm down dear," said Marjie. "It will come to you."

"Yes," Athena said. "Calm down and look within. Remember?"

"You know I hate that," Rosemary said, trying to breathe deeply, though the tightness in her torso made it impossible.

"There's no time like the present to change your mind and become its biggest fan," said Athena. "What did Granny Thorn's song say? Meditate in a forest of something?"

Rosemary wanted to argue and kick and scream, but there was no time for regressing to her childhood state and throwing the tantrum she felt was warranted. She had to take action. All her defence mechanisms were to run and hide, but that wouldn't work now. She had to take back control. She couldn't waste any more energy feeling panicked. Instead, she closed her eyes.

She listened to her own heart beat in her chest.

Calm, she instructed her body. *Calm down. Focus.*

She waited a moment longer until she felt a gentle easing and then took several deep, slow breaths. It was time to focus. There was no time to go to the actual forest now, like the song implied, but everyone kept telling her to bloody well look within, so, keeping her eyes closed she imagined she was in a forest.

The sounds around her faded to birdsong with a distant rumbling. The gales softened into a summer breeze. Rosemary wandered deeper into the forest.

It was so beautiful, so peaceful she could stay there all day, but an urgency tugged at her. She followed the humming sound into the darker and darker wood all around her, with barely any light filtering through. Then, up ahead, she saw it.

The giant light crystal shone through the vines from which it was trapped.

What do I do? Rosemary asked in her mind, seeking guidance from anyone who might hear her, but particularly from Granny.

You must have confidence in yourself, Granny's voice responded.

Thank goodness you're here with me, Rosemary thought, relieved.

I'm always with you, my dear. You just need to connect with your true self and you'll sense my presence. I'm always watching out for you.

Rosemary quashed her frustrations with Granny for the moment, figuring this wasn't the time to relitigate the 'why didn't you just tell me?' line.

Please give me solid instructions on what to do next, Rosemary replied.

First, trust in yourself. Have confidence...then, when you're absolutely sure of yourself, reach out and touch the crystal – not the vines and say the words I taught you.

What words? Rosemary asked frantically.

But Granny's presence had vanished again.

"Infuriating old bat!" Rosemary muttered. *Okay...so I just have to be confident. Rosemary. You are awesome. You've got this. Everything is coming up roses. This will be a piece of cake. The right words will come. It's obvious. Just go for it!*

She reached out towards the crystal, careful to avoid the vines. She managed to only hesitate slightly as her arm extended.

Her hand connected with the light crystal. A great jolt of energy coursed through her, making her feel powerful, indeed...and slightly high.

"Wowee! Okay. The words are...Blue, lace, dance?"

Nothing happened, except the vines began to bulge and creep tighter around the crystal, slowly inching closer to her hand.

"Oh, crud!" said Rosemary, then wished she could take it back, as "crud" clearly wasn't a magic word either.

She closed her eyes and took a deep breath.

I'm looking within...I'm being confident...I'm unbinding the family magic...

A shimmer of light swirled in the darkness in front of her. She could feel her wildness growing, blooming, breaking free from the cage it had been locked in.

Another voice broke through her thoughts, and this time it wasn't Granny's. It was an ancient voice, but light and airy and fresh at the same time.

You are not ready. You must connect to your elemental core to free the Thorn family magic.

"Drat!" said Rosemary as she was immediately jolted out of the forest in her. She found herself staring up at the ceiling of Thorn Manor.

CHAPTER
TWENTY-SIX

"Blasted bloody Hades!" Rosemary yelled.

Liam and Marjie stood over her, looking concerned.

"What's going on?" she asked. "Where's Athena? What happened to that massive chasm in the dining room?"

"I'm here, Mum," Athena said from behind Marjie. "And things seemed to have settled down in there.

Rosemary propped herself up, relieved to see her daughter, and doubly relieved that the chasm, along with its vortex of doom, had disappeared. "Well, I can't say that was a rollicking success," she said.

"What happened?" Athena asked.

"I was about to ask you the same thing," said Rosemary. "Not much at all happened on my end – I'll tell you that!"

Rosemary felt light and agile following her encounter with the huge crystal. She jumped up and gave Athena a big hug before attempting to assess the damage. The dining room was in chaos and the few remaining guests were keeping well clear. Some of them were even milling around outside the house. She checked the parlour to find that the decoy box was, indeed, missing, though she was pleased that the door to the library remained locked. When she opened it, the real box was still firmly in place on the table.

I hope Marjie's spell worked, Rosemary thought. *Otherwise, we're back to square one.*

She was even more furious with Granny Thorn than she had been earlier. *Couldn't she have thought to mention me needing to connect with my elements or whatever?! Perhaps left me a handy instruction manual?*

It was a strange thing for Rosemary to ask for, seeing as she never read the instructions properly on anything, preferring to just muddle through on intuition and blind luck. But this particular situation clearly called for a detailed set of guidelines.

She apologised profusely to the remaining guests and told them she'd invite them back another time, though most of them looked at her as if they'd rather not chance it.

She noticed some distinct absences, too. Elamina and Derse were gone, as were the gate crashers. Ferg was nowhere in sight, and neither was Mr June. To Rosemary's slight disappointment, Burk had also made himself scarce. She'd been wanting to find out more about the mysterious vampire.

Despina and Genevieve were also understandably absent. Rosemary had some sympathy for them. She certainly wouldn't want to have any child in her care near a nightmare like the one that just appeared in the dining room.

Constable Perkins, his cheeks still flushed from wine and sherry, insisted on sticking around to investigate. He promptly fell asleep at the kitchen table, snoring slightly.

Marjie discretely informed Rosemary that there was no hope of her tracking charm working since the vortex had scrambled all the energetic traces in the house.

"It looks like spaghetti," Marjie said.

"Oh, bother," Rosemary replied, disappointed that the evening she'd planned had been such a dismal failure.

Marjie insisted on sticking around. She and Athena had started on the dishes. Their clanking and chattering in the kitchen did not seem to disturb the police officer, who was clearly out of it. Rosemary made a note to ask Marjie what her secret was with getting teenagers to do chores so easily.

Aside from that, the last guests to leave were Liam and Sherry, who both kept offering to help clean up. Rosemary told them there was no need to do anything now, assuring them that if she needed help, she'd call them tomorrow. Sherry gave her a tight hug on her way out. Liam, however, lingered a little longer, his muscular frame taking up most of the doorway.

"Err, Rosemary?" he said, keeping his voice low so as to be out or earshot of the others.

"What is it?

"This might be a bad time, but...I was wondering, when things have settled down a bit...would you like to go out for a drink?"

Rosemary shrugged. "Of course," she said. "It'll be nice to have a bit of a catch up."

She was perplexed as to Liam's obvious discomfort and seriousness until, after a bit more erming and arring, he mentioned the word 'date.'

"Oh!" said Rosemary, taken aback. "Erm...What about Sherry? I thought you two were..."

"Sherry?" said Liam, his eyes widening in surprise. "Sherry's my cousin!"

"Oh...I didn't realise. I don't remember meeting your family. Thanks for...err, thinking of me," Rosemary said. "This is a really terrible time, and also, I don't date."

Liam's handsome face fell, and Rosemary felt a twinge of regret.

"But...if I ever do want to...err, go out. I'll give you a bell," she said.

Liam smiled, slightly sadly, and left without a goodbye.

Rosemary closed the door, baffled and embarrassed. There wasn't any space in her life for romances – despite Liam's sweetness and the good times they'd shared as teenagers. Rosemary was even more confused by the small candle she might be holding for a certain...vampire! Sure, both of them were charming and good-looking, but life was far too complex to add dating to the mix. It didn't seem like things would get any simpler in the foreseeable future, either.

No thanks to Granny! Rosemary thought sharply, daring her grandmother to respond.

What is it now, pet? Granny responded.

You didn't think to tell me I had to connect with the elements or whatever?

Oh, Rosemary, Granny replied. *You did more than enough of that when you were younger.*

Did I? Really? Before you addled my memory, you mean?!

It's all still there, silly. You just have to connect with your inner self.

"Aghhh! This is infuriating!"

"What is, love?" Marjie asked.

"Yeah, Mum, we've been watching you pace around the house, making funny faces, for the last ten minutes. Are you finally losing it?"

"Granny is in my head. Only she's being just as infuriating as she was before!" Rosemary grumbled.

"That is super weird," said Athena.

"Say hi to Galdie for me!" Marjie said, as if it was all perfectly normal to her.

"I'm starting to feel like I never really knew her," Rosemary said, sighing. "It's like the version of her in my head was just a tiny fragment of who she was, and I don't really remember her properly. Who was she? What did she even like doing?"

"Oh, Galdie was enthusiastic about so many things," said Marjie. "She was right into crafts. Loved embroidery. She spent a lot of time hiking in the bush, collecting wild herbs for her various magical workings...Oh, and the dancing of course."

"I remember the crafts and the dancing," Rosemary said.

"Oh, yes, Galdie loved a good cèilidh," said Marjie. "She'd get on her yellow dancing shoes with the bright blue laces..."

"Wait a minute!" said Athena. "What did you just say?" She shot Rosemary a sharp look.

"She'd put on her favourite dancing shoes," said Marjie. "That's all dear."

"Blue. Lace. Dance!" Rosemary made the connection, and a second later, she and Athena had bolted upstairs to check Granny's room again. Sure enough, in the top row of shoes in the wardrobe sat a pair of yellow suede shoes with electric blue laces.

"Interesting choice of colour combination," said Athena, as Rosemary reached up to grab the shoes.

"What now?" Rosemary asked.

"Look inside, silly!" said Athena.

Rosemary reached inside the soft suede of the shoes to find a small silver key.

"So, this was really what Granny meant?" Rosemary asked. "I wonder what it's for?"

"It's a double clue!" Athena cried, taking the key from Rosemary's hand and rushing to the small bedroom. "I bet there's a keyhole on that box somewhere. It's really clever of Granny Thorn, don't you think?"

"I've never seen a keyhole on that box in my life," said Rosemary dismissively, as Athena picked up the music box and spun it around, examining it.

"Look – here, it's just at the back next to the wind-up-thingie," Athena pointed to reveal that there was, indeed, a tiny keyhole.

"Okay, Miss Smarty Pants. What do we do now?"

"What do you think, Mum? Here." She held out the key for Rosemary to take.

Rosemary felt a tingle of nervousness and excitement. Clearly, Granny Thorn had put a lot more thought into this than she'd previously realised, not that Rosemary was ready to completely forgive her just yet.

She cautiously fitted the key into the lock and turned it, expecting sparks to fly and magic light to beam out all over the place. However, it was a perfectly ordinary latch.

It clicked open, revealing a false bottom to the jewellery box.

Inside was a stack of paper, an inch thick, covered in Granny's cursive scrawl.

Rosemary reached forward, but Athena was too quick.

"Hey!" Rosemary said as her daughter began scanning the pages. "Give that here!"

"You hate reading the manual!" Athena said in an accusing tone.

"It's a...manual?"

"Well, not exactly," said Athena. "But from what I can tell it's a whole lot of useful details."

Rosemary and Athena spent the next couple of hours poring over the notes Granny had written, interrupted only by Marjie, who seemed to know better than to ask questions, but delivered a tray of re-heated mutton and roast potatoes to the door before she left to head home. Rosemary and Athena gratefully scoffed the food while continuing to read.

As for the information they'd discovered, some of it was perfectly self-explanatory – like 'this is where I keep the keys to the car – make sure you get it serviced regularly. Take it to Daisy's on the west side of town, and whatever you do, don't let Ferg try to do it. He is not a trained mechanic!'

"Why did Granny Thorn keep that kind of thing locked up so secretively?" Athena asked. "It seems like basic useful information."

"Maybe because she thought it would be sensible to keep all the useful information in one place where we couldn't find it!" Rosemary said, exasperated. "And while it would have been great to know about the car keys when we first arrived. I haven't found anything remotely useful for our current situation yet. Half of these pages are gobbledygook."

"Look!" Athena said. "This page is all about the binding – there are little drawings of the vines and...ooh, it doesn't tell us anything we haven't already worked out."

"Let me guess? It says 'look within?'"

"Pretty much," said Athena, handing Rosemary the page. "Ooh – but this is useful!"

"What?!" asked Rosemary.

"It describes how the house and the Thorn family power are connected via another secret dimension – that explains where you've been popping off to when you lose consciousness."

"Great," said Rosemary. "If only knowing that helped us figure out how to break the binding. You know it's strange, when I touched the crystal before, I felt so...energised, and I still feel it a bit, now. It's like I'm buzzing with energy."

"That's funny," said Athena. "When you hugged me after you came to, it felt...well, it felt pretty wild actually."

"Wild how?"

"Kind of as if a wave of golden energy washed right over me," said Athena. "Maybe it's the Thorn magic, trying to get back to us in any way it can. I wonder if that's what settled the energy in the parlour down and closed up that cavern. Do you think that if you just went back in to the netherworld, or whatever it is, that you could just stand there and draw the energy out until it was all released from the binding?"

"I'm not a bloody car!" said Rosemary. "It's not as simple as fuelling up, you know. The crystal told me I wasn't ready, and besides, I didn't like the look of those vines. I was terrified they were going to come after me and choke me or something."

"It was worth a shot." said Athena. "I wish that more of this made sense." She held up some indecipherable pages.

"What's that one?" Rosemary asked, pointing to another page in Athena's lap. "Look! It says The Bloodstone Society on it!"

She grabbed hold of the page along with those immediately following it.

"What does it say?" Athena asked.

"The Bloodstone Society is an ancient secret society, blah-blah-blah."

"Mum – that actually sounds useful to know."

"You're right," Rosemary said. "It says here they grew powerful not only by drawing on the power of their members but also by stealing the power of old magical families."

"Like ours!" said Athena.

"Exactly. It says they were once the terror of the magical community – worldwide. The members bound their souls to the Society in exchange for power and are forever at the mercy of their tyrannical leader. Apparently, many old witch families went into hiding to escape them, including through resorting to the desperate measure of binding most of their own power so that it was undetectable. That way they just appeared to have the same level of power as regular magical people."

"So that's what Granny Thorn did?"

"It seems likely," said Rosemary. "It says here that the clan's power has been waning, which only makes them more desperate and dangerous. They must have come after Granny – figured out about the old family magic. That's probably what Granny's letter was talking about. Remember the one she left for us when we first arrived? They come by tooth, claw, and fang. It says here that some members are vampires and shapeshifters. I guess granny was cryptically alluding to it while trying to keep this secret."

"Why would she want to do that, though?" Athena asked. "If someone was trying to kill me, I'd be shouting their identity from the rooftops."

"I guess it's possible that the Bloodstone Society has ways of tracing the people who talk about them," Rosemary said and shuddered.

"But I guess they already know all about us now, so we're in no more danger by saying their name or anything," Athena said, though her tone was anxious and doubtful.

"Or maybe...the authorities are in on it," Rosemary said, feeling uneasy about the police officer supposedly asleep downstairs.

"Or that they are so powerful they make it impossible for people to talk about them – remember how Granny Thorn couldn't tell us who killed her?" Athena said.

"That's true. But don't you think we should check on the sleeping cop in our kitchen, just in case?"

"He's harmless," said Athena. "I'm sure of that – aside from his suspicions of us!"

Rosemary was about to argue, but then her eyes landed on something else. "Athena, look!"

"What is it?"

"It's a piece of a waxed seal that Granny must have stuck on here – and I know where I've seen the other part of it." She got up and raced to the library with Athena following close behind.

Rosemary unlocked the door to the library, relieved to see everything in the room was in place. She dashed in and began frantically searching the shelves. "It must be here somewhere!"

"The box is still on the table," Athena said.

"Good! But I'm looking for something else."

"What?"

"Hmm..." Rosemary ducked behind the desk and emerged triumphantly a moment later, clutching a piece of paper.

"What is it?" Athena asked.

"Look," Rosemary said, matching the substantive part of the seal she had just found with the piece remaining on the invitation.

"So, we have...a little coat of arms thing?"

"Yes! With a crow, snake, wolf, and a Celtic knot."

"Tooth and claw and so on?" Athena asked, sceptically.

"I've seen it before," Rosemary said, squinting at the shield. "I just know that I have..."

"Oh, no...not your memory again!" said Athena. "Anyway, enough about the stupid seal. How do we stop this awful secret society from killing us for our power?"

Rosemary took a closer look at the scrawled writing on the other page she was holding, on which Granny had taped the piece of seal.

"From what it says here, it seems like their power has been depleted slowly over the years, while ours only builds up more because it's connected to the earth. So, Granny was anticipating that our magic would have surpassed theirs very soon. In fact, it seems from this, like she was just about to try to release the binding herself and go after them when they snuck up on her!"

"I couldn't help but overhearing..." a voice boomed from the doorway.

Rosemary jumped, turning quickly to see Constable Perkins standing there in a posture clearly intended to bar their exit.

Was he actually asleep this whole time? Rosemary wondered. *Is he part of the Bloodstone Society, coming in here to finish what they started?*

The officer took a step towards them and reached into his pocked.

Rosemary flinched, terrified he was reaching for a gun or some kind of magical weapon.

Instead, he pulled out a large handkerchief and blew his nose loudly. Rosemary and Athena gave each other grossed-out looks.

"You're one of them, aren't you?" said Rosemary. "The Bloodstone Society."

"I take offence to that!" said Constable Perkins, stuffing his soiled hankie back into his pockets. "I happen to have been after that society for decades."

"So, you know they were the ones who killed Granny and not us," said Rosemary.

"I'm jumping to no such conclusions," he said. "After tonight's fiasco, it's hard to know what to believe. This whole thing could have been a set-up, staged by you two, including the conversation I just overheard."

"Are you meaning to tell me you've been after them for decades and that's the only hypothesis you've come up with?" Rosemary asked, flabbergasted.

"I'll have you know I have a number of suspects!" the officer said. "And they are a tricky bunch to catch. They all keep changing their identities, and no one – not even those in the society who I have apprehended over the years – knows who the leader is."

"Oh, yeah?" Rosemary asked. "Who are your suspects then?"

"Mum!" Athena whispered, trying to kick Rosemary, who stepped out of the way to avoid her daughter's foot.

"Proof," Rosemary demanded, "– or you're just making it up."

Constable Perkins glared at Rosemary, then fished inside his blazer pocket and pulled out a notepad. He flicked through a few pages then held it up for her to read.

POSSIBLE BLOODSTONE MEMBERS
Ferg – always involved in every little thing.
Mr June – power seeking.
Perseus Burk – nocturnally inclined and wealthy.

ROSEMARY WAS BLOWN AWAY by the banality she saw on the page, but before she could react. Constable Perkins stepped further into the office.

"I'm taking this box as evidence," he said, reaching out for The Box.

"No!" Rosemary cried, trying to get in Constable Perkin's way.

She was too late to stop him.

A sudden bang sounded, and a bright flash of light filled the room. It quickly faded to reveal the unusually dressed police officer lying on his back on the floor.

Athena gasped.

"He's alive," Rosemary said, checking his pulse. "But it looks like he's out cold. Oh, my goodness. This is not a good look! Quick, help me drag him out of here. I want him as far away from the box as possible when he comes to."

"We can't just drive him somewhere and leave him by the side of the road, can we?" Athena asked.

"I don't think that's wise," said Rosemary. "He's suspicious enough of us as it is."

It was tough work, but they managed to get him out to the lobby and then spent several minutes wondering what to do. Eventually, they decided there were no good options.

"We'll figure it out in the morning, I guess," said Rosemary. "It's well past midnight; we should sleep."

"What? With him down here?" Athena asked. "I don't think so. It's too creepy."

"Well, let's have a cup of tea to settle our minds, and maybe we'll think of something brilliant."

Brilliance wasn't required. As Rosemary and Athena sat on the window seats sipping their tea, they heard a cough from the lobby. On further investigation, Constable Perkins had gotten himself up off the floor, and seemed to be blushing, as if he'd quite embarrassed himself. He thanked them for a lovely evening and left, seemingly forgetting about the whole incident earlier.

Rosemary sighed in relief, then looked slightly concerned. "Do you suppose he's alright to drive? He looked a bit tipsy earlier."

"What? Him?" Athena asked. "He only had a tiny glass of sherry and another of red wine the whole evening. What a light-weight."

"Maybe the drunkenness was an act," Rosemary suggested. "People probably tell you all kinds of strange things when they think you're too drunk to remember."

"Do you think he's a double agent?" Athena asked. "He could be part of the Bloodstone Society and just pretending to investigate them. Maybe his idiocy is just an act."

"Could be," said Rosemary. "And what about The Boy?"

"Who, Finnigan?" Athena asked, rubbing her eyes.

"The very same," said Rosemary. "Don't you think it was suspicious how he showed up and then just disappeared? He could be one of *them*."

"Mum," Athena said, frowning. "Don't start."

"Seriously," said Rosemary. "That boy is a bad egg, I can tell."

"He's not an egg at all," Athena grumbled, but they were both too tired to have a proper argument about it.

"He did try to lure you away," said Rosemary half-heartedly, as she checked the front door to make sure it was locked. "I bet he was trying to abduct you. What is he, a shapeshifter?"

Athena had a strange look in her eyes that only made Rosemary more concerned than she had the energy to be.

"Don't be ridiculous," said Athena.

"How did he even know to come to dinner?" Rosemary asked. She took out her earrings and yawned.

"I invited him, remember? You said I could. I texted him, but he didn't reply."

"Unreliable, or too busy plotting against us?"

"You're wrong about this," said Athena. "I'm a good judge of character."

"Yeah, well so was I before I met your father."

"See, this is all really about you and your questionable life choices," said Athena. "My brain's broken. Need. Sleep." She zombie-walked upstairs, followed by her similarly exhausted mother.

Rosemary slipped into her pyjamas and into bed. As she drifted off to sleep, a connection flared in her mind.

Despina! she realised. *It was Despina who wore that same emblem on the seal on her badge the first time she came to the door. She must have been trying to send us a message – to show us she was powerful, even though we had no idea.*

"I knew she wasn't to be trusted. Estate agents are trouble," Rosemary muttered to herself as she scrambled up and wrote herself a hastily scrawled note so that she absolutely did not forget. After all that, she slept like a newborn baby – which is to say, she slept fitfully and woke several times in the night – but at least, she did get a little sleep.

CHAPTER
TWENTY-SEVEN

R osemary woke to the sound of clanking in the kitchen. The sun was already high in the sky, and though she was grateful for the sleep in, her entire body was filled with the led-weight of dread. She dragged herself out of bed immediately.

Athena's bed was empty. Rosemary rushed downstairs in terror, only to find her daughter making pancakes on the griddle.

"You scared me half to death!" Rosemary said.

"Don't be so paranoid then," Athena replied.

"Don't I have a right to be paranoid after all that's happened recently?" Rosemary asked, sitting down at the table and pouring herself some tea. She was still half-way through processing all the events of the past day. One memory in particular, as it flooded back, was enough to make her snort her tea in accidental laughter.

"What is it?" Athena asked.

Rosemary coughed and tried to clear her sinuses. "Oh nothing," she replied. "Did you know that Liam and Sherry are cousins?"

"Gross!" Athena cried. "I knew this was a small town, but that is *sordid*!"

"No," said Rosemary. "Not like that. They're not together."

"How do you know?" Athena asked.

Rosemary was silent for a moment, thinking back to the conversation she'd had quietly with Liam.

"He asked you out!" Athena shouted from across the kitchen.

"How did you know that?" Rosemary asked. "You're not that good at guessing."

Athena blanched. "I sort of...sensed it inside your head."

"How rude! Give a woman some privacy!" said Rosemary. "Wait a minute – how on earth...?"

Athena smiled at her mother, a slightly guilty expression on her face. "I think my powers are coming in."

Rosemary got up from the table and wrapped her daughter in a big hug, and then stood back and pinched her cheeks. "My little witch is all grown up."

"Shut it, Mum!" Athena complained, pushing Rosemary away.

Actually, let me try something.

"Try what?" Rosemary asked.

"Oh, my gosh! It worked!"

"What worked," Rosemary asked.

I said that only in my mind.

"You did?"

You see, my lips aren't moving.

"Wow!" said Rosemary. "Wait, let me try." *Bananas are pink,* she thought.

"They tend to be kind of yellow," Athena said.

"It worked!" Rosemary crowed. "I'm telepathic!"

"No. I am," said Athena. "I can read your mind. I don't think you can read mine."

Rosemary paused and tried to concentrate on Athena's thoughts. "Unless you're really thinking nothing, my telepathy isn't working, after all!"

"Maybe you don't have it," said Athena, shrugging.

"Not fair," said Rosemary, then she narrowed her eyes at Athena.

"Not that look. Wait, are you worried or suspicious?"

"Both," said Rosemary, her mind racing at the new revelation. "Firstly, are you okay? Do you think this could be dangerous?"

"I'm fine," Athena said, clearly downplaying the situation to calm her mother's fears.

"I'll take you word for it, for now anyway," said Rosemary. "But secondly, you've been keeping this a secret from me, haven't you? When did all this start?"

Athena lowered her gaze towards the pancakes and focussed on flipping one, then murmured. "Actually, it first started around the time I met Finnigan."

"What! Not him again. I told you he was suspicious," said Rosemary. "I can't believe you didn't tell me. That was days ago!"

"At first I thought it was just him I could read and who could hear my thoughts. He said we were the same in some way."

"Both telepaths, eh?" Rosemary asked, feeling even more apprehensive.

"I guess," Athena said. "That's kind of how we got to be friends so quickly. But I never heard anyone else's thoughts, well, not clearly."

"But you heard something?"

"Yes...but it was blurry, like little murmurs or tones, but nothing clear enough to understand. I felt a bit crazy, like my head was becoming an out-of-tune radio, picking up on all kinds of things, but nothing made sense. Last night, after you hugged me, it became a bit clearer, but it's still really annoying."

"And *why* didn't you tell me?"

"You seemed to have enough on your plate already, without having to look after a daughter who was losing the plot," Athena said. "I didn't want to worry you."

"Or share about your private interactions with a boy!"

"Or that," Athena admitted, walking over to the table with a big plate of pancakes.

Rosemary sighed, taking a pancake and squeezing the juice from a slice of lemon over it and then sprinkling on brown sugar in the traditional way. She then rolled it up and scoffed it, just like she always did.

"These are really good. Thanks," Rosemary said.

"You're mad, aren't you?" said Athena.

"Only a little. You know I want to know what's going on with you."

"Yes – and you also want to know where I am at every single moment. It's getting a bit much, Mum. You're smothering me."

"It's dangerous here!" Rosemary insisted.

"So what? The world's a dangerous place and I'm a teenager. I need my freedom."

"Give me a while to adjust, okay?" said Rosemary. "I've only known about magic and all this other scary stuff for a week. It's going to take me a while to let you wander in the woods alone."

"You're the one who's supposed to be wandering in the woods," Athena reminded her. "Chillin' with your inner self and all that."

"Don't remind me!"

"You really should do it, though," Athena said. "It's the only lead we've got at the moment, and things are looking dire. Who do you think is responsible for all this? And don't say Finnigan!"

A knock sounded from the front door.

Rosemary answered it to find there was no one in sight. A note sat on the doorstep, written on a pink card.

Despina!

Rosemary suddenly remembered her realisation from the night before. She rushed upstairs to check her hurried scrawl.

"Are you alright?" Athena asked, still seated at the table as Rosemary clomped back down the stairs.

"It's Despina!" Rosemary cried.

"The estate agent? Are you being prejudiced again?"

"No. I remembered it last night. Despina was wearing a strange brooch when I first met her. It was the exact same pattern as what was on that seal!"

"Really?" Athena said. "If that's true, why would she wear the Bloodstone Society logo it in public? Wouldn't that be too obvious?"

"Except that it's a super-secret logo!" Rosemary said. "So secret that Granny had to hide it and give us silly clues. Or maybe she's just so confident because she's in the upper echelons of the society. She doesn't need to hide because she's so powerful. She was sending us a message, but we didn't understand what it was."

"True," said Athena. "I couldn't find anything about them online, not even their stupid logo, which means wearing it only sends a message to people who are in the society or already know about them. If she's the leader, she can be as bold as she likes."

"And look – this note was just left on the door on pink cardboard. Can you think of a single other person who'd do that?"

"Erm..." said Athena.

"No! See. I told you! Despina's awful. That poor little niece of hers. Imagine having to put up with an aunt like that?"

"What does the note say then, Nancy Drew?" Athena asked.

Rosemary opened the card up and read it.

"Oh, no!" her face fell.

"What?"

"Oh, no, no no!"

"Mum?"

"The Spring Festival!"

"I thought we'd decided to skip it in light of everything going on here," said Athena.

"Read this," said Rosemary, holding out the note.

SEE *you at the Imbolc Festival...or else everyone there will burn!*

"WELL, THAT'S OBVIOUSLY A TRAP," said Rosemary. "There is no way I'm falling for it. Estate agents are not telling me what to do and neither are secret society leaders. Certainly not anyone who is both!"

"Maybe she knows we'll think like that," said Athena. "It's too obvious, otherwise."

"Then you think we should go?" Rosemary asked. "She's just going to sneak into the house and steal the magic!"

274

"If she was going to do that, why not try at any other time when we were out?" Athena pointed out. "They obviously need us for something."

"We have to go!" said Rosemary. "She won't suspect that. Ooh, unless she thinks we'll think that, and so she really does want us to go. Ugh, I hate being manipulated when I don't even know in which direction! Let's just go."

"And walk straight into a trap? Besides, what will we do? We don't really have any controllable powers."

"If they are planning something terrible, we can warn the people – get everyone out of the way. Children will be part of the festival, remember? Remember all those young, innocent faces? If they're at risk, they must be protected."

"Okay, fine," Athena said. "Let's go save the children, but don't say I didn't warn you."

Rosemary checked the box on the table in the library one more time. It looked innocent, but it was apparently powerful enough to protect itself from every other threat so far. It stood to reason that it – and the family magic – would be safe if they left the house.

They hurriedly got dressed and then jumped into Granny's car and drove to the town square. The whole place was packed with people, most of them wearing robes and carrying boughs of spring blossoms. Clearly, the entire town attended these things.

Once parked, they ran towards the circle within the square where everyone seemed to be gathering for the Imbolc ritual.

Rosemary looked around frantically for anyone who looked suspicious. She could see the young children in their little blossom costumes, all lined up and ready for the ritual to start. Ferg seemed to be instructing them on what to do next.

"Over here," Rosemary said, guiding Athena around the circle of people towards Ferg, who was wearing brown robes draped in a cherry blossom printed shawl.

"Should we warn Ferg?" Athena asked. "He seems like he's in charge. He could get everyone out if there's danger."

Rosemary looked at Ferg, suspicious. "No. We have to keep an eye on him."

"Do you suspect him?" Athena asked.

"Well, Constable Perkins does."

"I'm not sure that's an adequate reason," said Athena. "Besides, aren't we supposed to be warning people?"

"Change of plans," said Rosemary. "Let's be stealthy. Just watch for anything suspicious."

"Ah!" Ferg said, turning towards them. "Perfect timing. My spring maidens!"

"Your what, now?" Rosemary asked.

"You're not exactly dressed for the occasion," said Ferg, eyeing their jeans and dark coloured coats. "But you'll do. Here!"

He held out two flower crowns, adorned with ribbons and spring blossoms.

"What...?" Rosemary and Athena both said.

"Put these on and go and stand by the children. You don't have to say anything – just walk around the circle when it's time. The kids know what to do."

Rosemary tried to argue, but Ferg insisted, and besides, she reasoned they'd have a better view of the ritual from inside the circle, so she gave up and agreed despite Athena's glaring.

They put on the flower crowns and stepped inside the circle, next to the row of children.

"I feel ridiculous!" Athena hissed.

"Welcome to my world," said Rosemary. "I feel like this often."

"If you're suspicious of Ferg, why are you doing what he says?"

"I'm suspicious of a lot of people," said Rosemary. "I don't know who is helping Despina, but she's clearly the ringleader. Besides, he's right. It's much easier to see everything from inside here." She squinted at the crowd, trying to find the estate agent among the many faces there, but saw no sign of her.

"There must be two hundred people here!" Athena said. "Surely they can't all be in on the secret society, or it wouldn't be a secret."

"They all look pretty innocent to me. Just keep an eye out for that estate agent, or anything dodgy," Rosemary said.

The crowd hushed as the ritual began. Rosemary felt a stillness descend around them, a peacefulness. A few weeks ago, she would have assumed it was just in her mind, but now she was sure it was part of the magic of the ritual, drawing on the power that seemed to hang in the air above the town. Though she had always known Myrtlewood was special, she had never felt so aware of the town's magic as she did now. She could almost see it, the sparkle in the air, the shimmer, as a light breeze whipped around the circle.

Mr June, wearing a long blue grey cloak strode into the centre and waved his arms dramatically in the air. He performed a poem about the end of winter and the beginnings of spring. Despite his theatrics, Rosemary could feel the truth in his words, feel the natural environment surrounding the town as it willingly gave way to the seasonal change.

She allowed herself to close her eyes briefly, searching for something inside, her wildness, the disconnected parts of herself, perhaps even her magic.

Mr June stepped out again, and three women took his place, summoning in the new energies of warmth for the year and asking for the blessings of the goddess Brigid. Two of them held baskets of flower petals, which they began to scatter while the other one walked around, holding a large wand with an amethyst crystal at the end and "cast the circle" around everyone.

Rosemary could feel the energy condense around them, bringing them closer into the experience as many around the circle echoed her words. "This is sacred time, this is sacred space. I am fully present, here and now.

Rosemary knew she should be on the lookout for danger, but instead she found herself focussed on the present moment, the feel of her body, and the energy around them.

The women stepped back again. Other people standing at the four direction points announced they would summon the four elements.

"Pay close attention," whispered Athena.

"Why is there something suspicious?"

"No, this is elemental magic. Remember? You have to learn it."

Rosemary took note as the directions were called. Air from the east felt light and refreshing; fire from the south brought a burning warmth into the circle; water from the west a cool, soothing connection, and earth from the north was stable and solid.

"Now," Ferg said, stepping forward. "We all know the best way to bring in the warmer months is by dancing! The children and spring maidens will lead us in this dance! Go on!

Rosemary and Athena looked at each other and gulped.

"Err..."

"Come on!" one of the children said, grabbing Rosemary's hand and leading her and Athena into a free and frivolous dance. The children began skipping and twirling. Rosemary, Athena and the entire crowd followed suit, imitating the uninhibited way the children spun and jumped, gradually leading them all in a spiral towards the centre of the circle.

The dancing was tremendous fun. Even Athena seemed to be enjoying it, but Rosemary was keeping her eyes peeled for suspicious behaviour all the while. As the dancers made it to the centre of the circle and then turned around to spiral out again, she caught a glimpse of someone in a dark hood – someone ominous looking. Rosemary grabbed Athena's arm and pulled her in the direction of the dark hooded figure. They followed, ducking around various villagers as they ran.

The figure was headed out towards the boundaries of the circle.

"Rosemary!" Marjie cried, wrapping her in a big hug. "I didn't expect to see you here after such a late and troubling night, but I'm so glad you could make it."

Rosemary tried to reciprocate Marjie's smile, but kept her eyes trained on the figure, as did Athena.

"Excuse me," she said and continued to hurry after the suspicious character, only to lose sight of them near the lawyer's office building.

"Well, that was a dead end," said Athena. "You don't suppose they just vanished into thin air, whoever it was?"

"I bet it was Despina," said Rosemary.

Athena sighed. "It was too tall to be Despina."

"One of her cronies, then."

"Look, Mum. The ritual is wrapping up now with no incidents. The children are fine. You don't suppose this whole thing of making us come here was just a—"

"You're right," Rosemary said as dread condensed in her gut. "It was a triple trap, or maybe just a regular old trap. This was all a ruse to get us away from the house!"

"I thought so!" said Athena.

"Well, if you were so sure you should have told me," Rosemary replied. "Come on. Let's sneak away before someone else tries to chat to us and get back to Thorn Manor as fast as possible."

CHAPTER
TWENTY-EIGHT

As Rosemary and Athena neared the house, dark storm clouds were brewing in the sky directly over the property, despite the late afternoon otherwise looking rather clear and sunny.

Rosemary drove up the driveway to see dozens of dark-hooded figures, black masks obscuring their faces, surrounding the house. The shadows in the sky seemed to be growing above them, spreading out to cover the area around the house. They blocked out the sun, making it seem like night.

"This is bad!" said Rosemary. "This is very, very bad. Do you think we can just turn around and run away?"

"No," said Athena. "I think we're well past that."

Rosemary's heart raced as she realised it was true. Running away now would only result in more problems, which was annoying, because running away was by far her most preferred option. She continued driving, passing some of the figures, who turned to watch as the car pulled closer to the Thorn Manor.

"Mum...what are you doing?" Athena asked, fear rising in her voice.

"You're right," Rosemary said. "I need to confront this head-on. Stay in the car. I'll try to talk to them."

"I don't think they're here to talk, Mum. Besides, if you are going to talk, I think it's safer if I come with you to stop you putting your foot in it," Athena said.

"Not in a million years, kid," said Rosemary. "Stay right here. If talking doesn't work then at least the closer I get to the house the more likely the family power is to kick in and give me super strength."

She got out of the car, shivering from both the chill in the air and from the fear that pricked the skin on her arms, giving her goosebumps. As she turned towards the house, trying to maintain her composure, the hooded figures began chanting in low voices, uttering words in a language Rosemary did not understand but suspected was Ancient Greek or Egyptian, perhaps.

"Hello!" Rosemary called, trying to sound cheerful to dilute the atmosphere of tension and fear. "Err, is Despina about? I'd like to have a few words..."

A dark swirling vortex appeared above the house, as if summoned by the chanting. Rosemary watched, horrified, as an enormous shadowy beast emerged from the vortex. It was shaped like a huge Celtic dragon. Its scales glinted gold and red as it circled in the sky, and then, looking directly at Rosemary, it began flying straight for her!

Rosemary turned back to the car to see her daughter's expression of terror, mirroring her own.

"Athena! Run!"

Athena shot out of the car, and they both ran for the woods surrounding the house, jumping over brambles and dodging through thickets. The hooded figures were after them – chasing them through the trees. Rosemary tried to keep an eye on Athena as they ran, though it was a difficult task with all the obstacles in their way.

Rosemary shrieked as a bird swooped from the sky, transforming mid-flight into a hooded man, and falling into a nimble crouch on the ground.

"We meet again," the man said, pushing back his hood to reveal his scarred face. Rosemary recognised him as the crow man who had appeared unconscious in the house a few nights before. Verikus.

Athena shot her mother a terrified look as the sound of footfalls caught up with them.

"I've got no time for this," Rosemary said.

"Mum, duck!" Athena cried. Rosemary dived to the ground just in time as Athena hurled one of her home-made concoctions she'd stashed in her pockets towards Verikus, who screeched as a cloud of grey smoke burst from the charm, sending feathers flying.

"Nice one," Rosemary said as they kept running. There was no time to stop and assess the damage, as the rest of the Bloodstone Society were still hot on their heels.

Rosemary was almost out of breath. She tried to keep her eyes on her daughter, but Athena was too fast. She disappeared into a dense cluster of bushes.

Through here!

Rosemary heard Athena call out telepathically. She shot through the bushes, only to find a small clearing.

Athena was nowhere in sight, and neither were the hooded beings.

"Athena!" Rosemary yelled, and then held her tongue, not wanting to attract any more attention. Her heart thudded so rigorously in her chest that she felt it might leap right up into her throat.

She looked around the clearing, unsure of which direction to head. One path among the trees seemed lighter, as if it were glowing somehow.

I'll take that as a sign.

Rosemary followed it as it wound through the trees, her eyes darting all around for her daughter, fearing she had been taken by the enemy, hoping against hope that Athena was okay. She ran quickly at first and then slowed as the air began to feel unusual – lighter and denser at the same time, as if it was carrying more energy, laden with magical charge.

The further Rosemary progressed down the path, the brighter the air around her seemed to be, as if it was itself glowing. Golden.

This is a special place, she realised. *One of Granny's special places in the woods.*

At the end of the path was another smaller, circular clearing with a large boulder in the centre, a perfect size for sitting on.

Rosemary perched on the boulder. She took a deep breath and tried to calm her mind.

I need to find Athena and somehow stop Despina and her cronies – in that order, but I don't know how to do either of those things.

She closed her eyes and tried to listen out for Athena's telepathic voice – but there was only silence. Then a memory of Athena came back to her instead, urging her to meditate.

*Well. There's no time like the present...*Rosemary thought. *And at this point, what else can I do?* So many of Granny's words pointed to looking within, and to the forest, after all.

She sat cross-legged on the boulder and closed her eyes, just relaxing and breathing, listening to the sounds around her and allowing her mind to go blank, and from that blankness, she fell into darkness.

Rosemary found herself in the void again. Just like before, she held the crystal in her hands, but this time, it glowed brighter. She held it up above her head, allowing the light to shine over her. Then, intuitively, she held it to her heart.

As the cool glassy surface connected with her chest, Rosemary felt something shift inside her mind – an opening – and with that opening came a tidal wave of energy – a flood of memories and feelings; her childhood time spent wearing a bright-red felt cape, following Granny in the forest down the special path as Molly the cat wandered stoically behind them; learning about herbs, mixing potions in the kitchen, summoning the forces of nature; playing in the water, in the sea and streams, dancing with the wind; carefully lighting the sacred fires, lying on the very boulder that she now sat on, and connecting with the earth.

Granny was right – I do know this. I did all the elemental training I needed when I was a child.

She felt a strong sensation of unravelling in her chest.

Whatever had pulled her into pieces and bound those pieces to keep them apart all those years ago loosened. She leaned into the feeling as if unwrapping treasure, buried deep inside.

To her great satisfaction, the disparate parts sprung together like magnets.

From within came a purposefulness, a deep knowing. She was still that wild little girl that danced in the rain, even though the world had done its best to beat the joy and freedom out of her. She was sick of being a victim, at the mercy of fate, and now she understood that she didn't have to be. Not anymore. It was time to wake up and take control of her life. It dawned on Rosemary that she was unleashing a great power – not the old family magic, as yet – but her own power, which had been carefully bound along with it.

She was re-claiming a part of herself that had been taken away, and with that, all the walls and blockages of insecurity inside her came tumbling down. Rosemary connected with her own powerful confidence – her true self.

A huge wave of light rushed out from her. In her mind's eye, it swept across the surrounding land, vast and powerful, sweeping away the shadows, clearing the sky.

The dragon reared up. Rosemary could sense it above her body, seeking her out, just as she watched from the sky. It circled the house and then flew over the forest, diving towards the clearing in which she sat.

Oh, no, you don't.

From her aerial vantage point, she gathered the energy around her, the life force of the forest, the hum of magic from Thorn Manor, the new pulse of power inside her. Weaving all this together, Rosemary could feel her bond with Athena, feel her daughter reaching out with her mind, joining in with her own energy.

Rosemary pulled all these forces together into a powerful ball of energy and hurled it with all her mental might towards the dragon.

A wave of energy blasted through the air, sending Rosemary careening back into her body. She opened her eyes, raising her arms over her head. Above her, the light shone brightly through the trees. A feminine shape hung in the clouds above, somehow reminding Rosemary of the spring goddess Brigid. Rosemary smiled, and though she was sure it was probably an illusion, she issued a silent prayer just in case.

Thank you for your blessings, Goddess.

As Rosemary lowered her arms, the trees around her seemed to murmur in awe, rustling their branches.

She stood up, glowing with energy. She could feel Athena's presence now and knew exactly where to find her. Rosemary walked back along the forest path, heading directly for the house. The trees seemed to part for her, because there surely were no obstacles in her way as, with a flicker of gold in her eyes, she approached Thorn Manor.

CHAPTER
TWENTY-NINE

All was silent as Rosemary neared the house. The sky above had cleared and there was no sign of the black-clad beings or the beast, or even of any birds or insects for that matter. The wave of energy from Rosemary's mind really had swept them all far away just as she'd imagined.

There was no sign of Athena either. Rosemary's heart beat a drum in her chest, determined to find her. With magically enhanced senses, she could tell that her daughter was somewhere inside – taken by the Bloodstone cronies to use as leverage.

Rosemary entered through the front door. The house felt almost empty. Eerie. But she could feel her daughter's presence, and something else that set the hairs on her neck standing on end.

Mum! Get away! It's a trap! Athena's voice rang out in Rosemary's mind.

Rosemary walked directly to the library to find Athena there, sitting in the chair behind the desk, her wrists tied to the armrest. Rosemary felt equal parts relief that Athena seemed to be okay and horror that someone had restrained her like that, but both feelings were quickly overruled by a righteous rage.

"What are you doing here?" Athena cried, tears streaming down her cheeks. "I told you to get away!"

"I'm not leaving you," Rosemary said.

"Don't you see? She's got you right where she wants you..."

Athena's words trailed off as footsteps sounded outside the door.

Rosemary braced herself, still awash with her newly released magic, but cautious.

The door opened and little Geneviève walked in, wearing a silver pant-suit, her hair tied back in a tight bun.

Rosemary let out the breath she was holding. "Are you okay?" she asked. "Are you lost? Can you tell me where your aunt is?"

"Mum!" Athena said. "She's..."

"Cut that out," Genevieve said, her voice deep and gravelly. "I'm six thousand years old and I'm tired of being treated like a child."

Rosemary was stunned. "You're a..."

"A vampire, of course," said Geneviève. "I thought you figured that out already, despite being so dense. I must admit it did surprise me when you fed me blood-enchanted food. I suppose that was just Marjie getting things to run smoothly. Little did any of you know that I had other plans."

"You...?"

"The magic in the house already made it volatile. I just gave it a little nudge to generate that vortex. I needed to get rid of all those people and get you back on track towards unbinding the magic," said the very small, very young looking, very old person.

"You can do magic?" Rosemary asked.

"Being the leader of the Bloodstone Society has some advantages."

"The leader? It was really you driving all this." Rosemary said, aghast.

"Yes, I think we've covered this," said Geneviève, sounding bored. "You've done exactly what I planned you would do. Everything is working out exactly as I intended. Now give me the box or the girl dies," she pointed a finger at Athena, who shuddered.

"No, Mum. Don't do it."

"I think you're mistaken," said Rosemary. "It's just an ordinary box. Go ahead. Pick it up and see for yourself."

"Nice try," said Geneviève. "I knew full-well that that box in the parlour was a fake."

"So, it wasn't you who stole it?" Rosemary asked.

"Of course not. That would have been silly and pointless. I know all about this box, and I know you are the only one who can touch it."

"Except that I can't," said Rosemary. "Every time I've touched it, I get transported to who knows where."

"Try it again," Geneviève instructed. "I do believe that now you've unlocked your own magic properly – which that dragon gag was designed to do – it will work just fine."

"That was just an illusion?" Rosemary asked.

"Oh no," said Geneviève. "It was a manifestation of the Bloodstone power – which is much greater and vaster than you can imagine." Her expression was pointed, and her tone was cold and impatient. "So, you should be very afraid and do as I say. Now, if you'll just pick up the box and hand it to me – officially giving me the Thorn family's magic – I'll leave you alone, to rot, in peace."

It sounded a lot like a rather flippant business transaction.

"Erm..." Rosemary said.

"No! Mum! Don't do it!" Athena cried.

"Shut it, sweetie," said Geneviève, pointing her finger threateningly at Athena.

"I knew I didn't like you from the start," Athena said, glaring. "Mum, whatever you do, don't listen to her."

"Rosemary," Geneviève said with an edge in her voice. "Do exactly as I say if you want your daughter to live."

"You expect me to trust your word after you killed my grandmother?" Rosemary asked, as conflicted rage and the urge for vengeance clashed with fear and the absolute need to protect Athena.

"What choice do you have?" Geneviève asked. "Sure, I admit it. I killed the old bat. It took years of planning, and it was hard to even track her down, but once I set my mind to something, I achieve it.

Always. It's not easy being trapped in such a young body. No one takes me seriously, but it does have its advantages. I laid a trail to throw her off the scent. She knew someone was after her and I knew she suspected my 'aunt' just like you did. I was careful to use magic to mask what I truly am, so she never suspected me. And when I showed up looking distraught one night with my hair all tangled, she let me in and made me a cup of tea. When her back was turned, I set a trap and brought the whole clan in to make sure she didn't have a chance of getting the upper hand. She held us off for a while with her magic, but in the end, we broke through. I used a binding charm with my final blow to make sure she couldn't come back as a spirit and blab about me or the Society."

Rosemary took a deep breath. "Thanks for your honesty, I guess," she said. "But nothing you've said makes me trust that you'd let us live, so why should I hand you the box?"

"Stubborn." Geneviève gave a tired sigh and pouted. "Your Granny could have lived too if she hadn't been so stubborn."

"I don't believe that, Mum, and neither should you," said Athena. "Don't do anything she says."

"I don't have all day," said Geneviève sternly. "The box, Rosemary. Give it to me now or the girl gets vaporised!"

The gleam of gold flashed again in Rosemary's eyes. Only Geneviève was too fixated on the box to notice.

Rosemary felt the confidence of her own true power course through her in all its gleaming wildness, and in that moment, she knew exactly what to do. She walked over to the desk and picked up the box to find that Geneviève was indeed correct. She didn't black out or find herself on another plane this time.

Mum...no!

Despite Athena's continued telepathic urging for her to drop it, Rosemary did not, nor did she hand it to the very young-looking old vampire.

Instead, urged on by the centre of energy within her, she opened it.

Rosemary found herself back in the other world – but this time it was on her own terms.

Darkness still surrounded her, though the light crystal she held shone much brighter. The space around her was no longer a total void but was illuminated, revealing shimmering cave walls all around.

She knew instinctively where to go. She walked purposefully through the cave to see the elder standing before her.

"You have arrived," the elder said, her silver hair shining brighter and her eyes glinting with pride. She gestured for Rosemary to walk ahead towards the familiar sight of the thick dark green vines wrapping around the huge, shining crystal.

This time, Rosemary did not hesitate. She moved forward with self-assurance to stand before the centre of the Thorn family's bound magic. She reached out and confidently took hold of the elder's hand, lifting her other hand to connect with the crystal.

A wave of light rushed through her.

You are ready, the power said, light and bright in Rosemary's mind. She closed her eyes and sang the words she now knew intuitively were the ones she had been taught for this very purpose all along.

COME AWAY MY LITTLE CHILD,
    through the forests of the wild.
    Feel the pulling deep within,
    Trees will dance and trees will sing,
    until they die and fall
    elemental magic calls,
    until we let the light shine through, rise up, and seize it all.

AS SHE SANG, the elder's voice joined hers in harmony. The song reached deep into her heart, into her soul, into their shared genealogy and twisted like a key.

Around her, the sounds of a thousand voices rang out in harmony.

Her ancestors were around her, behind her, supporting her. The newly reunited parts of Rosemary Thorn breathed a collective sigh as the old family magic flooded in, coating her from the inside out in strength and grace, nourishing the neglected parts of her spirit and psyche.

This was it. This was her destiny.

Rosemary let all her elemental memories flow through her mind, and her magical recollections of Granny, of being in the forest, of being connected to nature and to the old family magic.

A cracking sound pierced the air.

They watched as the crystal shattered, the vines shrivelled up and everything around them seemed to break apart into pieces.

Rosemary opened her eyes to find she was in the library, still standing this time.

"What happened?!" Geneviève demanded, clearly flummoxed. "There was a bright light and I couldn't see. I thought I would melt! What was that?" She stepped forward to take the box from Rosemary's hands, only to find it empty. The power was no longer contained. It was hovering in the air, throbbing through the house, pulsating in the veins of the Thorns.

"No!" Geneviève shrieked, her eyes glowing red just as smoke began to coil up from her shoulders.

"The Thorn family magic has been released," said Rosemary, her own eyes glowing golden. "And it's more powerful than the Blood-stone Society's."

"It is not!" cried Geneviève. "You'll pay for this, Rosemary Thorn!"

A torrent of flame burst out from Geneviève's small frame. It built up into a furnace, and another dragon remerged, smaller than the one summoned by the group of Bloodstones, but somehow fiercer. Some books caught alight and others fell to the floor as it circled in the air, stirring chaos through the room, before roaring towards Rosemary.

But Rosemary was prepared. She let the power surge up inside her, even stronger than before, now that she had unbound the Thorn magic. She did not falter, did not waver as the flaming beast shot towards her. She simply raised her hands confidently and released her power. A wave of magical water burst out, cool and refreshing, dowsing the flames in the room, but not dampening anything.

Geneviève shrieked and blasted another wave of power out towards Rosemary. It was black as night this time. Rosemary met it head on with a bright beam of golden light, blasting Geneviève's own magic back at her.

Rosemary and Athena watched as the small, ancient, innocent-looking evil being burst into dust, leaving the box to tumble to the floor where it lay open. Silvery particles, which had once belonged to the ancient evil being floated in the air and then moved swiftly towards the empty box as if being sucked in. The lid swung shut with a click.

Rosemary ran to Athena and untied her, then wrapped her in a big hug that her teen didn't even try to push away.

After a moment of silence, their eyes flicked towards the box.

"Do you think she's dead?" Athena asked.

"I suspect so, seeing as she was vaporised," said Rosemary.

"Good riddance," said Athena.

"I know she wasn't really a child, being six thousand years old and all," said Rosemary. "But it still feels wrong."

"She kind of had that coming, though," said Athena. "You did well, Mum."

"Thanks," said Rosemary. It felt odd accepting the praise, but she'd take it, as positive feedback was rare from her teenager. "Ick…" said Rosemary. "It feels so wrong. I'm glad that box did the clean-up. I would hate the idea of having to get her essence out of the carpet!"

THIRTY

R osemary and Athena made their way out of the library towards the kitchen, clearly in need of a cup of tea, but a humming sound distracted them.

They checked the front windows to see a small crowd appeared to be gathering outside Thorn Manor in the evening light.

"What's all this?" Rosemary asked, warily.

"It looks to me like...friends," said Athena. "Look. There's Margie and Sherry...oh, and Constable Perkins!"

"I suppose we'd better go and see what this is all about," Rosemary said with a fleeting glance of longing in the direction of the tea kettle.

She opened the door and stepped out towards the group, ready to meet them.

Constable Perkins approached.

"You're both under arrest!" he shouted.

"What?! What for?" Rosemary asked, surprised.

"For...for...disorderly behaviour and...and...disturbing the natural order of things, that big flash of light and all them clouds and the blimin' dragon came from here, they did!"

"Stand down, constable," said a cool and confident voice.

Rosemary looked over Perkins's shoulder to see a woman with arrow straight black hair and flawless porcelain skin, wearing a sleek black suit.

"Err, Neve," Constable Perkins said, looking disgruntled. "It's okay, love. I've got this."

"I said, stand down. And as your superior, you'd best obey me," the woman said, stepping forward to shake hands with Rosemary. "I'm Detective Constantine Neve," said the woman. "But everyone just calls me by my surname, Neve."

"Constantine is your first name?" Rosemary asked.

"Indeed, it is. My parents had a strange sense of humour. Anyway, I apologise for my colleague's behaviour. He likes to think he runs the roost, especially when I'm out of town on business, but he knows I'm also the acting head of the local police station since Captain Sledge retired."

"Oh...erm...nice to meet you," said Rosemary, trying to make a good impression.

Detective Neve, in her sleek black suit, seemed rather normal, aside from her name, and for a moment, Rosemary wondered if she actually knew about all that magic stuff...until she opened her mouth again to explain.

"I've been on the case of the Bloodstone Society for months. Only they led me on a wild goose chase half way around the country. I knew Despina Crepe was involved, but I figured she was a minor level member. I had no idea about Geneviève."

"I suppose someone so powerful and experienced would have a habit of staying off the radar," said Rosemary, empathetically. "I thought Gen was a sweet little girl."

"What happened to Despina?" Athena asked.

"There's no sign of her, I'm afraid," said Neve. "Or of the others."

"I suppose that's a good thing," said Rosemary. "If I never see them again, that will be just fine. But how did you know what just happened up at the house?" she asked, narrowing her eyes a little.

Neve laughed. "You're shrewd. I don't blame you. Like I said, I was travelling all over the place, trying to follow the trail, which was clearly all a set-up. Only it took me two weeks to realise it. They clearly wanted me out of the way. I came back in time to consult my scrying mirror and see what happened up at the house just now. That was brilliant. Thank you for what you did today. Congratulations on a job well done!"

Rosemary and Athena both beamed, delighted by this turn of events, while Constable Perkins scowled.

"Alright, Gerry," she said, putting a hand on Perkins's shoulder. "Let's get you back to the station before you end up red-carded again." She led him away, making space for Marjie to rush forward and wrap both Rosemary and Athena up in a big warm hug.

"You both did your Granny proud today!" she cried. "Now, if you don't mind, I'll pop inside and put the kettle on and rustle you both up some dinner since you missed the Brigid's Day feast."

"There was a feast?" Athena said. "Why did no one mention that?"

"Of course there was!" Marjie said. "There's always a feast after a ritual. But don't worry. I brought plenty of left-overs and lemon cake for dessert!" She held up a big cloth bag bulging with cake tins.

"That sounds perfect," said Rosemary. "I'm starved."

No sooner had Marjie bolted for the front door, then Sherry came forward and hugged them, too. "I knew you could do it. Excellent work – all round. Come over to the pub tomorrow for lunch or dinner on me!"

Athena nodded enthusiastically.

"Thanks, that would be lovely," said Rosemary, noticing Liam hanging back behind Sherry, rather than coming forward to chat. She wondered how long it would be before he was comfortable speaking to her after that previous awkward conversation, but she didn't have much time to think about it before Ferg stepped up, holding a small box wrapped in a yellow bow.

"What's this?" Rosemary asked, taking the box, cautiously.

"A small gift of my own homemade fudge," Ferg said. "I heard through the grapevine that you were quite the connoisseur of confectionary in your youth."

"Ooh...how thoughtful," Rosemary said. "Thank you."

"Thank *you*, madam." He lifted his brown Saturn-day cap and tipped it to Rosemary and then to Athena. "Mademoiselle. Good day to you both."

Rosemary and Athena looked at each other, slightly puzzled, but smiling warmly.

"Excuse me," a familiar deep and silky voice said. Rosemary was pleased to see that it was Burk. "I came here to apologise," he said.

"For what?" Rosemary asked.

"For disappearing during your dinner party. I wish that I could have helped you more, only...I was trying to lay low. I've been on the run from the Bloodstone Society, and I knew they were after you."

"Oh...why?"

"I used to be a member...a long time ago, I had to earn back my soul, only they weren't happy about it. They came after me and I had to magically obscure my identity from them. I didn't want to get too involved here, in case they found me out. It's a strange sect, you see. None of the members know who each other are, unless they choose to reveal themselves. Only the leader knows who all of them are...I only tell you this to keep vigilant. There are bound to be society members lurking around Myrtlewood."

"You were a part of them?" Rosemary gaped.

"I was," said Burk. "But I left over two hundred years ago."

"You're really...old," said Rosemary, and then blushed as she realised that had sounded quite rude.

"I told you, it's a long story," said Burk.

"I hope to hear it sometime," Rosemary said, smiling before she was whisked away to be greeted and thanked by Mr June in his official capacity as Mayor.

Mr June gave a speech in which he declared that even the Goddess Brigid herself had blessed the town with her presence and was spotted in the air above Thorn Manor.

Athena gave Rosemary a questioning look.

"Ah, so that's possibly what I saw in the woods..."

Athena shook her head, incredulous.

Mr June ended his speech and then bowed and proclaimed Rosemary and Athena as both VIM's – Very Important Myrtlewoodians. He even handed them little gold brooches depicting an M with a myrtle tree growing behind it.

"Uh, thank you," said Rosemary, surprised by all the spontaneous gratitude as the crowd around them cheered.

A few people scampered out of the way as a shiny Rolls Royce pulled up the driveway, driven by a chauffeur.

"This can only mean one thing," Rosemary muttered to Athena.

Elamina wound the back window down and beckoned Rosemary and Athena over with her index finger. Rosemary kept a safe distance from the clouds of lily of the valley perfume that wafted out of the car.

Burk came over to stand with them, too, though whether out of curiosity or protectiveness Rosemary couldn't tell.

"The family magic is flooding back," Elamina said, a look of astonishment on her face. "I don't know how you did it, but it worked."

"Great," said Rosemary.

"You exceeded my expectations," said Elamina, coolly, while Derse maintained his usual sneer on the seat beside her.

"When I discovered Granny had left you the house, I was beside myself." Elamina continued. "My apologies regarding your Burkenswood office, by the way," she said to Burk. "I didn't mean to set it on fire. I just lost control of my power when I heard about the house going to Rosemary. I didn't believe she would have what it takes to release the family magic. Oh, and about this..."

Elamina reached out and handed Rosemary the decoy box. "Here," she said. Clearly, she'd been the one to steal it from the party.

Rosemary glared at her cousin. "Thanks," she said flatly.

Elamina gave a little shrug. "I didn't think you'd have what it takes to release the binding," she explained. "I tried to take matters into my own hands, but you tricked me."

"I'm not going to apologise for that, you realise," Rosemary said. She certainly wasn't planning to grovel for forgiveness when Elamina hadn't apologised to her.

"Very well." Elamina turned to Athena. "Aren't you charming?" she said. "Sorry about all this fuss. Goodbye, sweety."

Rosemary balked as Elamina gave a little wave and the window slid up.

The Rolls Royce retreated back down the driveway and Rosemary grumbled. "She apologises to everyone but me! Typical...Still, at least I was right about one thing. I was sure Elamina was responsible for that fire!"

"I'll give you some credit for that one," said Athena.

They looked around at the somewhat disbursed crowd.

"Well, this was all kind of...grand!" said Athena. "I suppose we can get back to normal, whatever that means now."

"That's right, school starts next week!" said Rosemary. "Which is the day after tomorrow."

Athena groaned. "Just when I was starting to relax."

"Clearly, the fun never stops around here!"

Just then, Athena turned her head in the direction of the driveway. Rosemary followed her gaze to see Finnigan, looking like a perfectly innocent teenager.

Athena shot her mother a pleading look. "It clearly wasn't him," she said. "You had no right to be suspicious."

"You never know," said Rosemary. "It *was* another young-looking person, but okay, fine, I'll admit you are a much better judge of character than me."

"Can I hang out with him, then?"

"Oh – go on then" Rosemary said.

"Really?"

"Yes. Go and spend time with your friend for a little while before dinner, but stay within shouting range of the house and be sensible!"

"I'm always sensible," Athena said, flicking her flaming red hair over her shoulder as she walked off towards The Boy. "It's you who should be following that advice," she muttered.

"I heard that!" said Rosemary and smiled as she turned and headed back for Thorn Manor, and tea, and dinner, and cake.

LATER THAT EVENING, Rosemary and Athena sat on the window seats, drinking tea as they looked out the windows towards the forest.

They were feeling full and satisfied after eating more of Marjie's wonderful pasties and cake, and they'd even opened the fudge Ferg had given them as a gift which was surprisingly delightful.

"This is really good," said Athena.

"Yes," Rosemary agreed. "Smooth and rich with a hint of elderflower."

"Who would have thought Ferg was an excellent confectioner."

"I wish *I* was a confectioner," said Rosemary. "You know how much I love chocolate."

"Well, you can be whatever you want now, Mum," said Athena. "Your destiny is in your hands."

"Thanks," said Rosemary. "I'm not sure if that's wise, epic or just an incredibly cheesy thing to say."

"Why not all three?" Athena asked. "And while we're at it, I think we've learned something today."

"Like don't trust innocent-looking tweens?" Rosemary suggested.

"Yes, that, and also you learned to use magic on purpose, not just by accident, which makes you at least thirty percent less ridiculous than usual."

"Gee, thanks," said Rosemary. "Do I get an award?"

"Smugness is its own reward. You should enjoy it. Besides, you have nothing to complain about. Your magic actually works, whereas I still don't have any cool powers apart from a buzzing brain with occasional telepathy."

"It's probably a good thing," said Rosemary, taking another sip of tea and smiling at her daughter. "I'm not ready for you to be all-powerful yet. You're already enough of a know-it-all."

"Hey," said Athena, laughing and giving her mother a playful shove.

"I wonder where Dain is," Rosemary said, becoming more serious. "It's strange how I still keep forgetting him, even though I've remembered almost everything else...at least I think I have."

"I'm trying to forget he exists, actually," said Athena. "Seriously, Mum, we're better off without him."

An owl hooted, and they looked back out into the garden.

"Do you think they're out there, watching us?" Athena asked.

Rosemary shook her head. "No. Neve thinks they've cleared out of town. After that performance, it seems like Despina won't be showing her face for a while."

"But the others," Athena said. "We don't even know who they are."

"True," said Rosemary. "And now that their power has diminished, they'll want to keep it that way. Besides, from what Burk said, a bunch of them will be relieved to be able to cut ties with the Bloodstone Society."

"Burk *and* Liam, hanging off your every word," Athena teased.

"Don't start that again," said Rosemary. "Anyway, back to the subject at hand. What did you learn today?"

"I've learnt..." Athena started, and then her eyes went wide. "Mum!"

"What?"

"Something is watching us again!"

Rosemary looked out the window to see a pair of glinting eyes in the darkness, reflecting the moonlight. "An animal...?" Rosemary started, but whatever it was began moving closer, a dark shape, low to the ground, darting towards the house.

"What?" Rosemary started, but Athena had already run towards the door. "Don't open it!" Rosemary cried, but it was too late. "Athena!"

Athena opened the door and bent down to retrieve the creature.

She turned back towards Rosemary, holding a fluffy black kitten with dazzling green eyes.

"We're witches, right?" Athena said. "Apparently, that means we attract cats."

Rosemary stepped closer, and the little black floofball leapt into her arms. "What in Brigid's name!?" she said, cradling the adorable purring creature.

"You've done well, dears," said a kind and familiar voice, coming from the mirror across from the door.

"Granny!" said Rosemary, realising the resentment and anger she had felt for the old woman had evaporated, most likely over the course of unlocking her magic.

"You've done well and I'm proud of you both."

"Ahh, thanks," said Rosemary, stroking the cat. "I think I get it now; why you had to do what you did."

"I'm not perfect," said Granny. "I could have done a thousand things differently and possibly better, but it was the only way I could think of at the time to keep you both safe until you were ready, and now you clearly are." She smiled warmly.

"Can you explain this, then?" Athena asked, nodding towards the kitten.

"It's Rosemary's familiar, dear," said Granny.

"Familiar?" Rosemary asked. "It really is just like fiction."

"Why does Mum get a familiar?" Athena asked, scratching the kitten's head. "Where's mine? I've always wanted a cat."

"We can share," Rosemary suggested. "I've always been afraid to get a pet in case I can't look after it properly. It's hard enough keeping both of us alive, clearly."

"Don't worry, Athena," said Granny. "Yours will come in time, as soon as your powers properly kick in."

"Molly was your familiar, wasn't she?" Rosemary asked, remembering Granny's old mottled cat.

"Indeed, she was, and she was with me right until the end. Familiars last as long as their witches, all going well."

"I can't wait!" Athena said. "I really will get cool powers *and* get to have a cat. Livin' the dream!"

Granny nodded sagely. "Indeed. But for now, just look after your mother. I think she's going to need it in the coming weeks," she winked. Athena laughed and Rosemary gulped.

"What's that supposed to mean?"

"You'll soon see," said Granny. "I'm fading now, but farewell, my lovelies. I'll see you again soon!"

"That woman!" said Rosemary. "Exasperating."

Athena laughed again, taking the cat from Rosemary. "It must run in the family," she said.

Rosemary smiled and wrapped her arms around Athena and the small purring kitten. It might be bizarre and dangerous, but their lives had also changed so much for the better in such a short space of time. It would be remiss of her not to appreciate it.

EPILOGUE: THREE DAYS EARLIER

Dain pulled up to the old house. It was just as he remembered it, though it had been years since he'd been there. Rosemary's grandmother had warned him off, and he wasn't fool enough to mess with someone as powerful as Galderall Thorn.

Even now, he was wary of ringing the bell in case she answered and blasted him to another realm.

He parked the car and began unloading boxes.

His daughter's things.

Rosemary's things.

He knew he didn't deserve them – these women who had somehow become the most important part of the tornado of his life.

He had wronged them too many times, stole from them, lied to them, left them, only to return again, and start the whole cycle over. Dain had wanted things to be different, every single time, and yet there was only so much he could control.

This was the least he could do, pack their things into boxes and drive them over here. Rosemary even said he could keep the car and sell it. She knew him too well, knew he would need the money. Dain sighed.

The last box was loaded onto the porch, and he could hear them talking inside – Rosemary and Athena. Their voices were soothing to him. They anchored him here in this world where he had no real place.

He wanted to see them, but he was afraid of the old woman, and something seemed to be holding him back.

It must be Galderall's power. She's trying to keep me away from her family...from my family.

It wasn't strong enough to stop him and his instinct was to push through, but he hesitated again, unsure whether they would want to see him or not.

Hesitation was unusual for Dain who'd never had any particular form of self-control. *It must be the magic holding me back,* he thought, and that was enough to get him to push through, no matter how scared he was of Granny Thorn.

He reached up to the door and knocked. Then he turned around. He could hear it. From far away, a familiar sound roared towards him faster than anything of this world.

No...they've found me.

A swirling mist appeared, enveloping Dain in white, and he disappeared from the human world.

Order Myrtlewood Mysteries book 2 now!

A NOTE FROM THE AUTHOR

Thank you so much for reading this book! I had a lot of fun writing it. I love Myrtlewood with all it's quirky characters and cozy magical atmosphere.

I wanted to write this book, in particular, because I've hardly ever come across solo parent main characters in fantasy, urban fantasy and paranormal mystery books.

The inspiration came, one day, in an Urban Fantasy books group, when someone posted a request for books a bit like Gilmore Girls, but with magic. She particularly wanted a magical village with lots of interesting characters, like in Stars Hollow. I followed the recs with interest. There weren't many options and so I decided to write this series!

I was raised by a solo mother, and have also been one, myself. I've noticed that there aren't many books, movies and shows that focus on this kind of experience, so I wanted to bring this project to life.

I've also always been interested in magical things, consider myself a bit of a kitchen witch and also belong to a Druid grove. Writing magical books allows me to draw on my own witchy experience and boost it with fantastical elements. For instance, you may notice that this book is based around a traditional magical festival, as are the following episodes in the series. They are a lot of fun!

If you have a moment, please leave a review or even just a star rating. This helps new readers to know what kind of book they're getting themselves into, and hopefully builds some trust that it's worth reading!

If you're keen to read more, you can order Myrtlewood Mysteries book 2 now!

You can also join my reader list or follow me on social media. Links are on the next page.

A big thanks to GiGi Kent, Jason LeVaillant and Jackie Lee Morrison for all the helpful feedback you provided in the making of this book!

ABOUT THE AUTHOR

Iris Beaglehole is many peculiar things, a writer, researcher, analyst, druid, witch, parent, and would-be astrologer. She loves tea, cats, herbs, and writing quirky characters.

facebook.com/IrisBeaglehole

twitter.com/IrisBeaglehole

instagram.com/irisbeaglehole

Printed in Great Britain
by Amazon

eafc0f56-440e-49ae-ab43-36cc7cface08R01